DESERT FIRE

Phil Campion, author of *Born Fearless*, is a veteran of military operations in just about every conflict-prone corner of the world, both as a soldier in the regular Armed Forces, an elite operator and as a mercenary. He lives with his partner, Wendy, and their children and continues to work as an operator on the private military circuit.

DESERT FIRE

NO RULES. NO LOYALTY. ONLY THE MISSION.
A STEVE RANGE AND BLACKSTONE SIX THRILLER

PHIL CAMPION

Quercus

First published in Great Britain in 2012 by
Quercus
55 Baker Street
Seventh Floor, South Block
London
W1U 8EW

A CIP catalogue record for this book is available from the British Library

PBO ISBN 978 0 85738 444 7
TPB ISBN 978 1 78206 327 8
EBOOK ISBN 978 0 85738 442 3

10 9 8 7 6 5 4 3 2 1

Text designed and typeset by Ellipsis Digital Ltd
Printed and bound in Great Britain by Clays Ltd, St Ives plc

For the real Tony Hogan, late of the Beaujolais wine bar and the world – rest in peace. Gone but not forgotten.

I'd like to thank the small but very clued-up band of operatives from across the disciplines who helped me with the research for this book. You know who you are. Your advice and input was bang on the nail and it is hugely appreciated. Whilst *Desert Fire* is a work of fiction, it is anchored in facts – and it reflects the dark reality that we are only now waking up to, and from which we will very likely reap the whirlwind.

Chapter One

The French air force cargo aircraft lurched alarmingly, its giant turbines fighting to gain traction on the hot desert air. It was 0400 hours, the coolest time of night to fly such a mission, yet still the weight of arms and ammunition strapped into the aircraft's hold dragged it downwards. The pilot, Captain Le Favre, knew he had to gain height and quickly, or they'd be forced to abandon the mission.

Up ahead loomed a fearsome apparition – a shadowed mass boiling on the dark horizon like a devil's cauldron. The Captain eyed it nervously, the hot Saharan wind that was gusting behind it showing up like a giant, whirling ghost glowing eerily in his night-vision equipment. The aircraft was flying on black light – showing no lights whatsoever – and only the faint glow from the computer consoles lit his and his co-pilot's features.

The intense, glowing darkness before them was building to around 3,000 feet, its seething mass extending to ground level and blocking out all vision beyond. Even though they were still some ten kilometres out, the Captain could tell that this was no normal cloud formation: it was a super-giant, violent, boiling sand-storm.

Captain Le Favre could attempt to fly around it, but the storm had to be fifty kilometres or more at its base, and blooming like a mushroom cloud as the winds pulsed out from the epicentre. More to the point, the drop zone they were heading for lay somewhere to the centre of that storm front, and most likely deep within its sand-blasted interior.

Normally, the aircraft that he was flying – a state-of-the-art $200 million Airbus A400M Atlas – would be the perfect plane with which to weather such a storm, but there was every chance that tonight it might force them to abort. Le Favre had been trimming the aircraft for maximum fuel efficiency, as he circled the intended drop zone at low altitude, scanning the desert for the signal they were searching for.

But not any more.

Now he had no option but to keep forcing forward the throttles to drive the four turboprops to ever-greater speed, their eight-bladed Scimitar propellers screaming at increasing revolutions as the giant aircraft struggled to gain altitude.

'Captain, what the hell is that thing?' a voice echoed over the intercom.

It was Major Goderiaux, the man from the Direction Générale de la Securité (DGSE) – the French equivalent of the Central Intelligence Agency, or Britain's Secret

Intelligence Service (MI6). The Major was perched in a fold-down seat to the rear of the cockpit, and he was leaning forward and staring anxiously through the aircraft's windshield.

'*Tempête de sable*,' the Captain replied. 'This is the time of the Harmattan – the Sahara's seasonal wind. From time to time it blows up giant sandstorms, like this one. Tonight we are unlucky.'

'Unlucky like how, Captain?'

'Unlucky in that I cannot see how we will find the drop zone with this storm raging. Unlucky because without being able to positively identify the DZ, I don't see how we can make the drop.'

'Activate the video link,' the Major ordered.

Much as he hated having to do so, it was time for Major Goderiaux to consult with his boss at the Paris headquarters of the DGSE. Back in the good old days, more or less everyone at the DGSE bar the secretaries was military or ex-military. But in the politically correct reality that was modern-day France, some sixty per cent of the agency's staff were civilians. The person he was about to speak to – the DGSE's Operations Director – was one such person, and to make matters worse, a woman.

As Captain Le Favre dialled up the aircraft's secure video link, the Major reflected upon his mission. Dropping weapons to Libyan rebels didn't sit easily with him, even at the best of times. In his view, as a military man, he saw the rebels as a disorganized, unruly mob, and hardly one capable of toppling the Libyan strongman, Colonel Gadaffi. But orders were orders. And like their British and American so-called allies, France seemed to have embraced the misguided ideology that regime change on behalf of 'the people' was always for the good.

In the circles that Major Goderiaux hailed from, strongman dictators made the best leaders in the Arab and North African worlds. Men like Colonel Gadaffi were hardly angels, but they were forces of iron control with whom France could do business. And she had, very lucratively and to the nation's great benefit, until this rebel uprising had reared its ugly head. Now men like him were being ordered to arm and train the rebels, disregarding the fact that no one knew – less still seemed to care – where their allegiances would lie in the long term, and whose interests they might protect.

It was a leap into the great unknown, and as far as the Major was concerned keeping Gadaffi in his post would have been infinitely preferable. But what worried him most was the nature of the weaponry they were about to drop to the rebels. Small arms would be bad enough. But as for the few dozen MANPADS – man-portable surface-to-air missiles – they were preparing to kick out into the lawless void, well, in his view it was sheer lunacy.

He glanced behind through the open doorway connecting the dimly lit cockpit with the aircraft's shadowy rear. The A400M was a stupendous piece of engineering, and the Major felt a momentary surge of pride as he ran his eye down the cavernous hold. The largely French-designed aircraft was unique in that its four giant turbines rotated counter to each other, each cancelling out the other's torque and boosting the aircraft's stability and lift. As a result the Atlas could carry 32 tonnes of equipment, far more than any comparable aircraft.

Right now, a few hundred kilograms of that payload was made up of six dozen SA-24 Grinch missiles. The Russian-made Grinch surface-to-air missile was one of the most potent and deadly on the market. It rivalled – possibly even surpassed – the capabilities of the French equivalent, the Mistral. It employed an infrared 'heat-seeking' system that homed in on any hot part of an aircraft – most usually its engines. It had a range of six kilometres – further than that of the Mistral – and with its impact-proximity fuse it could destroy a target without actually hitting it, by detonating within the 'kill range'.

No doubt about it, it was a fearsome weapon to drop into the hands of the Libyan rebels. The DGSE had chosen to send them the Grinch, as opposed to the French missile, for two reasons. One, the Libyan military already possessed a few Grinches that they'd purchased direct from Russia, so there would be defectors from the Libyan army who should know how to use them.

Two, if the missiles fell into the wrong hands – as

Major Goderiaux feared they would – France could always claim it had nothing to do with them, for what would the French be doing supplying Libyan rebels with Russian-made weaponry? This way their mission had maximum 'deniability', and that had been the deciding factor.

'Connection through, sir,' Captain Le Favre announced.

The Major glanced at the computer screen to his front left. 'Madame Director, it's a pleasure. We have a problem with the mission. A *tempête de sable* has blown up over the location of the drop. We may be forced to abort.'

The DGSE's Director of Operations frowned. 'Have the rebels given any of the pre-arranged identification signals?'

'We have detected their IR strobe, Madame, yes. Our aircraft's forward-looking infrared sensors can see through even such a storm. But as for the K-marker, no sign of it, Madame.'

'What's your visibility?'

'Within the sandstorm itself, Madame, I would imagine one hundred metres at best. And it looks to be a good kilometre high, sitting right over the drop zone.'

'Captain Le Favre, how long can you remain in your present orbit?' the Director of Operations demanded.

The pilot flicked his eyes over various icons on the computer screens. 'Madame Director, on present fuel consumption rates we have one hour's loiter time. But as we climb to keep above the *tempête*, our fuel-usage rises, and our loiter time falls.'

'Remain over the drop zone for as long as you are able. But do not – I repeat do not – complete the drop unless you see both pre-arranged ID signals: IR strobe, and the K-marker. Leave this video link live and keep me informed.'

Captain Le Favre pushed his aircraft towards a 5,000-foot cruise ceiling, which should take them out of the reach of the *tempête*. As they scrambled to gain altitude, the giant aircraft was dwarfed by the shadowed mass bearing down upon it. The storm reared before them like the wall of a dark and angry tsunami.

As the towering darkness thundered ever closer, Major Goderiaux noticed that the video connection was breaking up. For a few seconds the image pixellated terribly, struggling to stabilize, and then it seemed to give up completely, disintegrating into a blank screen, the aircraft's speakers set to either side pushing out a hollow void of wailing static – the screaming 'voice' of the sandstorm.

They clawed their way over the roof of the vortex, and it began to take on an animal form, fingers of wind-blown sand reaching up thousands of feet from the desert floor like vicious talons stretching around and above the aircraft. The mass of the storm was darker at its base, where the wind sucked and tore at the sands, and lighter at its tumbling peak where moonlight rent the blackness.

And then a rising finger of the storm was upon them, the steady progress of the aircraft broken as the wind grabbed and shook it like an angry child throwing around a toy. The storm screamed and wailed, its voice deafening even inside the soundproofed cockpit, sand grains blasting in blinding waves against the glass.

The aircraft disappeared for several seconds as it was swallowed whole into the roiling belly of its darkness. Captain Le Favre wrestled desperately with the controls, fighting to keep the heavily laden plane airborne in such appalling conditions, when suddenly they were through and spat out into the relative calm of the far side.

Having climbed through the storm, the Captain trimmed his aircraft once again, settling into an orbit that would provide maximum endurance. Before him the plane was encased in a massive wall of glass, the entire cockpit one transparent shell. This was one of the design triumphs of the A400M, for it provided all-around visibility. Right now, it enabled them to search the desert in every direction for the signal. But as they scanned the terrain, all they could see was an ominous, boiling cloud of wind-driven sand.

Le Favre scanned the goldfish bowl of darkness that had become his world, one eye keeping check on the air-speed, altitude and artificial horizon indicators.

Flicking his eyes downwards he checked the electronic flight page of the computer. The forward-looking infrared (FLIR) scanner was still showing a regular, rhythmical burst, as an IR beacon at ground level kept flashing. Down below, in the heart of that storm, someone was signalling to them. They just needed a glimpse of the pre-arranged visual marker, and the drop was on.

Of course, some of the massive parachutes under which the weapons crates would fall might not survive the strong winds of the *tempête*. Others might, but be scattered across the desert sands. Such were the risks of covert operations like this. The Captain felt a tap on his shoulder. He turned to see his co-pilot, Philippe, gesturing to a point somewhere to the port side of the aircraft.

'Break in the *tempête*,' he intoned over the radio. 'Some 1,000 metres forward of us the visibility clears.'

The Captain glanced where his co-pilot was pointing. He could just about make out the ragged edge of the storm racing across the open desert. Behind it, the air seemed remarkably calm and clear. As he drew his eye back towards the nose of the aircraft, he figured he'd spotted something. Or had he? He couldn't be sure. Then there it was again – a pinprick of fierce light burning like a drop of molten gold in the darkness.

As he stared at it, an outline of glowing dots seemed to shimmer out of the thinning storm. A shape became visible. Three lines of fire had been lit at ground level to reveal a burning 'K'. It was the signal. He checked the location of the IR strobe: his visual fix on the fiery K and the strobe coincided. No doubt about it, this was the drop zone. He flashed a look at his co-pilot, and he knew that Philippe had also seen it. One glance behind at the Major, and he could see that he had too.

'We're on,' the Major announced grimly. 'Get us onto your fastest line of approach. I'll see to things in the rear.'

He unbuckled his seatbelt and headed aft, to where a dozen parachute dispatchers were preparing the loads that were to be rolled out of the aircraft's giant hold. As he did so, he felt the Atlas begin a slow, ponderous turn, as Captain Le Favre brought it onto the correct approach path for release.

Each pallet of weapons would be rolled off the aircraft's rear ramp, with the parachute attached to a fixed line. As soon as the load had dropped a certain distance from the aircraft, the parachute would open automatically and the weapons would drift to earth – assuming the parachutes weren't torn to shreds by the storm.

The Major began barking orders, and figures scurried across the cold steel floor. He figured if they were going to drop such a lethal load to a bunch of rebels they couldn't even see due to the storm, they might as well get the distasteful business over and done with. After all, orders were orders.

Five thousand feet below him desert nomad Moussa ag Ajjer eyed the heavens. To his people, the Tuareg, the blasted desert wastes of the Sahara were their ancestral home, one they'd inhabited for countless generations. They had always been here, and with their long indigo headscarves – their *cheches* – wrapped tightly around their hair, face and eyes, they could wait out all but the most atrocious of sandstorms.

With the present storm starting to abate, Moussa ag Ajjer had loosened his *cheche* to reveal just his eyes and his ears.

He tilted his head and cracked a thin smile. 'I hear it.'

At his side, a figure murmured a reply. 'Yes, *amghar* – chief – it is coming.'

'Waste not one moment,' Moussa ag Ajjer announced. 'As soon as we have it, then is our moment of revenge. Strike for Gadaffi, our one and only true friend . . .'

There was a crack in the air above them like a ship's canvas being torn by the wind, and the ghostly form of a parachute emerged from out of the belly of the storm. As the pallet hit the sand it disintegrated, throwing crates of weapons in all directions. Figures scurried for the nearest, feverish hands grabbing the straps and lifting them onto strong, sinewed shoulders. The first of the French weaponry was now in Moussa ag Ajjer's hands.

The crates were rushed across to the tribal chief's position and loaded onto a fleet of waiting Toyota pickups. But one that was larger and heavier than the rest was dragged to one side. A fierce-eyed individual bent over it and let out a harsh, ululating cry. He tore at the fastening straps, ripped the lid off and rose to his feet, a long tubular weapon perched upon his shoulder. For a second he hefted it there, assessing its weight and balance, before dropping it tail end down before him.

His hands flicked around the device, expertly punching buttons and ratcheting levers. With his free hand he reached into a second crate and removed a sleek, compact, snub-nosed missile. He pulled back the launcher's breech, slotted the warhead into place and hefted the tube onto his shoulder again. With his right hand supporting the tube at its far end, his left curled around the trigger grip set halfway along.

With the sandstorm obscuring the aircraft from view, he was tempted to wait to get visual with it. But he had a sound fix at least, which gave him a general launch direction, and he had to presume that the missile's infrared eye would be able to see through the storm and pick up the heat from the aircraft's engines. He flicked it onto automatic mode, which meant that the missile would choose its own lead and elevation, and turned towards his chief.

'The Igla-S,' he announced excitedly. 'There is none better. I am ready.'

The Igla-S is the Russian name for what NATO terms the Grinch. His Russian instructors had taught him to always leave his trigger finger lying beside the trigger, in line with the weapon, until the very moment of firing – as a precaution to avoid a premature launch. This he did now, as he eyed Moussa ag Ajjer excitedly.

The Tuareg chief nodded at the heavens. 'Proceed. If God wills it, revenge will be ours.'

The lean desert warrior raised the tube to an eighty-degree angle, for the aircraft sounded as if it was still circling more or less directly above. He curled his finger around the trigger, and gently, almost lovingly, he increased the pressure. As he did so a momentary break in the receding storm revealed the barest flash of a silhouette outlined against the moonlit heavens – the Atlas.

He adjusted his aim, and the missile left the device in one smooth burst of blinding flame, the launch-man holding the tube as steady as a rock, just as he had been trained. Never before had he had cause to fire the Igla-S in anger, but now he did so with a fierce rage burning in his heart.

He turned to the chief. 'It is done. Nothing outruns the Igla.'

High above them the last crate left the A400M's fuselage, and the ramp started to whir shut. Up front Captain Le Favre set a course for home – Paris – which meant turning the ponderous aircraft through one hundred and eighty degrees. She felt noticeably lighter and more responsive with the cargo gone from the hold. As the plane turned towards the north, the pilot's eyes were drawn to an icon that had flashed onto his screen.

Barely had his brain begun to process what it meant, when a robotic-sounding voice started blaring out a warning that resounded around the aircraft.

The A400M is fitted with the multi-colour infrared alerting sensor (MIRAS) – a state-of-the-art missile warning and evasion system. The MIRAS's defensive sensors had detected an enemy missile launch and lock-on, and the weird, disembodied female voice of the warning system had begun to identify the threat, whilst simultaneously computing how best to counter it.

'SAM. Launch! Launch! Launch! Launch! 090 degrees. Speed . . .'

The weird, metallic voice sounded like some sinister version of a satnav system, and to Captain Le Favre and his co-pilot those words were absolutely chilling. He knew in his heart it had to be a Grinch that was inbound – he'd studied the capabilities of just about every missile that might be used against his aircraft. The Grinch utilizes a 'two-colour' infrared seeker system, which is all but impossible to defeat. He could just imagine the missile's seeker head scanning with its iris inside the glass nose dome as it tore towards his aircraft.

The A400M has a top speed of 780 kph. The missile now bearing down upon them would have reached terminal velocity by now, and be scorching ahead at some 570 metres a second. It would be upon them in an instant. Before the Captain could act, the MIRAS system had kicked in, and there was a massive flash of blinding light as all around the aircraft a fountain of white exploded into the night sky.

Scores of flares fired off from the Atlas's rear, side and front launchers, surrounding the aircraft in a sea of burning fire, and transforming the darkness into a harsh metallic daylight. Each flare burned with a ferocity that far outmatched the heat from the aircraft's exhausts, enveloped as they were in the aircraft's cooling system. The dense cloud of flares provided a confusion of different hot points to confound the missile's guidance system. In the few moments remaining the hope was that the missile would lock onto a flare, and miss the aircraft completely.

The Major snapped his head towards the video link, which finally had stabilized. 'Madame Controller! We have a SAM inbound–'

His words were cut short as the 2.5 kilogram high-explosive warhead detonated barely a metre away from the aircraft's bulbous nose. As the storm of shrapnel tore into the cockpit, Major Goderiaux had a split second in which to understand that his worst fears had been realized before a chunk of jagged, razor-sharp steel tore through his windpipe at a speed of 4,000 metres per second, severing his spinal cord. He died instantly. As the aircraft shuddered horribly and began to keel over into a slow and ungraceful dive, the pilot and co-pilot slumped lifeless over the Atlas's controls.

Some three thousand kilometres away, Madame

Enée, the Operations Director of the DGSE, stared into the video feed in utter horror. Her hand had gone to her mouth involuntarily, and she just kept crying over and over and over, '*Mon dieu! Mon dieu! Mon dieu! Qu'est-ce qu'on a fait?*' – My God! My God! What have we done?

The feed lasted long enough for her to witness the carnage, and for the aircraft to begin its terrible descent towards the dark Libyan desert. And then it flashed white for an instant, before being – mercifully – for ever lost.

She turned to a figure beside her. '*Mon dieu!* Who in God's name did we drop those weapons to? They are shooting our warplanes down with our own missiles!'

A nervous tic pulled rhythmically at her assistant's cheek. What on earth was there that he could possibly say in response?

'Get me Major Hermionne, and Saint-Egury,' Madame Enée barked. 'And whoever else drew up the damn intelligence file on this mission . . .'

As the assistant hurried off to fetch the two Libyan desk officers, he could hear his boss muttering away to herself in horrified disbelief. She lifted her head and cast a withering glance around the handful of figures seated in their plush operations room at the DGSE's new Noisy-le-Sec quarters. Constructed in the 1850s as a fort from which to defend Paris against marauders, Noisy-le-Sec was an island of ancient impregnability, set amongst an expanse of manicured gardens. The move to the refurbished building had only just been completed, and Madame Enée could hardly think of a worse way to have christened their new headquarters.

'Not a word outside of this room until we have some answers,' she snapped. 'If news of this leaks out to our British allies, or, heaven forbid, the Americans, we will be a laughing stock and worse. Not to mention if it reaches the world's media . . .'

She shoved back her chair, got to her feet and stalked towards the door. 'NOT A BLOODY WORD! You hear me?' she snarled over her shoulder, as she hurried off in the direction of the Director-General's office. 'NOT A BLOODY WORD!'

Chapter Two

Steve Range lowered his burly frame into the chair and cast his eyes around the room. A dozen of the old faithful were gathered, and with several he exchanged a glance of welcome and a few words – mostly wisecracks about absent friends or speculation about the coming mission.

As was the norm with Blackstone Six (B6) operations, none of the private operators knew what the mission entailed until they gathered for the briefing. If they took the tasking, they'd deploy directly from here to a forward mounting base and under strict communications silence.

They'd hand in their mobile phones and other comms devices, so there was no chance of the nature of the task before them leaking out following an indiscreet phone call home. It wasn't that the men didn't trust their close families, but it was always possible to make someone talk under the right kind of torture.

At the front of the room, the man they knew as The Colonel was having an easy chat with Tony Hogan, the boss of Blackstone Six. The Colonel played some kind of shadowy liaison role between the Secret Intelligence Service (SIS), the various branches of the armed forces, and people like those gathered in the room. Range liked The Colonel and trusted him as much as you could anyone in this kind of business.

The door opened and a tall figure slipped into the room. As far as Range was concerned, Nigel Champion was the opposite of men like The Colonel, or Tony Hogan, the boss at Blackstone Six. To those in the business of ultra-covert black operations, Nigel Champion was known simply as 'The Fixer'. His role was to take orders from his political taskmasters and translate those into language men like Range and his fellow private warriors could understand. Plus he was the firewall. The politicians spoke to The Fixer. The Fixer spoke to Blackstone Six. That was the key link in the chain of deniability that surrounded all of their missions.

The Fixer made his way across to the battered desk at the front of the room, his feet gliding across the linoleum floor almost without lifting them, as if he were a human hovercraft. With his long, chalky, effeminate-looking hands, his snow-white hair and lifeless pale-blue eyes, The Fixer had a distinctly alien look about him. He had briefed Range on several previous occasions, and with each Range's dislike and distrust of the man had grown. He was the last kind of bloke that Range would have wanted beside him when the bullets started to fly.

Fortunately, their only contact today was going to be the overall mission briefing: the tasking. Once that had been outlined in full, The Fixer's job was done, and he'd hand over to The Colonel plus one or two of the Intel boys so they could get down to the real business of planning the thing. That's if Range and the others from Blackstone Six decided to take the mission.

The Fixer exchanged a few words with Tony Hogan and The Colonel before turning to face the room. 'Gentlemen, if I might have your attention. Thank you for coming. The mission I am about to outline is being contracted by Her Majesty's government only. There are no private partners or funders, and no other governments with any role – so no other interested parties apart from HMG. Consequently, above and beyond the normal expectations of secrecy, this mission will remain off-limits to our usual allies, including the Americans.'

The Fixer paused for effect, letting his words hang in the air. As every man in that room fully appreciated, for a black op to be secret and deniable even where Britain's foremost ally, the Americans, were concerned, it had to be some kind of hyper-sensitive tasking.

'As you are all aware, the former Libyan leader, Colonel Muammar Gadaffi, was toppled from power by a rebel coalition. This took place within a wider movement that has been called "The Arab Spring". Part and parcel of the Libyan uprising was the hunting down of

Colonel Gadaffi and his family. Mostly, they were captured by the rebels and dealt with – ahem – rather summarily.'

'Executed, you mean,' Range interjected. 'Slotted on the spot.'

'They were dealt with in a way which our new allies, the Libyan Freedom Coalition, feel was appropriate.'

'Dead's still dead.'

The Fixer stared at Range in silence for a long second. Range stared back into his unblinking, lizard-like gaze.

'However the Gadaffi family may have met their end is not germane to this briefing,' The Fixer grated. 'What matters is which of the Gadaffi family members *are still alive*. The Libyan leader is believed to have had perhaps a dozen children. There are rumours of many illegitimates and bastard offspring—'

'They can join the club, mate,' Range muttered.

A ripple of laughter ran around the room. The Fixer's lifeless gaze took on a distinctly icier hue.

'The offspring that interests us is one of Gadaffi's legitimate children, his last and youngest son, Sultan Gadaffi. Before you on your desk you'll find a buff envelope. If you decide to take this mission, there are photos in there to ID the Gadaffi son. Officially, all of the Gadaffi family is either dead or in the hands of the rebel coalition authorities. However, we happen to know that Sultan Gadaffi escaped the net. Your mission is to go in and get him.

'You are all familiar with the term The Maghreb?' The Fixer continued. 'It refers to the region of North Africa that largely equates to the Sahara desert. The Maghreb encompasses southern Libya and Algeria, plus parts of Niger, Chad and Mali. It is inhabited by a nomadic desert tribe, the Tuareg. They call themselves "The Free People": they move across this vast, lawless region largely without let or hindrance. Traditionally, they ran trade caravans across the trackless wastes. More recently, several thousand of them were recruited into the late Colonel Gadaffi's armed forces, becoming his most loyal fighters.

'Gadaffi championed the Tuareg, and they in turn championed his regime. When the rebels began to win the war – with us and our French allies providing joint military support – the Tuareg melted into the desert. They took several of the Gadaffi family with them, providing sanctuary. One only interests us: Sultan Gadaffi. Your mission it to head into their territory and to snatch him, so as to bring him back to the UK to face justice – essentially on charges of war crimes.'

The Fixer gestured to the two men standing behind him. 'Tony Hogan, your boss at Blackstone Six, is briefed in more detail on the mission, and he believes it is one that you will want to take. As per usual, The Colonel will be your liaison. He is able to brief you on the minutiae of the tasking, including what, if any, support Her Majesty's armed forces can provide. Are there any questions?'

'Only one for you,' Range remarked. 'Why us? Why not give it to The Increment?'

The Increment – formerly known as the Counter-Revolutionary Warfare Wing, or The Wing for short – was the British government's own black ops outfit. It employed serving members of the Special Forces on black missions, carrying out official government business that was best kept quiet. By contrast Blackstone Six did the ultra-deniable work – the kind of stuff that even The Increment couldn't risk dirtying its hands with.

'Range has a point,' Tony Hogan remarked. 'It's something that troubles me. This is a classic mission for The Wing. It's not dirty enough for us. So why not use them?'

'For reasons I'm not able to go into, it's seen as being too risky for The Increment to get involved,' The Fixer replied. 'It needs to be rather more at arm's length than the Inc can deliver, so hence we've come to you.'

'Bullshit,' Range snorted. 'You're asking us to go after a suspected war criminal so he can be tried for war crimes. We did just that in the Balkans when myself and several others present in this room were serving with the SAS. We tracked down and nabbed Milan Kova-something . . .'

'Kovačević,' a voice interjected. It was Mike The Kiwi, a hard-as-nails New Zealand operator sitting just behind Range. 'Op Tango. I remember it well, mate, especially when you fell out of the bloody chopper.'

'Piss off,' Range retorted. 'I only fell out 'cause I'd necked a bottle of that rough-as-fuck Serbian hooch – what's it called?'

'Slivovitch.'

'I was celebrating capturing Kovačević.'

'Range is right,' The Kiwi remarked, turning back to The Fixer. 'Grabbing Gadaffi is the kind of mission the Regiment could well handle, let alone Inc. It doesn't need us. Not unless there's something about it you're not telling us.'

The Fixer narrowed his gaze imperceptibly. 'That's as may be, but it's not your need-to-know. This mission needs to be considerably more off-the-books than Inc can deliver. That's as much as I can say, and probably more than I am cleared to tell you.'

'Fair enough.' Range shrugged. 'That's likely the least of our worries. If you don't mind me saying, Tony, this one's too much risk for the money.'

The Hogan smiled, indulgently. 'Absolutely, Range old boy. I couldn't agree more. I'm never one to baulk at trying to bargain up Blackstone's fee for the job.'

Range and the boss at Blackstone Six had as close to a father–son kind of relationship as you could imagine when there was no blood relation. Range had been abandoned at birth and brought up in a string of kids' homes. He had no real family to speak of. 'The Hogan', as he was known, had two sons, but both had chosen a career in investment banking, and he felt he had little in common with them these days.

The Hogan had hands the size of shovels, and he'd been a prize boxer in his youth and whilst serving in the military. But he'd never made it into an elite regiment and he'd never seen any significant combat, although not for the want of trying. To The Hogan, Range was everything he'd wanted to be, or at least how he'd have liked one of his sons to turn out.

'For our normal rates,' Range continued, 'a grand a day after The Hogan there has taken his cut, you're expecting us to fly down the gun barrels of a bunch of desert warriors who outnumber us a thousand to one, I'd imagine. We're to do so in the heart of their territory, which has been Tuareg Central for centuries. It's hardly going in to battle at the time and place of our choosing, is it? And what will it be, a week-long mission at the most? So we'll walk away with seven grand apiece if we're lucky. It's never worth the hassle, is it?'

'We suspected that might be your position,' The Fixer smiled, oilily. 'So, there is the mission-plus option. More risk, but potentially fantastic rewards.'

'Go on,' Range nodded. 'Mission-plus sounds better than mission-zero.'

'In essence, we pay you nothing to go in and do the job. The Tuareg do.'

Range snorted. 'We go lift the Gadaffi boy, murder most of the Tuareg in the process, and they pay us handsomely for doing so, is that it? I may be thicker than a whale omelette, but I seem to be missing something vital here . . .'

'You are.' For an instant a sneer flashed across The Fixer's features. He did his best to hide it, but it wasn't lost on Range. 'The late Colonel Gadaffi bought the Tuareg's protection. He paid for it, and very handsomely. We estimate the Gadaffi gold is worth in excess of one hundred million dollars at today's values. It's stored in the same fortress as the Gadaffi son. We're happy to pass you all our intel on the gold, if that'll convince you to take the mission.'

The Hogan let out a delighted chuckle. 'Ingenious suggestion, old boy. My men get their usual fee, plus the gold as a bonus, I take it?'

'We were thinking of something a little more equitable,' The Fixer replied. 'If you go for the mission-plus option, you reduce your fee to zero, and we allow your men to keep the gold. We – HMG – turn a blind eye, as it were.'

'I always did say if I turned fifty and hadn't made a million I'd go rob a bank,' Range remarked. 'I've got five years before I've got to grab my sawn-off and pop down to my local Halifax. This sounds like a far better option.'

'That's the spirit,' The Hogan smiled. Then, to The Fixer: 'But Blackstone will need fifty per cent of its normal fee guaranteed.' There was a hardness that had crept into The Hogan's voice that belied his cheery exterior. 'The gold remains a high risk. How certain are you that it's there for the taking?'

'We're entirely certain. You'll get our full dossier of intelligence on it, including satellite images of the underground bunker where it's stored.'

'What logistics and back-up do we get?' Range asked.

'You get your airborne means of insertion and extraction,' The Fixer replied. 'You'll be going in by helicopter, I presume. No way to penetrate into the heart of the Sahara unnoticed overland, not even for you boys. That's as far as HMG's support goes. There's no air support, not this far into the territory of a sovereign nation with whom we are not at war. We'll ferry you back and forth, but that's about it.'

'Same as normal, then. Only this time, you ferry us *and the gold* in and out, right?'

'Absolutely,' The Fixer confirmed. 'Absolutely.'

'I'll be sure to get the paperwork watertight on that one, Range,' The Hogan added. 'The last thing we'd want is HMG snaffling up the gold as illegal contraband or something, wouldn't you agree?'

The Fixer waved a hand dismissively. 'I'm sure we can get all of that squared away. It's the Gadaffi boy that we're after. Bring him to us, and you're welcome to the gold. After all, you and your men will have more than earned it.'

Chapter Three

The vote had been a mere formality. At the mention of the gold, everyone had wanted to take the mission. All were freelance warriors, and The Hogan could compel no man to take a Blackstone Six tasking. Neither would he want to. As much as possible he ran B6 as a meritocracy, wherein all decisions were made freely, and the willingness to soldier and prosecute the most challenging of tasks went duly rewarded.

It was via a similar process that Range had come to be seen as the ideal leader for missions such as this one. He had no formal education. In fact, he'd left school at sixteen having had to cheat to gain his one qualification in life – his Cycling Proficiency Certificate. But hailing from the most utterly shitty of backgrounds had given Range an uncommon hunger to succeed, and the one thing for which he had an undeniable gift was fighting. He'd made that his career, the pinnacle of which had been making it into the military elite – the SAS.

Yet there was something else about Range that The Hogan valued, a degree of value-added that was quite unique. His lack of a conventional education meant that his mind was unusually uncluttered by any norms of thought. As a result, Range was willing to consider just about anything as being possible. In the SAS those that had this unique quality were said to be able to 'use The Force'. It enabled such men to think wholly outside of the box, and to come up with the most unconventional and unexpected ideas. The more lateral and crazed an idea, the less likely your enemy was ever to have thought of it, and thus to be prepared to defend himself against it. And as The Hogan well knew, in thinking the unthinkable and doing the unexpected Steve Range had no equal.

Once the vote was passed, The Colonel and his intel officer briefed the men of the specifics of their mission. The target was a desert fortress situated near the Libyan border with Niger. Nestling in the midst of the trackless desert wastes, it was hardly possible to imagine a more deserted or desolate part of the earth – that's unless you were a Tuareg nomad. To them, this was the realm of *Tinariwen* – the sea of deserts.

To the Tuareg, the Sahara consisted of many types of desert, just as the Inuit people of the Arctic could name many different types of snow. The vast sand-dune seas were called *Tenere*. The flat gravel plains, the mountainous deserts, the sand-sculpted rock deserts – each had its own unique name: *Adrar*, *Tagant*, *Tawat*, *Tanezrouft* . . . It was unfortunate that the toppling of Gadaffi had so alienated the Tuareg to the West. Traditionally, they were moderate Muslims who had no truck with terrorism or kidnapping – the two scourges that were sweeping the Maghreb now that al-Qaeda had set up operations there.

Exploiting the West's rift with the Tuareg, and the lawless vacuum of the desert, al-Qaeda had set up one of its more murderous franchises there. Al-Qaeda in the Islamic Maghreb – AQIM for short – had gained a foothold in many parts of the Tuareg's traditional territory. As they had with Gadaffi, the Tuareg had at first been happy to consider an alliance with those who might offer a powerful friendship. In the aftermath of Gadaffi's demise, bitter and angry Tuareg had been recruited to al-Qaeda's cause, and some had joined the ranks of AQIM.

But the alliance was starting to turn sour, as the Tuareg – a noble and proud nomadic people – witnessed the lack of respect foreign Arab operators had for their ancient desert culture and way of life. Increasingly, there were clashes between the more heavily armed factions of the Tuareg and the AQIM teams operating in their territory. This hadn't stopped the Tuareg doing deals with AQIM when there was money to be made, for these accomplished desert traders never missed the chance to make a somewhat dishonest buck.

'Sultan Gadaffi was caught up in just such a transaction,' The Colonel explained to the B6 team. 'In essence, once Colonel Gadaffi was dead the Tuareg knew that alliance was finished. At that stage, their loyalty to the Gadaffi family was trumped by their loyalty to each other – to the Tuareg clan. In a harsh environment like the Sahara, survival is all. In short, they sold the Gadaffi son up the chain to AQIM, and so it's al-Qaeda that hold the fort you are going in to assault. Make no mistake, you're up against diehard AQIM fighters who will give no quarter. And if any man amongst you is captured – well, keep a bullet for yourself.'

'Yeah, anyone need these?' Range pulled a Leatherman out of his pocket and opened up the pliers.

The Kiwi shook his head in bemusement. 'Mate, like what for?'

'You can pull out all your own teeth now, so as to rob this AQIM lot of the pleasure.'

'Standard answer, mate: you first, I'll follow.'

'Typical bloody Aussie!' Range snorted. Nothing wound up The Kiwi more than Range pretending to mistake him for an Australian. The Aussies are to the Kiwis what the French are to the British – traditionally the best of enemies.

'I'd rather have The Kiwi follow me, than have to follow a bloody Englishman,' a red-haired monster of a bloke remarked, speaking in a thick Scottish accent. He turned to a small, bearded figure sat beside him and jabbed him in the ribs. 'Or a bloody beardy Yankee dwarf for that matter.'

Range held up his hand, palm blocking out the giant

redhead's features. 'Speak to the hand, Jock, at least until you've learned to buy your own round.'

'Yeah, or until Scotland manages to beat America at rugby,' the bearded figure added. 'How many times is it now that we've kicked your sad asses? Not much to celebrate up in grim Glasgow, is there, buddy?'

Patrick 'Pat' O'Shea was an Irish-American, and an ex-US Navy SEAL – a Special Forces unit every bit the equal of the SAS. Together with Euan 'Jock' McGregor, the hulking great Scottish redhead and SAS veteran, they made up the third and fourth members of what Range called his Old Dependables.

Pat O'Shea had left the SEALs with the rank of Lieutenant-Colonel, which meant that he far outranked Range, who had only ever made it to Staff Sergeant. Range was seen as being too much of a spirited maverick to ever make officer. The Director of Special Forces had famously said of him that he was the type of operator who should be 'locked in a cage, and only let out in the face of the enemy'. Range had seen that as the ultimate accolade. In Blackstone Six – as it should be with any elite, bespoke unit – merit and freethinking experience took the lead regardless of rank, which was why Range was commanding the twelve men gathered in that room.

'So, that's who you're up against,' The Colonel cut short the banter, 'al-Qaeda in the Maghreb. As to the target and the kind of defences you can expect, this is a desert fortress from the time of the Ottoman Empire. For those of you who don't know your history, that means it's a good two hundred years old, though that doesn't detract from its value as a defensive structure. There are detailed satphotos in your dossiers, but suffice to say it consists of four round towers set at the corners of a quadrangle. The walls are thick enough to stop more or less any kind of a round, and they have more than stood the test of time.

'The walls and towers have walkways,' The Colonel continued. 'During the Second World War the Italians cut holes into them at walkway and ground level, to provide gun ports through which to fire. You'll be twelve lightly armed men, and I think it's fair to say there's no way through or over those walls. And in the time available you won't be tunnelling under them, that's for sure.

'Now for the upside, if there is one.' The Colonel paused briefly to catch his breath. 'During World War Two British forces laid siege to the fort and broke through via the western wall, a good thirty-foot section of which remains a rubble-choked ruin. This AQIM lot appear to have shored up the breach a little, but if anywhere is the weak point then that I would suggest is it.

'Defenders will have small arms, plus light and heavy machine guns situated on the towers, and they're bound to have rocket-propelled grenades. We estimate from intelligence gathered that it's garrisoned by some sixty AQIM fighters. Their level of training and discipline will vary greatly, but if they are anything like AQIM fighters we have experience of elsewhere, they will fight with suicidal ferocity.'

'Nelson will get his eye back before that lot surrender?' Range quipped.

'Precisely,' confirmed The Colonel.

He went on to explain how British and American forces were training the elite armed forces of Mauritania, the country that lies to the western end of the Maghreb. Those forces were penetrating overland to Mali, Niger and even as far as Libya, to hunt down the AQIM terrorists. From those missions – which, more often than not, had British and American Special Forces teams embedded within them – HMG had formed a good idea of how fiercely AQIM tended to fight.

'One final point which is absolutely critical to how you prosecute the mission,' The Colonel added. 'The area around the fort is totally devoid of habitation, so there are any number of potential landing zones where a helicopter could put down. However, we believe that AQIM may have got its hands on several MANPADS – man-portable surface-to-air missiles. The danger of your insertion helicopter getting shot down is very, very real.' The Colonel glanced around the room. 'Any questions, or suggestions how we go about doing this?'

'How big is the interior of the fort, inside the four walls?' Pat O'Shea queried. 'Is it large enough for us to, you know, fast-rope directly in and take it from inside?'

'Nice idea, shame about the SAMs,' Range responded. 'To fast-rope in, the helo's got to hover right above it, which is like saying – hey guys, put a missile up my arse!'

'Och, that's an easy one: we put down say fifteen kilometres away from the fort in the open desert,' Jock remarked. 'We move in on foot, slip through the breach in the wall, and we're all of us 8.333 million dollars better off.'

Range snorted in derision. 'Typical – he's worked out already just how much money he's going to make, the stingy Jock bastard. Still wouldn't stretch to a round at the bar, though, would you, mate?'

'If I get in and out with my 8.333 million, I might just manage to buy ye a beer,' Jock replied, with a twinkle in his eye. He had a soft spot for Range, in spite of all his wind-ups and his needle-sharp wit. 'So, what about my suggestion?'

'One problem,' said Range. 'To be out of visual and hearing range of the fort, we'd need to put down a good fifteen kilometres away, maybe more. Think how far sound carries in the desert, especially when there's not another engine for hundreds of miles around. I'd say we'd need a good twenty-five kilometres to be safe – about a third of the endurance march on SAS selection. Selection takes what, eight hours? The desert night doesn't even last for eight hours. We'd never get in, get the job done, and get out again during the hours of darkness.'

'Range – always the goddamn smart-arse,' O'Shea remarked to the others. 'So what's your big idea?'

'First off, we leave the bloody Yanks and the Aussies behind. Scots too, if I had my way. Second, we don't go in via air, or at least not like you lot are suggesting.' Range glanced in The Colonel's direction. 'Colonel, presumably you could make a whirlybird available?'

The Colonel sucked his teeth. 'Well, I wasn't exactly expecting to have to, not on a mission such as this. But I'm sure I could rustle one up from 47 Squadron, if we really need to. What exactly do you have in mind?'

'There's only one possible route in,' Range continued, speaking with absolute certainty. 'We take a C130 Hercules in at 30,000 feet. That way, we're ten thousand feet or more above the maximum range of any SAMs they may have in that fort. We're also totally invisible and inaudible to the fort's defenders. We HALO in at night, pull the chutes at 5,000, and the stick leader puts us down right at the very fort.'

HALO stands for High Altitude Low Opening, a type of parachute insertion practised by only a few of the world's absolute elite military forces. In a HALO jump, the blokes would pile off the C130 transport aircraft and plummet to earth in a monster freefall. It offered the fastest and most covert way of getting rapidly onto target, but as with all insertion methods it did have its downsides.

'We'll be forced to carry a lot less firepower if we jump,' O'Shea objected. 'Plus you can't use your weapon as you go in to land, so if they do wake up to the attack we're gonna get a whole load of lead up our backsides.'

'True,' Range conceded. 'But we can scavenge ammo and weaponry off the dead, plus we don't need to put down at the fort. If we go in offset a thousand yards, bundle up the chutes and tab in from there, we'll take 'em by surprise.'

'It's a good plan,' said The Colonel. 'There's only the one problem I can see. To HALO in you'd need the C130 directly over the fort. That puts it bang over the target and bang on everyone's radar screens. The Libyans. The Israelis too. The Americans. Once the raid becomes known about, they'll have proof a British C130 was directly over the target the night the fort was taken. It blows our deniability.'

'So we don't HALO,' said Range. 'We HAHO. If we HAHO in, we'll be offset a good eighty kilometres from the target when we bomb burst out of the Herc. That way, no one can claim it was a British aircraft put us lot onto target.'

HAHO stands for High Altitude High Opening. With a HAHO jump, each parachutist's canopy opens at 30,000 feet automatically, as each is attached to a static line. You can jump many kilometres away from the target and glide in.

'We'll need the Herc, plus a dozen BT80 parachute

rigs, and the high-altitude breathing kit to go with them,' Range continued. 'HAPLSS I think it's called. Everyone here's HAHO-trained, aren't they?' He glanced around the men for confirmation. 'Right, HAHO it is, unless anyone's got a better suggestion.'

'So, we have a workable plan?' The Colonel queried. 'We're all agreed?'

There were a series of nods and grunts in the affirmative.

The Colonel turned to The Hogan. 'Tony, are you happy?'

The Hogan smiled. 'My military days are long behind me, and I was never at the level of these boys. If my men are happy, I'm happy.'

'I'll need to make some calls, that's some fairly specialist kit you're after,' The Colonel added. 'But this one has backing from the very top, so it shouldn't pose any great problems. Timescale: if I can ready all that specialist kit, you're to be good to go in twenty-four hours. We don't want to risk this AQIM lot moving the Gadaffi boy. Is that doable?'

The Hogan shrugged good-naturedly. 'We've got nothing else cooking, old boy. Give us the tools and we'll do the job.'

'One last thing: codenames and comms,' The Colonel added. 'It would be useful to have call signs for your unit and an operational codename. Something simple, easy to remember and of the essence.'

'Saladin,' O'Shea suggested. 'Saladin One is Range, Saladin Two is my good self, Saladin Three The Kiwi, and so on down the fire teams.'

O'Shea was big into his ancient history, and Saladin was the legendary desert warrior who had fought against Richard the Lionheart during the Crusades.

'Wasn't Saladin on the wrong bloody side?' Jock queried.

'There are no sides, old boy,' said The Hogan. 'No sides where Blackstone business is concerned. Only contracts, and the bigger the better.'

'Garibaldi,' Range suggested. 'Operational codename. Like the biscuit. Sounds a bit like Gadaffi. And we can each take some with us to munch on and so we don't forget.'

The Hogan let out his signature chuckle, deep and rumbling and with his shoulders rocking in time to the laughter. 'Excellent suggestion, and classic Range, if I might say so.'

'Perfect,' The Colonel smiled. 'Saladin is your call sign, Op Garibaldi the mission codename. And may I suggest The Joker as codename for your target, Sultan Gadaffi.'

'The Joker,' confirmed Range.

'Radio and comms silence is key on this one, obviously,' The Colonel continued. 'You aren't supposed to be there, and the mission doesn't exist, so let's keep the airwaves very, very quiet. All we need from you – and all we'll expect – is the call to bring in the helo, and we'll get a Chinook inbound to lift you out. Use standard operating procedure to guide the helo in to your chosen LZ. Any questions?'

There were none.

Assuming The Colonel could rustle up the C130 Hercules aircraft and the jump kit, Operation Garibaldi was on.

Chapter Four

It was six o'clock in the morning, and approaching time to load up the Lockheed Martin C130J Super Hercules and take to the skies. The venerable C130 Hercules has had the longest continuous production run of any military aircraft in history. For decades, C130s have ferried British, American and allied forces into the remotest corners of the earth and to all major theatres of war.

The C130J is the newest and most powerful variant, with greatly increased air speed and lift capabilities. But from the outside, it looks pretty much the same as the first Hercules that rolled off the production line more than fifty years ago. A fleet of Super Hercules was operated by 47 Squadron RAF, the Special Forces support unit, and for want of a better departure point the Blackstone team was using one of their remote satellite bases.

Rarely had a 47 Squadron Hercules crew been tasked with a mission such as this one. After a seven-hour flight, a dozen men dressed in a motley collection of uniforms culled from half the militaries around the world would pile off the rear ramp of their aircraft, above the night-dark wastes of southern Libya. The C130 aircrew had not the slightest idea what mission those men were tasked with, or who exactly they might be. It wasn't their need-to-know, and they sensed it might be better to keep it that way.

Range strolled along the deserted runway seeking a few minutes to himself. The feeble February sun was peeping above the leafless trees to the east of the air-base, below a rumpled mass of grey cloud. The airstrip lay deep in a densely forested valley, serried ranks of pines marching up the slopes to either side.

From above a buzzard emitted a lonely, high-pitched wail as it called to its mate. There was an answering cry from a nest atop one of the tallest of the pines. Range gazed in that direction, wondering if the pair of birds could really be nesting in February. It was early to have started the breeding season, but it had proven to be unusually warm and muggy since the turn of the year.

Growing up in the kids' homes the one escape Range had known was the great outdoors. At every opportun-ity he had gone over walls, out windows or through doors, absconding for days on end and living rough in the countryside. By age eleven he'd learned to catch fish with his bare hands, set snares for rabbits, and to build a functional and watertight basher – a makeshift sleep-ing platform in the trees – out of what he could find in your average British woodland.

Range loved the escape from the violent discipline and abuse, plus the call of the wild. And in a sense –

although he hadn't known it at the time – it had been the perfect training ground for a life in the Special Forces, or for a career spent as a private warrior with B6 for that matter. These days he felt just as at home in jungle, mountain or desert environments, and there was a part of him that thrilled at the prospect of getting parachuted deep into the Sahara.

He'd served in Iraq and Afghanistan, so he'd experienced the desert at first hand, but nothing close to this. The pure, simple, wind-driven vastness of the Sahara, with its dune seas as wide as any ocean, was a massive pull. It was the Sahara that had spawned the world's very first Special Forces when David Stirling formed his Special Air Service, whose remit it was to penetrate hundreds of miles across the Sahara desert in open-topped jeeps and strike far behind enemy lines.

In a sense, this mission was taking Range and his men back to where it had all begun. Like Stirling, Range was leading a band of warrior-desperadoes into the North African desert and into the very jaws of death. Stirling's unit had been made up of a murderous Danish psychotic, an Irish jail-breaker and a London conman, with a good smattering of lunatic English eccentrics thrown in.

In The Kiwi, Range figured he had the psychotic, for his New Zealand teammate was a merciless killing machine when the red mist of combat descended. In Jock he sure had the jail-breaker: one too many beers inside him, and the giant redhead turned into The Great Destroyer. He figured O'Shea was the trickster – wowing Irish ladies with being an American, conning American girls that he was Irish, and all the while telling the English that he was a blond Italian named Rico.

Which left only 'lunatic Englishman' for Range. He was happy enough with that. Many had considered Stirling to be a mad and misguided fool, until his unit's record of success had silenced them. With their hit-and-run tactics, Stirling's SAS had destroyed so many Italian and German warplanes on their desert airstrips that Hitler had decreed any SAS men captured would be shot on sight. Execution awaited those unfortunate enough to fall into enemy hands.

For a moment Range considered what fate would await him and his men, should any get taken alive by al-Qaeda in the Maghreb. It didn't bear thinking about. He, like the rest of them, would put a bullet in his brain before that happened.

Having reached the far end of the runway, Range turned to face the lone hangar, where his team was making their last-minute preparations. The airstrip was so decrepit it didn't even seem to possess a working control tower. Not that it mattered much: other than the waiting C130J, there were no other aircraft visible on the pitted runway, which was here and there sprouting thick tufts of grass.

Range figured the place had to date back to the thirties, and it didn't look as if it had been used much since the Second World War. But it was fine for their purposes, and far away from any prying eyes, which was the key.

En route back to the hangar Range paused by the bulbous nose of the Super Hercules. The cockpit sat some fifty feet above the runway, right on the roof of the aircraft. He saw a window slide back and a head poked out. It was the pilot.

'Weather report's unchanged,' he called down to Range. 'L-hour in ninety, if you're good with that?'

Range nodded. 'Yep.'

L-hour stood for lift-off hour, or the moment the C130 would take to the skies. It struck Range that the pilot had a face like a sack of claw hammers, not that it particularly mattered. This wasn't a beauty contest. 47 Squadron were the best in the business, and Range had every confidence these guys would get them to the exact point in the sky at which they needed to jump.

'Any music you want?' the pilot queried. 'You know, like for P-Hour?'

P-Hour was Parachute Hour, when Range and his men would hurl themselves off the tail ramp of the Hercules and into the unknown. Range had done enough jumps to know the form. Normally, the unit making the jump would bring along a particular track of music. They'd get it blaring out of the aircraft's speakers, which boosted the adrenalin and got the pulse hammering as they prepared to freefall into war.

Range shrugged. 'No, mate. Nothing. No time. What you got racked up on the system?'

'Well, classical mostly,' the pilot replied. 'That's unless you fancy a Cliff Richard number?'

Range smiled. 'You're taking the piss. Tell you what – you choose. Only don't make it "Living Doll".'

The pilot laughed. 'Got it. I'll find something . . .'

Range strode across to the hangar. Everywhere he looked blokes were hunched over their Bergens, stuffing in a few last magazines of ammo or grenades. You could never have enough firepower on such a mission, and with all their ammo, water and personal kit they'd be jumping with a good eighty pounds in their Bergens, not to mention the weight of their weaponry and specialist parachuting gear.

Range let his eyes wander around the dark interior of the hangar. Eleven good men, twelve with himself included. He knew each man personally, having served with them in the military or on the Circuit, as the world of private military operations was known. Some he knew less well than others, but they came highly recommended from fellow operators he trusted. That was how this business worked: people came to Blackstone Six only via the personal introduction of a B6 veteran.

His twelve-man team broke down into three four-man sticks – the four-man unit being the standard used in the Regiment. Range led the headquarters stick, consisting of himself, O'Shea as his second-in-command, plus The Kiwi and Jock as the gun-toting meatheads. Fire team two was led by Tak, a brick-shithouse of a Fijian. At six foot two and built like a barn door, Range was hardly small. But Tak and Jock – the two monsters in the unit – pretty much dwarfed even him.

If it ever came to a punch-up between the two of them, Range would be hard pressed to decide who he'd put his money on. But on balance, Tak probably had it by a whisker. There wasn't a man in the Regiment who had earned a more fearsome reputation. Tak was a living, breathing war machine, and there was nothing he wasn't prepared to do when fighting on behalf of his brother warriors. There was a long tradition of such Fijians serving in British Special Forces, and Tak had added much to the legend.

Fire team three was led by Randy, a good-looking, rangy Afro-American. O'Shea had brought Randy into B6, for he was a fellow ex-SEAL. Randy wasn't his real name. He'd earned the nickname within the unit because he was such a hit with the women. British girls just couldn't seem to get enough of his cool, laid-back American charm. Once he'd got used to the British sense of humour, 'Randy' had warmed to his nickname.

He had a lean, hard, lightly muscled torso, and he was said to have come from one of the Chicago projects – the no-go areas of that hard city that were awash with drugs and teenage killers with guns. Either way, he walked and talked as if he'd been born with a shooter in his hand, and he was a demon with explosives.

Range didn't give a shit about the ethnic origin or nationality of any on his team. He'd happily command a bunch of aliens if they brought with them the right military pedigree. He knew that every man in that hangar had passed selection and served with either the SAS, the US Navy SEALs, or sister units. It meant that each had been proven to have the physical and mental stamina, plus the aggression and expertise to take himself into the extremes of war and beyond.

Range bent over his rucksack, checking his webbing kit one last time. He wore a South African Defence Force (SADF) chest-and-belt-kit hybrid, for the simple reason that it allowed him to strap more mags of ammo to his person than any other rig. Happy that all was as it should be, he stuffed the webbing into his bulging Bergen. None of his men would parachute wearing their full war-fighting gear. There was too much danger of a strap getting caught as you jumped, or a pouch falling open during the descent and losing half your ammo.

Range had his back-up weapon stuffed deep inside his Bergen. Every man could choose what arms he took, and most carried a Sig Sauer P226 super-capacity tactical (SCT) as their back-up. The compact pistol packs a twenty-round magazine of 9mm bullets, and boasts TruGlo sights which light up under night-vision goggles, so enabling the operator to aim even when operating in darkness.

But Range preferred to take his first love as his back-up weapon. Nestling inside his Bergen was the ultimate in combat shotguns, an Auto-Assault 12. The AA-12 was a totally indestructible piece of hardware. It could be dropped in water, mud, sand or whatever, picked up and unleashed, and the twenty shotgun rounds would hammer out of the weapon's drum magazine at a rate of 300 per minute. As a close-quarters combat weapon it had no equal, and Range figured they'd be doing a lot of fighting up close and dirty on this one.

He'd parachute with his main weapon, an M249 squad assault weapon (SAW) – a fearsome light machine gun – slung over his left shoulder, barrel downwards. Range had opted to bring the 7.62mm variant, known as the 'Maximi'. The NATO-standard 5.56mm weapon – the 'Minimi' – was a fine gun, but on this mission they'd likely need to scavenge rounds off the enemy. Taking the 7.62mm SAW not only gave them greater firepower, it offered Range the chance to use the enemy's own ammunition against them – for their main weapon would be the AK-47, which also used 7.62mm rounds.

When doing a HAHO jump you always carried your main weapon, plus several spare mags of ammo, strapped to your person. It was always possible that during the jump you'd lose your Bergen, in which case it was vital to have your main weapon to hand. With his rucksack packed, Range tightened every last strap one last time, then stuffed it into an over-sack made of a thick and tough canvas material. This was the jump sack, which would hang from the front of his harness as he fell towards earth.

Originally, the SAS had used a parachute system that strapped to the jumper's back with the Bergen attached below it. Trouble was, that made the jumper backside-heavy. When he fell through the aircraft's slipstream the vortex could send him into a violent spin, which could render him unconscious. The parachute would still open automatically at a certain altitude, but with the jumper falling on his back it would open under him. The jumper would fall through his own chute and he'd plummet to earth like a stone.

The new system that Range and his team were using was designated the BT80. The chute strapped to the jumper's back, but the Bergen hung in its canvas bag from the front. That way, even if the jumper did fall unconscious, the weight of the Bergen would force him to fall front-first, so when the chute was triggered automatically it would open above him and properly inflate.

Together with their HAPLSS high-altitude breathing equipment, each man was jumping with some £100,000 worth of kit strapped to his body. With the twelve of them, that was over a million pounds' worth of specialist gear, not counting all their weaponry and ammo. It was testimony to the priority given to their mission that all of this had been made available without question, and with such alacrity.

Range glanced at his watch. He wore an Omega Seamaster, and at £3,500 a shot it was one of the most expensive purchases he had ever made. Immediately before boarding the aircraft they'd synchronize watches. It sounded like a cliché from some James Bond movie, but exact military precision was everything when jumping onto the enemy's guns.

Range glanced over at The Kiwi, who was lovingly packing the last few items into his rucksack. Beside him on the floor lay his main weapon, a compact VSS Vintorez 'thread cutter' sniper rifle. The Kiwi would have some kind of sub-machine gun stuffed in his Bergen, most likely a Heckler & Koch MP5, but he would be parachuting in with the sniper rifle slung over his shoulder.

The Kiwi chose to use the Russian-made VSS because it was a third of the weight of most of its competitors, whilst still being able to fire a twenty-round magazine. Most sniper rifles were bolt action, each round having to be chambered separately. With the 'thread cutter', you could hit twenty targets in quick succession, with an effective rate of fire of 800 rounds a minute.

But most importantly, the VSS was designed specifically as a silenced weapon, and it could not be operated without its wrap-around suppressor. Broken down into its main components, the VSS could be packed into a compact case, which made it the ultimate portable sniper weapon. It was in use with the Russian Spetnaz – their equivalent of the SAS – and was perfect for fast-moving, covert assassination work.

'You got your Bergen ready, mate?' Range remarked. 'L-hour in sixty.'

'Yeah, mate. But one thing.' The Kiwi levelled his light green eyes at Range. There was something of a snake about to strike its prey about them. He moved over until he was beside Range. 'I've been studying the satphotos of the target. Something troubles me.'

Range knew The Kiwi better than any other bloke on his team. He wasn't just a steely-eyed bringer of death; he also had a brain as sharp as a pin. He knew that The Kiwi was something of a loner, and that he didn't suffer fools gladly. But in spite of his somewhat abrasive character, Range knew him to be as loyal as they came, and he had learned to listen well to whatever he had to say.

The Kiwi spread some images on the rough concrete floor. He was an inch or so taller than Range, but he had to weigh a good few kilograms less. There wasn't a scrap of fat on him, and Range knew him to be unbeatable at hand-to-hand combat. A master at Krav Maga, the Israeli hybrid martial art – a blend of kung fu and raw street fighting – he was as fast as a striking cobra, and just as deadly.

Unlike most martial arts, Krav Maga is all about bringing a fight to an end as quickly as possible by doing maximum damage to an enemy. There are no rules, and all moves are aimed at hitting the most vulnerable parts of the body – the eyes, nose, neck, groin and knee. The golden rule of Krav Maga is: *always use the nearest tool for the job.* You train wearing footwear, to replicate real-world situations, and with whatever comes to hand – planks of wood, metal bars, broken bottles even.

'Right, this is the image of the entire fort,' The Kiwi muttered, indicating four satellite photos spread out on the floor. 'And this' – he pulled out another photo – 'is the underground bunker where the gold is stored. Tell me, is there anywhere within the fort that corresponds to the location of the loot? 'Cause if there is, I can't see it.'

Range studied the satphotos for several seconds, flicking his eyes back and forth between the images. Try as he might, he couldn't seem to detect any shape or form of an underground structure within the grounds of the fort. What was it – an acre square at most? – yet no below-ground structures seemed to be visible.

'I've checked repeatedly,' The Kiwi added, 'and it just doesn't make sense. It's like there's no building in that fort like the one on the satphoto which holds the gold.'

'Maybe it's the angle the photo's been taken from,' Range suggested. 'Or the time of day and the light. Either way, the Gadaffi kid's got to know where his daddy's gold is stored, hasn't he? If we can't get the photos to match on the ground, we'll beat it out of the bastard.'

The Kiwi eyed Range. 'That's if it's there, mate. That's if the gold is actually there.'

Range glanced at his watch again. 'L-hour in fifty, mate. Too late to worry about it now. Either way, the mission's happening, and we'll find out when we hit the ground.'

Chapter Five

Being the most experienced parachutist on the team, O'Shea, the ex-SEAL, would lead the stick out of the aircraft. HAHO and HALO training is incredibly expensive, and the British military was forever short of aircraft from which to do practice jumps. By contrast, the Americans faced no such challenges, and it was hardly surprising that O'Shea had racked up more parachuting hours that any of the others.

For a guy his size – O'Shea was five foot seven, with a whippet-like frame – the American had an unbeatable stamina over distance. He was an ultra-marathon runner, which meant he raced over insane distances – anything up to 1,000 miles over several days. Range didn't really see the attraction. His thing was more of a stomp over the Brecon Beacons in the rain for a good while, ending up steaming in a pub over a few beers.

Still, he had a real soft spot for O'Shea, although the American had never quite got his head around the British sense of humour. What he valued most about the ex-SEAL – and why he used him as his second-in-command – was his absolute unquestioning loyalty, and the certainty that he would never baulk at an undertaking, no matter how risk-laden it might seem.

There was an incredible strength concealed within O'Shea's compact frame. He was one of the few tandem masters on the team, which meant he could HAHO or HALO another person, a sensitive piece of kit, or even a war dog into target, strapped to his own person. Range would have loved to take a dog handler and war dog on this mission. There was little this AQIM lot would fear more than an attack dog at their throats. But freelance dog teams were as rare as rocking horse shit at this level of the game.

'Wheels-up in forty-five,' O'Shea remarked to Range. 'Best we load up the packs.'

'It's *Bergens* and *L-hour*, mate,' Range shot back at him. 'You might get away with "wheels-up" in America . . .'

'Yeah, buddy, like I give a shit. You guys had an empire once, but not these days. This is the American Century.'

The men stomped out to the waiting C130, mounted the open tail ramp and dumped their packs in the order they were going to jump, with O'Shea's nearest the exit. The Kiwi would follow O'Shea, with Jock directly behind him. That way you got a sniper and a machine-gunner – Jock was carrying a fearsome M240 general-purpose machine gun – on the ground alongside your stick leader.

Range was placed somewhere in the middle of the stick. You'd never put the mission commander on point, in case you dropped into a barrage of enemy fire. Randy, O'Shea's fellow former SEAL, was last man out, for he was another of the most jump-capable on the team, and it would be his job to watch everyone's back.

In a way, each man's favoured weapon reflected who he was, both as an individual and as a soldier. Range favoured the tough, unbreakable, brute ferocity of an automatic shotgun – providing maximum up-close killing power. The Kiwi was wedded to his silenced sniper rifle – providing the ultimate in long-range, clinical lethality. O'Shea favoured the snap fighting power of the Colt Diemaco assault rifle – the lightweight, Special Forces version of the trusty M16 – the perfect weapon for a video-game shoot-'em-up lightning-fast war. And as for Tak and Jock, both wielded the big M240 – providing heavy-duty smash-it-up firepower.

Bergens and weapons loaded, Range led the guys back into the hangar. To one side, several blokes in British army fatigues were waiting – the parachute packers and dispatchers (PPDs). These guys had the somewhat unglamorous job of looking after all the specialist parachuting gear that Range and his team were about to use. Range figured the para-systems had to be on loan from the SAS at Hereford, for only a handful of elite units ever got to use such gear.

Two figures were chatting easily with the PPDs: one was The Colonel and the other The Hogan. They'd set up a temporary operations base in an adjacent building, which would be shut down just as soon as the mission was done and as if it had never existed. Range strolled over, exchanged a few words with The Colonel, and was introduced to the PPD team leader.

'You ready, mate?' the PPD commander queried. He nodded towards a dozen parachute packs lined up against the hangar wall. 'You've used this gear before? You know what you're doing, right?'

Range grinned. 'Does a bear shit in the woods?'

'Best get your Gore-Tex on, then,' the PPD suggested. 'It's going to be colder than the Arctic up there, especially as you're doing a HAHO.'

Range and his team proceeded to suit up. On a private operation such as this, dress was down to personal preference, but the one thing everyone had to be absolutely certain of was that his combats had been sanitized. Brand names and manufacturers' labels were cut out of clothing, and all forms of ID – even photographs of loved ones – were left behind. That way, if any of the team were captured or killed there would be little means of identifying them – and HMG would have a better chance of denying any knowledge of their mission.

Each man pulled a thick and cumbersome Gore-Tex suit over his fatigues – ones that had been specially designed for HAHO jumps. It was a real pain having to wear them, for the first thing they'd have to do when they hit the desert was to discard the suits. But without such protection they'd freeze to death during the long drift at altitude. At 30,000 feet they were a good few thousand feet higher than the peak of Everest, and in the permanently frozen dead zone.

Once Range and his men had suited up, The Colonel grabbed them for a moment. With Libya running on a different time to the UK, and with several air assets – a C130 Hercules, and shortly a CH47 Chinook heavy-lift helicopter – flying in on the mission, they needed to synchronize watches. It would be pointless Range calling in the Chinook to lift them out of the desert if either they or it arrived at the landing zone an hour late due to time differences. All needed to be working to a standardized time, known as Zulu time.

'In one minute it'll be zero-eleven-ten Zulu,' The Colonel announced.

Each of the men moved the second hand of their watches to one second ahead of eleven-ten.

'Forty-five seconds,' The Colonel warned. He glanced up from his watch at Range. 'All good? Got all the kit you need? You ready?'

Range nodded. 'As we'll ever be.'

The Colonel nodded. 'Twenty-five seconds . . . Zero-eleven-ten Zulu in fifteen seconds . . . Ten, nine . . . three, two, one: mark!'

On The Colonel's call each man set his watch running. They now knew that all assets brought to bear on the mission would be working to the exact same second. Not a man amongst them was wearing a cheap timepiece. Equally importantly, none was wearing anything particularly flashy. The golden rule was the fewer buttons and gizmos the better. The last thing anyone wanted was a watch with a light or a bleeper that might be triggered accidentally whilst creeping through the desert night.

Range's Omega Seamaster boasted a coaxial mechanism, one that made it more accurate than any other comparable timepiece. Encased in black ceramic and liquid-metal alloy, its case was four times harder than normal stainless steel, so pretty much indestructible. Waterproof to three hundred metres, he could rely on it keeping perfect time no matter what punishment he put it through.

Having synced watches, Range stepped forward to the first parachute pack and checked the seals were in place. After each jump the PPDs repacked the chutes and sealed the pack with red cord. That way the next jumper to use it would know that it hadn't been tampered with. Range had no doubt the seals were intact, but it would demonstrate to the PPD boys he knew what he was doing, and it didn't hurt to put their minds at ease.

The seals inspected, Range turned around so the lead PPD could lift the para-pack onto his shoulders. He wriggled into the shoulder straps, pulled them tight, then fastened the heavy metal chest buckle with a solid thunk. Lastly, he looped the restraining straps tight around his thighs. He now had the equivalent of a large sack of potatoes strapped to his back, and this was only the beginning.

The PPD fussed around some more, further tightening straps and buckles until the pack was immovable. This was vital. When doing a HAHO jump they would drift under the chutes for approaching an hour, and if a strap were loose the pack would shift and saw about, rubbing the jumper's skin raw. The last thing you needed were a raw groin and shoulders when you were poised to move forward and take on a heavily defended enemy target.

Range pulled on his headgear, which resembled a khaki green open-faced biker's helmet. The PPD strapped Range's personal oxygen canister to his chest and passed him his mask, which was linked to the canister by a ribbed rubber tube. Range clipped the mask onto the lugs on the helmet, pressed it into his face and breathed hard to check it made a good, airtight seal. At 30,000 feet there was basically no oxygen, and if the mask or the breathing system failed for just a few seconds he'd be a dead man.

Range gave a thumbs-up, and the PPD switched on the canister. He felt a wild rush of euphoria as the pure, cold oxygen hit his brain. That done, he pulled on his leather gloves, followed by the thick Gore-Tex overmitts. The gloves were partly for the warmth, but more to protect his hands during the jump.

During his days in the SAS they'd most often used chutes operated with foot toggles – ones that left the hands free for holding a weapon. But the BT80 systems they'd been given for this mission were hand-operated units. Using the canvas hand toggles he was going to have to guide himself in whilst hanging suspended under an oblong of silk the size of a large truck. Without gloves, his hands would get torn to shreds, which would leave him in no fit state to fight.

With their HALO kit fitted, the dozen men exited the hangar and made towards the waiting Hercules. Burdened by all their gear, they shuffled forward like a bunch of zombie space astronauts. As the first man – The Kiwi – hit the ramp, the Hercules emitted a high-pitched whine as the starter motors began to fire up the giant turbines. There was a cough and a splutter, and the first of the massive, hook-bladed propellers began to spool up to speed.

The twelve men shuffled over to one side of the aircraft's dark interior, and one by one with the PPDs' help, they lowered themselves into the fold-down canvas seats. As Range took his, one of the PPDs buckled him in and plugged him into the aircraft's oxygen system. They'd breathe from the C130's oxygen tank until it came time to make the jump.

The noise inside the bare shell of the aircraft was deafening. The ramp whined closed, and the instant it did so the rear of the aircraft became a dark tunnel of shadow. They would be flying in showing no lights, and if all went to plan they'd be over the Libyan desert at just after last light. They'd pile out of a darkened aircraft and into the night sky, twelve men clad in black, faces daubed in camo cream, and suspended beneath twelve matt-black parachutes. They would be invisible, and inaudible, to any watchers on the ground.

The aircraft jerked forward and began to taxi along the rough and pitted runway. Designed for take-off and landing from just about any patch of roughly level ground, the Hercules would have no problem with the tufts of grass and ruts. Range leaned forward and gave a thumbs-up to the men on his team. He got a series of raised middle fingers and V-signs in return – *piss off, mate*. It was good to see that everyone was sparking. The time to get worried was when blokes like these started to get serious.

Range felt the aircraft slow at the end of the runway, and then the turbines screamed as it spun itself around on the spot. He felt a surge of adrenalin as the engines roared ever louder, the big aircraft straining to get airborne. The pilot would be doing a last-minute check with The Colonel before releasing the brakes. Inside the hold the air was thick with the heady smell of burning avgas as the fumes seeped in from the howling engines.

As he sat there waiting for the pilot to get the 'go', Range realized that he couldn't remember saying a last goodbye to The Colonel or The Hogan. He was certain they'd have been there, standing to one side of the C130's ramp, but he must have missed it. Rigged up in all his HAHO gear, it was hard to keep a perspective on things, constrained as he was in his own, ever-narrowing world. Plus the oxygen tended to put you into a heightened state of being – like having a massive cocaine rush, but without the worry of the after-party hangover.

A thought came into Range's mind. He remembered the last time he'd been on a mission as crazed as this one. Back in 2000, he'd flown into the African jungles to assault the rebel base of the West Side Boys in Sierra Leone. Pure lunatic, drugged-up killers, the rebels had taken hostage a group of young British soldiers on peacekeeping operations. Range had been at the tip of the spear as the Regiment descended from the dawn skies and wreaked bloody vengeance upon them.

Then, he'd been part of a sixty-strong SAS force, backed by a couple of hundred men from the Parachute Regiment, and with helicopter gunships in support. They'd faced odds of ten-to-one against, but still they'd blasted that rebel base and rescued all the hostages. Here, they were twelve men with nothing and no one in support. They faced similar odds or worse, in terms of their chances of taking that desert fortress and the Gadaffi son alive. But there was one crucial difference: back in Sierra Leone, Range had done what he had done for the Queen's shilling. Here, he was hoping to seize riches beyond his wildest dreams.

There was a sharp change in the howl of the turbines outside, and in an instant the C130 was powering forward. Less than a thousand feet later it lifted off and began clawing its way into the winter skies. Range reached behind and plugged himself into the C130's intercom, so he could tune in to the pilot's chat. It always served to calm him when preparing for a jump.

'Airspeed 300 knots. Altitude 3,000 feet. Rate of climb . . .'

The only threat to Operation Garibaldi would be if a storm blew up over the Libyan desert. As Range well knew, the winter months were the time of the Harmattan, a seasonal wind that came off the Sahara. Where the hot dry winds came up against the wet monsoons of the tropics, massive storms could blow up. At 30,000 feet, the conditions were always pretty much the same: icy cold, calm and stable. But a storm could make conditions at ground level unsurvivable.

The C130's aircrew would be patched into the mission operations centre, and from there they'd get regular updates on the weather conditions on the ground. Range just had to hope it all stayed fine at the target.

'Altitude 15,000 feet,' the pilot's voice intoned. 'Airspeed 348 knots. Approaching cruise altitude.'

As he listened in on the radio chat, Range felt a rush of nausea. As a rule, he didn't get airsick, or seasick for that matter, and he didn't particularly fear the mission. Sure, it was one of the ballsiest jobs that Blackstone had ever taken, but set against the potential rewards the risks were more than worth it. It wasn't fear of flying or of the coming combat that unsettled him: it was the thought of making the jump.

Prior to getting HAHO-trained, every operator has to undergo a series of tests to check natural resistance to low oxygen levels and disorientation. First, you were placed in a compression chamber, one that took you up in stages to the kind of atmospheric conditions you'd face at 30,000 feet. At each stage you had to take a massive in-breath, rip off your mask and yell out your name, rank and serial number, before slamming the mask back on.

If you passed that test, you were placed in the dreaded centrifuge – a giant drum like a monster washing machine. It spun you around and around until you were on the verge of passing out. Before losing consciousness you 'greyed out' – your vision starting to fade into shades of grey. You needed to know when you were about to grey out, so you could recognize it in real jump situations and get yourself out of a spin. After you were done in the centrifuge they gave you a video as a keepsake. Greying out wasn't pretty. Your eyes bugged out, your face was like a skeleton and your cheeks distorted all to hell.

During his years in the SAS, Range had served with Mountain Troop – the wilderness being the domain in which he thrived. Every operator was said to dread most the SERE training, which was designed to prepare you for getting captured by the enemy. Survival, Evasion, Resistance and Escape was seen as being the real man-test of SF soldiering – the moment when your ability to evade the enemy and not to crack once captured was tested to the full.

But Range had loved SERE. For days on end he'd lived rough in the woods, scavenging food and being pursued by an enemy hunter force. He was one of the very few not to get captured. At the end they dragged the hessian sack over his head anyway, and so began the Resistance and Escape phases – the most brutal of all.

The mind-games during simulated capture were evil. He'd seen grown men and supposedly hard men bawling their eyes out. It was a hellish week, especially when he was forced to choose others to be tortured. But it had taught him – it taught all who passed – to survive the worst.

During his earliest years as a fighter, Range had learned that the best way to defeat an enemy was often to wait for him to make the first mistake and to be ready. It was the same during SERE. He focused on surviving the worst, and remaining alert to his captors making a mistake. When they did he seized the moment. He'd escaped the main capture facility – a simulated prison camp – twice, which was something of a record, though both times he'd been recaptured. The key was to never let your captors break you, and to keep alert to your chances, because that kept your spirit alive.

Range had proven a natural at SERE. It had been the compression chamber and the centrifuge that he'd dreaded, and each had proven a horrific trial. Ever since the kids' homes, he hated being locked up or constrained. And whilst he was fully jump-trained, he was never going to kid anyone that getting all trussed up in a suffocating HAHO suit was his thing. He'd suggested they go in by HAHO for the simple reason that it was the only method that would get them onto target undetected.

But truth be told, he was dying to get the jump over and done with, and to have his boots on the desert sand.

Chapter Six

'P minus sixty,' the pilot announced. 'MET conditions and flight path unchanged.'

It had taken a ten-hour flight to get the Super Hercules to its present position, some 400 kilometres north of the release point. Normally, from the months of December through to March, the Harmattan blew south from the Sahara, so the weather conditions should be fairly predictable. It blew as a steady and gentle dry wind, which should present no problems to Range and his men at ground level.

A set of complex calculations – taking account of wind speed and direction at 30,000 feet and at all altitudes from there to ground level – had provided the exact release point from which they should jump. From there, it was a seventy-kilometre glide directly into the fort.

At first, Range had killed time on the long flight studying the satphotos. He had a good idea how they might take the fort, but you never knew exactly until you had eyes on the target. Yet try as he might, Range had been unable to reconcile the images of the fort with those showing the bunker where the gold was supposedly secured. The Kiwi was sharp. He'd sussed out long before that there might be a problem, but, to be fair, Range had been focused on how to get in and do the mission.

For a while on that long flight Range had considered sharing his and The Kiwi's misgivings about the location of the loot with the rest of his team, but he figured there was no point. The only way to prove it one way or the other was to get on the ground and take that fort. In a sense, it was better that the others didn't know, for the worry might distract them from the job in hand.

A couple of hours into the flight Range had dropped off, and he'd dozed until the pilot's voice woke him. He felt stiff as a board, for there was a bitterly cold draught blowing in from the aircraft's rear. He rubbed his hands together vigorously to try to get some warmth into them. He'd kill for a brew.

'P minus thirty,' the pilot intoned.

All along the line of seats figures levered themselves to their feet, stamping stiff legs to try to drive out the cold. Range turned to face the C130's icy bulkhead, as the nearest PPD hefted his canvas-bag-cum-Bergen onto the seat that he'd just vacated. Range bent forward, and the PPD clipped it onto the front of his parachute harness, using a series of massive steel karabiners to do so. When he straightened up, the Bergen was left hanging from his chest on a simple pulley system.

'P minus 20,' the pilot announced. 'Cruising altitude 30,000 feet.'

Range was carrying a thirty-five-kilogram pack on his front, a similar weight of parachute gear on his back, plus fifteen kilos of personal weapons and oxygen-breathing gear. It made walking all but impossible, and it was now that the PPDs would really earn their money. As much as anything, their job was to assist the twelve men as they shuffled towards the aircraft's rear.

The same PPD reached for Range's oxygen tube, unclipped it from the C130's tank, and in a flash had it slotted into the exit valve on Range's tank. Range took a gasp of oxygen, the alien suck and blow of the gas roaring in his ears. His system seemed to be working perfectly well, which was reassuring.

The lead PPD stepped back so that all twelve men could see him. He flashed up ten fingers: *P minus ten*. None of them could hear the pilot any more, for they'd unplugged from the C130's intercom system. During the jump they'd not be able to use their personal radios – used for comms between each man on the operation – for the rush of air would rip the earpieces away.

Range reached up and pulled down his HAHO goggles, which had been perched on his helmet. Resembling a deep-sea diver's mask, the goggles served the same purpose as a motor biker's visor – keeping the wind out of your eyes at speeds in excess of 100 miles per hour, the sort of velocity they'd reach before the parachutes opened.

The lead PPD held up one fist and blew into it, his fingers opening as he did so. Immediately thereafter he held up five fingers: wind speed at the target was five knots, about normal for the Harmattan, and fine for making the jump.

The PPD moved along the line of men, pausing before each to flash three fingers in front of his goggled face: three minutes to the jump. Range turned with the rest of them to face the rear of the Hercules. As he did so he half expected to hear the first notes of whatever track of music the pilot had chosen blasting out of the aircraft's speakers. It was at the three-minutes-to-jump mark that they'd normally start it playing.

Instead he heard a hollow thunk from the rear of the aircraft, which was followed an instant later by an icy inrush of air. The rear ramp was starting to lower, and with each foot it descended a howling gale of wind blew ever more powerfully into the hold. As Range started to shuffle forward, trying to lift the Bergen with one hand and using the other to hold himself steady against the aircraft's side, he figured the pilot must have decided he had nothing in his CD collection worthy of such a moment.

Fair enough. The times were few and far between when twelve men would have jumped into a mission such as this one.

To either side of the ramp the PPDs were strapping themselves to the airframe, so as to prevent themselves getting torn out into the wind. Range glanced forward, and he could see the form of his point man, O'Shea, silhouetted against the howling night. During the long flight his eyes had adjusted well to the darkness, and they'd be making the jump using only their natural night vision.

The secret to making a successful HAHO was to keep your spatial awareness: knowing exactly where you were in the stick of parachutists, and keeping a fix on the others. If you lost someone during the jump, you couldn't exactly radio him to find out where he was. Night-vision goggles tended to mess up your spatial awareness, and they were stashed in the Bergens, along with all the other specialist gear.

Range came to a stumbling halt on the open ramp, with blokes lined up before and aft of him. For an instant he glanced outside. Nothing. A whirlwind of raging darkness. They were on the very roof of the world, the realm of the starlit heavens. He felt his guts drop into the pit of his stomach, and a rush of nausea hit his throat. This was the moment that he dreaded most: *making the jump*.

He'd had a quiet word with The Kiwi at the start of the flight. If he froze on the ramp, The Kiwi had strict instructions to rugby-tackle him out into the darkness.

The PPD started yelling at them, screaming to make

himself heard above the noise: 'Tail off equipment check!'

Each man did a final visual check on the guy in front, to ensure that none of his straps were tangled or snagged.

'TWELVE GOOD!'

'ELEVEN GOOD!'

As each yelled out his ready status, he thumped the guy in front on the right shoulder, in case he hadn't heard. No thump, and you knew the guy behind you was having problems. Range felt a massive whack from the seventh man – no surprises there, for it was the giant Fijian operator, Tak.

Before the words could freeze in his throat, Range forced himself to yell out: 'SIX GOOD!' He thumped the bloke in front, and the shout went down the line. Figures shuffled further forward. Too much separation in the night sky and they'd lose each other. Range glanced at the jump light, which was flashing red: *get ready*.

He got his head down and steeled himself to drive forward and go. There was no way out of this aircraft now but the jump, and no way into that fortress but the long glide through the heavens. So be it. He was going to make this jump even if it killed him.

He felt the wind tearing at his helmet and trying to rip the goggles from his face. Out of the corner of his eye he saw the red light turn green.

In that very instant the PPD stepped back: 'GO! GO! GO! GO! GO!'

Suddenly O'Shea was diving forward and plummeting into the darkness. Figures went after him, each tumbling into the howling void until the ramp was clear for Range. He tried to force his legs to work, but he felt frozen. He was screaming at himself to move, but his limbs wouldn't react. Then he felt an impact like a truck had driven into him from behind, and he was cannoned out of the open ramp. Tak had played rugby for the Regiment, and he hadn't messed around.

Range plummeted into the juddering darkness and hit the aircraft's slipstream. It picked him up like a giant's hand and threw him around and around. An instant later he broke free from the raging air current, starring out his arms and legs in an effort to stabilize the dive. Above him he saw the solid form of Tak doing likewise, whilst below him there was a barely audible snap, as number five parachute in the stick was triggered.

Range pushed his head into the dive, and for an instant he felt like a mini-version of the Shuttle plummeting towards earth. Then there was a sharp tug on his para-pack as the static line triggered his chute, and it shot out behind him in a tower of blossoming silk.

The chute caught, filled with air, and wham! – his 100-miles-an-hour fall hit a brick wall. He felt his shoulders grabbed by this massive, irresistible force, and an instant later he was hanging almost motionless in the still night air.

Range glanced up at the chute to make sure it was good. He grabbed the steering toggles and gave a sharp pull on each to force air into the chute. But whilst the left toggle felt good and responsive the right was stiff and immovable. Range tugged again, but all it served to do was send his chute into a spin, as the right toggle pulled the right edge of the chute downwards, and the left failed to have any effect.

Like this, his parachute was next to useless. If he couldn't use both toggles he'd have trouble keeping with the stick. And when it came time to land it would be nigh-on impossible to turn himself into the wind, which was the only way to slow up and make a safe landing. Even now, barely a minute after making the jump, O'Shea would be setting a course for the impact point (IP), the patch of open desert where they planned to land.

Either Range kept with him, or he was lost. And that meant sorting out his bloody toggle.

Blanking all other thoughts from his mind, he reached across with his right hand to his left shoulder, and pulled his knife free from its sheath. In Range's book any soldier who carried a massive dagger or machete was generally best avoided. All you needed was a blade large enough to deal with the kind of problems he was having now, without it getting in the way of things or stabbing yourself accidentally.

The only people who used knives to fight were drunken yobs on the streets of Britain's seemingly lawless cities. In war, if it came to close-quarters combat, you'd win every time by shooting your opponent from close range in the head. It didn't matter much whether you used an automatic shotgun, one that would pepper the entire room with leaden death, or a well-aimed round from a Sig Sauer, but the man who chose to fight with a knife was invariably the dead man.

With the knife gripped in his right hand Range reached up and began to try to unhook the lines that had become trapped. He could see that two or three of the parachute's panels were barely functioning, for the tangled lines were preventing them from inflating properly. As he worked away furiously, he felt the chute starting to spin out of control, as the semi-inflated half dropped below that of the fully functioning one, forcing it to revolve ever faster in that direction.

If he didn't clear the lines, and quickly, he'd spin out completely. In a matter of minutes, the spin would become so bad the entire chute would collapse, and he'd be history.

As the chute whirled faster and faster, twisting Range beneath it like a spinning top, he tried to force his mind to focus on the last few lines he had to work free. But he could tell that the 'grey-out' was approaching as his vision started to blur and fuzz around the edges, and his mind drifted further and further away.

'Focus, you wanker!' he cursed at himself, shaking his head to try to free it of the blinding confusion. 'FUCKING FOCUS!'

He didn't care which of the others might hear him yelling to himself like a lunatic at 28,000 feet, and he sure as hell wasn't about to get overheard by the enemy. With a superhuman effort, he heaved repeatedly at the lines and the final one came free.

The instant they did so, Range started to pump with the toggles to readjust the trim of the chute and counteract the forces that were causing it to spin. Within a few minutes he'd brought it safely under control. Just as soon as he'd done so, he checked the night sky above and below him. His main worry was the position that he'd ended up in and that he might have lost the others.

If they hadn't noticed that he was in trouble, they might have formed up the stick and set off for the IP without him. He glanced down and scanned the velvety darkness. Finally, he caught sight of the faintly glowing cross marking number five chute. He glanced upwards, and above him silhouetted against the stars he counted six parachutists snaking in line behind.

True professionals, the lads had used Range as the marker upon which to converge, once they'd see that he was in trouble. His chute was far from perfect now, but by keeping pressure on one of the toggles he could even up the giant oblong of silk and try to maximize its glide ratio (the distance it could cover for each degree of fall).

The BT80 had one of the best glide ratios of any parachute, and he had to rely on that now to get him to target.

Range's world had gone from one of a swirling, dizzying, turbulent confusion, to one largely of calm silence and stillness. For a few moments he struggled to bring his heartbeat under control and to properly clear his head and relax into the glide. It was only ever the moment of the jump itself that freaked him: once he was into the fall he was pretty much okay.

He knew that one way or another The Kiwi would have bundled him off the ramp of the Hercules when he'd frozen, but he didn't have quite the same steamroller impact as did Tak. Range made a mental note to whack the big Fijian back, just as soon as he got the chance.

Strapped to his left wrist was an altimeter. He checked its faintly luminous dial: 27,000 feet. He glanced at the SP-GPRS, or 'spugger' as they called it, a metal plate with a compass and a military-spec GPS strapped to his chest rig. From that he could tell that they were drifting due south and had sixty-four kilometres still to go to target.

They'd fallen 3,000 feet and covered six klicks. At this rate, they should be good for making their intended IP. As they neared the ground the wind speed would increase, and so would their glide ratio, so they should reach the fortress with a good few kilometres to spare.

O'Shea would be scanning the earth for recognizable landmarks, and Range found himself doing the same. Each man had taken time to memorize the maps, for you obviously couldn't use a map during the drop. It was best to double-check the location shown by the GPS using visual means, for the devices had been known to fail. From this altitude, all Range could make out of the landscape were the different shades of grey, marking out dry wadis and sun-baked desert plains.

There, below him and just to the south was the form of O'Shea's chute, a blacker square against the dark terrain. As number one jumper, O'Shea had the responsibility of choosing the exact spot upon which to land. He'd be scanning the ground as it drifted towards him, searching for an area free from obstructions, and he'd be checking that it was free of hostile forces.

From now on the glide should be steady, silent and stealthy – that's unless anyone else suffered a malfunction with their chute, which was unlikely. Any such problems were almost always experienced directly after diving out of the aircraft. Keeping the stick together was now the absolute priority, so they reached the IP as one functioning war-fighting unit.

Most regular armies and militias don't use night-vision kit, and they don't like to operate in the hours of darkness. They fear the night, and shun the unknowns it brings. Range and his team were the opposite: they felt most comfortable when deploying and fighting under cover of darkness.

As they drifted through the silent night, Range began to feel more and more at ease with himself, and as if he were coming home.

Chapter Seven

There were barely a couple of thousand feet to go, and Range had spent the last forty minutes struggling with his chute, all the while adjusting its trim so as to keep pace with the others. For the last five minutes O'Shea had been performing a spiral descent, which meant that they had to be more or less directly above his chosen IP.

In spite of the rise in air temperature as they neared the night-dark desert, the extremities of Range's body felt frozen due to the long minutes spent at altitude, plus his hands were aching like hell from continuously working the toggles.

After diving out of the C130, this was the next-most dangerous moment. In addition to the risk of making a bad landing, there was no way to operate a weapon when flying under a chute, for both hands had to be kept free to work the toggles. As they drifted towards the desert, Range and his men were completely defenceless.

Range checked his altimeter: 1,000 feet to go. He reached forward with one hand, unfastened the pulley system and let his Bergen drop away into the void. It came to a stop some fifty feet below him, which meant that it would hit the ground first, so taking the weight of its own fall.

As Range concentrated on following O'Shea's line of approach, he felt his Bergen impact the earth with a clearly audible thud. He pulled back sharply on both toggles, keeping extra pressure on one so as to balance out the damaged chute. He felt the vast expanse of silk flare above him, slowing his descent as he turned into the wind. His feet hit the ground, and he stumbled forward a few paces to keep pace with the chute before letting it drift past him on his left side.

As his chute came to the ground, Range flicked his eyes up to check on the parachutists above, and to make sure they weren't about to land on top of him. As the further chutes came swishing to earth to the left and right, Range unstrapped his para-harness, oxygen gear and helmet, and dropped it in a heap, alongside the bundled-up expanse of silk.

He unslung his Maximi machine gun, slid a drum of ammo out of the side pocket of his Bergen, slotted the drum onto the weapon and chambered a round. He was good to fight.

Range fished out his night-vision goggles from his pack and began a three-sixty-degree scan of the terrain, checking for any movement or the enemy. He presumed the area all around was devoid of hostile forces. It had certainly looked that way as they descended from the heavens. But as years of elite soldiering had taught him, presumption was the mother of all fuck-ups.

They'd landed amongst a featureless expanse of barren rock. It looked as if a steamroller had driven across a world of gravel and sand, squashing it dead flat, before the sun had baked it hard as concrete. In the eerie green wash of the night vision, it seemed to Range as if they'd arrived on an utterly lifeless, alien planet. The one upside was that they'd apparently got here totally unopposed and unobserved.

For a moment Range gave himself a silent congratulation. On this mission, the infiltration to target was always going to be one of the toughest challenges. They'd got stage one – the para jump – done, and pretty much without a hitch. And then he spotted it: a flash of movement, maybe five hundred yards to the east of his position.

He kept his gaze focused on that point, and there it was again – something moving through what looked like a line of rough, scrubby vegetation. Vegetation meant water, and the linear formation suggested a dry riverbed, or wadi. In the Sahara, rivers were strictly seasonal. They only ran on the rare occasion when it rained, but the course they cut through the surrounding desert meant they provided ideal cover to move through terrain unobserved.

It struck Range that maybe their arrival here had been observed, and that maybe they had an enemy force creeping up upon them, using the wadi as cover. He spotted the movement again, as someone or something slipped along the wadi rim, half obscured by vegetation.

If they did have an ambush force approaching, Range and his men were in the shittiest of defensive positions. O'Shea had chosen a great landing zone: a patch of terrain empty of any features. But the downside was that they had zero cover. Range felt his pulse notch up a gear as he reached up and flicked his NVG onto infrared mode.

His vision was instantly transformed into a skein of grey, upon which any heat source – anything that threw off the faintest infrared heat signature – would appear as a white-hot glowing figure. The lifeless desert terrain was pretty much devoid of any heat sources – apart from whatever it was that was moving through that riverbed. Range traced the glowing form as it crept ahead, seemingly using the vegetation to mask its every move.

And then as he tracked its progress, the glowing outline paused for a moment and stabilized. As it did so, it revealed itself to have an arched neck, a small head with big stand-up ears, plus four slender legs. It had paused not to level a weapon at Range and his men, but only to nibble on a bush. Range let out a long sigh of relief. It was some kind of small desert deer.

His scan complete, Range felt pretty confident there was no one out there poised to attack. He sniffed the night air. There was a faint breeze that carried with it the smell of hot rock, desert spice and sun-baked camel dung. A blood-red crescent moon hung low on the horizon, and the constellations glittered crystal close and clear. He felt a faint chill, for the cold had begun to seep into him, but it was dry and crisp, and as soon as they got moving they'd warm up.

Range took a second to catch his breath, admiring the wild, empty beauty of the moment. These were almost perfect conditions in which to make the attack. He'd have preferred it a little darker to mask their approach, but the light was more than enough to make good use of the NVG. They worked by boosting ambient light, so you needed a good moon, or, as in this case, bright stars, to be able to use the night-vision kit.

Range grabbed his compass from out of his smock pocket, found north, and orientated himself on the nearest landmark, which happened to be the fortress itself. It appeared as a squat black mass a good thousand yards to the south of their position. He noticed that the line of vegetation marking the wadi ran all the way to the fort's walls. He made note of that. He felt sure it was going to prove very, very useful.

That done, Range struggled out of his Gore-Tex suit and dropped it in a heap with the rest of his para-gear. He flipped open his Bergen, shrugged on his webbing, lifted the pack and slung it onto his back. He gathered up his chute and oxygen gear, hefted his Maximi, and made his way over to the muster point, which was O'Shea's position.

Twelve figures converged silently upon the stick leader. By the time they were gathered, Range had done a quick map read and double-checked it with what he could see on the ground.

'Right, we need to stash the chutes,' he whispered. He pointed due west. 'There's a dry riverbed two hundred yards that way. Tak, take as many blokes as you need and stash the gear. Camouflage it as best you can, but way-mark it on your GPS just in case we need to find it in a hurry.'

'Got it,' Tak confirmed.

'One more thing,' Range added. As Tak turned his way, Range threw a punch at his chest. His fist made contact with what felt like a wall of concrete. The Fijian glanced at him, raising one questioning eyebrow. Clearly, he'd barely felt anything.

'That's for shoving me out of the aircraft,' Range grunted, as he tried to shake the pain out of his fist. 'Hurt me more than it hurt you.'

The Fijian's teeth showed white in the darkness. 'Any time.'

Range dug out a Sophie thermal-imaging sight from his Bergen and focused in on the fort. Via the sight any hot object – a human body, an animal, a fire, a recently used vehicle – would appear outlined by its heat signature. The Sophie magnified the image, so it was fine for use over such distances, and perfect for identifying where any sentries had been posted.

As Range scanned the target, to the left and right of him his team spread out into positions of defence. They didn't for one moment think that their arrival had been observed, for they'd dropped silently out of the darkness like wraiths, but you could never be too careful.

The target was named *Qaser El Jebel* – Fort of the Mount – due to the fact that it perched on a low hill. That made it fine for defensive purposes, but it had also proven one of the fort's major shortcomings. There was no well inside the grounds, and the only source of water lay in a small oasis at the base of the hill. Range could see its location marked by a clump of palm trees.

Had they all the time in the world they could take the oasis, and wait for the castle's occupants to start dying of thirst. As it was, they had only the hours of darkness in which to complete the mission. The Chinook was scheduled to be inbound at first light the following morning, as long as they sent the message to call it in.

His study of the fort done, Range called the guys in for a Chinese parliament – a final mission-planning session. He could sense the tension and urgency amongst his men. They had been on the ground for a good forty minutes and time was running.

'Right, this is what I see,' Range began, scratching a rough outline in the sand. 'Just like The Colonel briefed us, four round towers, plus linking walls with battlements and regular gun slits. I've seen three sentries on each tower, manning what look like heavy machine guns – probably Dushkas. You don't have that kind of artillery unless you're expecting to get hit by something pretty significant, most likely a vehicle-borne attack, or possibly a helo-borne assault.'

The Dushka is the Russian equivalent of the NATO .50 calibre heavy machine gun. It unleashes its chunky, armour-piercing, high-explosive rounds at the rate of 600 per minute. Designed as an anti-aircraft weapon, it's also devastating in a ground attack role, which was how it had been configured here. Its 12.7mm rounds could tear their way through walls and trees, and a direct hit from one of those would rip a limb from your body, or blow your head clean off.

Colonel Gadaffi's Libya had taken delivery of scores of Dushkas from the Soviet and then Russian regimes. In 1988, during the conflict in Northern Ireland, a pair of Dushkas had been smuggled from Libya into Ireland, and used to shoot up a British army Westland Lynx, the fastest helicopter in the world. The Lynx had been hit some fifteen times and forced to crash-land.

At that time Colonel Gadaffi had been a major sponsor of terrorism worldwide, and his was viewed as a pariah state. It was only in more recent years that Gadaffi had been brought in from the cold, and his terrorist-sponsoring ways supposedly put behind him. But the legacy of the Dushkas imported during his reign would long outlast him, as so many of the fearsome heavy machine guns had made their way into rebel, militia and terrorist hands.

'You all know what damage a Dushka round can do,' Range continued. 'So, thank fuck we didn't try to helo in and fast-rope onto target. The breach in the wall is clearly visible, here.' Range marked an X in the centre of one wall. 'If you get a good look at it, it also gives a sense of the thickness of the walls. There's an outer and inner layer of stone blocks, with the cavity filled with rubble and sand.

'In short, the fort looks as solid as the Tower of London,' said Range, 'only it's defended by a bunch of AQIM lunatics with some serious hardware. I don't doubt we can take the place, as long as we can get past those Dushkas and get into it. But there's no way anyone's blasting through or scaling those walls. If we try to go in that way, we'll be all over the place like a handcuffed crab.

'The only obvious route in is via the breach, but you have to ask yourself: why have they left it undefended? It doesn't make sense. You could argue they're a bunch of lazy Arabs, but we know from The Colonel's briefing this AQIM lot don't do things in half-measures. Rebuilding that breach would have been no great trial, or at least rigging up a wooden barricade as a defence.'

Range turned to The Kiwi, who had his eye glued to the scope of his sniper rifle. 'Mate, check out the ground underfoot at the breach. What do you see?'

'It's what I don't see,' The Kiwi murmured. 'Not a sign of any foot traffic passing either way.'

'Exactly,' confirmed Range. 'The breach appears completely free of passage, which is weird. Bearing in mind it's on the opposite side to the main gate, you'd expect it to have become a makeshift back entrance. It doesn't make sense, especially when you consider that the oasis with the only water lies directly below the breach. It's the obvious way to collect water.

'So why no path through?' Range paused. 'Only one reason I can think of: the breach is protected by something we can't see, and that means a minefield. So, probably the breach isn't the best way into the fort. Probably—'

'I'd kill for some sarin,' The Kiwi cut in, speaking half to himself as he studied the fort through his scope. 'Creep up to the walls, lob a few canisters in through the lower gun slits, and you'd gas the lot.'

'Yeah, but we don't have any sarin,' said Range. 'Plus we need to take the Gadaffi kid alive. According to The Colonel, he's being held in some kind of underground chamber, which brings me onto my next thought. The one thing the satphotos failed to show us was that the fort is built upon a sizeable hill. It looks like a crown sat upon a bald head – a bit like Jock's sad excuse for hair, now I come to think of it.'

There was a ripple of quiet laughter. The big Scot had

a fringe of long, scraggly red hair running around a bald scalp. If only he'd shave his head he'd look totally fearsome. As if was, the ragged orange fringe made him look like a Viking biker on acid, not that anyone was going to tell him that to his face.

'We have to presume it's hollowed out inside,' Range continued, 'which means . . .'

'Jock's head or the hill?' The Kiwi interjected, without removing his eyes from the scope.

'Will ye shut the fuck up about my heid!' Jock hissed.

Range grinned. 'The hill beneath the fort is hollowed out, and that's where they've stashed Sultan Gadaffi and the gold.'

'That's if the gold is there,' The Kiwi muttered.

'Only one way to find out, and that's to take the fort,' Range retorted quickly. The last thing he needed now was any dissent within the ranks. 'So, to sum up. One: the Dushkas are the main threat and we've got to prioritize hitting those. Two: the back door – the breach-cum-minefield – looks a bit of a challenge. Three: stealth and surprise are the only ways we'll do this. Any suggestions?'

The Kiwi glanced up from his scope. 'Presumably we've all remembered our silencers? I say let's use them. Give me five minutes and a couple of mags of ammo, and I can deal with three of the Dushka teams without alerting anyone in that fort. The fourth is out of sight, hidden to the south side of the castle. But presumably I could skirt around the fort and take that too.'

'Presumably,' said Range.

'Right, that deals with the Dushkas, and hopefully without the alarm being raised. Of course, if they have a change of sentries they'll realize the present shift have all been slotted, so once I've hit the towers we'll have to seize the advantage and press ahead immediately with the attack.'

'All good so far,' Range confirmed. 'Dushka teams slotted. Plan of attack for the fort?'

'Okay, hear this one out, you piss-taking British bastards,' volunteered O'Shea. 'The Kiwi mentioned lobbing some sarin through the gun slits. That got me thinking. They're cut horizontally into the walls, more like apertures for firing cannons through. And while we don't have any sarin, how about we lob a couple of us through? We move forward and someone like Jock hoists me up and shoves me through—'

'Rat up a bloody drainpipe—'

'Shut it,' O'Shea hissed. 'It'll be dark as the grave inside, and there must be passageways running through the tower walls. I'll go in on NVG and with a silenced MP5. I can see them, they can't see me, and they can't hear me killing them, either. Ten minutes and I'll have the place clear, and there won't be an AQIM asshole left standing.'

'The first original thought an American has had,' Range announced quietly. 'A true peach of an idea. Randy, you're wiry enough to slip through one of those gun ports, along with O'Shea?'

Randy rolled his eyes. 'Man, but I am real scared of the dark.'

'Not as scared as they'll be of you,' Range told him. He glanced at his watch. 'Here's the plan of attack. At 2200, that's fifteen minutes from now, we launch stage one: The Kiwi and me move forward and take out the positions on the towers. I'm allowing five minutes to kill all three towers visible from here. At 2205 we'll set off south-west and take out the final gun crew on tower four.

'Meantime, fire team two and three – that's Tak and Randy's lot – get stage two underway, with O'Shea in command and big Jock for some company. Soon as The Kiwi's done for the last of the Dushka gunners, we call you lot in. You advance, sticking to the cover of that wadi that runs more or less to the fort walls. It's key you reach the front entrance undetected. Once there, you prepare to blow the gate off its hinges. Randy, you got enough explosives to do the job?'

'Man, I got enough to start a third world war,' the rangy American drawled.

'You got to let someone else light the fuse,' Range continued, ''cause I need you to go through one of the gun apertures. You take the wall to the right of the gate, and O'Shea, you take the one to the left. Get Tak and Jock to hoist you through, but only once me and The Kiwi have confirmed we're in position by the breach in the rear wall of the fort.'

'Yeah. Got it.'

'Once you're in, you'll work away from the main gate through the towers, killing any AQIM you find. Those left on the gate only trigger the explosives if and when it all goes noisy. That way, we stay covert for as long as possible.'

O'Shea grinned. 'Long fuse, slow burn, big bang kind of thing.'

Range returned the smile. O'Shea had just stolen his favourite catchphrase – *long fuse, slow burn, big bang* – and both men knew it.

'Stage three of the assault: The Kiwi and me go through the breach if and when you need us. If it all goes noisy, which means O'Shea and Randy are in trouble, blow the gate and go through it like a whirlwind. If the gate gets blown we'll come through the breach, so they'll be taking fire from both sides. Any questions?'

'Silly one, this, but how will ye get through the breach?' Jock asked.

'Trust me, there's a way,' Range answered, adding evilly, 'I'll send the Aussie first . . . Oh, and one last thing.' He levelled his slate-blue eyes at his men. Normally, they were sparking with energy and irreverence; now they'd gone cold and deadly as ice. It was the look of a man you wouldn't challenge if he crossed you in a bar. 'We take no one alive, apart from Gadaffi. I want them dead, every last one.'

'The lot?'

Range closed his eyes slowly and opened them, revealing the same look as before. 'Yeah. You slot the lot.'

'Jesus, man, but there'll be women and children in there . . .' O'Shea objected.

'Women and kids is different,' Range conceded. 'But every last AQIM male of fighting age, I want dead. Very. And with even the women and kids I want them locked away somewhere underground – very, very secure.'

'What's the big deal, buddy?' O'Shea asked.

'Once the fort is in our hands, we've got one hundred million in gold bullion to retrieve from below ground and load aboard the Chinook. Ideally, we need the helo parked up pretty much outside the front gate. If one of this AQIM lot gets away, and so much as gets his hands on a working Dushka, he can blast us out of the sky. Plus we know they may have SAMs. We can't afford even the slightest risk. All of the enemy have to end up dead, and that's just how it is.'

Chapter Eight

'Which tower first?'

Range was belly-down in the sand beside The Kiwi, studying the fort through his Sophie sight. He was acting as The Kiwi's spotter, helping him prioritize targets and call the shots. The two men had crept forward a good six hundred yards to get the fort's towers within range.

'South-east,' The Kiwi muttered, his eye glued to the scope. 'Then north-east, then north-west.'

The Kiwi's VSS sniper rifle fired heavy, subsonic 9mm rounds. Subsonic ammo was used to prevent the weapon from making a sonic boom – the characteristic thump as the bullet went through the sound barrier. It was pointless using a silenced sniper rifle if each time it fired the bullet emitted a deafening crack as it approached terminal velocity.

The 9mm rounds were tipped with a tungsten point to enable them to pierce light armour. Due to their low muzzle velocity, they lost energy more slowly than high-velocity rounds, hence the remarkable range of the weapon for its weight and size. The 9mm rounds also tended to ricochet less when striking solid objects, which reduced the noise of the impact at the target.

The accurate range of the VSS was 500 metres maximum, less than a half that of many sniper rifles, but it only weighed in at 2.6 kilograms. Its nearest rival – the Russian Dragunov – had twice the range but also twice the weight. More importantly, the Dragunov couldn't be fitted with a silencer, which was the key reason The Kiwi favoured the VSS.

He lay prone on the dirt, the hollow, tubular stock of the VSS nestling in the crook of his shoulder, its thick silenced barrel supported on one elbow. Back home in New Zealand he'd grown up on a farm, and he'd spent his childhood hunting deer and bush pig. A sniper rifle was only ever as good as its operator. There was none better than The Kiwi, especially when he was on a covert mission and hunting in the dark. And there was no weapon that could rival the VSS as a silent night killer.

The Kiwi had fitted the weapon with a specialized four-times magnification night sight, one that enabled him to compensate for bullet drop, plus wind speed. With the wind blowing at around five knots, he'd adjust the sight to fire one mark to the left of the target and two chevrons above it, to allow for the fact that the weapon was being used at the limit of its range.

The Kiwi slowed his breathing and talked himself into the calm and absolute focus that a sniper needs. He was under no illusions as to the challenges before him. With each tower he had to hit the three gunners in rapid succession, or the first kill would alert the others, and one might get time to yell out a warning.

The VSS emits no muzzle flash, so the rounds would come tearing out of the dark and silent night with little chance for the enemy to return fire. But one cry of alarm and the covert nature of the assault would be blown.

'Okay, I'm looking at the south-eastern tower,' Range whispered, keeping his head as near to The Kiwi's as possible without obstructing his line of sight. This close to the target, they needed to keep noise to an absolute minimum. 'I see three targets seated round the Dushka, side-on to us and looking east. Head and shoulders only visible, with the nearest figure part-blocking the view of the guy furthest away.'

'I'll take the nearest first,' The Kiwi whispered, 'take him down to clear the shots for two and three.'

'Two is four feet to the right of target one, three is directly behind one, but maybe ten feet to his rear.'

'Got it,' The Kiwi grunted. Via the telescopic sight he was only able to focus in on one target at a time, so Range's commentary was vital to give him a sense of where he needed to shift his aim, so as to kill successive targets.

'You'll get head shots only,' Range added. 'That's all there is.'

'Dead's still dead.'

The Kiwi spent a few seconds rehearsing the moves he'd use to take down all three of the targets. Happy that he was ready, he let out a long breath.

'Engaging now.'

There was a faint phut! Without pausing to check if the bullet had hit its mark, he swung the weapon a fraction right, fired again, swung back left and squeezed off a third round. The entire move had taken barely three seconds.

'Targets have disappeared from vision,' Range confirmed.

Range had seen each of the figures twitch and jerk as the bullets struck, before slumping out of view.

'Doesn't mean for sure they're dead,' The Kiwi muttered.

'It doesn't. We'll keep watch for sixty. If there's no movement or noise from the tower, we'll consider them slotted.'

The Kiwi didn't move his eye from the scope and he didn't respond. He just kept watching, silently, like a cat sizing up its prey. The sixty seconds ticked by with no noticeable movement at the tower.

Range broke the silence. 'I think it's safe to say that if their brains were made of chocolate there's not enough left to fill a Smartie.'

'Nicely put,' said The Kiwi.

'Target two, the north-eastern tower. I see three figures seated, but this time they're face-on to us. You're going left to right?'

'Left to right.'

'Okay, this time you've got head and shoulders visible above the tower wall. The figures to either side of the Dushka are clear shots, but the guy in the centre's got the barrel of the Dushka half obscuring his head.'

'I'll go left and right with body shots, a head shot for the central guy, so the round clears the gun.'

'Makes sense,' Range confirmed.

Body shots were easier, as there was more of a target to aim for, but they were less immediately lethal. He saw The Kiwi slip a finger down to the weapon's mode selector and flick it from semi-automatic to fully auto. In semi-automatic mode the VSS uses a ten-round magazine. The twenty-round mag could only be used in fully auto mode. The Kiwi was working in both modes, and he had seven bullets left in his ten-round mag for three kills.

'If you hadn't noticed, they're smoking,' Range added. Via the Sophie sight, the glowing butt-ends showed up like fiery pinpricks each time one of the figures inhaled. Other than that, they appeared as featureless heat-blobs in his sight. 'That has to mean they've heard and seen nothing of the hits on the first tower.'

'Someone should tell them smoking kills . . .' The Kiwi let out a long breath. 'Engaging now.'

Phut! Phut! In rapid succession two 9mm rounds left the barrel. Almost without taking his finger from the trigger he swung right and unleashed a further two shots. As the bullets tore into the chests of the gunmen to either side of the Dushka, he swung a fraction left and fired one shot at the central figure's head.

There was a faintly audible tzzsing! The sparks from the tungsten-tipped bullet ricocheting off the barrel of the Dushka lit up the centre of Range's Sophie sight a burning white.

'Hit the Dushka!' he hissed. 'Target three is on his feet. Re-engage.'

As Range gave the warning, he was acutely aware that The Kiwi had just the two rounds remaining in his magazine. An instant later the VSS spat again, and as the figure on the tower turned to call out a warning the rounds tore into his left shoulder, spinning him around and slamming him into the roof of the tower.

'Third target down but not out!' Range reported. Through one of the gun slits he could see the figure crawling towards the rear side of the tower.

The Kiwi ripped off the empty mag, snatched up a new magazine of ammo that he'd laid beside the weapon and slotted it into the breech.

'He's visible through the third gun slit from the left, crawling . . .'

Phut! Phut! Phut!

'He's stopped moving now,' The Kiwi remarked, taking his finger off the trigger mechanism.

'Nicely done. We keep watch for sixty?'

'Sixty,' confirmed The Kiwi. 'But is it just me, mate, or is the visibility dropping?'

Range tore his gaze away from the Sophie and glanced into the night. There was a vague opaqueness to the sky above, as if a haze of smoke had drifted between them and the stars. But it wasn't likely to be smoke, not here in the midst of the Sahara desert where there was sod all to burn. It had to be the beginning of a sandstorm.

'Dust in the air.' Range returned his gaze to the Sophie. 'Wind's got up a bit. Let's get this done.' He shifted the sight until tower three came into view. 'Okay, the south-western . . . Hold on, we've got a fucking problem. Two guys are on their feet with AK-47s, and they're gesturing towards the tower we've just hit. The third guy's crouched astride the Dushka, like he intends to use it. Get the–'

Phut-phut-phut-phut-phut-phut-phut!

Range's words of warning were cut short as The Kiwi unleashed on automatic, pumping seven well-aimed shots into the targets on the third tower. Range watched as each was hit, body shots blasting the enemy gunmen off their feet. One of the standing figures collapsed backwards, his skull coming to rest with a sickening crack against the hard steel of the Dushka's breech. The figure manning the big machine gun slumped forward, ending up stone-cold dead on the barrel of the gun.

The third had been standing right by the near side of the tower, and he came to rest with his torso hanging half over the outer wall.

'Three down,' Range hissed. 'One still visible, and may be seen by the enemy.'

All it would take was one glance from the central gateway and the dead man hanging over the wall could be spotted. The Kiwi already had a fresh mag on his weapon.

'Phut!' A single aimed shot to the head threw the dead man back over the wall, and neatly out of sight.

'Sorted,' The Kiwi breathed.

'Let's wait sixty, then get moving.'

Once he felt certain there was no one left alive on any of the towers, Range led The Kiwi in a slow belly-crawl back the way they'd come. They moved away from the fort and began to skirt westwards through the open terrain to bring the last tower within range. As they did so, Range heard a faint squish of static in his radio earpiece.

'In position.' It was O'Shea, radioing confirmation that they'd made it to where the wadi met the base of the fort.

'Affirm,' Range replied, speaking into the mouthpiece clipped to the top of his webbing. 'Wait out.'

But as he and The Kiwi moved further west – their bodies bent double to present the least visibility to any watching enemy – Range noticed the conditions steadily worsening. The wind was blowing at approaching ten knots, and the dust was becoming ever thicker on the air. By the time they'd reached a position from which tower four could be engaged, it was lost in a shimmering brown haze. The two men paused to exchange a few hurried words.

'Fuck it,' Range cursed, gobbing out a mouthful of brown spit into the sand. The dust was getting right into his throat. 'Any point in trying to get any closer?'

'Not a lot. In conditions like this they'll have as much chance of spotting us as we'll have seeing them, which cancels out the advantages of having a silenced sniper weapon.'

'Right then, let's forget it. This is the tower furthest from the front gate, so it presents the least threat. We'll leave it and skirt around to the breach.'

The Kiwi nodded. 'One minute.' He crouched down, unslung his Bergen and pulled out the padded case for the VSS. He glanced up at the dust-laden skies, then back to the sniper rifle. 'Pity, 'cause she's a fine weapon, but not when this shit comes down.'

Range watched in fascination as The Kiwi disassembled the sniper rifle. Within seconds he'd got it broken down into its four constituent parts: stock, silenced barrel, trigger and firing mechanism, plus sight. He packed it away, pulled out his stubby MP5 sub-machine gun, slotted on a magazine, cocked it and slid shut the dust cover.

'Let's go, mate.'

The two men hurried onwards. There was little need to hide their progress, for the storm enveloped them in a soupy brown smog. Via compass and GPS they found their way around to the southern wall, and stopped a hundred yards short of where they figured the breach had to be. They were now in the thick cover provided by the palm trees at the fort's one source of water – the oasis.

'In position,' Range radioed the force on the far side of the fort. 'Proceed as planned. But tower four has not been neutralized. Repeat, tower four has not been taken out.'

'Affirm,' O'Shea replied.

In his mind's eye Range could just see the wiry American preparing to be lifted up and posted through the first gun port. The motto of the Navy SEALs – arguably America's finest Special Forces unit – was 'to find a way or make one'. O'Shea was more than living up to that maxim now, and, not for the first time, Range was reminded of how he valued having him on his team.

Range readied his Maximi light machine gun, retrieving a spare drum of 200 rounds and stuffing it into one of his chest pouches. He reached into his Bergen, pulled out a handful of high-explosive grenades and stuffed them into the remaining pouches of his webbing.

He glanced at The Kiwi. The MP5 sub-machine gun

looked like a small but deadly toy in the tall New Zealander's hands. 'You fit?'

The Kiwi shrugged. 'About that minefield . . .'

Range flashed him this look. 'What minefield? Pretty soon, there won't be one.'

'Like how?'

'It's an old trick I learned from the Afghan mujahideen, back when they were fighting the Soviets. You're too young to remember, but a couple of us grey-heads took in some Blowpipe missiles to shoot down Russian gunships. The Blowpipe was about as much use as an ashtray on a motorbike: a totally shit piece of kit. But whilst we was with them, the muj gave us a demo of how to cross a minefield.'

The Kiwi rolled his eyes. 'A bit like Jesus on the water, was it?'

Range flashed him a crazed smile. 'Just watch, and do as I do, and you'll be fucking all right.'

'I thought we were only going in if it all went noisy?'

Range gestured at the dust blowing all around them. 'With this shit coming down, I reckon they'll need all the help they can get.'

With Range in the lead, the two men crept forward, following a path that snaked through the palm grove. The area was well used, a testament to how often those in the castle must come here to fetch water. Discarded palm husks lay underfoot, and above his head Range could hear dry palm leaves clashing against each other in the wind, like the bones of some giant skeleton.

The grove petered out at the foot of the hillock upon which the castle stood. The fortress itself was all but invisible now, a darker, angular mass against the rushing shadows of the dust storm. Range paused. The path they'd been following turned sharply east, exiting the palm grove and skirting around that side of the fort. He guessed it led all the way to the front entrance, the one and only safe way in.

A hundred yards directly ahead lay the breach in the wall, and he knew for certain now there had to be some hidden factor preventing anyone from using it.

He glanced at his watch: 22.45. They were three-quarters of an hour into the assault. Practically all militaries around the world managed their sentry duties on two-hour rotations. Any longer, and the alertness of those on guard tended to tail off rapidly. A good hour and fifteen minutes had passed and they'd not seen a change of guard. There were forty-five minutes to go, max, before the new shift went up to the towers and stumbled into The Kiwi's handiwork. The change-over could be scheduled for any moment now, at which time the element of surprise would be blown.

Range stared ahead into the gloom. He steeled himself for the next move.

Now to do it.

Chapter Nine

With his Maximi levelled at the shoulder, Range dropped the muzzle slightly so it was pointing downwards and to the front twenty degrees off the horizontal. He cast his mind back to how he'd seen the mujahideen do this, the mad bastards. He tightened his finger on the trigger, and turned to The Kiwi.

'Ready?'

The two of them locked eyes. Range could tell by the look on The Kiwi's face that he knew what was coming. The Kiwi gave a thin smile. 'You crazy fucker, I'm right behind you.'

Range turned back towards the breach. As he did so there was a massive explosion echoing from the far end of the fort, the reverberations muffled by the all-enveloping dust storm. Jock, Tak and the others must have blown the front gate, which had to mean that it had all gone haywire in there. And that in turn meant that there were ten good men against fifty or more of the enemy, and God only knew what weaponry the AQIM lot might bring to bear.

Range surged forward and opened fire with his

machine gun. The Maximi is an 'area weapon', which means it sprays out a cone of rounds to saturate terrain immediately surrounding a target. As Range hammered forward, a solid funnel of bullets tore into the earth some thirty feet to his front, ripping a blasted, smoking furrow through the hard crust of rock and sand.

Range was screaming at the top of his voice as he pounded up the slope, which was just as he'd seen the mad Afghans behave as they'd charged across the Soviet minefields. The muj had refined this method of attack so as to hit the Soviet Red Army from the least-expected direction – from their flanks protected by minefields – which was just the kind of effect Range was hoping for now.

The trouble was, the machine gun as mine-clearance tool had at best a fifty per cent success rate. Generally, there were two or three shortcomings. One, the funnel of rounds somehow missed a mine, failing to detonate it. Two, the runner put a foot down outside of the bullet-cleared furrow. Three, a round set off a mine, and the whirlwind of shrapnel blasted out far enough to disable the runner, leaving him trapped in the midst of the minefield.

As he pounded up the incline, Range tried to blank such thoughts from his mind. He figured he was halfway to the breach in the wall when the inevitable happened: the trigger went click! He was less than twenty seconds into the mad dash and two hundred rounds of ammo down.

He came to a juddering halt, dropped the machine gun butt down, ripped off the empty ammo drum and slammed in a new one. The whole ammo change had taken less than five seconds. He cocked the weapon, pulled the trigger and sprinted onwards, determined this time to make the breach or to go down trying. But as he surged ahead, a thought struck Range: he'd yet to see a single mine detonated by his rounds.

The Maximi shuddered and shook, its barrel smoking hot as it churned out the 7.62mm and tore up the terrain, but he was still to see a major explosion rip apart the earth. There was a gust of wind from behind, a sharp downdraught and out of the gloom before him reared the wall of the fort, a jagged saw-tooth smile showing where the wall was breached, the nearest shattered blocks of stone lying just a few yards ahead.

Range came to a jarring halt, his lungs fighting for breath after the adrenalin-pumping insanity of the charge up the incline. An instant later he felt something cannon into him, knocking him sideways off his feet and into the cover of the wall. For the second time in as many hours, one of his team had rugby-tackled him from behind, and this time The Kiwi landed right on top of him.

Range was about to unleash verbally on the New Zealander when there was a blinding flash of light and his world erupted in a whirlwind of shock and pain. A wall of blasted rubble and dirt engulfed him, the terrifying power of the explosion punching and pounding him like a rag doll. The violence of the blast tore the air from his lungs, forcing him into the hard earth.

Range felt his body tense for the burning agony of injury or worse. He choked and gagged on a mouthful of sand, but still he came up breathing. How the hell was he still *alive*? And what about The Kiwi? He'd been lying on top of him, fully exposed to the gut-wrenching blast. Surely he must've been peppered full of jagged, razor-sharp steel.

After the thunderous roar there was a deafening silence, the air thick with choking, blasted debris. For a second Range just lay there, The Kiwi pressing him down into the dirt. He tried lifting his head, but either The Kiwi was dead or he just wasn't moving. Range tried wriggling out from under him, but he was pinned down, his head ringing and pulsing with agony from the shockwave of the blast.

'Command-wire IED,' said a voice from above. It was The Kiwi, but his words sounded as if they were coming from down the end of a very long and echoing tunnel. 'Time to go kill the bastards that triggered it.'

The Kiwi stumbled to his feet. He was plastered in dust from head to toe, but otherwise he seemed unharmed. No doubt about it, he'd saved both of their lives by hurling them into the cover of the wall the instant before the improvised explosive device detonated. The defenders in that fort were no fools. They must have heard the front gate get blown in, but a force of fighters had remained here, watching over the breach and waiting for an attack.

The Kiwi levelled his stubby machine gun, turned to Range and indicated with his head the route he was taking. 'Cover me.'

'Got it,' Range confirmed.

The wiry New Zealander vaulted into the breach and was gone. He started to climb to the right where the broken wall stretched upwards at a forty-five-degree angle. All around him swirled the thick dust from the blast, mixed in with the murk of the gathering sandstorm. The rubble underfoot made for tough progress, but The Kiwi kept moving upwards, his gun firmly in the aim.

Presumably whoever had triggered the IED must have thought they'd got the both of them, which just went to show how presumption was the mother of all fuck-ups.

Range slipped off the Maximi's drum, hefted it, and by the weight alone he could tell that it was all but exhausted. He slapped on a third, flicked down the bipod from the barrel, and placed it at shoulder height on the lip of the wall. That way, he could put down sustained and accurate fire in support of The Kiwi.

The Kiwi's lean figure disappeared into the dust and darkness, like a coiled snake waiting to strike. His weapon was the MP5-SD3, the silenced variant of the sub-machine gun. From out of the heart of the whirling darkness above him Range heard a barely audible series of shots. There were two in quick succession, followed an instant later by two more: Pzzzt! Pzzzt!

A figure came charging down the broken wall, and from his wild-eyed stare alone Range knew this was the enemy. He opened up, a short and savage burst from the Maximi practically cutting the runner in two. His body was blasted backwards, tumbling down the far side of the wall.

An instant later The Kiwi was back at his side. 'There were three: a spotter, a triggerman and one standing security. That's the one that almost escaped.'

'He ran the wrong way,' Range growled.

'The other direction and I'd have got him.' The Kiwi paused. 'There was no minefield. They'd rigged the breach with a daisy chain of IEDs. They *wanted* an attacker to try to come in that way.'

'How the fuck did you know?'

The Kiwi shrugged. 'Luck, mostly. Whilst you were spraying death into the ground at your feet, I spotted a wire snaking down the side of the breach. It just didn't look right.'

'Well, thank fuck you did. And thanks.'

'No worries.'

The two men turned and stepped through the breach into the fort. The noise of battle from the direction of the front gate was fierce, as Range's main force traded fire with the fort's defenders. Here and there muzzle flashes speared the darkness, and Range could tell that the bulk of the gunfire was at the level of the walkway looping around the fort walls.

All of his men were using muzzle suppressors or silencers – even on the big M240 general-purpose machine guns. Those flashes of flame at walkway level meant that the enemy had the high ground, and as far as he could tell his force was getting hit from all sides. They had one slight advantage: none of the enemy would know that he and The Kiwi had made it through the breach.

There was a squelch of static in Range's earpiece. 'We're pinned down at the entranceway.' It was O'Shea, and whilst he sounded calm enough, Range could hear the deafening snarl of weaponry in the background. 'If you're through the breach, you're welcome to join the party.'

'We're on our way,' Range confirmed.

There was a sudden, savage burst of fire from his left – the clunking, rhythmic bark of a truly heavy weapon opening up: Chthunk! Chthunk! Chthunk! Chthunk! Chthunk!

Range knew instinctively what it was. Only one weapon made such a noise: the Dushka. The team on the fourth tower – the one that The Kiwi had been unable to take out – had joined the battle, and they were hitting his force at the front gate.

Range gestured to The Kiwi. 'We've got to get through to relieve them. Take the right-hand walkway, and I'll take the left. We'll meet somewhere on the far side.'

In answer, The Kiwi brought his weapon into the aim and prepared to move.

'Wait one,' Range added. 'Cover me.'

He unslung his Bergen, reached inside and hauled out the AA-12. Never a better moment for an automatic shotgun. He slotted a twenty-round mag onto the weapon, fastened the Maximi onto the side of his pack with a pair of quick-release straps, and slung it onto his shoulders again. It was exhausting fighting under the weight of the Bergen, but no way was he about to ditch any of its contents. He needed all the ammo and firepower he could muster.

Without another word they parted company, The Kiwi climbing up the broken wall to the right, and Range pounding up the forty-five-degree incline to the left. He reached the top, and stepped out onto the walkway that ran around the fort. To the outside, a thick wall reached up to chest level. To the inside, the walkway ended in a drop thirty feet or more to the ground.

He saw long tongues of flame stabbing out from the tower ahead of him, as the Dushka unleashed on automatic, pounding out its big, murderous rounds. In all the swirling, shadowed mayhem it was likely doing as much damage to the enemy as it was to his own men. But he figured that didn't matter much to these guys:

there were dozens of AQIM fighters here, so they could easily lose a few. Range couldn't afford to lose even one of his team.

He powered ahead, the shotgun pulled tight into his shoulder. He'd made thirty paces when the first human figures emerged out of the shifting gloom. The enemy had placed a blocking group on the walkway that led into the Dushka gunners' position. The nearest figure spotted Range a split second before he opened fire. He tried to bring his AK-47 around to engage, but Range was quicker.

Without slackening his stride he opened up with the AA-12, six rounds of buckshot tearing into the group of enemy fighters in quick succession. KA-BOOM! BOOM! BOOM! BOOM! BOOM! BOOM!

The raw power of the weapon threw the figures backwards, slamming them into the outer wall of the fort. He leapt over their twisted, bloodied bodies, keeping his finger firmly on the trigger as he hammered into the centre of the tower. He swept right with the shotgun, spraying the heavy machine gun position with a solid wall of fire, and blasting its operators to the floor.

He came to a halt in the cover of the big steel gun. He was keeping count of the rounds fired: he was fourteen down, with six still to go. Keeping to the cover, he reached around the edge of the big weapon's mount and unleashed in the general direction of where he figured the second blocking group had to be, operating the

AA-12 one-handed as if it were some kind of giant pistol.

KA-BOOM! BOOM! BOOM! BOOM! BOOM! BOOM! Klick!

Range crouched down, slid the empty drum from the weapon, grabbed a spare from his webbing and rammed it on from beneath the smoking gun.

The amazing thing about the AA-12 was that it had practically zero recoil. A system of springs set in the butt absorbed just about all of the kickback – which meant Range could remain in cover and throw it around and unleash merry hell, as he'd done just now. Point it in the general direction, pull the trigger, and whatever was in front of it was pretty much obliterated. For close-quarters combat in the midst of a dust storm at night, the AA-12 was a dream.

Range broke cover and skirted around the outer wall of the tower, which jutted out from the fort in a semicircle. He reached the far corner, poked the gun around the edge, and unleashed a further three rounds. As the smoke cleared he stepped out into a scene of utter carnage. He figured the first burst from the cover of the Dushka had done for the enemy fighters positioned here. The three rounds that he'd just unleashed at close to point-blank range had only served to chew the bodies up still further.

Range vaulted over them and pressed onwards. He was now heading due north, towards the last tower on his side. Up ahead he could make out the staccato crack-crack-crack of assault rifles firing from the walkway, and the pencil-thin stabs of flame from their muzzles.

By the trajectory of the rounds cutting through the air, and the direction of the muzzle flashes, Range was pretty certain the enemy was focused on the fort gateway, which meant none of them were onto him yet. He sprinted forward, unleashing with the AA-12 at the first shadowy figure that appeared, the wave of buckshot ripping through his back and throwing him off the walkway.

He hit a second and a third enemy fighter, blasting the last one into a crumpled heap at the entranceway to the tower. Seconds later Range found himself amongst the Dushka team on the north-western tower, those that The Kiwi had hit with his silenced sniper weapon. The three gunners were lying dead by the big machine gun, and for a moment it struck Range as odd that the surviving enemy fighters hadn't turned the big gun on his main force.

Its massive steel pipe of a barrel was pointing out into the empty desert, which meant it was useless against a force that was already inside. And then it struck Range as to why: with the Dushka positioned to cover the outer approaches to the fort, there was no way it could be swung around and brought to bear against anyone inside it. The angle made it unusable, which explained why the enemy on the walkways were sticking to using small arms.

There was the burst of an incoming message. 'Man down! Man down!' It was O'Shea, and the tough American was panting heavily from the exertion of battle. 'They got us pinned down!'

'We're moving in!' Range yelled into his mouthpiece. 'Me from the western tower, Kiwi from the east.'

He wondered who the fuck it was had taken the hit. He felt the red mist of rage sweep over him, as he readied his weapon for the final leg of the walkway assault.

There was a sudden, savage burst of fire from behind him – from the area that he'd just cleared. Range saw rounds sparking off the thick steel of the Dushka right in front of his eyes. As he swung the AA-12 around to return fire, he felt a searing stab of pain in his right leg.

He opened fire to his rear one-handed: KA-BOOM! BOOM! BOOM!

Out of the corner of his eye he saw the whirlwind of buckshot tear into the fighter who was engaging him. It was the last of the enemy figures that he'd hit on the walkway. He'd gone down but he'd managed to keep hold of his weapon. As the buckshot raked across his prone form, his head snapped backwards with a sickening crunch, and the AK-47 was torn out of his hands.

Range was pretty certain he was dead now. Keeping a one-handed grip on the shotgun, he reached down with his free hand towards where he'd been hit. Many times he'd seen what horrific damage even a small-calibre round could do to human flesh. A 7.62mm short – the standard AK-47 round – hits a human body at a velocity of 715 metres per second. The bullet ricochets off bone and rips an erratic course through the victim, before tearing a ragged exit hole.

He felt around his calf, where the round had slammed into him. His combats were torn and his hand came up covered in a slick of warm, sticky blood. But he could find no shards of bone, nor any fragments sticking out of his torn flesh, so it looked as if it was only a flesh wound. The adrenalin was pumping through his veins in bucketloads, and it was blanking out the agony, but as soon as the fighting stopped the pain would hit him like a speeding truck.

Since he wasn't about to bleed to death he hauled himself to his feet, levelled the AA-12 and made a move towards the final length of walkway. The haze was worse than ever now. As the wind gusted ever more strongly, it brought thicker banks of dust scudding across the sky. But the lack of visibility was playing to their advantage, rather than that of the enemy. All his men needed to do was to aim for their muzzle flashes, and they could kill the last of them.

Mustering his strength, Range started to hammer along the final stretch that would take him to the tower at the gate. The first enemy gunman appeared. He was leaning out over the edge of the walkway in an effort to put rounds down onto the force just below him and to the left. Range fired once, and at near point-blank range the shotgun round tore into the enemy gunner's head, throwing him forward and off the walkway.

Range put a second round into him as he fell, just to be sure. These AQIM fighters were tough, as the one who'd shot him had just proven, and he was taking no chances that any more might survive a round to the head. He charged onwards, the tower above the gate drawing ever closer, and he kept the shotgun hammering out the rounds, blasting apart a further four fighters as he went.

But as he neared the gate he realized the tower itself was packed with a seething mass of figures. It made sense that the siege was at its fiercest right here, above where his team was pinned down. If he'd been counting correctly, Range figured he'd just fired the last round from the AA-12. There were three fighters in that tower, maybe more, and any second now they were going to spot him.

He dived forward, the AA-12 and his webbing taking the force of the fall. There was fuck all cover, so he had to make his body the smallest possible target.

As he came to a skidding halt lying prone on the walkway, a muzzle spat fire just to his front, and a long burst of rounds went tearing over his head. He felt a savage tug to his back, as bullets hammered into his Bergen.

If the enemy gunner dropped his aim just a couple of inches, he'd be sending the rounds right into the top of Range's skull.

Chapter Ten

In a flash of movement, Range reached behind him, feeling for the quick-release straps that fastened the Maximi to the side of his pack. At any moment he was expecting to get half of his arm blown off by an AK round. Then one of his massive hands closed around the pistol grip of the machine gun, and he dragged it free.

In one smooth movement he swung it forward, flicked off the safety and opened fire. The silencer on the Maximi doubled as a flash-suppressor, killing any muzzle flame that the weapon would otherwise emit. The deafening clatter of the mechanism was right by Range's head as he opened fire – the hard judder of the firing pin, the harsh rattle of the ammo belt as it chewed through the breech – but now he sensed that he had the advantage.

As he traded fire with the gunners on the tower just twenty yards ahead of him, he had definite points at which to aim, whereas they faced an adversary prone on the deck in the midst of a dust storm and firing an invisible weapon. He took aim at the nearest enemy, and as AK rounds tore apart the air all around him, he put a short burst into the target a foot below and to the left of the muzzle flash.

He heard the distinctive hollow thump that bullets make when impacting a human's chest cavity, and the weapon just ahead of him ceased firing. He shifted his aim, squirted out two further short bursts, and finally the guns on the tower fell silent.

He punched the 'send' switch on his radio: 'I'm moving on to the tower directly above the gate. Send two to hold it.'

'Affirm. Not a moment too soon, buddy!'

Range moved forward until he covered the stairwell that led down to the gate below. He heard boots pounding upwards, echoing on the rough sandstone steps. He stepped back and readied the Maximi, just in case they weren't friendly. A bald head shot out of the stairwell, with a sweat-soaked fringe of red hair framing a pair of mad, staring eyes.

'A moment later and I'd have fucking slotted ye myself!' the big Scot roared.

The front of Jock's combats were soaked in a slick of blood – whether his own or someone else's Range couldn't tell – and massive sweat patches were spreading out from under his arms. Range figured he probably didn't look a great deal better himself.

'The tower's yours!' he yelled back at Jock. 'Hold it.'

With that he dived into the stairwell and charged down to ground level. As he hit the deck he heard The

Kiwi's voice over the radio, reporting that the eastern approach to the tower above was now also secure. O'Shea sent up two men to relieve his position, and the wiry New Zealander came tumbling down that stairwell to join Range.

They turned right, and immediately before them were four of the B6 team, two to either side of the inner gateway and trading fire with the enemy. A slick of empty shell cases crunched underfoot as Range inched forward to join the unmistakable compact form of O'Shea.

'Fucking tell me,' he yelled, as he came up on his shoulder.

'Six with flesh wounds,' O'Shea yelled back, as he squeezed off a three-round burst from his Diemaco assault rifle. He had a makeshift bandage wrapped around his bloodied head. 'We'll live.' He paused. 'But Randy's down, and probably out. Unless we can get him to a hospital, and there's fuck all chance of that . . .'

Range roared out a string of curses. 'Right, let's fucking win this one! NOW! Tak and Kiwi, take the high ground and lead a counter-attack from the walkways. Mallet the fuckers with all you've got.'

Range delved into his Bergen and pulled out a fourth drum of ammo for the Maximi. This one had a loop of black gaffer tape wrapped around it – marking it out as packed full of tracer rounds. As a rule, they weren't using tracer, for it would give away their position to the enemy. But right now he had real need of it.

He grabbed the Sophie sight from where it was stowed in his pack and slotted it onto the sight rail. That done, Range rolled out of cover and into the centre of the gateway, until he was lying prone on his stomach facing the enemy, the Maximi supported on its bipod.

'Watch my tracer!' he yelled into his radio. 'Where I fire, that's where the enemy are!'

He brought his right eye up close to the Sophie sight and scanned the wall of opaque dust in front of him. For a moment the sight was blank, but as he swung the weapon gently left a glowing figure emerged. The infrared scanner was powerful enough to see through the dust storm and find those he wanted to kill. There were several enemy fighters clustered behind the cover of some sort of vehicle, from where they had a clear line of fire into the gateway.

Range squeezed the trigger and put a burst of red-hot tracer rounds into the heart of the target. The moment he did so, two M240 machine guns, and a battery of Diemacos and MP5s opened up on the same target. Just seconds after the murderous barrage of fire erupted there was a massive flash, as the fuel tank of the vehicle went up in a searing sheet of flame.

Range figured one of his tracer rounds must have hit the jackpot, the fiery projectile cooking off the wagon's diesel. Via the Sophie he watched several figures stagger away from the inferno, trailing smoke and flame like incandescent scarecrows.

'Burn, you bastards, burn,' he roared.

He was already sweeping right with the Sophie, scanning for more targets. A dozen enemy fighters were hit in this way, their heat signatures proving their death sentence, before the handful of survivors broke cover and ran for the only route of escape, the breach in the fort's rear wall. Range and his team chased them with harassing fire, but eventually they were lost to even the heat-seeking eye of the Sophie.

Range ceased firing, his men doing likewise the moment his gun fell silent. An eerie stillness settled over the fort.

O'Shea stepped over to Range, and helped pull him to his feet. 'Nice work, you crazy fucker.' He glanced at Range's blood-soaked leg. 'You're wounded.'

'Fuck that. I'm still standing.'

O'Shea nodded in the direction that the enemy had made their escape. 'What do we do about the leakers?'

'I'll go after them,' The Kiwi cut in.

Range threw him a look. 'You'll never manage it, not in all this dust storm shit.'

'You've never had me hunting you,' The Kiwi replied, with a voice like ice.

'Listen, I know you're good,' Range growled, 'but correct me if I'm wrong – within thirty minutes the storm will have blown away every trace of the fuckers. Footprints. Piss stops. Shit stops. The works.'

'Maybe you're right,' The Kiwi conceded.

'So what do we do?' O'Shea prompted.

Range shrugged. 'We let them go. There's not a lot they can do this side of Christmas. There's no settlement that's not several days' march away, unless I've missed something, so they can hardly raise the alarm.' Range paused. 'Tell me – what happened your end of the mission. The short version.'

O'Shea shrugged. 'All was good with the plan, until Randy hit trouble. He got halfway through his gun port, but he's bigger than me. I squeezed through. He didn't.'

'And when you got in?'

'NVG proved useless, what with the dust storm blocking out all the light. I switched to flashlight, which meant I could see them but they could see me. In the confusion a good half a dozen of them must have got away and alerted the others. That's how it all went noisy.'

'Fair enough. And Randy?'

'Pulled himself out of the gun port and went and blew the front gate. But as soon as he'd done that the crazy fucker went charging through it, just as he always does. He was halfway up the stairwell to the tower and trying to take the high ground, when he had a fuckin' stoppage. One of the AQIM lot lobbed down a grenade, and Randy took a bucketload of frag to his chest and legs.'

Range fixed O'Shea with look of cold steel. 'So he's dead.'

'As good as. Like I said, he needs a proper hospital . . .'

'Well there ain't no fucking hospitals this side of heaven, mate, so Randy's dead.' A beat. 'What about Gadaffi?'

'No sign of him. But we've not been able to search properly . . .'

Range waved a hand to silence him.

'Orders,' he snarled, pressing 'send' on his radio. 'Jock, I want one bloke on each of the four corner towers, and see if you can't get them manning those Dushkas. The threat will come from outside of the fort, so be ready.'

'Got it,' Jock confirmed.

'Tak, take one bloke and secure the breach at the rear. Use Claymores to murder any fucker who tries to come through.'

'Got it,' Tak confirmed.

Claymores are a type of simple but deadly anti-personnel device. Once triggered they fire out a devastating wall of hundreds of steel ball bearings that scythe down any human being caught in their path.

'Kiwi, keep a couple of blokes on the tower above the gate, and set Claymores at the gateway itself, in case anyone tries to come through. But I want you tending to Randy just as soon as.'

Of all his men, The Kiwi was the most skilled as a medic. He might have been a killing machine in battle, but ironically he was also a superlative lifesaver.

‘Got it,’ The Kiwi confirmed.

‘O’Shea, take a couple of blokes and search the entire fort. Check for any enemy, and find where Gadaffi’s being held. Plus the gold. And anyone who can bring me an AQIM fighter still half alive gets a gold star.’

‘Good to go,’ O’Shea confirmed.

He turned and jogged off into the dark haze that blanketed the fort. There were a few seconds’ delay before he reappeared with a bloodstained figure draped over his shoulders. He dropped him unceremoniously face-down at Range’s feet.

‘I got one.’

Range used his boot to roll him over. The front of the guy’s blue robe was soaked with blood, and he had a horrible, sucking chest wound that was leaking congealed gore. He was still just about living, but Range figured he wasn’t long for this world. His left arm had also taken a round, and Range could see the ivory white of shattered bone poking through the skin.

He lifted his boot and went as if to stamp his heel violently onto the wound. He halted it just short of the mark.

‘*Mushkilla* – big problem,’ he growled, his voice thick with threat and pending violence. ‘*Ayna ajedu* Gadaffi? *Ayna ajedu* Gadaffi? – where is Gadaffi?’

One of Range’s specialisms in the SAS had been languages, and he was a passable Arabic speaker. The wounded fighter’s eyes stared up at him, full of a blind defiance and a terrible, unspeakable pain.

Range crouched down so he was eye to eye with the wounded figure. 'Listen, mate, I wouldn't cross the road to piss on you if you were on fire. And I don't do sympathy. So, once again and for the last time, where's Gadaffi?'

In answer, the guy tried to spit in Range's face, but the fleck of bloodied phlegm fell short. Where there should have been fear in his eyes, Range could read only a burning, diehard hatred. He'd seen such a look in the eyes of terrorists before, and it sure made it a whole lot easier to torture the bastards.

Range straightened up, lifted his good leg, and slammed his boot down onto the broken arm. There was a piercing scream of agony, and the wounded figure went into a series of jerking convulsions, as Range kept the sole of his boot stamped hard into the wound. He removed it, and gradually the dying man's screams abated.

Range was just about to put the question to him again, when there was a call on the radio. It was O'Shea. 'I'm at the south-west tower. I figure I've got the Gadaffi hideout. Maybe the gold too.'

'On my way,' Range confirmed.

In spite of the injury to his leg, Range was over at the tower in seconds. Excitement drove him on. Inside, O'Shea showed him to a wooden trapdoor that was set into the floor. It was securely padlocked, and Range figured it might be booby-trapped as well. Either way, there was no time to pussyfoot around.

He dropped his Bergen and dragged out the AA-12. Range slotted on a new drum of ammo, stood back from the trapdoor and roared out a warning in both Arabic and English.

'*TAQUF BA'ED 'AN AL-BAB*! STAND BACK FROM THE DOOR!'

Then he let rip. He put four rounds through each of the four sides of the door, and by the time he'd stopped shooting, the thing had all but ceased to exist. He stepped forward, slammed a boot into the middle of it, and it crumpled and fell in. Range flicked on the tiny Maglite he had attached to the weapon. He shone it into the smoke-filled interior. A set of stone steps could be seen leading down to a dark floor.

With his weapon held at the ready he inched himself down, step by cautious step. The first thing that hit him was the smell. Over and above the reek of burned cordite from the shotgun blasts, there was the sickly-sweet, nauseating smell of a human being left to rot. Plus the smell of human shit and piss was mixed in there somewhere, just for good measure.

Range reached the bottom steps and flashed the light around the room. It came to rest on a pair of eyes staring at him, animal white in the darkness. Range advanced to find a man crouched on a bed of stained, rat-eaten rags and blankets. He flashed the light in the guy's emaciated face and into his terrified eyes.

No doubt about it: Sultan Gadaffi.

Range turned to the figure on his shoulder. 'We got him.'

'One down, one to go,' O'Shea smiled.

Range moved his torch beam around the room some more, but apart from a lone piss bucket, it was empty of anything save for the tools of torture. A car battery, crocodile clips attached and looking sickeningly well-used. Iron bars, stained with God only knew what. Chains and hooks suspended from the ceiling. The poor bastard had been entombed here with only the tools of his torture for company.

A grate set high in one wall let in a feeble seep of fresh air, and possibly some light during the hours of daylight. Range used the flashlight to search for a doorway or a passage that might lead to a further chamber, in which there might be secreted one hundred million dollars' worth of gold. But nothing.

'I'll go search the rest of the fort,' O'Shea volunteered. 'Maybe there's another like this below one of the other towers.' With that the wiry American was gone.

Range turned back to the skeletal figure. He was chained to the wall with an iron hasp around one ankle. Where the rough metal had bitten into the man's flesh, it was rubbed bloody and raw. Range could see the marks of torture on the guy's exposed skin, and it looked as if he'd been burned and beaten horrifically.

'Hardly the Dubai bloody Hilton, is it, mate?' Range remarked, gently.

The pair of eyes stared back at him – blank, petrified, uncomprehending.

'You are Sultan Gadaffi,' Range tried. 'I am Steve Range. British soldier. We're getting you out of here.'

Still not even the flicker of a response. For a moment Range wondered whether the horrors this AQIM lot had put him through had fried the guy's mind. Maybe he was totally gone. He certainly looked it. What on earth was the point in taking a guy like this back to Britain to face war crimes trials? He'd clearly suffered more than any man should ever have to.

Range lifted up the leg iron. 'This needs to be gone.'

He levelled the AA-12 and got his bulk between Gadaffi and the blast. Range fired once, tearing apart the iron links in the chain, the sheer power and noise of the gunshot echoing deafeningly around the room.

He turned back to the Gadaffi figure and smiled. 'You're free, mate. Let's go.'

Maybe it was the shock of the blast that had done it, but there seemed to be the hint of a light in the man's eyes, as if he was starting the long crawl up whatever hellish tunnel he'd retreated into.

'Can you stand? Walk?' Range asked. 'Stupid bloody question. Of course you can't.'

He reached down with one powerful arm, lifted up the emaciated figure and threw him across his shoulders. The stench from the guy was overpowering, but what struck Range most was how little he weighed. He was just a skeleton with a sack of skin around it, and he'd been left to starve half to death down here.

As he climbed the steps, Range muttered to himself: 'Don't suppose you know where the bloody gold is, you poor bastard.'

There was a faint outrush of breath where the Gadaffi head lolled by his left ear. 'There . . . is . . . no . . . gold.'

Range froze. 'Sorry, mate, did you say something?'

Barely a murmur, but clearly audible. 'There . . . is . . . no . . . gold.'

Range powered up the stairwell, feeling his heart thudding in his chest. He lowered the figure carefully from his shoulders and propped him against the wall adjacent to the tower's open door. He figured after how long – weeks? months? years? – locked in the dark, the guy's eyes wouldn't be able to cope with the light. It was still dark outside, but there were blokes charging about with flashlights checking over the fort. He'd keep him here for now.

Range crouched down so he was at his eye level. 'So, Mr Gadaffi, tell me about the gold.'

'Water.' A croak. Parched and pitiful. 'Water.'

Range cursed to himself. Of course the guy needed water. Food too, most likely, though what he'd be able to keep down Range didn't exactly know. He delved into his pack and pulled out a litre bottle. He held it to the guy's lips and helped him take a few meagre mouthfuls.

When a man is starved to the degree that he had been, his stomach would shrink to the size of a prune, and it would be almost impossible to get food or liquid into him.

'You need to eat,' Range told him, in Arabic.

He gave a weak shake of his head. 'No need Arabic,' the figure whispered. 'English.'

'Fine, English,' Range confirmed. 'So, you've got to eat. At least something. You've got a long journey ahead of you, and you'll need food.' Range rummaged around in his pack and pulled out some energy bars. 'By rights, you should be hungry enough to eat a dead dog stuffed between two pissed mattresses . . . In the meantime, Granola energy bars will have to do.'

Range devoured several himself, and he made sure Sultan Gadaffi got at least a few mouthfuls down him.

'Okay, so as you probably figured, we're getting you out of this hellhole,' Range told him, once they were done eating. 'But first, tell me, the gold?'

The hint of a smile flashed across Sultan Gadaffi's features. 'There is no gold. At least not here. There never has been.'

Chapter Eleven

Range got Sultan Gadaffi relocated to the main gate and then broke out a collapsible, British army hexy stove – a fold-up metal cooker not a lot bigger than your average cigarette packet. He dug a shallow scoop in the dirt to make a fire pit, and to shield it from the Harmattan that was blowing steadily now. Range pulled out some opaque, whitish fuel blocks much like household fire-lighters, held a lighter to them, and got a brew going.

'Tea or coffee?' he asked.

'I would love to taste coffee,' Sultan Gadaffi replied. 'It has been so very long. But perhaps tea is gentler for the stomach.'

His voice was weak, but he spoke a rich, cultured, formal kind of English, with the strong overlay of a guttural Arabic accent. Range handed him a massive, pint-capacity brew mug, the tea laced with several spoonfuls of sugar.

'I'll be back in two,' Range told him. 'Just going to check on my men.'

With guards placed on every exit point, wall and tower, the Gadaffi son was going nowhere. In any case, he was barely able to stand. Range figured the bloke had to be no more than in his late twenties, but after what they had done to him he looked like a hunched and shrivelled old man.

He sought out O'Shea and gave him a quick heads-up. Sultan Gadaffi's affirmation that there was 'no gold' tallied with O'Shea's findings. Other than the Gadaffi dungeon there were no further underground chambers in that fort.

'Fucking unbelievable,' Range muttered. 'How's Randy?'

'The Kiwi's done his best,' O'Shea replied. 'He's still alive.'

'Got many enemy wounded?'

'Practically none. Those that were left behind saved a last bullet for themselves.'

'Just as we would,' breathed Range. 'If there are any left throw 'em into the dungeon where they kept Gadaffi. Rig up a makeshift door, and make sure it's secure. Let's give them a taste of their own medicine.'

'Water? Food?' O'Shea queried.

'Nope. Nothing. No medical care either. We'll leave 'em to sweat and bleed, just like they left the Gadaffi son to suffer and die.'

Range delved into the map pocket of his combats and pulled out the satphoto showing the supposed location of the gold. He studied it for a good few seconds. He glanced at his watch: 2400. They'd been on the ground for four hours, with maybe six left until first light. The Chinook would be launching from the nearest British base, but it would still need a good two hours to fly in to their location and do the pick-up.

'I'll go speak to Gadaffi some more,' Range told O'Shea. 'Find out what he knows.'

He returned to the gate and found Sultan Gadaffi dozing, his back propped against the wall. The mug of tea was a third empty, which was a good sign. Range figured the shock of the last few hours must have further exhausted him. He shook him gently awake.

'Tea was good? You're feeling better?'

Sultan Gadaffi nodded. 'A little.'

'Great. I want to show you something.'

Range handed him the satellite photo. Sultan glanced at it for a second, his eyes darting from the photo to the date and time details imprinted around the edge.

'What, please, is the date?' he asked Range. 'One loses track of time . . .'

Range showed him the face of his Omega. 'Date and time, mate. Take it you've been here a good while?'

Sultan Gadaffi shuddered. 'A lifetime . . .' His eyes went back to the satphoto. 'So, this is very recent – just a few days old. And it shows the location of what was once my father's gold.' He glanced at Range. 'You were given it by whom – your government?'

'We were,' Range confirmed. He saw no point in hiding anything from the man. Quite the contrary. It was via him that he just might get some answers to all the questions and the dark thoughts that were whirling through his mind. 'We were given that photo and told the gold was here, located in this fort.'

Sultan Gadaffi levelled his grey-brown eyes at Range. There was a little more colour to his face now, but still those eyes were racked with unspeakable suffering.

'You have been lied to,' he declared, quietly. 'There are no underground chambers here, apart from the dungeon in which you found me. It seems inconceivable that your government took these photos, yet somehow by accident gave to you the wrong location.'

'Doesn't it,' Range grunted, in confirmation.

'Perhaps if you explain something of why you have been sent to – rescue? – me, I can shed some light on the matter of this gold.'

'We've not come to rescue you,' Range replied, bluntly. 'We were sent to get you to face a war crimes trial, which after this place probably does feel like a bloody rescue. A cell in The Hague is going to be sheer luxury after the Qaser El Jebel dungeon. A few days' hospitality here and you'd end up with an arse like a wizard's sleeve . . .'

Sultan Gadaffi fixed Range with this haunted look. 'The phrase is unfamiliar, but I think I understand your meaning. Mr Range, the sexual abuse was as nothing . . . Here, they found ways to torture my very soul.'

'What did they want from you? The location of the gold?'

'No. Not the gold. They have that already. You see, the Tuareg were my father's most loyal friends. But when he was deposed the alliance came to an end. The surviving family sought protection from them, of course, and we paid for it – as you know – with our gold. But with my father gone, and his rule at an end, the alliance was over. At that moment the Tuareg's loyalties reverted to their own. Fairly quickly they realized they could make some money – a great deal of money, in fact – by, how do you say it? – selling me up the chain.'

'To this mob – to al-Qaeda in the Maghreb?'

'Exactly. First they sold me, and then, when the price was right, they sold my father's gold. It all went to AQIM. AQIM had millions – maybe billions – of terrorist dollars they needed laundering. Cash can be frozen in bank accounts. Gold cannot. It is untraceable. It has no signature and no serial number. It offered them the perfect way to launder their money. But, of course, you wouldn't put your two most valuable assets in the same place, would you? Hence, I am here, but the gold is not.'

A figure appeared at Range's shoulder. It was O'Shea. 'Mind if I listen in, buddy?'

Range shifted to allow the American to join them. 'Mr Gadaffi, this is Pat O'Shea, one of the Americans on my team.'

Sultan Gadaffi nodded. 'An American. If you had a Frenchman too, all my father's former friends would be here . . .'

Range spat. 'France: a good country ruined by the French.' He turned to O'Shea. 'By way of a quick catch-up, Mr Gadaffi was just telling me where the gold is, so we can go liberate it.' He turned back to Gadaffi. 'Weren't you?'

'Perhaps. Maybe it is possible.' He paused. 'But I would wish for something – how do you say? – in exchange.'

Range smiled. 'Or I could just beat it out of you.'

'You could. You could torture me, but look at me. I might not even survive it. Plus, it would take too long, and time, I sense, is not on your side. Bear in mind if AQIM catch up with you . . . Well, it is better for you to do a deal.'

Range nodded. 'I'm listening.'

'Of course, I could lead you to the gold and you could still betray me, whatever we may have agreed. I know that. But I don't think you will – not when you know what I know . . .'

'Like I said, I'm listening.'

'Tell me: why did the French and your own government ride to the rescue of the Libyan rebels? Why did they intervene in Libya, and not in Syria, or Algeria, or even Sudan for that matter?'

Range shrugged. 'Search me.'

'It is because they knew what the rebels would stumble across were they to topple my father. They knew their dirty secrets would suddenly be revealed, and with the media crawling all over Libya, very likely to the world. That they could never allow happen. So they sent in their military and their intelligence people alongside the rebels – sometimes, in front of them – to clean up . . .'

'I'm interested in the gold,' Range interjected, 'not government shit. Weren't they always this dirty?'

'They were. But this you do need to understand, because it explains why your own government has lied to you, and why it is necessary to do a deal with me and keep me alive.'

'Fine. But get a move on, 'cause time's running.'

Gadaffi took a glug of his tea, as if to give him strength for what was coming. 'France has a massive uranium mine, at Adjaney, just across the border in Niger. In my father's last stronghold, Sabha, in the southern Libyan desert, he had many secret military projects. You may have heard of some of them. Yes, there were chemical weapons. But mostly they were old and obsolete. That wasn't his obsession, at least not in the last years of his life before he was murdered . . .'

The young Gadaffi paused for a moment, as if remembering his father's death at the hands of the rebel mob.

'As any dictator and megalomaniac might, my father was desperate to join that most exclusive of clubs – the nuclear club. France was ideally positioned to help him do so. They had a ready supply of uranium just across what is a lawless and porous border. In the deserts south of Sabha, they used their nuclear expertise to construct an underground facility. It was most of the way to completion by the time the rebel uprising began.'

'Like I always said, the only good Frenchie . . .'

For the first time since they had dragged him out of his stinking cell, Sultan Gadaffi gave a faint smile. 'Yes, I know of this English saying. Of course, the French did the same for Saddam Hussein in Iraq. But the Israelis stepped in and bombed the reactor from the air. My father knew of that threat, and the reactor is sited so far underground as to be immune to air strikes. The French shipped yellowcake uranium across a lawless frontier populated only by desert nomads. Hence the unholy alliance was born: Libya's Great Dictator, the Tuareg, and the Perfidious French, as I think you British often had cause to call them.'

'We have,' Range confirmed. 'But this isn't a British scandal. It's got nothing to do with us. It's got Made in France stamped all over it.'

'It does, but only if it had stopped with the French. As we all know, the British have the best intelligence service in the world. Much as they tried, my father and the French couldn't keep this business secret. Your government challenged my father over this and what they knew. They threatened to take my father to the International Atomic Energy Agency and the United Nations, for treaty violations. They threatened to blow his big secret wide open.'

Sultan shot Range this piercing look. 'You seem to me

to be a thinking man's soldier, Mr Range. As you know, only a select group of nations are permitted to be part of the nuclear club. If Libya's Gadaffi was allowed in, who next? Venezuela? North Korea? Iran? My father was a clever man. Mad, but clever. And he was stupendously wealthy. Money was literally no object to him. Your government extracted a high price for its silence and its complicity. My father used our country's oil wealth to buy off the British, by giving you the most lucrative deals–'

'You talking of buying off a government, or individuals?'

'Well, both really. My father bought your government's silence by issuing massive oil contracts . . . And in certain cases, certain individuals in positions of influence were paid off very handsomely . . .'

'Two questions,' said Range. 'One: you talk about your dad as if you didn't like him much? Two: how do you know all of this, especially if you didn't much get on with him?'

'My father was both a genius and a madman. The traits often run side by side, no? He was a dangerous lunatic and a megalomaniac, someone who would do anything for power. Had he got the bomb, I shudder to think what he might have done with it. Yet for all of that, he trusted me. Unlike my siblings, I was the quiet, studious, retiring one. My father trusted me with his darkest secrets. He trusted me to cut his dirty deals, to keep quiet and never to talk. I was known as The Laundry Man, for he trusted me to wash all his dirty secrets. And in that he was completely mistaken, for I was the one above all others who betrayed him.'

'Like how?'

'It was I who passed the information to your Secret Intelligence Service about my father's nuclear programme.'

'You're telling me you're a British spy?' Range asked, dumbfounded.

'Not a spy, no. But an "asset", I think is how your SIS would refer to me. My codename was Tawariq. It means "those abandoned by God". I chose it. In the last ten years of my father's rule, as his madness deepened, I felt we Libyans truly had been abandoned by Allah . . .'

'All right. But if you're a British spy, why didn't the Brits just call you in once the fighting began? You could have slipped away and handed yourself in.'

'Regimes change. Alliances shift. Friends become enemies. Those in your country who negotiated the deals with my father lost power. And overnight, my father went from being a friend of the West to being demonized. As the world disowned him, those who had done deals with my father realized what dangers they faced. They were terrified their secrets would out. And as my father's son and The Laundry Man, I am the one person in the world who knows every detail of their dirty deals with the late Colonel Muammar Gadaffi.'

'Okay, so we've listened.' Range exchanged a glance with O'Shea. 'On the level of the gold, which is what matters to us, d'you know where it is? And is it within striking distance? If you take us to it, what do you want in return?'

'I know where it is,' Gadaffi confirmed. 'It is in another fortress, not too dissimilar to this. Heavily guarded, but men like you no doubt could liberate it. In exchange for taking you there, I want my freedom. I want you not to hand me over to whoever commissioned your mission, which I happen to doubt is your own government.'

Range ignored the last comment. He was himself starting to question who exactly it was had sent his team in, and why. But such doubts – and maybe revenge – could come later. Right now, the focus had to remain one hundred per cent on the gold.

'All right. So, you lead us to this other fort. Let's say we seize the place, waste the AQIM lot, and lift the gold. What happens next? If we fly back to the UK with a tonne of gold and no Sultan Gadaffi, we're deep in the shit. You can guess what'll happen. And if we fly back with you—'

'Then I am a dead man,' Sultan Gadaffi finished the sentence. 'There will be no highly public war crimes trial, that is for certain. I am not, anyway, a war criminal. I have never, to my knowledge, killed anyone. I will simply be disappeared.'

'Probably,' Range confirmed.

'So, my only safety lies in speaking out. I was a pedantic recorder of all of my father's deals, and I have a detailed dossier stored online, on a secure server. If I expose all of this to the world's media, no one will then benefit from silencing me. Heads will roll. At the very top of your own and the French regimes. But no one then gains anything by snuffing me out. Revenge, perhaps. But hopefully those seeking revenge will be safely behind bars.'

Range nodded. 'You'll buy yourself a few years.' He glanced at O'Shea. 'And for sure we'd like to see those fuckers go down hard. But Mr Gadaffi–'

'Sultan, if you please.'

'Sultan, what exactly are we supposed to do: fly you back and drop you off for a London press conference?'

'I had something rather more subtle in mind. And Mr Range, bear in mind we share an agenda here. Even if you do not find what your people have done unacceptable, surely you object to the fact that they lied to you and your men. The satellite images are of the right building. It just happens to be in a fort several hundred kilometres away. Presumably they knew you would never take this job without the promise of the gold. They lied to you, and all to protect – how do you say? – their own backsides.'

Range shrugged. 'I'd expect nothing less of 'em. But yeah, I'd like to get more than a little even. O'Shea?'

'We've got ourselves shot to pieces, and we're gonna

lose Randy,' said O'Shea, angrily. 'I'd like to string the bastards up by their balls, and that's just for starters.'

'You know what the French are doing now?' Sultan Gadaffi added. 'As soon as the guns fell silent, at that very moment they stopped telling their British allies anything. Your forces fought shoulder to shoulder as brothers-in-arms to oust my father, but when the last shot was fired the French stopped dealing with the British completely, and that's when they began their massive clean-up operation.'

'No surprises there,' Range grunted. 'Listen, if there's a way to do a deal with you and to get away with it, I'm all for it. But if there isn't, I'll need to get the gold and hand you over regardless. That's just the way it is. I've got a family to feed, and a bunch of blokes to go find that gold for. You understand?'

'I appreciate your honesty.'

'So, you need to give me a plan that gets us and the gold out of here, satisfies our government that we got you, and keeps you alive. I can't see it myself . . .'

'Mr Range, you should want to get even with these people. They were happy to double-cross all of you to protect their secrets. You should want to get out of my country with the gold, *and to get even*. And I have a very good idea how you – well, we actually – might do this.'

'Let's hear it.'

'You see, there are a few things your Secret Intelligence Service were never told.'

Chapter Twelve

'So, the question is: do we trust him?' Range grunted, as he and O'Shea strode away from the gate. 'And remember, it's make-our-minds-up time, 'cause we've got to get that Chinook inbound.'

'No, buddy, I don't trust him,' O'Shea replied. 'But I do figure he's telling the truth.'

'And the deal he's proposing?'

'We take it. Even if we don't take it because it enables us to fuck those who sent us in here on a lie, we take it 'cause it offers us the best chance to get in and out with the gold.'

Range turned to face the wiry American. 'Right, I'm getting the lads in for a heads-up. But first, we need to appoint someone to take over command of Randy's fire team.'

'He's not dead yet.'

'Maybe, but we're not kidding ourselves he'll last to the morning. In any case, his fighting days are over.'

'Let's make it Tiny.'

Range nodded. 'Good choice. Tiny it is.'

After Tak and Jock, James 'Tiny' Smith was the third-biggest of the men in Range's unit. He'd earned his nickname in the regular British army, where his size had been pretty remarkable. In the SAS, the unit he'd graduated onto, such imposing physical presence hadn't been so unusual, but by then the name had stuck.

Tiny was an inch shorter than Jock, and he wasn't as broad in the beam, but he had a boxer's nose and a tattoo for every day of the week. He was known as a hardened street fighter who was happy to lead from the front when the bullets started to fly.

'Tak, Jock, Kiwi, Tiny – heads-up at the fort gate in five,' Range announced over the radio.

The men gathered at the main gate, out of Sultan Gadaffi's earshot. Range explained that Randy wasn't doing great, and that Tiny was taking over command of his fire team. He outlined the gist of what Sultan Gadaffi had told him – that the gold wasn't there, and that they had been misled and lied to by those who had tasked them with the mission.

'I doubt if The Colonel is in on this,' Range announced. 'I'd find that hard to believe. And The Hogan obviously isn't. But The Fixer – this has him written all over it.'

Range ran his gaze over the five men before him. There was an anger burning in their eyes now, plus the cold, hard realization of betrayal. What he needed to do was take that anger and channel it into a renewed fighting spirit, one that would enable them to carry out the next – and wholly unexpected – stage of this mission.

'Now the good news,' Range continued. 'The gold exists all right. I've shown the Gadaffi son the satphotos, and he's confirmed that's where it is. But it's in another fort 150 klicks east of here.'

'150 kilometres ye say?' Jock queried. 'That's a long walk on a dark night . . .'

'Yeah, but who's talking about walking?' Range cut in. 'There's no doubt about it, HMG sent us in here on a lie. All they wanted was the Gadaffi son. Well, we got him, and I say we go get the gold.'

For the second time that night, Range scratched the outline of a fort in the desert sand. 'Bear in mind this is rough – it's only from what the Gadaffi son's told me from memory. But Qaser Wadi-al-Kabir – Fort of the Great River – sits in the crook of a bend in one of the few seasonal rivers here in the desert. It's a giant wadi, so it flows only when it rains. The fort lies at the base of the Jebel Arkanu – the Mountains of Tomorrow. When it rains on the Jebel the wadi becomes a raging flood, hence its name – Fort of the Great River.

'The fort's older than this place, and it's much larger and with a more confusing layout. The key factor is this.' Range jabbed a finger at the southern end of the diagram he'd scratched in the sand. 'Here lies a tomb within which the clan that built the fort used to bury their dead. The tomb was long ago cleared and robbed of all its loot. But right now it's stuffed full of what was until recently the Gadaffi family gold. The satphotos The Fixer gave us: they're from the Fort of the Great River. So, we take the fort and rob the tombs and we've got ourselves our gold.'

Range held up his hand to silence any objections. 'Before you blokes say a word, O'Shea and I have come up with a plan, with the Gadaffi son's help. So hear us out, and leave any bone-stupid comments to the end. One: we call the Chinook in as soon as. The helo arrives, we load up two of the wagons we've captured here. We take the ones with the best weaponry and that are most serviceable.

'We get the Chinook to ferry the wagons and six of us to a forward base, as close to the Fort of the Great River as the pilot can get without alerting its occupiers. The Chinook drops the vehicles, returns here and picks up two more, plus the remainder of us lot. We RV at our forward base, and we get all of that done during the hours of darkness.

'The next stage is a massive risk, but I can't see any way around it,' he continued. 'We lie up all day with the wagons and the helo. The Gadaffi son reckons he knows a patch of cover where we could do so without being detected. At last light we mount up the wagons and head in to take the fort. We do so dressed like locals, and with Sultan Gadaffi up front in the lead wagon to talk us in.

'We'll look like a bunch of AQIM fighters and we'll be

driving their vehicles. Once Sultan talks us through the front gate we'll open up on the fort's defenders. We are the best at what we do, and firing accurately from fast-moving vehicles is one of our greatest strengths. It'll be hard for the enemy to hit us, and we'll have the advantage of night-vision and infrared kit. Whilst three wagons mallet the fort, wagon four makes for the tomb and takes it before those guarding it can wake up to the assault.

'That done, we load up the wagons, drive back to the Chinook with the loot and take to the skies. We're in and out in a matter of hours, and we're each of us as stinking rich as we hoped we'd be when we HAHOed in here. So – thoughts, questions, ideas, utterly stupid suggestions – whatever – let's have 'em.'

'What'll you tell The Colonel when you call in the Chinook?' Jock asked.

'Nothing. I'll just tell him to come get us.'

'So, when the aircrew turn up expecting to extract with Gadaffi, how d'ye get them to undertake a whole new mission?'

'We tell them the Gadaffi son's been moved, and we're going in to hit the fort where they've got him.'

'The Chinook's going to have to fly two missions, not just the one,' Jock persisted. 'What about fuel?'

'O'Shea?' Range prompted.

'47 Squadron RAF operates MH-47s, the Special Forces version of the standard Chinook.' O'Shea was a walking encyclopedia when it came to weaponry, war machines and airframes. 'It's got a standard range of 1,380 kilometres, and a ferry range of 2,250 klicks.'

'Which means?'

'It'll have a minimum range of 1,380, and a maximum of 2,250. Depends whether they've fitted extra fuel tanks. Either way it'll be flying out of the UK, but refuelling en route. Last refuelling stop will likely be in northern Libya, where we know the Brits have their own operational bases.'

'In short,' said Range, 'fuel shouldn't be an issue.'

'What about ammo?' asked The Kiwi. 'I dunno about the rest of you, but I used up a shedload taking this fort. And local clothing. To look like AQIM we have to dress like AQIM.'

'You scavenge the lot,' said Range. 'You discard all non-local weaponry that you can't easily hide, and equip yourselves with what you can take from this place. Likewise clothing. Find a dead bloke your size and go local.'

'And the bloodstains?' The Kiwi queried.

'Added authenticity,' Range replied.

'So what about the Gadaffi son? You can't claim to be going to hit fort two to capture him, when we've already got him with us.'

'Not necessarily.' Range shifted uncomfortably. 'Twelve of us set out on this mission. Twelve of us will board the helicopter for stage two.'

'Twelve of us plus Gadaffi makes thirteen,' said

O'Shea. 'Or at least it did last time I counted.'

'It does. But you said yourself Randy ain't going to make it.'

'Dead or alive, he's still one of us. And dead or alive, he's coming with us. We leave no man behind.'

'In an ideal world . . .' Range shrugged. 'But look around you. This world ain't ideal.'

'You're proposing we leave Randy behind?' The rumbling voice was that of Tak, the giant Fijian. He was a man of few words, and when he spoke people tended to listen.

In answer, Range turned to The Kiwi. 'How long d'you figure he's got?'

'He's been in a coma for the last two hours,' said The Kiwi. 'I've got him on a saline drip, which might keep him going for another hour or two. But come daybreak he'll be gone. He suffered massive internal injuries and trauma, and he needed emergency surgery hours back. He didn't get it. He'll be dead by sunrise.'

The big Fijian flicked his dark eyes back and forth between Range and The Kiwi. 'You're happy to leave him behind because he's black?'

'I'd leave anyone if he was dead and it helped us get the gold,' The Kiwi replied, his voice deadpan and matter-of-fact. 'You included. That's just how it is.'

'Tak, when was race ever an issue in the Regiment?' Range added. 'Come on, mate – never has been, never will be.'

'The man who is dying is a black man,' Tak growled. 'Would you leave one of your white brothers so easily?'

'I don't give a flying fuck about the colour of his skin,' Range rasped, his eyes flashing angrily. 'I care about how he fights and dies, and about the mission. Randy fought like the best of us, but the man is dead. His wife and kids aren't. If he could talk he'd tell us to do whatever it takes to go get that gold, and deliver his share to his family. He needs that far more than he needs us to get his body home. Those are the brutal facts.'

'So what the hell d'you propose we do with him?' O'Shea demanded.

'We bury him as best we can back where we stashed the chutes,' Range replied, 'which is where we'll call in the helo.'

'US Navy SEALs have died on operations,' O'Shea growled. 'But you know what – we've never once left a man behind.'

'You're not in the SEALs any more, mate. You're in B6. You're on a mission barely halfway done, and we've been right royally lied to and betrayed. So, we'll do whatever it takes.' Range raised his voice to address everyone. 'Unless anyone has any better suggestions, I propose a vote. One: who votes that we pursue stage two of this mission – the second fort assault?'

Six sets of hands went up, which made it unanimous. There had been little doubt in Range's mind on that one.

'Two, who votes we leave Randy buried in the wadi? It's not what I want, but it's necessary. The Chinook crew will have been briefed to collect thirteen blokes – that's the twelve of us plus Gadaffi. If we're thirteen, they'll know we've got him, and that'll be stage two of the mission blown.'

Range raised his hand. 'I vote we leave him.' The Kiwi, Jock and Tiny followed suit. After a few seconds, Tak raised a reluctant hand. But O'Shea's remained stubbornly down.

'It's not unanimous, but it's carried,' Range announced. 'Tak and Tiny, go brief your guys. If anyone has misgivings about what we're about to do, send him over to have words with me. This has to be a joint decision, and every bloke can have their say.'

'Will do,' Tiny confirmed.

'Got it,' Tak grunted.

'And Tak, no hard feelings, mate,' Range added.

The Fijian's gaze met that of Range. 'There are none.'

'Get your blokes scavenging as much weaponry and ammo as they can lay their hands on, plus local dress, and load it all into the four most usable vehicles.'

Tiny paused. 'One thing. Why don't we ditch the uniforms and make like locals now? It'll save time and there's less to carry.'

'If you were the pilot of that Chinook, would you want to land if you saw us lot dressed in desert robes and headscarves, and with local vehicles and weaponry?'

Tiny shrugged. 'I guess not.'

Tiny was a tough and reliable soldier, and as hard as they came, but not for the first time it struck Range that he wasn't the brightest tool in the box.

As the two figures headed off to brief their teams, Range, The Kiwi and O'Shea moved back towards the gate.

'You figure it's time to stop the drip?' Range asked.

The Kiwi checked his watch. 'It'll be done by now anyway. I won't renew it.'

'Is there anything his family might want to have?' O'Shea asked. 'Like, you know, to remember him by?'

'There's a body,' The Kiwi replied. 'A blood-soaked set of camos. His weapons. His Bergen. That's it. Take your pick.'

O'Shea stopped and eyed The Kiwi angrily. 'You're a heartless fucker, you know that?' he snapped.

'I've seen a lot of people die,' The Kiwi replied evenly. 'It's always ugly. If I were his brother, I wouldn't want anything to remember him like he is now. That's just how it is.'

The Kiwi split from them and went to check on the dying man. Range and O'Shea headed into the tower above the gateway.

'You got the radio?' Range asked.

O'Shea fished around in his Bergen and pulled out the team's main comms system, a PRC319 secure HF radio. The 319 dated back to the 2003 Iraq war, but its great strength was that it was all but immune to detection or interception. Its 'black box' technology incorporated a computerized brain, one that scanned the airwaves for bad, marginal bandwidth, and sent the message on those borderline-usable frequencies. It hid the comms amongst the noise and chatter, and did so using barely a quarter of a watt of electricity.

The 319's ultra-low energy usage meant that any message it sent was next to impossible to detect by means of an enemy's direction-finding (DF) kit. And with each transmission the radio picked up new encryption codes – so even if a listener did manage to intercept a message, it would be indecipherable.

Without a word, O'Shea began to set up the radio. It involved erecting a wire aerial and plugging together various gizmos that Range didn't pretend to understand. High-tech really wasn't his thing. Whilst O'Shea was doing that, Range went to check on Gadaffi. He seemed to be growing stronger with every sugar-laden brew that Range got into him, which was encouraging.

'Mr Range: I think, perhaps, there is something else you need to know,' the Gadaffi son volunteered. 'Al-Qaeda in the Maghreb, they paid a large price to buy me off the Tuareg. Why do you think they believed that I was worth it?'

Range shrugged. 'Because you are your father's son.'

'In a way, yes. But more specifically, because of my knowledge of his nuclear secrets. Even if they can just get hold of a small amount of fissile material, imagine what they could do with it. They could build themselves a so-called dirty bomb, and hold the entire world to ransom.'

'And did you tell them all of his secrets?'

'Yes. I am ashamed to say I told them everything. But I think, Mr Range, even a man like you would have done the same, had they done to you what they did to me.'

'Probably. I'd prefer to have put a bullet in my brain before they got the chance. I don't suppose you had that option?'

'I did not.' Sultan Gadaffi paused. 'You must understand: the fort you are going in to assault – it holds the sister force to those who were stationed here. They were preparing a mission to seize some of the fissile material resulting from my father's nuclear programme. I was to go with them, as their guide.'

'Well, now you'll be coming with us as ours.' Range smiled grimly. 'I'd say that's a fine turnaround.'

'It is. But that is just the point. You have what, twelve men?'

'Eleven. We're just about to lose one.'

'I am sorry.' Again, the pause. 'But there are as many as ten times the fighters there as you encountered here. The numbers do not, perhaps, look too good on . . . our side.'

'How many are we talking exactly?'

'It varies from day to day. Maybe 300. Possibly as many as 600.'

Range fixed the Gadaffi son with this hard look. 'You having second thoughts?'

'No.' Sultan Gadaffi shook his head. 'You came. The decision has been made. It is the right one. Let this be finished, one way or the other.'

'Mr Gadaffi, we have a saying: fortune favours the brave.'

'Mr Range, we also have a saying: it is what it is.'

Range made his way over to the radio. Truth be told, the news of the numbers they were up against was a bit of a blow, but there was no turning back now. In any case, he'd known elite warriors such as his overcome such seemingly impossible odds before.

'It's ready,' said O'Shea, handing Range the 319 handpiece.

'No hard feelings, mate?' Range asked, as he took it.

'If we can take Randy with us, we take him,' O'Shea replied.

Range punched 'send' on the radio, which put him live on the airwaves. 'Sunray, Spartan One.'

'Spartan One, Sunray,' a familiar voice answered.

Range gave The Colonel the codeword. 'Coordinates of LZ: 894725.'

'Affirm: LZ 894725. Expect Lifter One in one-twenty.'

'Affirm.'

Range cut the line. The whole conversation had taken a little more than ten seconds. He glanced at his watch. They had a Chinook – call sign Lifter One – inbound, and it'd be with them in two hours' time.

They had a shedload to do before the cavalry arrived.

Chapter Thirteen

The next hour or so was a frenzied rush of scavenging weapons, ammo and enough usable clothing off the dead, whilst keeping a watchful eye on the desert wastes outside of the fort. Not a man amongst them had forgotten that a good half-dozen of the enemy had got away. There was always the danger of a counter-attack, and no one was in any doubt that those who had escaped would stand and fight if they got the opportunity to do so.

At 0230 Range went and found O'Shea, who was standing by the front entrance, in amongst the shattered remnants of the wooden gateway. Randy had used a series of shaped charges to blow apart its giant iron hinges and tear the lock asunder. O'Shea was staring out into the open desert, and Range had a good idea what was on his mind.

'Randy's gone,' he remarked. 'The Kiwi went to check not a minute ago, and he's slipped away.'

'God rest his soul,' O'Shea whispered. Born and raised a Catholic, O'Shea had lapsed a little in recent years. Still, he made the shape of a cross on his body, touching his hand lightly across his chest. 'God rest his soul.'

'Yeah. Give the man peace, wherever he's gone.'

Range hadn't been born and christened anything. He hadn't ever had a religion to lapse from, and if he believed in anything now it was getting his hands on that gold.

'There is another option,' O'Shea remarked, as he gazed out into the empty, dust-blown wastes.

'Mate, believe me, we need to leave Randy here. Let it go.'

O'Shea shook his head. 'Not Randy. The assault on the Fort of the Great River. There is maybe another way in.'

'Tell me.'

'I was speaking to the Gadaffi kid.'

'How is he?'

'Better. Positively thriving on the brews you keep feeding him. He even asked me for another Granola bar.'

'Result.'

'You know that fort sits on a wadi – Fort of the Great River and all that?'

'Yep.'

'Gadaffi says when the wadi runs with water it flows right into the fort, or at least there's a duct takes water inside the fort walls. Makes sense. Means you don't have to leave the fort to fetch water. Means you can withstand a major siege. Even when the wadi's dry, there's a spring-fed oasis that forms a sizeable lake, and that carries fresh water inside.'

'And your thinking?'

'SEALs like Randy and me.' O'Shea crossed himself again. 'Our specialty is – *was* – fighting on or under the water. Maybe that oasis and the duct into the fort offer an alternative route in.'

'You've got zero gear,' Range pointed out. 'No dive kit, no scuba gear, masks, tanks, the works.'

'We've got zero scuba gear,' O'Shea confirmed. He had his eyes fixed way out on the desert, staring in the direction of the wadi in which they had stashed their parachuting gear. 'But you know what we do have? HAHO oxygen bottles and breathing masks. It's not scuba kit, but it should work well enough and for long enough to get us across the lake, into the duct, and through into the fort.'

Range let out a long, low whistle. 'That's the second original thought I've ever known an American have . . . Pure fucking genius. So what's the plan?'

'If we can get a couple of us through that water channel we can cut through the fort, take the gate and have it open without anyone even knowing.'

'In case Gadaffi can't talk us in.'

'In case of that. Or in case he's not as trustworthy as he makes himself out to be. You never know who you can trust these days.'

'It'll need more than you alone,' said Range.

'I'll need two. Me and one other.'

'Who?'

'There's only one candidate. Big fuckers like you might float across the lake all right, but I'd never get you through the chute. I'll need The Kiwi. He's lithe enough, and have you ever seen the guy swim? He's like a human eel.'

'You okay with that?'

'Why wouldn't I be?'

'You didn't seem to like the way he dealt with Randy's dying, that's all.'

'I didn't much like your attitude either,' O'Shea remarked. 'I've dealt with it. The thing about The Kiwi, it's like there's no emotion there. No soul. Like there's no human inside the soldier.'

'Mate, I've known him the longest of any bloke here, yourself included. And you know what, he's the best there is. More to the point, he's loyal to a fault. And totally incorruptible. He just doesn't know how to show his emotions much. That's Kiwis for you. Brits are pretty much the same. We don't let it all hang out, like you Americans do. It doesn't mean that we don't feel . . .'

'Okay, cut the pop-psychology crap. You approve of the plan?'

'I do,' Range confirmed. 'Tell me. You're a geek about machines. Does the CH47 carry an inflatable, in case it has to ditch on water?'

O'Shea nodded. 'It does. One big enough to carry a four-man crew.'

'That's your route in. You use the helo's inflatable

and you infil via the wadi or lake or whatever patch of water you find there. You take one of the satphones and you call us when you're in position to go through the duct. Seal the satphone in a ziplock bag, you guys go through, open the gates and call us in.'

'Piece of cake.'

'Let's hope so. We need things to start going our way.'

'It's war, buddy. People die in war.'

'Yeah, but we can't afford to lose any more on this one. You know how many AQIM there are in that fort?'

'About the same number as we had here?'

'Gadaffi reckons anything up to six hundred.'

'Holy shit.'

'Exactly. We're eleven against six hundred. We need every man we've got.'

Thirty minutes later the four Toyota pick-ups formed up and pulled through the open gate. In a snarl of powerful diesel engines they left the Fort of the Mount behind them and drove out into the open desert, the rear vehicle in the convoy carrying Randy's body. They made for the wadi, navigating on GPS to the location where they had stashed their HAHO gear barely eight hours before.

The wagons drew up in all-around defence. Two of the open-backed pick-ups sported Dushkas mounted on tripods, which were bolted to the wagon's floor. The others had PKM drum-fed light machine guns mounted in the rear. The PKM is the Russian equivalent of the

GMPG, and a fine and reliable weapon. In addition to the machine guns, the wagons were piled up with as much ammo as it was possible for them to carry.

Each vehicle must have had the top of the cab sliced off with a welding torch at some time, leaving the front open to the air. Range had seen such makeshift vehicle modifications before, most recently on B6 operations in Somalia. The open-topped look was a new craze in the world of Toyota pick-ups with rear-mounted machine guns – or what in this part of the world were more commonly known as 'technicals'.

They cut the engines, and the silence of the windswept desert descended all around. Range sent one team into the wadi to retrieve the HAHO gear, whilst another scouted for a suitable landing zone for the Chinook to put down. The helo was thirty minutes out, and there was still a lot to do.

When the team returned with the HAHO kit, that too was piled into the wagons – all except one length of dark silk that was unrolled before the last vehicle. O'Shea and The Kiwi lifted Randy's body out of the wagon's flat bed, and placed it onto the material. They rolled it up until it was enshrouded within a massive wrap of silk.

The matt-black cocoon was carried into the wadi, laid on the dirt, and the men began to heap stones on top of it. Soon they had raised a sizeable cairn, one that would prevent any scavenging animals from getting to the corpse. Entombed within the folds of silk, the body would mummify in the hot and dry desert air. There was always a chance that his family – or possible even his fellow warriors – might return to this spot, so the body could be retrieved and given a proper burial.

The men gathered in a semicircle, and O'Shea said a few words over the grave. They stood with their heads bowed as they remembered a good friend and a fine brother warrior. The angry words of earlier were forgotten now, as the men united in their loss. Randy had been popular – one of the most likeable guys in the unit – and he would be missed by all.

Range noted that even Sultan Gadaffi had joined the short ceremony. He stood a little to one side, with his head likewise bowed, and he swayed noticeably in the wind as O'Shea gave the short eulogy. Range figured it was taking all of his strength and willpower to stand there and pay his respects, and he liked the man for it.

The Gadaffi son looked pretty out of place, dressed as he was in Randy's combats. The camos hung off him like a skeleton. The dirty bandage wrapped around his head did a fine job of obscuring his features, and the bloodied holes torn in the uniform only strengthened the impression of him being one of the barely walking wounded. Range just hoped it would pass muster with the Chinook crew. It would have to. It was the best they'd got.

The short funeral done, Range sent a team out to mark the chosen LZ. It was 0255, which meant that the

Chinook was five minutes out, and closing fast on the six-figure coordinates Range had given The Colonel. Four men stood at the corners of the chosen landing spot, each with an infrared marker attached to a length of string.

Once the helo became visible, they would whirl those IR markers around their heads, creating a halo of IR-light marking out the square. Even thought the air was thick with wind-blown dust, the Chinook's forward-looking infrared sensors would see through it, picking up the IR markers, which would provide a foolproof fix for the helo to put down on.

Then, as Range fully knew, the talking would begin. Somehow, he had to convince the aircrew to fly them on to a completely new location, lie up in the open and hostile desert for a day in their forty-five-million-dollar state-of-the-art aircraft, and help them lay waste to another fort of war, not to mention load up the best part of a tonne of gold. He figured they'd take some convincing.

The Kiwi was the first to hear it. The giant helo must have come in skimming the sand dunes, for just as soon as the thwoop-thwoop-thwoop of the rotors had become audible it was all but upon them. As the Chinook descended from the dust-enshrouded sky, its massive, triple-bladed twin rotors – one set forward and one aft of the machine – blew up a choking brownout of a dust storm.

By the time it had cleared enough to make the

Chinook visible, the giant helo was down and the rotors had all but come to a thwooping stop. The ramp was lowered, and from the rear of the CH47 a loadmaster – the airman who oversaw loading in the hold – was waving the men forward and up the ramp.

Range raced ahead, his body bent double to avoid the worst of the downdraught. He paused by the loadie.

'I need to speak with the pilot,' he yelled. 'Bit of a change of plan.'

The loadie pointed him towards the cockpit, and continued to wave the rest of the men aboard.

Range poked his head through the open crew door. Pilot and co-pilot were hunched over the controls, big bulky earphones blocking out the noise of the giant turbines. Range placed a hand on the shoulder of the pilot. He leant his head back and lifted one earphone, clearly expecting it to be his loadmaster with some kind of a message.

'Steve Range. Blackstone Six. There's been a change of plan.'

The pilot turned his head and his eyes crinkled into a smile. 'Range. Heard a lot about you from The Colonel.' He extended his hand. 'Bill Walters, 47 Squadron. What's up?'

'We took the fort, but the Gadaffi kid's not there,' Range answered without missing a beat. 'The Colonel said he mightn't be. Turns out he's not. Sod's law, 'cause the bastards only just moved him. We tortured a few of them and found out where he is. So we'll hop over there, lift him and get ourselves gone.'

Range had realized long ago that it didn't so much matter what you said, it was how you said it. Likewise, the *what* you knew didn't cut the ice anything like the *who* you knew.

'Right, so you don't actually have him?' the pilot queried.

'No, but we've found out where he is, which is as good as. Like I said, a short flight and we'll roust him out of there and be on our way.'

The pilot eyed his co-pilot. 'Check fuel status, will you, Mike?' Then, to Range: 'Any idea how far? As you'll appreciate, this dust storm's not the best of conditions to fly in. Wind-blown sand gets into the engine intakes. Not a happy helicopter.'

'It's 150 klicks, or thereabouts. Shouldn't be too much trouble for one of these birds. An MH-47, ain't she? A proper piece of kit – 2,250 klicks in the fuel tanks, or so I seem to remember.'

'It is an MH,' the pilot beamed. 'Flies like a beauty too. She does have a two-two-five-zero range, but only on ferry, mind you. We should have enough juice. We'll need to clear it with The Colonel. I'll put it on speaker and see if I can raise him'

The pilot flicked a switch on the control panel and spoke into his radio. 'Sunray, this is Lifter. The Joker has been moved. Reassigning pick-up.'

‘Lifter, this is Sunray,’ came back the voice of The Colonel. ‘Negative. Joker is static at your present location. Collect and RTB.’

The pilot turned to Range. ‘Higher says he’s here. And to return to base.’

‘Well he isn’t. We know where he is. We need to go get him.’

‘Sunray, this is Lifter, ground force commander is adamant . . .’

‘And so am I. Bring the Joker in.’

The pilot turned to Range and offered him the radio. ‘Best you speak to him.’

‘Sunray, this is Saladin One. The Joker’s not here. He’s been moved in the last few hours prior to our going in. Looks like they had warning we were coming . . .’

‘Negative, Joker is at your location. Bring him in.’

‘Sunray, you’re not here on the bloody ground. I am. The Joker isn’t here. We need to go get him.’

‘Saladin One, this flies in the face of all available intel.’ The Colonel’s voice sounded unusually strained. ‘You need to bring him in.’

‘There’s no time to argue this over the air. We’ll bring him in, but there’ll be a short detour and a bit of a shit fight to do so. Out.’ Range turned to the pilot. ‘Sometimes, there’s just no telling them, is there? Let’s get airborne.’

Range could tell that the pilot was torn. Short of ordering them to return to base, The Colonel had made it very clear that he wasn't buying it.

'Trouble with men like The Colonel, you're damned if you do and damned if you don't,' Range continued. 'He likes things to be done just right. Bringing in your bird with twelve blokes and no Gadaffi would go down like a turd in a punch bowl, I reckon. That's kind of career-ending stuff.'

'How many are you?' the pilot asked.

'Twelve, though I got two or three walking wounded. Well, one who can hardly walk at all, in fact. But we're good to go.'

The pilot sat there in silence for several seconds. Range could just imagine what he was thinking. If he proceeded with Range's version of the mission, he'd be going against The Colonel's wishes, if not his explicit orders. But if he returned to base without the Gadaffi son, when Range had made it crystal clear that they hadn't got him, he didn't want to think what might happen.

'One hundred and fifty klicks?' the pilot queried. 'To this new pick-up point.'

'Thereabouts.'

'Mike, we have the fuel capacity?'

'More than enough,' his co-pilot confirmed.

'Right, we'll fly you,' the pilot announced. 'What's the bearing? And is there anything else I should know before we get airborne?'

'We're bringing a couple of wagons with us, if it's all

the same with you. Might be useful for getting into and out of the new pick-up point.'

'Right, well, get them and your men loaded. And the bearing?'

'Zero-six-twenty degrees.'

'Zero-six-twenty,' the pilot repeated.

'Plus I'll get you the grid we need to put down on.'

The pilot turned back to his controls and began to flick switches and buttons in preparation for take-off. 'The sooner we're out of here and have your Gadaffi boy, the quicker we're on our way home and we can prove to The Colonel this detour was entirely justified.'

'That's the number-one priority,' confirmed Range.

'And tell your guys to hold on to their hats,' the pilot added, ''cause we'll be going low and fast, to avoid any ground fire.'

CHAPTER FOURTEEN

Range returned to the rear. 'Get two wagons aboard,' he hissed at O'Shea. 'We're coming back for the others if and when I can think of a way.'

The two technicals sporting the Dushkas were backed into the aircraft's hold, one carrying Sultan Gadaffi so he didn't have to walk. Once they were in, Range helped him to one of the fold-down canvas seats along the helo's side, and strapped him in.

'Took a load of frag pretty bad,' Range yelled at the loadie above the roar of the turbines, which were spooling up to speed. 'Maybe it's the shock of it, but he can't seem to talk much. Nothing that a good kip won't heal!'

'Poor bastard,' the loadie yelled back. 'Get one of the door-gunners to unleash a minigun in his ear. That'll bring him back to his senses!'

'Nice one!' Range feigned a smile. 'Right, that's us I reckon. All aboard.'

The loadie did a final count of the men who'd come aboard. 'Twelve pax, two vehicles,' he radioed to the pilot. 'Good to go.'

'You got us the grid?' Range yelled at O'Shea, as the

turbines screamed above them and the aircraft began to rise.

'832746,' O'Shea yelled back. 'Remains of a long-extinct volcanic crater. Desolate. Completely devoid of life. Sounds perfect.'

Range felt the aircraft pull away from the desert, and barely had it lifted when the nose tilted lower and it began to power forward, accelerating towards its cruising speed of 250 kph. Up front in the cockpit the MH-47's state-of-the-art terrain-following radar displayed a three-dimensional ground map of the route to be flown by the pilots. Forward-looking infrared systems mapped that same terrain, but by temperature alone, picking out any heat spots. Four-screen night-vision scanners rendered that same territory into a fluorescent green daylight, so the aircrew could see exactly what they were flying over.

Via such aids the pilots could fly their ship using 'nap-of-the-earth' tactics, at below 100 feet and hugging the contours, and Range and his team were expecting one hell of a ride. At that altitude, a helicopter was all but impossible to shoot down. But just in case it was targeted, a complex system of jammers, automatic hand-off systems, laser warning systems, missile warning systems, pulse chaff and flare dispensers kicked in to defeat any threat.

As the Chinook banked towards the east, Range could see the door-gunners scanning the terrain below them for any threat. He leaned across to O'Shea, and shared an idea that was fast coalescing in his mind.

'Is there any part of an MH-47 you can remove relatively easily?' Range yelled into his ear. 'So as to temporarily disable it?'

O'Shea threw him a look. 'Dunno, buddy. Let me have a think . . .'

'Just in case we need to persuade these guys to stay put in the desert and wait for our return.'

'Maybe the crypto fill . . .'

O'Shea's comments were cut short as the Chinook swung violently to port, throwing him and Range against the aircraft's side. An instant later, a flaming projective went tearing past the helo's open door, as the sky around the speeding aircraft erupted into a violent starburst of burning daylight.

'Holy shit!' O'Shea cursed. 'That, buddy, was a SAM. Either that, or an RPG. But it looked too big and nasty for a grenade round.'

Range gave voice to what they both were thinking. 'The leakers from the fort?'

'Got to be. Though where in God's name they got a SAM from . . .' O'Shea shrugged. 'Only reason they didn't get us is 'cause the pilot flew some awesome evasive manoeuvres. Let's hope they aren't loading up another . . .'

Five minutes into the flight the helo hit its cruising speed of approaching 225 kph. Range figured they were out of the SAM kill zone, and he headed for the cockpit.

The Chinook seemed to have settled into a rhythmic, rollercoaster-like motion as the pilot weaved it through the gently undulating night-dark desert landscape.

Range was forced to hold tightly to the side of the fast-moving helo as he moved through the aircraft. As he appeared in the dimly lit, glass-fronted nerve centre of the helicopter, the vision of the night-dark desert speeding past below took him by total surprise. He couldn't believe how low they were, or that the aircraft wasn't about to plough into the dirt.

The pilot passed control of the Chinook to his co-pilot. 'Mike, your aircraft.'

'My aircraft,' the co-pilot confirmed.

That done, he leaned back towards Range and slipped off one earphone so they could talk. 'Enjoying the ride?'

'Can't you get any lower?'

The pilot grinned. 'We're lower than a snake's belly as it is . . . You have the grid of the LZ?'

Range gave him the coordinates. 'Apparently, there's the plug of a volcano that stands up like a giant black finger of rock, so you can't miss it. If you put down just to the west of that, you should find reasonably flat terrain between there and the remains of the crater rim. It's a desolate and deserted spot, so should be clear of any threat.'

The pilot cracked a smile. 'Just like your last LZ? That was a SAM, by the way. Missed us by a good few feet, thank God.'

'Yeah. Well avoided.'

'Only just, actually. Infrared-guided. Lord only knows where they get them from. But a helo as big as this one, moving relatively slowly just after take-off . . . Well, they should have had us. Must have been an inexperienced operator.'

'I thought the MH-47 was pretty much bulletproof? Just how vulnerable is this thing to ground fire?'

The pilot glanced at his flight computer screens. 'Right now, flying at seventy-five feet above the desert and at 225 knots, pretty much untouchable. By the time they've seen us, we're long gone. But at take-off and landing, it's like a big, slow lumbering invitation to put a missile up our backside.'

Range smiled. 'Nicely put.'

'One of the main advantages of flying an ultra-low-level-capable aircraft is that once we're moving, we're pretty much safe.' He fixed Range with a piercing look. 'The other is that we're flying at well below radar level, so we're off anyone's radar screen. No one knows where we are.'

Range nodded. 'Sometimes, it's best to keep it that way.'

'Sometimes.' The pilot glanced at his controls, checking that all was as it should be. 'You have any satphotos? Always good to get a sense of the lie of the land that we're flying into.'

'No. Nothing more than your bog-standard maps.'

'Still, you seem remarkably well informed as to the terrain around the LZ, and as to the nature of any threat there.'

Range smiled. 'One of the tricks of the trade, mate.'

'Right, well, we'll get you in there all right. Once we're down, get your wagons off the ramp. How long do you expect us to need to wait? We should be on the LZ forty-five minutes after lift-off, so by 0350, which still leaves a good three hours of darkness.'

There was no subtle or gentle way to do this, so Range decided to go for the nuclear option. 'As much as twenty-four hours, mate. We're not doing the Gadaffi pick-up before nightfall. Can't, and largely because we'll need you to fly another shuttle to go back and fetch the other vehicles.'

Walters stared at Range in silence for several seconds. Then he turned to his co-pilot. 'You good with her for a few minutes? I need a proper talk with Mr Range.'

'I'm good,' the co-pilot confirmed.

The pilot reached down, flicked a lever and swivelled his seat around to face Range. Range figured Bill Walters had to be in his late forties, so just a few years older than him. He had crew-cut grey hair, and an unmistakable sparkle in his grey-blue eyes. He also had the nose of a fighter, and Range figured he would make a tough adversary when up against someone he didn't particularly warm to. There was something vaguely familiar about Walters, but Range had a crap memory for faces, and he couldn't place him.

'Listen, Range, I can stretch this thing to daybreak,' Walters told him, speaking slowly and deliberately. 'I can fly you and your men the one extra leg. But going off radar for twenty-four hours, and on an unsanctioned mission?' He shook his head. 'I'll get murdered for it. It's just not doable.'

'Would it help if I gave you no option?' Range suggested. 'I've asked one of the Americans on my team – an ex-SEAL – which part of a Chinook we might remove so as to temporarily disable it. If we did that and rendered you unable to fly, presumably you'd have no choice but to wait for us?'

Walters locked eyes with Range. 'But that would amount to hijacking my aircraft.'

'Exactly. Perfect excuse for you when you get back to headquarters. All you need to say is: *That lunatic Range disabled my aircraft and practically held us at gunpoint. He forced us . . .*'

'And are you holding us at gunpoint?' Walters cut in.

'I'd prefer not to, mate.' Range paused. 'But violence is golden, as they say in our line of business. And trust me, with the stakes as high as they are on this one . . .'

'Well, instead of menacing me and my crew, why not let me in on what this is all about?' Walters countered. 'Correct me if I am wrong, but right now I am still in command of my own aircraft. I think I deserve that much from you if you are going to commandeer it.'

'Happy to, mate.' Range squatted down until he was eye to eye with the pilot. 'We got Gadaffi. He's there in the rear of your aircraft, and dressed in the uniform of one of my men who was killed in that fort.' The pilot darted his head around, to get a look into the helo's echoing hold. 'He's the guy with all the bandages around his head,' Range added. 'Only way we could think to disguise him.

'The point is, the AQIM lot tortured him and messed him up pretty bad,' Range continued. 'They were after some very specific information: the location of the late Colonel Gadaffi's nuclear reactor, which was built with the help of the perfidious French. The Gadaffi boy spilled the beans. Who wouldn't, after what they'd done to him? We're going in to lay waste to the main AQIM force, those who plan to go get themselves some fissile material. In layman's terms, they're trying to build a dirty nuke and we're on a mission to stop them.'

'Then why not simply plot a course for England, deliver the Gadaffi son, report all that you've found and let the powers that be deal with it?' Walters asked. 'Why go AWOL on a mission that's likely to get you all—'

'Look, mate, I don't pretend to know it all,' Range cut in. 'But there are those high up in our administration who don't want all of this to out. I can't explain it all – it's too complicated. But trust me, we have to deal with this here and now, our way. If we don't, there will be a nasty little cover-up and it may never be brought to an end.'

'So, you're planning to drive in and attack this AQIM force, to deny them the opportunity to raid Gadaffi's nuclear facility and build their bomb. Is that it?'

'In a nutshell,' Range confirmed. 'Now, obviously we need your help. And I'm happy to hijack your ship – plus whatever else I need to do – so you and your crew come out of this completely blameless and smelling of roses.'

'So, if I understand you correctly, I and my crew have no choice in this matter?'

'Exactly,' Range confirmed. 'None.'

A hint of a smile crept across the pilot's features. 'In that case I think we're good. I think we understand each other: if you hijack my ship, Mr Range, you leave me no choice but to assist you in your undertaking by all possible means.'

Range returned the smile. 'Pretty much.'

'I'd prefer it not to take any longer than the twenty-four hours you've asked for – sorry, *demanded*. But one question: what happens to you and your men when we fly you back to the UK?'

'Sometimes in life you get fed a shit sandwich. And sometimes in life you just got to get the ketchup on it and get it down you.'

'Rather you than me, Mr Range. But you do know what you're doing?'

'I do.'

'Right.' Walters glanced at his instruments. 'We're fifty kilometres out from the LZ. We'll be there in twelve minutes. Get your men and vehicles ready. There are some camo nets stored in the racks in the helo's hold. You might want to use some of those – sorry, take them at gunpoint – to camouflage your vehicles.'

'One more thing,' Range added. 'It may seem like an odd one, this, in the midst of the Sahara desert, but I need to steal your inflatable dinghy.'

Walters raised one eyebrow. '*Our dinghy*. Mind if I ask why?'

'There's a wadi runs right up to the walls of the fort, plus some kind of lake and oasis. We reckon we might be able to get a couple of the blokes in covertly that way.'

'Smart. The inflatable's in the rack adjacent to the camo-netting. Inflates automatically. Ask the loadie if you can't work out how.'

'Thanks.'

Range turned to go, but Walters put out a hand to stop him. 'Any idea how big this river is, or how low below the surrounding desert it flows?'

'No. But the Gadaffi lad is sure to know. Why?'

'I once flew a mission into Sierra Leone,' Walters replied. 'Op Barras. Hostage rescue mission. You probably know of it. We flew in using the river to mask the sound of our approach until the very last moment. It worked a treat.'

Range held out a hand to Walters. 'Thought I knew you from somewhere. I was on the mission. Probably in the rear of your aircraft's hold.'

Walters shook Range's hand. 'Unforgettable, wasn't it?'

'Awesome. The best.'

'I've never forgotten how we made that approach up the Rokel Creek, crocs jumping off the sandbanks as we passed.' He turned and scanned his instruments. 'I wonder, would we even have enough fuel? Mike, my aircraft if you will.'

The co-pilot handed back the controls. 'Your aircraft.'

'Mike, the refuelling point in Libya: I need to know how far north-west of here it is, and I need an exact computation as to the mileage we can cover with what's left in the tanks, okay?'

'Give me a couple of minutes, and I'll have some answers.'

'One more thing,' Walters remarked to Range. 'D'you mind if I make an announcement to the crew that we've been hijacked by you lot? The black box recorder stores all comms, so it would be something extra with which to defend myself when the bullets start to fly back in the UK.'

Range shrugged. 'Be my guest. Better still, I'll make the announcement myself if you like.'

'Perfect.' Walters turned to his co-pilot. 'I presume you've heard most of what Mr Range and I have been discussing? How d'you think the loadie and the door-gunners are going to react to being hijacked?'

The co-pilot laughed. 'What I wouldn't give to see their faces when the big guy says his stuff.'

Walters handed Range the handset for the intercom. 'Listen up,' Range announced. 'This is Steve Range, Blackstone Six, and I have taken command of your aircraft. I'm up front with your pilot, and I guess you could say he's relinquished control. He had no choice, really. You've been hijacked.' Range paused. 'One more thing,' he added. 'We won't be serving you any drinks and refreshments, but the in-flight entertainment – it'll be to die for.'

Range got some decidedly odd looks off the aircrew when he returned to the Chinook's hold.

He spent the remainder of that short flight running through his assault plan. It was inspired by some of the most infamous British Special Forces operations of the Second World War, ones that had taken place across the desert over which they were now flying. Stirling's SAS had hit German and Italian airfields at night, driving between the rows of aircraft and shooting up anything in sight. They'd trained relentlessly for firing accurately from fast-moving vehicles, which gave them the ability to destroy dozens of targets at a time. More often than not, the enemy was caught so totally by surprise that by the time they'd mounted any kind of defence the shoot-'em-up was done.

Range's plan of attack was pretty much a carbon copy of such missions. He intended to get into that fort and to have it shot all to hell before the enemy had woken up to the attack. He and the men would be doing so from highly manoeuvrable technicals, sporting heavy and light machine guns. They'd rely on the element of shock and surprise, plus their superlative vehicle combat skills, to tear apart the fort's defences.

The major problem that Range could foresee was they'd have to hold the fort for as long as it took to remove the gold from the tomb, load it up and make their escape. But with a Chinook waiting to whisk them out of there, there was little the enemy might do to come after them and hunt them down.

Or so Range hoped.

Chapter Fifteen

It was 0800, and the harsh Saharan sun was creeping over the jagged, razor-toothed rim of the crater encircling their position. The Harmattan had abated, and the dust was rapidly thinning from the skies. In all directions lay an utterly wasted and barren landscape. Towering spines of sharp, black volcanic rock were interspersed with bright yellow sand dune seas, and to Range it looked as if they had landed on some alien, lifeless moonscape.

Having dropped the first two vehicles, plus six of the Blackstone team, they'd flown a relay mission back to their previous LZ to collect the further two technicals. At some stage the pilot had come aft to reassure his crew that this was a fairly benign form of hijacking, and not to worry unduly – they were all basically on the same side.

By first light they'd got the vehicles and the Chinook parked in the lee of a giant spur of jet-black rock, and sheeted over with desert-camo-netting. To the casual observer, the massive helicopter and four wagons would resemble nothing more than a patch of shade. Not that there were likely to be any passers-by in this godforsaken wildness to which the Gadaffi son had directed them.

That done, Range and the pilot found themselves a patch of shade in which to get a much-needed heads-up. For it to be convincing, the 'hijacking' would need some detailed planning and thinking. Bowing to the inevitable, Walters explained to Range the simplest method of disabling his aircraft, one that as a bonus would be etched indelibly on the Chinook's in-flight computer systems.

At the start of each and every mission the crew was given a drive that slotted into the flight computer. It contained all information pertinent to the coming operation: satphotos, mapping, call signs, weather reports, codewords, the works. If Range removed the drive and 'forced' Walters to wipe the information from his in-flight computer system, the aircraft would be rendered more or less unusable.

They would no longer be able to navigate properly, and they'd certainly be prevented from flying at nap-of-the-earth level. With the threat from SAMs, it would be suicidal to attempt to fly anywhere at anything less than ultra-low level, and Walters's aircraft would in effect be grounded.

'Stealing the drive has one other upside,' said Walters. 'It means I can't receive or send secure comms. The drive contains the crypto fill – the encrypted communications software for the present comms routine. Without it, I can't speak to The Colonel and vice versa. He's tried to make radio contact several times since you spoke to him. I've been ignoring his calls. This makes it all very explainable.'

'Great,' Range enthused. 'You're getting right into the spirit of things, aren't you, mate? A part of me can't help wondering why. I mean, don't get me wrong, I'm grateful. Very. But it ain't exactly without some degree of risk on your part, is it?'

A shadow seemed to pass across Walters's features. 'You remember the July 2005 bombing of the London tube?'

'Only too well, mate. I was in the counter-terrorism squadron at the time, down at the London barracks, and we were right royally scrambled.'

'My niece was caught in the attack,' Walters remarked quietly. 'On the Piccadilly Line. You know what saved her? She had her laptop computer slung around her front, as opposed to where she normally carries it. It took the brunt of the blast. Saved her from death, or at least ending up in a wheelchair. They got it back from the police, once the inquiry was over. An Apple Mac PowerBook. Scorched; smashed screen; keyboard half melted. But it saved her.'

'I'm sorry. How is she now?' Range asked.

'All things considered, she's not so bad. Her back's never been the same. Her hearing was permanently damaged from the blast. But considering when they got her into casualty they thought she might never walk again – well, she's doing fine. Just got married. Trying for a first child. Bowed but not broken.

'And you know what,' Walters continued, 'if those bastards could have got their hands on a dirty bomb, a poor man's nuke, they'd have used it. They'd have detonated it beneath London and irradiated half the city. You give me a proper alibi, Range, and I'll back you all the way on this one. I'd slaughter every last one of the murderous bastards if I had the means and the chance.'

For a moment Range was tempted to share with Walters the secret of the gold. Together with his co-pilot and crew they were five, and Range and his team could afford to share a few hundred grand's worth of the loot with each of them. In spite of the cover of the hijacking, he felt as if they were pulling together as more or less one team now. But something still held him back.

'How bulletproof is the stolen drive alibi?' Range queried. 'Will it hold up when the shit starts to fly back in the UK?'

Walters shrugged. 'It's good, but it's not perfect. In theory I can still fly. With no crypto, comms, mapping and no low-flying capability it'd be pretty suicidal, especially when we know they have IR-guided SAMs. But in theory, I could get her airborne and make it back to base.'

'What about if we booby-trapped the helo?' Range asked.

'Booby-trapped like how?'

'Claymore rigged to a trigger wire. One end attached to the helo, the other to a stake in the ground. You take off, the claymore blows and blasts your aircraft with steel ball bearings. It's the kind of thing The Kiwi can rig up with his eyes closed. You take a few photos of that, and you've got your cast-iron alibi.'

Walters fixed Range with this look. 'What about if you don't make it back? What then? There's no one in my crew would want to try to unrig that kind of a thing.'

'You think we won't make it back?'

'There's always a chance. It's not Dad's Army you're taking on, is it?'

'Fair enough,' Range conceded. 'Murphy's Law: if it can go wrong it will.'

'Exactly.'

'We'll rig it up so it looks convincing, but we won't arm the claymore. That way you take off and fuck all happens.'

'Okay, let's do it.'

Range said that he'd get The Kiwi onto it, and then O'Shea appeared to have words.

'We're pretty much sorted for tonight's mission,' he announced. 'The guys were wondering about grabbing some shut-eye before getting the show on the road.'

'Just a couple more things,' said Range. 'One: give the wagons a good going-over. Tyres, fuel, water, oil – the basics. Just so we can be sure they'll get in and out without piling in on us. Plus you'll need to smash out all the windows in whatever way's easiest. We're going to take serious fire in that fort, and the last thing we want is windows going in on us.'

'Gives better all-around fire, too, I guess.'

'You got it. Two: I want us to go local from now on. I want us to grow into our AQIM glad rags, so by tonight we're pretty much feeling at home in them. That's how we need to look and act when we hit that fort.'

'Got ya, buddy,' O'Shea confirmed. 'What about zeroing in the weapons? The Dushkas and the PKMs?'

Range considered this for a second. The present location was perfect for checking that the sights on the machine guns that they'd liberated from the Fort of the Mount were zeroed in properly. They could mock up some targets against the rock wall of the crater and pound some rounds into them. The upside was the extra confidence this would give them, knowing that they were going in with pinpoint-accurate firepower. The downside was the noise of the weapons firing. On balance, Range figured it was better to take the risk. There didn't seem to be a soul moving anywhere around.

'Yeah, get a good few rounds down,' Range confirmed. 'Do it in the heat of the day. There's unlikely to be anyone moving anywhere then.'

'At some stage The Kiwi and me need to rig up our HAHO scuba kit,' O'Shea added. 'Should be simple enough. Clip into the para-harness, attach the oxygen bottle to the front and the mask to the face, and we're good to go.'

Range eyed the American's stubble. 'Don't forget to scrape the bum-fluff off, mate.'

The latex rubber of the oxygen mask wouldn't make a proper seal with the skin unless it was freshly shaven. Even a day's growth would allow the outside air – or in this case, the water – to leak in.

'So, how d'you figure you'll do the water-borne infil?' Walters asked. 'The river passes not so far from here, doesn't it?'

'Yeah, about four klicks to the east,' O'Shea confirmed. 'But it's not rained for years, and it'll be a bone-dry wadi right now. I guess the wagons will have to drop us on the approach to the fort and we'll do the rest on foot, at least until we reach this lake or oasis. But we'll be slower than the vehicles, and there's only a certain number of hours of darkness to get the job done.'

'There is perhaps another way,' Walters remarked. 'We fly you in. Once Range has got the wagons, say, a klick out from the fort, we load you up and whisk you down to Blackpool-by-the-Water. We're thirty klicks short of the fortress?'

'Thirty-five, to be exact,' said O'Shea.

'That's less than ten minutes flight time. We drop you on the riverbed a kilometre out from the fort. It sits on a tight bend in the river, so they'll not be able to see us or to hear us if we keep below ground level. The river banks will shield the noise, as will the vegetation that lines those banks.'

'I thought you couldn't fly now I've stolen your drive?' Range asked. 'I thought that meant all your mapping was gone?'

'Water's different. Well, unless it's the sea, and even then it's fairly predictable. A river's perfectly flat, especially one meandering through a desert landscape. We don't need the computer mapping.'

'D'you have the fuel to do it?' Range asked.

Walters rubbed his chin, pensively. 'Probably. Just. We'll be sipping on air by the time we reach our refuelling stop in northern Libya. But what mission was ever won that wasn't flown by the seat of the pants?'

'Appreciate the offer,' said O'Shea, 'but it's too risky. On the rare occasion that it does rain that wadi'll be a raging torrent. It'll carry all before it: trees, rocks, boulders. They'll get scattered over the riverbed, which means it won't be a flat and predictable route to fly. With terrain-following radar and computerized mapping, I'm sure you'd make it. But at night and with no navigational aids . . . No offence intended, buddy, but I'd rather walk.'

Walters shrugged. 'You're probably right. That was perhaps my Dambusters moment. Maybe it's best if we sit this one out.'

'We lose the Chinook we're totally and utterly fucked,

mate,' said Range. 'Stay grounded, stay safe, but be ready to get us the hell out of here.'

'I've been hijacked, remember?' Walters replied. 'I'm doing exactly as I'm told.'

'You know, I've been thinking about the infil,' Range remarked to O'Shea. 'You get into that fort unnoticed and undetected, simply to open the gates and let us in. Seems like a wasted opportunity to me. Sultan Gadaffi was in that fort before they moved him to where we nabbed him. He should have a good idea where the quarters are that house the guards.'

'Yeah, I figure he should,' O'Shea confirmed. 'Shall I go get him?'

'No, not now. Let him sleep. But imagine this. Imagine if you go in through that waterway, and come up into that fort carrying all of Randy's PE4. I mean, did he bring as much as he usually does?'

'Yeah, totally over the top,' O'Shea confirmed. 'Slabs and slabs of plastic explosives, plus rakes of detonators.'

'I thought as much, God rest his soul.'

'God rest his soul,' O'Shea echoed.

'Seems a shame to waste it, especially as this mission cost him his life. So, what about you and The Kiwi carry it in and plant charges on all the buildings where this AQIM lot are billeted? You use decreasing fuse times as you go, so that the last charge you plant has say, a sixty-second fuse. That way, they all go up pretty much at once. Do that, and we'll blast the place apart even before the battle proper has been joined . . .'

'And we plant our last charge on the gate, so as to blow that and let the cavalry in,' said O'Shea.

'Exactly,' Range confirmed. 'Beats Plan A, which was driving up to the gate and asking to be let in.'

By early afternoon the heat had become unbearable. The sun was beating down remorselessly from a cloudless blue sky. The only source of shade was the camo-netting slung over the wagons and the aircraft. The Blackstone Six team plus the Chinook crew were clustered together, some trying to snatch a few hours' much-needed kip, whilst others were getting a brew and a feed on.

American military 'meals ready to eat' (MRE) ration packs had been ripped open, and the chow was being swapped, bartered and generally shared around. Once the Blackstone guys had eaten, O'Shea pulled together the drivers and gunners on the four vehicles so they could go do a spot of shooting. Despite being in the shade of the netting, O'Shea figured you could boil an egg on the metal sides of the wagons. They'd already split the eleven men – twelve with Sultan Gadaffi included – three per vehicle, each taking the role either of driver, machine-gunner or navigator-cum-vehicle commander.

As the rounds from the big, vehicle-mounted machine guns echoed across the deserted landscape, Range sought out Sultan Gadaffi. The heat of the afternoon was still intense, but there were a few bigger-picture aspects of the mission they needed to iron out. They gathered with O'Shea and Walters.

'Very Lawrence of Arabia,' Walters remarked, when he spied Range in all his local gear.

Range was wearing a long, blue flowing Arab robe, albeit slightly bloodstained and bullet-damaged, and he had an indigo *cheche* – a traditional Tuareg headscarf – wrapped around his neck, plus the back and top of his head. It left his nose, eyes and mouth showing, but covered up his razor-cut, greying hair.

'Seeing as I've hijacked your aircraft, I'd watch the lip,' Range retorted. 'Now, what's your refuelling stop en route back through Libya? A name, and better still a grid, would be great.'

'I'll fetch the charts,' Walters volunteered. 'We do still carry a few of the good old reliable paper types, thank God.'

'This is English humour?' Sultan Gadaffi enquired, once the pilot had hurried off to fetch his maps. 'This hijacking the aircraft is an English joke?'

'It is not,' Range told him. 'I have hijacked his aircraft.' He delved into the pocket of his combats and pulled out the drive. 'See? Without this Captain Walters is pretty much unable to fly. Effectively, he is trapped.'

'Then why is he still so happy to help us?' Sultan asked. 'It is very confusing.'

'Don't worry. Unless you're a Brit you wouldn't get it.

It's a tribal thing.' Range struck a pose. 'So, tell me, how do I look in my local garb?'

'At a distance, half convincing,' Sultan Gadaffi smiled. 'But up close, the blue eyes are a giveaway. You and your men will need to cover your eyes with your *cheche* when we come to talk our way into that fort.'

'*If* we need to talk our way in,' O'Shea corrected. 'Hopefully, the gate will have gone kaput under several charges of PE4.'

Sultan Gadaffi smiled. 'Indeed, let us hope so.'

'You know, we were targeted by a surface-to-air missile back at the Fort of the Mount,' Range remarked. 'You may have felt a violent lurch just after take-off. Walters taking evasive action.'

'Just after take-off? So, well within the range of an Igla-S.' Gadaffi's eyes met Range. 'You know the Igla-S? In NATO countries I think you call it the Grinch, an odd name . . . My late father's armed forces possessed a few before the war, although mostly they were ill-maintained. But early in the conflict, your forces airdropped several consignments of Igla-S to the rebels. Or at least, so they thought. In reality, one such airdrop went directly into the hands of the Tuareg, who, as you know, were my father's most loyal fighters.'

'We did the drop?' queried Range, in disbelief.

'Well, I say your forces. I mean your key ally, the French. The Tuareg chief, one Moussa ag Ajjer, had captured a rebel leader. From him, he learned the identification system to signal in the airdrop. He lured in a French transport aircraft and they dropped the weapons consignment, including several dozen state-of-the-art Iglas. The French cannot claim they didn't know what they had done, either.'

'Why's that?'

'One of Moussa ag Ajjer's men had been trained on the Igla-S. He unpacked one of the missiles and used it to shoot down the French transport aircraft. As you know, the Tuareg bitterly resent those who helped topple my father, because he was the only champion they had in the world. There are some five million of the desert nomads, and they are marginalized and disempowered in the countries they inhabit. My father was their champion.'

'The Igla's got a range of five kilometres?'

'Six, actually,' Sultan corrected Range. 'And in case you were wondering, the Tuareg would waste no time deliberating whether to shoot down a British warplane. As to al-Qaeda in the Maghreb, the Tuareg have of course traded them some missiles. And AQIM would love nothing more than to blast you out of the sky.'

'Correction. Not just us. As things presently stand, you as well.'

'Indeed. But I told you that whoever planned this mission—'

'Here it is,' Walters remarked, cutting off Gadaffi. He

spread out a chart before them on the hot sand. 'Took me a while to find it. Mike's not great at keeping the cockpit shipshape. Younger generation, you know? They just don't seem to have the same respect for paperwork. Think it can all be done in cyberspace.'

'Before you get all nautical with us over your charts,' said Range, 'Sultan here was just telling us what kind of SAM capability they have around here. Apparently, the French airdropped a load of Igla-S missiles to the bad guys, just as the war was gearing up. They've found their way into AQIM's hands and all.'

'Then it probably was an Igla-S that targeted us back at the LZ,' Walters remarked. 'It was certainly IR-guided. Any idea how many?'

'Several dozen,' Sultan Gadaffi confirmed. 'Perhaps as many as seventy-two. All found their way south, either to the Tuareg or to AQIM.'

'Bloody hell.' Walters shook his head in dismay. 'You're saying there are as many as seventy-two Iglas stationed around here?'

'Yes. Well, seventy-one after the one they just fired at us.'

'Even so . . . That's one hell of a lot of MANPADS to have to avoid.'

'Generally, you should be safe if you keep six kilometres away from any human habitation,' Sultan Gadaffi suggested. 'And the Libyan Sahara is very sparsely populated. The trouble is the Tuareg are nomadic. You never quite know where they are. And of course, AQIM do have these mobile patrols.'

Walters turned to Range. 'Bloody marvellous. That's seventy-one SAMs, and we don't have a clue where they are.'

Chapter Sixteen

'Whatever else you do, keep the helo's flight-drive safe,' Walters warned Range. 'Do not get it shot, drop it in the river or lose it. I'll be needing that to get us safely out of here.'

Range felt around in the map-pocket of his combats. 'Just checking it's still there. Tell you what, why don't you keep it? Anyone ever tells me not to lose something, I generally end up losing it.'

'I really need you to keep it,' said Walters. 'Or one of your team. When the Spanish Inquisition starts I need to be able to tell headquarters you took it off me, at least for the duration of the unauthorized legs of this mission.'

'O'Shea, you take it,' Range suggested. 'You're a smart, efficient, well-organized American. You never lose anything.'

'Is it good in water?' O'Shea asked.

Walters shook his head. 'Very un-waterproof, I'd say.'

'I guessed not,' said O'Shea. 'Range, I'm the scuba team, remember? Guess you got to keep it.'

'Right,' remarked Walters, as he smoothed out the chart, 'that refuel point you asked me about. It's a

Special Forces base set way out in the western Libyan desert. It's where you lot – well, the Regiment I should say – got sent in, right at the start of all the Libyan trouble. A load of British expats and oil workers needed evacuating and the Regiment rode to their rescue.'

'Remember it well, mate,' said Range. 'A classic NEO: non-combatant evacuation operation. They flew in a couple of whirlybirds and lifted a load of civvies out.'

'They did,' Walters confirmed. 'Here it is. Tiny little place called Wadi Idhan. Not a lot there, but a small base under canvas, and a couple of fuel bowsers. But they've got a helipad of sorts and aviation fuel, and that's all we need.'

'Can you show Sultan the exact spot?' Range asked.

Walters looked askance at Range. 'It's an SF base. It's somewhat erm . . . sensitive.'

Range nodded. 'I know. But trust me, it is his need-to-know.'

Walters shrugged. 'Hey, I've been hijacked. I do as I'm told. Mr Gadaffi, come closer.' Walters pointed out the remote desert outpost, using a pencil tip as his indicator. 'Right there. Camp Stirling to us. Wadi Idhan to a local like you. Its grid is: 947528.'

'Thank you,' Gadaffi replied. Then, to Range: 'I know of the place. I have never been there myself, but I know of it.'

'Will it work?' Range asked. 'Can your guy make it there in the time we've got available?'

'He should be able to. After all, Libya is now a free country, so they say, and any Libyan should be able to travel freely anywhere.'

'But a friend of your father's?' Range queried. 'Sorry, a friend of your late father's.'

'Even a friend of my late father still has friends in positions of power,' Gadaffi replied. 'People tend to think of our country now as being either rebels or Gadaffi forces. There were many in the middle, and many more who switched sides.'

Range could tell that Walters was watching this exchange very closely. It hadn't escaped Sultan Gadaffi's notice, either.

'As you know, my late father was a despot,' Sultan Gadaffi remarked to Walters. 'He was a power-crazed madman. He was no doubt a danger to himself, his people and maybe even the world. But he was a man of iron will, and under his rule he kept Libya together for decades. And you know something else: he kept the extremists – al-Qaeda in the Maghreb, call them what you want – out of our country. Will those who have taken over do likewise?' He shrugged. 'The answer is all around you. Al-Qaeda is here. I fear for my country greatly.'

'We don't make the policy, Mr Gadaffi,' Walters told him. 'We just execute the actions.'

'Yeah, and right now, Sultan, we need to know if your man can make it to Wadi Idhan in time for our refuelling stop,' said Range. 'Walters, what time will it be? Somewhere around 1100 hours tomorrow morning?'

Walters thought for a second. 'If we're airborne at first light, we should be up around Camp Stirling by 1000. But if you don't mind me asking, Range, who exactly are we rendezvousing with? And why?'

Range fixed Walters with this steady, level gaze. 'There are some things it's best you don't know. If you knew the answer to that question, The Colonel – or more likely those above him – could use it against you. So, I can't tell you and I won't tell you, and it's for your own good, mate. You okay with that?'

'I guess I'll have to be. But reassure me on one thing: this is all part of the bigger picture of putting the kind of people who blew up my niece where they belong, which is six foot under?'

'It is,' Range confirmed. 'Very much. You have my word on that.'

'That's good enough for me.' Walters got to his feet. 'Unless you need more of me, I'll leave you guys to talk. I sense there's stuff it's best I don't hear.'

'Thanks, mate,' said Range. 'And Bill, you don't fully understand how much we'll make this all worth your while. But you will. Lest we forget.'

'Lest we forget,' Walters confirmed, before heading back to the shade of his aircraft.

'O'Shea, you got the satphone?' Range asked.

O'Shea handed him a Thuraya hand-held satellite

phone. It was as insecure a means of communication as your average cell phone, but the upside was that it was reliable, portable, simple to use, and could pick up a clear enough signal just about anywhere in the world. Because the number that Range was calling was that of another Thuraya, it would be insecure both ends, but there was bugger-all he could do about that.

Range's team had three Thurayas between them, one per fire team. Normally, the Thuraya provided the backstop in their 'lost-comms' procedure – the last form of communications they would resort to if their radios went down. They were Blackstone Six pieces of kit, and Range and The Hogan had made sure that they were registered to an anonymous offshore company in the British Virgin Islands. That way, if any Thuraya call was intercepted by those they didn't particularly want to listen in, it would be difficult to trace the call back to B6. It was no secret that international electronic interception agencies – eavesdropping facilities like Britain's own GCHQ – worked on the basis of 'key words'. Millions of international calls were scanned automatically, but only those from flagged numbers – those of known interest – or those triggering interest would be scrutinized. If a call was kept free of keywords – 'terrorist', 'explosives', 'bomb-maker' being some of the more obvious – it should go through pretty much unnoticed.

The Thuraya had become the default means of private comms for Special Forces, and for freelance operators like B6. The number that Range was calling was that of a good mate of his who was still serving with the SAS. Right now he just happened to be working in the western Libyan deserts, and it was time to call in a favour that had long been owed. Whilst the Thuraya searched for satellites – it needed to lock on to more than one before it had a reliable signal – Range talked through the final details of the plan with O'Shea and Gadaffi.

The Thuraya let out a bleep to indicate it was ready. Range dialled the number, and true to form the Thuraya-to-Thuraya call went through more or less immediately.

Range spoke into the handset. 'Planky? Yeah, it's Range. How you doing, mate? Yeah. Good, it's all good.'

Range made some small talk, before getting down to business. 'Listen, mate, I'm on some ultra-sneaky-beaky mission down south of where you are. I'll be passing through tomorrow morning on an MH-47 with a team from B6. We're on a refuelling stop, so we won't be hanging around for long. I need a favour. A big one.'

For a long moment Range listened to whatever was being said on the far end. 'Piss off, mate, you knew I'd call it in sometime. So, listen: this mutual friend of ours will turn up at Camp Stirling with a Libyan in tow. The Libyan's name is Al-Khofra. The mutual friend needs no introduction. I need you to shovel the Libyan aboard our helo, plus a few dozen para-packs he'll have with him, and no questions asked, okay?'

Again, Range listened for a good few seconds to the speaker on the far end of the connection. 'Yeah, a lot of beer, mate. This all goes to plan, I'll have more than enough wonga to keep you minging for a month. So, we're on? Fantastic. I owe you big time for this one.'

Range cut the line. 'Sorted.' He smiled. 'Here.' He passed the phone to Gadaffi. 'Phone your Al-Khofra friend and let him know we're on.'

Sultan Gadaffi took the Thuraya and dialled a number seemingly from memory alone. He spoke into the handset for several minutes, but it was in a fast guttural Arabic that even Range found hard to follow.

'You think The Hogan's up to this?' O'Shea asked, as Sultan Gadaffi paced back and forth, deep in conversation. 'I mean, he's hardly a spring chicken, is he?'

'The Hogan? There's no one better for this kind of work,' Range confirmed. 'I'd trust him with my mother's life, not that I ever knew her.'

At shortly after seven that evening the sun sank below the eastern horizon, but for an hour more the desert remained a wide expanse of fierce, burnished red. Walters was in his pilot's seat doing a round of flight checks. It was a long while since he'd flown a Chinook – hell, any aircraft for that matter – devoid of crypto, mapping, satphotos, comms, the works.

He concentrated on ensuring that he and his co-pilot would have the best chance of getting airborne and avoid ploughing into the desert sands, just in case Range didn't return from the coming mission. It hadn't escaped Walters's notice that the odds weren't exactly stacked in favour of the B6 team.

Range had told him that if they hadn't put in an appearance by 0900, he was to consider them missing in action and to try and get his aircraft out of there. Range had given him Blackstone's third Thuraya satphone, in case of emergencies. So if it came to it Walters figured he could call in a rescue helo, or at least one that could deliver to them a replacement computer drive.

Range popped his head around the door that led into the aircraft's cockpit. 'Shipshape?' he asked. 'Don't worry, we'll be back before you know it.'

'Last time I had to fly a crate by manual means alone I seem to remember it was powered by steam!' Walters glanced at his watch. '2000 hours. Leaves you thirteen hours to do the mission. Unlucky for some . . .'

Range laughed. He held out a hand to the Chinook pilot. 'Thanks for everything, mate. And if they throw you out of the military, there's always a place for you at Blackstone.'

Walters arched one eyebrow. 'Will there still be a Blackstone Six after all this is over?'

'The Bible is wrong, mate. It should read: "And on the seventh day God created Blackstone Six." We've survived worse. We're always in need of the finest of aircrews, and you'll get one hell of a pay rise if you throw your lot in with us.'

'I'll think about it. Now, get your wagons on the road.'

'See you in a jiffy, rotors turning and ready to get us out of here,' Range replied. 'Don't go leaving without us.'

Range turned to O'Shea and The Kiwi, who were manhandling the Chinook's inflatable dinghy out of the hold. 'You guys ready?'

'Good to go.'

The three men jumped down from the Chinook. Having loaded up the inflatable, they mounted up the four-vehicle convoy, and with a snarl of engines it pulled out into the deepening night.

Range had sorted a line of march for the wagons, one that shouldn't be broken. That way, each would know where the others were at all times. He'd put Jock in the rear, because it was vital to have an experienced operator to backstop the convoy. They'd only ever break the line of march if they were ambushed, and if the wagons needed to fire-and-manoeuvre, falling back as each gave the other covering fire.

The vehicles were showing no lights whatsoever, and when they'd checked them over earlier in the day, O'Shea had thought to disable the brake lights by removing the bulbs. That way, even when the convoy slowed, there would be no telltale row of red stoplights blinking in the darkness. A darkened convoy, carrying twelve men dressed in dark desert robes and navigating on NVG – they would flit through the desert night as invisible as ghosts.

For tonight's mission Tak was the driver on Range's wagon. They figured the front vehicle needed the greatest concentration of brown-skinned blokes, just in case they did need to talk their way into the fort. Gadaffi was in the rear, alongside The Kiwi, who was manning the Dushka heavy machine gun.

Once they exited the volcanic crater and had driven a good distance, Range called a brief halt. Grabbing some old hessian sacking, he and his men made sure to brush away any tracks left by their vehicles leading into the crater, just in case there were any hostile or curious passers-by in the night hours.

Range paused to check the night sky. Above him were the old faithful constellations, and he sought out the North Star. As its name suggested, the point on the horizon directly below the North Star would be due north. Having found that, Range flicked his eyes east, and his gaze came to rest upon another distinctive constellation, this one resembling the tunic and dress of a warrior. No matter where you were in the world, Orion – often known as 'The Hunter' – rose on the horizon due east, and set due west. It was a key navigational marker.

'Right, mate,' Range announced to Tak. 'For now, head north-east on a bearing of 060 degrees. For the first twenty kilometres keep three fingers to the left of Orion. It's open desert all the way, so choose your own route through. Once we're closer, I'll give you a more accurate bearing.'

'Got it,' Tak grunted.

By holding his hand in front of his face, and steering at a point several fingers' widths to the left of Orion, Tak would keep the convoy on a rough north-east bearing. It was the quickest and simplest way to do a navigation check whilst on the move, and without needing to consult a map, compass or GPS.

When driving on NVG and black light as they were, the use of the GPS had to be kept to a minimum. The light thrown off from the electronic gizmo's screen could be enough to betray their position – especially when driving through terrain totally devoid of man-made light.

Tak eased the wagon forward, pushing along at no more than 30 kph. The 3.0 litre diesel engine of the Toyota purred softly in the still night, the tyres making just the faintest, crunching hum. Men like Tak and Range had drilled and drilled and drilled for this kind of noiseless cross-country driving. The secret was making no sudden movements: no noisy accelerations, no engine growling, no gears grinding, no spinning of tyres on the dirt. All was smoothness and silence, the convoy's passing being as soundless as the wind.

Range turned to face the night. It wasn't a conscious

thing, but his senses were hugely heightened as they pushed into the open desert. They'd left the protective screen and the cover of the volcanic crater behind them, and they were out on their own. In every direction stretched a dry, undulating landscape, one that was awash with a sea of silvery-blue light. The moon was up, and it provided more than enough ambient light by which to see and to drive.

Everywhere he looked, Range could see flat, open, empty terrain. There were no Tuareg desert caravans, no AQIM patrols and no human settlements as far as he could make out. He sensed that their four-vehicle patrol was utterly alone in this desert wilderness, and the sense of isolation here rendered his mind unusually calm, quiet and clear.

There weren't a hundred different thoughts crashing through his head, as there had been for most of the day. All of that was behind him as they set out for the Fort of the Great River. As Range tuned in to the night-dark desert, he opened his mind and his senses to any changes in the surroundings, and he was hyper-alert to any threat, but there was nothing that he could detect.

Range turned and spoke to the figure crouched in the vehicle's rear. 'You comfortable back there? You good?'

'I shall survive,' Sultan Gadaffi replied. 'I would not miss this journey for the world.'

'Great. But listen – you do as I do on this one, okay? You keep quiet and don't say a fucking word unless I tell you to. Stealth and surprise is going to be key. We've trained and trained for it and we do it well. Just do as we do, or don't do anything at all.'

'I understand.'

'And the state you're in, you'd best stick with the vehicle, that's if there is any dismounted fighting to be done.'

'So, do I get a weapon?' Sultan Gadaffi asked. 'To defend myself? After all, we are going in to assault this fort together.'

Range turned to face Gadaffi, and the two of them locked eyes. This was the moment of truth. Did he trust this bloke enough to allow him to carry a weapon? He hadn't considered the question much before, but now that he came to think about it he figured that he probably did.

'When we reach the target, you get one,' Range confirmed. 'You're going in alongside us. That makes you one of the team.'

Having given Tak his navigational instructions, it was up to the big Fijian to feel his way forward and seek out the best route. His massive bulk was hunched over the Toyota's controls as he wove the vehicle through the darkened landscape, skirting around the occasional rent torn in the flat terrain by seasonal rains and flash floods.

To the east lay the swirling, jagged-toothed massif of the Jebel Arkanu, the Mountains of Tomorrow. When it rained up there, within minutes a series of dry wadis criss-crossing the desert plain would be transformed into wild torrents. It was such flash floods that had carved out the gouges in the plateau that Tak was now doing his best to avoid.

If he drove over one of those, he could bring the rest of the convoy in on top of him, for all the vehicles were following his lead. They were driving tactically, keeping a good hundred metres between wagons, so that if the lead vehicle was ambushed those to the rear could put down covering fire. But nonetheless there was a real danger that one wrong move by Tak would prove disastrous for the others.

In spite of the few hours' sleep they'd snatched during the day, Range knew how knackered they were in his vehicle, and the other teams had to be similarly exhausted. During the midday heat it had been pushing fifty degrees, even in the shade, and it had proven next to impossible to get any proper rest. It was that, plus the constant tension, that was the biggest potential killer.

After forty minutes of such driving Range issued a new set of navigational instructions. A dry ravine had pushed the convoy too far north, and he needed Tak to compensate. He told him to steer a route south-east whenever he could, using Orion as his celestial fix, plus the distinctive form of the Southern Cross. By the time they were approaching the Jebel Arkanu, an hour or more spent staring into the artificially boosted luminosity of night vision had taken its toll. Range could feel the strain as an added tightness around his eyes.

The nearer they got to the mountains, the more nightmarish the terrain was becoming. For the last twenty minutes Tak had been trying to steer a route through an increasingly pockmarked and ravine-strewn landscape. It would have been difficult enough in broad daylight, yet here they were doing so with only the fluorescent green video-game glow of NVG to guide their way.

The Jebel loomed before them, a vast black form silhouetted against the star-specked night. To the left and right, enormous boulders that had been washed down from the mountains loomed out of the darkness. The Jebel rose to over 6,300 feet, making it twice as high as any peak in England. At over fifty kilometres across, the Mountains of Tomorrow stretched into both Egypt and Sudan, forming four separate plains linked by narrow, rock-cut valleys, with plunging rock faces on all sides. The landscape's rugged vastness provided a perfect trans-frontier wilderness in which the likes of AQIM could thrive.

Range could well appreciate why the terrorist movement had made this their main base here in the Sahara. They were heading into the lion's den.

Chapter Seventeen

Range figured they'd made thirty kilometres max, but in terms of the distance driven overland – wherein they'd been weaving crazily between ravines, wadis and giant boulders – he reckoned they'd covered more than double that distance. They were into the badlands on the western edge of the Jebel, where the mountains met the desert plain in a confused jumble of all but impassable terrain. It made for horrendous going, and for long stretches Tak had been managing less than 15 kph.

They were less than two klicks short of the target, and by Range's reckoning they were approaching the western edge of an escarpment, one leading into a sunken depression on the western edge of the Jebel. At the far side of that depression stood the Fort of the Great River and its lakeside oasis. The entire depression – called Karkur Guelta, Valley of the Oasis – would flood when it rained, but that only ever happened once every ten years or so.

In spite of that, the spring-fed oasis never ran dry, which explained why the fort was built there. And if there was water, O'Shea and The Kiwi could dive it, which meant they should have a covert way to gain access to the fortress.

Range led the convoy to the lip of the escarpment and into a dry wadi. They nosed into a patch of dense palm groves and spiny undergrowth. Tak pushed ahead until he reached a position where he figured they were well hidden. The thick vegetation provided cover from view. It would stop them being seen, but it wouldn't stop a bullet, so provided little cover from fire. However they couldn't push any further into the undergrowth, for there was a wall of tangled palm groves stretching east into the Valley of the Oasis.

The relative availability of ground water here meant that the way ahead was thickly vegetated right up to the walls of the fort. There was only the one route through– an ancient track that snaked its way across the depression. Range called a halt so they could do a recce of the lie of the land before them.

The four wagons pulled up in line abreast. The Kiwi swung his Dushka around to cover the terrain to the west, and the gunners on the other wagons each chose an arc, until the convoy could put down all-around covering fire. They were now in a snap ambush – just in case any curious AQIM forces did decide to venture out of the fort.

Range ran a finger across his throat, the signal for *kill the engines*. In the dead quiet that followed, he could clearly hear the pinging of metal, as the hot motors began to cool. The searing heat of the day had dropped considerably after sundown, but still the drive across the desert had been hard going for the Toyotas.

Range checked his watch, cupping the faint glow in the palm of his hand to shield the light. It was 2155. They'd been on the move for approaching two hours.

The vehicles were close enough for Range and his men to have a Chinese parliament – a group heads-up – without moving out of them. They flipped up their NVGs. For a good few moments everyone remained silent and listened out for any sign of the enemy, or that their convoy had been detected. But apart from the regular, rhythmic beat of the cicadas chirruping away, it was as still as the grave out there.

Range and O'Shea checked the map, using a torch with a length of black gaffer tape fastened over the lens. A tiny pinprick pierced the tape, allowing a thin laser-beam of light to shine through. With hands cupped around that they could map-read with almost no risk of any illumination leaking out. They nailed their position, compared notes on anything that they'd seen since leaving Walters, and readied themselves for the next stage of the operation.

Range, O'Shea and The Kiwi moved off on foot, together with Sultan Gadaffi. They scaled the edge of the wadi, from where Range used his Sophie on night-vision mode to scan the terrain ahead. Before them stretched the shallow, bowl-like depression, which from this level was a mass of feathery palm trees. On the far side lay the stretch of water, upon and under which O'Shea and The Kiwi would make the first foray into the target – but for now it remained out of sight, hidden by the mass of palm trees.

Further ahead was the form of the fortress itself, set against the dark wall of the mountain. From their vantage point, its configuration was relatively clear, and Range listened carefully as Gadaffi talked them around it. There was a hexagonal set of walls, with a tower set at the apex of each. Across the middle of the fort ran a dividing wall, with a gateway set at what marked the very centre of the fortress.

Adjacent to that gateway on the wall's southern side was the fort's ammo store, one of the key targets upon which O'Shea and The Kiwi had been briefed to rig their explosives. To the opposite side lay the fort's headquarters building, which was also where the AQIM commanders were believed to have their sleeping quarters. Again, it was a key target for the bombing team: by hitting that they would be cutting off the head of the snake.

At the north-western corner of the complex, and set into a massive tower, lay the fort's one entranceway, which was barred by a thick gateway of iron-studded wood. That was another of O'Shea's and The Kiwi's key targets. Sandwiched between the entrance tower and the tower on the north-eastern corner were two, more modern-looking, wooden buildings, which were the barracks for the AQIM forces garrisoning the place. A few well-placed charges on those and they should go up like matchwood.

Set in the centre of the southern half of the fort was the main stable block. These days, it was occupied by vehicles, as opposed to horses or camels, and Range wanted that rigged with explosives too. By hitting the fort's transport, it should ensure that none of the enemy would be able to pursue him and his men as they made their getaway – that's if there were any survivors.

Against the southern wall of the fort was the tomb itself, and Range let his Sophie sight linger on that for a good few moments. There, underground, stashed in the ancient catacombs, was a cool one hundred million dollars' worth of gold – that's if Sultan Gadaffi had told them the truth about the location of the loot.

Range threw a sideways glance at the man. He figured he'd had little cause to doubt him up until this moment, and now more than ever his life and his liberty lay in Range's – and the Blackstone Six team's – hands. If they so decided – and if they survived the mission before them – they could deliver him into the custody of whoever it was had set this mission in train. And if they did that, Range didn't doubt that would be the last anyone ever saw of the last surviving Gadaffi son.

Range switched his Sophie to thermal-image mode and scanned the area before him for heat signatures.

From this distance, and behind the thick stone walls, there was little showing from within the fortress itself. But between them and the fort were a score or more glowing pinpricks of light. He passed the Sophie to Sultan Gadaffi.

'What's with all the fires?' he whispered. 'Between here and the fort – it's full of them.'

'Tuareg,' Sultan replied. 'Their campfires. This time of year they drive their cattle up onto the Jebel, for the grazing. They take them to the high plains, and block the narrow entrance with stones. They leave them there for three months to graze on the bush and trees, then return to collect them. These will be some of the cattle-herding party.'

'What're their relations like with the AQIM lot? And how come AQIM have the fort?'

'Money. AQIM are renting it off the local Tuareg leader, Moussa ag Ajjer. As long as the money keeps flowing, they will be friends of convenience. As soon as it stops, the Tuareg will retake their fort and show little mercy. They are a fierce warrior nation, and they do not gladly suffer foreign aggressors in their midst.'

'So they'll be pretty pleased to see us lot pitch up,' Range muttered.

'On the contrary, the Tuareg and AQIM will be united in enmity against you.'

Range eyed Gadaffi. 'Correction: united in enmity *against us*.'

Sultan Gadaffi held Range's look. 'Listen, my friend, they are the very people who betrayed my family and sold me to al-Qaeda. After what AQIM did to me, I hate them with every breath in my body, but the Tuareg also are far from being my favourite people.'

Their recce done, the three men scuttled back to the wadi. There was a quick heads-up amongst all present and the final touches were put to their plan of attack. Whilst they were talking, Range watched The Kiwi reassemble his sniper rifle – his trusty VSS Vintorez 'thread cutter'. He was reassured to see that the wily Kiwi was going in with his silenced, long-distance killing machine. It was the perfect weapon with which to cover O'Shea and to silence anyone who might challenge them, as the American set his charges around the fort.

The Kiwi and O'Shea shouldered their Bergens, grabbed their makeshift scuba gear and the folded inflatable, and they were ready. They'd only get it to self-inflate if and when they decided to use it, which would depend on the extent of the water they encountered, and whether they could more easily swim across.

'Remember the comms procedure,' Range told them. 'You call when you've made it through the valley and you're ready to go wet.'

'Got it,' O'Shea confirmed.

'We won't expect to hear from you again until the charges blow. We see the fort go up, we come screaming in. Radio in your location as soon as we're within range, and keep your IR strobes going. That way, we should be able to see you just as soon as we hit the fort.'

'Got it.'

'Follow the wadi right to the oasis,' Range added. 'That way you should avoid the Tuareg camped in the trees. Good luck. And when you reach the rock pool, keep an eye out for the crocs!' With that the two figures turned, and within moments they were lost in the shadows.

Range figured it would take them a good thirty minutes to sneak their way through the Valley of the Oasis. Another half-hour would get them through the water and into the fort. Thirty minutes more to plant their charges, and they'd be poised to blow. An hour and a half, he reckoned, and battle would be joined, which meant they would hit the fort at around about midnight.

The remaining force started their vehicles' engines. Range did a time check. They'd been static for twenty minutes – that was all the time it had taken to make decisions that might cost many of them their lives.

After the quiet and stillness of the night, the throb of the diesel motors sounded deafeningly loud. The rhythmic beat of the cicadas – breeeep-breeeep-breeeep-breeeep-breeeep – seemed to falter for a moment as the engines caught. It had been the marker to the silence here, the call of a million tiny insects beating time as they fine-tuned their plan of attack.

Range's vehicle led off, bumping and kangarooing over the rough terrain towards the track that led across the Valley of the Oasis. It was dark and silent in that direction, and there wasn't a thing to be seen. As it reached the fringes of the dirt track, the convoy halted in a patch of thick cover. It was here that they would wait for the fort to go up when O'Shea and The Kiwi triggered their explosives.

It was some forty minutes after they'd cut their engines when Range first heard it: voices speaking in a guttural language sounding something like Arabic, drifting across to him on the cool night air. Whoever it was, they were talking loudly and animatedly, and moving ever closer to his position.

Range presumed it had to be Tuareg, moving down the track into the Valley of the Oasis to join their brethren already camped there. The voices grew louder. There was dense undergrowth all around, so he couldn't yet see them, but in the eerie silence and stillness their voices sounded deafening. Range figured they had to be speaking Tamajaq, a language unique to their tribe, and as a result he couldn't make out a word of what they were saying.

With The Kiwi gone, Range had taken over as the rear gunner on their wagon, and Sultan Gadaffi had taken his place in the front passenger seat. That way he could do the talking, if there was any that needed to be done. Few, if any, AQIM could speak the Tuareg dialects, and so Arabic was the language used to communicate between them and the desert nomads. As a native Arabic speaker, Gadaffi should be able to pass as an AQIM operator without too many problems.

Range swung the big machine gun around to target the threat. The gunners on the other wagons had done likewise. If the figures on that track so much as levelled a gun in their direction, two Dushkas firing 12.7mm armour-piercing rounds would tear them apart, not to mention all the other weaponry that could be brought to bear from the vehicles.

But right now that wasn't the point. Right now that was the last thing Range wanted. They had to try to remain covert until the last possible moment – when the explosives blew the target sky-high. If not, those in the fort would be alerted to trouble and stand their forces to. All it would take was a general call to arms in the Fort of the Great River, and O'Shea and The Kiwi would be caught as they prepared to blow the place all to hell.

Equally importantly, if they were Tuareg, and Range and his team wasted them, the gunfire was sure to be heard by their brothers in the valley. It was going to be challenge enough taking down the AQIM fighters garrisoning that fort, and Range had little desire to pick a fight with the Tuareg desert nomads as well.

Range had no idea how they would react when his men hit the fort. He hoped they'd melt away into the night, leaving AQIM to take the punishment. Either way, all they could do was proceed with the plan of attack, and cross that bridge if and when they came to it.

Range was a firm believer that if you thought too hard about any given mission or battle, if you tried to consider every angle and outcome, you'd end up taking no action at all. In situations like the one they were going into right now, they would be given no second chances. Survival would depend on decisive and immediate action, and it would be better to risk making the wrong decision than to make no decision at all.

Even if you made the wrong call, if you saw it through with total determination you could still adapt and refine it as you went. During his years in the SAS, the one thing all had been desperate to avoid was analysis to paralysis. It was far better to make a snap decision, and to have a chance of adapting it and winning through, than to do nothing and condemn yourself to the worst.

A group of figures appeared on the far side of the track. Range could see their sandalled feet below the thick bush that lined the route, their heads above it, but little else. They were some thirty yards away, and it seemed impossible that they wouldn't spot one or other of the vehicles. Range was frozen, his only movement being his hunched shoulders following the figures in slow motion with his gun sights.

His finger was achingly tight on the trigger, a hair's breadth away from opening fire, his heart pounding in his ears. As the figures drew level, Range could make out more about them. They were tall, rangy, incredibly fit and hardened-looking. Each was dressed similarly to Range, in dark robes and with heads wrapped in indigo *cheches* – headscarves. But each also had a distinctive *takoba* – a straight, metre-long sword – swinging in a leather scabbard at his side.

As he studied the figures through his iron gun sights and at such close quarters, Range could make out the ornate carvings on the scabbard nearest to him, and the pointed silver pommel of the weapon. And slung across the backs of these Tuareg warriors were the distinctive forms of folding-stock AK-47s, the tried and trusted assault rifle so common to rebels, terrorists and tribes all across Africa.

The AK was a fine enough weapon: reasonably accurate at short range, one hundred per cent reliable and practically maintenance-free. It was the perfect weapon for desert-dwelling nomads, and Range didn't doubt for one moment that these tough-looking Tuareg knew well how to use them.

The last in line had the long, bulbous form of a rocket-propelled grenade launcher slung over his shoulder. The RPG-7 was another classic weapon of guerrilla fighters and rebel armies, and it was unmistakable with its hollow, flared exhaust. Like the AK, part of the beauty of the weapon was its ruggedness and brute simplicity.

In the hands of a skilled operator, the RPG-7 was a fearsome weapon, and this guy looked as if he'd been born with one in his hands. Whether used against a British Land Rover in Afghanistan, or a US Black Hawk helicopter in Mogadishu, Somalia, it was the weapon of choice for militias the world over.

As the Tuareg's voices faded away into the tangled, brooding bush, Range let out a long sigh of relief. It seemed as if they hadn't spotted his hidden force. But for several minutes he and his men remained absolutely still and silent, just in case there were more of them coming, or the force that had just passed was doubling back to attack their position. Yet there was no further sign of them.

Now Range knew a little more about those camped in the valley below. They were well armed, and they carried their rugged, effective weaponry as if they knew how to use it. After taking that fort, the last thing he wanted was to pick a fight with that lot.

Once all was silence and stillness again he gave voice to his concerns, and Sultan Gadaffi was the first to respond. 'From what I know of these people,' he volunteered, in a hushed whisper, 'if they have no clan leader with them – an *amghar* – they are unlikely to attack. Their tribal structure is strictly hierarchical, so nothing happens without the *amghar*'s say-so.'

'So will their chief be with this lot in the valley?' Range demanded.

'It is unlikely. He will be in the mountains, overseeing the grazing rights. Those here are likely camped with their cattle, en route to the highlands.'

'So, they'll need to clear it with their *amghar* before having a pop at us lot?'

'I believe so. That is, unless we do harm to one of their number. For the Tuareg, what matters above all else is the survival of the *Kel* – their clan. If an outsider attacks or hurts any of their *Kel*, they will unite and take immediate action against him. These are the rules by which they have lived since time immemorial.'

Range put the word around his men that the Tuareg were to be left alone wherever possible. If Blackstone Six showed respect to the clan, maybe the clan would show respect back.

Maybe.

Chapter Eighteen

The first explosion rent the darkness, the ear-splitting violence of the blast cushioned by the thick vegetation that surrounded Range and his men. The fort was hidden from view by the bush, but the jet-black rock face of the Jebel was visible above it, lit up in the fiery orange of the detonations.

The noise of that first blast echoed across the depression, the shockwaves reverberating over the once peaceful oasis. As a second and a third explosion went off in quick succession, it seemed as if a savage lightning storm was playing across the entire face of the mountain.

That first blast was the signal for the wagons to move. Within seconds, Range and his men had the technicals nosing onto the track that snaked into the valley. As the lead wagon swung right, Range was relieved that they'd thought to lower the tyre pressures during the long wait in the bush, for the way ahead wound through soft, clogging sand and would be impassable otherwise. The engine growled throatily as Tak put pedal to the metal and urged it ahead. Vehicles two, three and four swung into line behind, and the convoy accelerated down the incline.

Range had decided they would go in lights-on. There would be little point in trying to remain covert with explosions and burning buildings lighting up the valley. Their convoy was bound to be spotted – by the Tuareg, if not the fort's defenders – and any force trying to sneak its way in would clearly be allied to the fort's attackers, whereas they wanted to appear like fellow AQIM heading in to help defend it.

Range glanced behind. The wagon was kicking up a cloud of dust, which was lit up silvery-yellow in the following vehicle's headlamps. A momentary glance was enough to convince him that his force did indeed appear like a local AQIM contingent heading in to help their terrorist brothers. Driving captured wagons sporting captured weaponry, and dressed in captured local clothing, there was little that from a distance could give them away.

They rounded a bend in the track and a stupendous blast tore apart the night, the shockwave hammering into Range's wagon and rocking it backwards on its springs. A pillar of fire jetted skywards like an erupting volcano, the explosion billowing out into a giant mushroom cloud that spread its dark and oily mass above the mountains.

The massive blast was followed by countless more explosions, as shells, grenades and ammo cooked off in a ferocious firework display. No doubt about it, the ammo store had just gone up, and Range couldn't help but smile to himself at the fantastic job that O'Shea and The Kiwi were making of things.

The weapons dump was situated adjacent to the fort's headquarters building, and it was inconceivable that that had survived the enormous blast. Hopefully, they had just cut the head off the snake, leaving the surviving AQIM fighters confused, shocked and leaderless.

Range's concentration was dragged back to the route ahead, as figures came hurrying out of the palm trees about a hundred yards in front. Tuareg. Maybe a dozen or more. They paused on the track, as if transfixed by the monstrous light show before them. All were armed, and they were staring in the direction of the burning fort and gesticulating wildly.

Range felt Tak's eyes upon him. 'Keep it turning and burning,' he growled. 'Keep it steady, like we've got all the right in the world to be here.'

They picked up speed, the wind blowing in their faces, and Range found that he felt strangely calm. He sensed that these were the last few moments of peace and relative stillness before the coming storm. He leaned forward from his gun position to have words with Sultan Gadaffi.

'You ready to do the talking?'

'I am ready. Leave it to me.'

In his lap, the only surviving Gadaffi son cradled an

AK-47, one that Range had liberated from the Fort of the Mount. Come what may, they were all in this together, Range figured – the Gadaffi son and the men from Blackstone Six. He deserved to have a weapon. More importantly, it helped with the overall disguise that those in the lead vehicle were seen to be packing local weaponry, Sultan Gadaffi included.

Range double-checked that he had a round chambered in the Dushka. He had an ominous feeling about this Tuareg lot, as if the convoy was driving into a whole world of trouble. As the lead wagon bore down on the figures ahead, the rearmost desert nomad turned in their direction. He must have spotted the headlamps out of the corner of his eye. He studied the convoy for a good few seconds, before shouting something at his brothers.

They turned as one and eyed the approaching vehicles. The nearest figure started to wave and yell at Range's wagon, and Range caught snatches of broken Arabic in between the roar and crackle of ongoing explosions from the direction of the fort. Arabic wasn't the first language of these desert nomads, and many spoke it haltingly at best.

'*Ahlan sadiqui! Asre! Mushkila al Qaser!*' Friend! Hurry! Trouble at the fort!

For a moment Range figured the Tuareg were going to wave his convoy through, but then a couple of them raised their hands in a clear gesture for the lead wagon to halt. Range tightened his grip on the big machine gun, as he braced himself to unleash hell.

Sultan Gadaffi turned to speak to him. 'I suggest we hold fire. I can talk my way through.'

'Do it,' Range snapped. 'Tak, ease off the gas.'

The lead vehicle slowed. As it rolled to a halt the light sand thrown up by the tyres drifted forward, catching like gold dust in the beams of the headlights. Sultan Gadaffi leaned out of the left passenger side of the wagon to greet the tallest of the Tuareg. They brushed hands and brought them back to touch their hearts – a greeting Range was familiar with from his travels around the Islamic world. It meant: I bring your peace into my heart . . .

There were a few rapid words of greeting exchanged in Arabic, before the conversation switched to what sounded to Range like Tamajaq, the Tuareg dialect. Gadaffi must have picked up some of the local lingo when staying as a guest of the desert nomads, before they decided to sell him out. The conversation ended with a few quick words fired back and forth between the tall Tuareg and some of his men, and then he plus one other climbed aboard Range's vehicle.

The two desert nomads came to rest on either side of Range, who was standing manning the tripod-mounted Dushka. They crouched down, their swords tucked under them and their AKs cradled in their hands. Range figured it was best to remain silent and keep staring straight ahead down the barrel of his weapon. He had his eyes all but covered by the *cheche*, and he just had to hope the thin indigo material would mask their true colour.

As Tak eased the wagon into motion again, another massive explosion shook the fortress, the white glow of its blast lighting up the entire convoy as if in broad daylight. Range cursed to himself. A few more light shows like that courtesy of O'Shea and The Kiwi, and their Tuareg escort was bound to be on to him.

For a moment he wondered what the hell Sultan Gadaffi was doing, letting the desert warriors ride in their wagon. They had to be coming to investigate what was happening up at the fort, and probably with a view to reporting back to whoever was in control of the group camped in the oasis. He figured that Gadaffi probably had no choice but to let them on.

He was torn out of his thoughts by a smattering of phrases that he realized he understood. The Tuareg had been jabbering away at each other in their own dialect, but these last few words had been spoken in Arabic and clearly directed towards him. '*Sadiqui, men ayna anta?*' – Friend, where are you from?

For an instant, Range wondered whether they'd sussed him, before he realized that the question was a pretty obvious one to ask of any AQIM operator. As with all their unholy terrorist franchises, al-Qaeda in the Maghreb populated its ranks with volunteers from all parts of the Islamic world. Range could be from just about anywhere, and the question was probably asked in all innocence.

'*Ana men Almaghrib*' – I'm from Morocco, Range muttered, trying his best to mask his accent and keep his eyes forward and down the barrel of the Dushka. Morocco was the first country that had come to mind. It was one that was far enough away for these Tuareg geezers not to have visited it on their trans-Saharan travels, but near enough to be reassuringly familiar.

Tak swung the wagon around a sharp bend in the track, the tyres slewing through the soft terrain and the rear of the vehicle sliding outwards in a cloud of soft sand. As the wagon righted itself, a further blast tore through the fortress. Range reckoned O'Shea and The Kiwi had just blown the main gate. They were less than four hundred yards out, and battle was shortly to be joined.

Range wondered what the hell they were going to do with their unwanted passengers, before it struck him that they had both fallen ominously silent. He glanced across at the figure to his right, and he realized in an instant what had happened. The guy was staring down into the well of the pick-up, and his eyes were fixed on Range's Maximi light machine gun.

Range and Tak had stashed a bunch of very un-local-looking gear under a tarpaulin in the rear of the Toyota. It was the kind of stuff without which they just couldn't see themselves going to war. NVG. Sophie sights. Claymores. Field dressings and medical kits. A dozen bottles of water and a couple of ration packs, plus Tak had his M240 general-purpose machine gun, and Range his Maximi.

Most of the kit was stuffed inside their Bergens and well hidden. Tucked into cover like this, Range had figured there was little risk of the weapons being seen as they drove into the fort. He hadn't bargained on having a couple of eagle-eyed Tuareg riding with him, or on the rough terrain shaking the Maximi free from the heavy sheeting.

No one in this part of the world carried a Maximi M249 squad assault weapon – not unless they were American or British Special Forces sent into the desert to hunt down the bad guys. The Tuareg warrior flicked his eyes up and across at his brother. As he did so, he made a momentary connection with Range. He tried his best to avert his gaze, but Range had seen the look in his eyes. There was a momentary freezing of the mind, as if the guy was thinking: *Who in Allah's name are these guys?*

Everything seemed to wind down to ultra-slow motion. Range could see the Tuareg's mind scrambling for some kind of comprehension, some sliver of understanding as to what and whom this convoy that had appeared from out of the desert night might be carrying. He opened his mouth and blurted out a stream of words in the local dialect. Range could just imagine what he was saying: *Take a look at the weapon this guy's got at his feet. That's no AQIM bit of hardware. And get a look at the guy's eyes. Grey-blue, like the water of the oasis at dawn.*

Range had few options open to him. He couldn't exactly engage them with the Dushka, for it sat too high on the wagon and its barrel was too long to fire at the figures perched on either side of him. The Maximi was out of reach, and if he went for it he knew the Tuareg would use their weapons first.

He turned away from the machine gun, and leaned across to the first guy as if to have words with him. All he could think of saying to distract him was: '*Sadiqui, ma esmouk?*' Friend, what's your name?

As the Tuareg went to reply, Range brought his head down in a savage thrust, using his bull neck to drive his forehead into the bridge of the desert warrior's nose. As he did so, his right hand grabbed the figure by the scruff of his robes and pulled him up sharply to meet the blow, so doubling the impact. There was a sickening crunch as the guy's nose collapsed, the bone being driven inwards into his face.

At the same instant he twisted around, and as the other Tuareg raised his weapon to fire he brought his boot down hard, stamping into his groin. A split second later he reversed the move, bringing the knee up hard under his chin and snapping the guy's head violently backwards. The weapon in the Tuareg's hand fired, but

Range's move had thrown him, and the bullets went hammering into the bush on the far side.

In one smooth motion Range lifted the Tuareg up and heaved him over the wagon's side. He spun to face his first opponent. The Tuareg had blood streaming down his robes, and the front of his face looked as if he'd done a hundred-yard dash in a ninety-yard room. He'd dropped his AK-47, and there was no room to wield his sword, but in his right hand he held a *sheru*, a long and cruelly curved dagger.

The guy slashed at Range's stomach, and he sensed the tip of the razor-sharp blade cutting into him, a burning pain shooting through his torso. He was faced with an opponent armed with a fine weapon for close-quarters combat, and Range had nothing with which to defend himself but his hands. The three moves he'd pulled so far were classic Krav Maga ones – designed to cause maximum damage and to end a fight as quickly as possible.

But a golden rule of Krav Maga was also to be prepared to run and make good your escape, if faced with an opponent far better armed than you were. The only way out of this was to vault from the vehicle, and Range didn't figure he could make it before the Tuareg got the knife into him again. Already, he could feel a warm slick of blood seeping from his stomach wound into his boxers, as if he'd pissed himself.

He had zero room for manoeuvre, trapped as he was

in the rear of the speeding pick-up. The Tuareg slashed at him again, the curved blade slicing past just inches from his windpipe. The pain from the guy's smashed face had to be excruciating, and Range could hear the horrible bubbling suck and blow of his breathing, as he struggled to draw breath. But at the same time he could see the glint in the fighter's eyes as he realized he had Range cornered.

The glistening blade came at him again, nicking him in the forehead, but as the knife arm went past, Range stepped forward and slammed his fist into the bloodied mess that was the front of the guy's head. It was another golden rule of Krav Maga that you struck again and again at the point where an opponent was most badly injured. Range was nowhere near as fast or as lethal at Krav Maga as The Kiwi, but his blow packed a punch like a sledgehammer.

Range drew back as the knife came at him again. A wild animal was at its worst when wounded, and Range sensed that the Tuareg warrior had thrown caution to the wind in a desperate effort to kill him. The fighter held the blade before him as if taunting Range to risk an attack. But as he tried to move away from the menacing blade, he realized the Tuareg had tricked him. Whilst his eyes had been glued to the blade, he'd slipped out a leg and tripped him.

Range fell hard, his shoulder slamming into the body of the Dushka with a jarring impact. He glanced upwards, only to see the bloodied warrior above him, and with the curved form of the *sheru* held high, its blade flaming in the light thrown off from the burning fort. As the Tuareg prepared for the savage down thrust, Range readied his arm to block the blow.

He'd take a horrific wound to the forearm, but as long as his artery wasn't severed he'd survive. As the knife struck, he'd use his other arm and the Tuareg's momentum to pull him downwards, and slam his head face-first into the hard steel of the Dushka's tripod where it was bolted to the wagon's floor.

But as the knife began to descend there was a deafening blast in Range's left ear, and the Tuareg's features disintegrated under the force of a high-velocity bullet fired at close to point-blank range. The body was propelled backwards, and Range saw it topple from the speeding vehicle and disappear from view.

Range struggled to his knees. There in the passenger seat was Sultan Gadaffi, a smoking AK-47 levelled at the shoulder. There was a split second in which the two men stared at each other – the Blackstone Six team commander and the last surviving Gadaffi son. No words were needed, and none were spoken. Range knew that Gadaffi had just saved him from serious injury at the hands of the Tuareg warrior, and maybe worse.

'If they didn't think we were the enemy, they fucking will now,' Range yelled, above the noise of the speeding vehicle.

Sultan Gadaffi shrugged. 'It is what it is. One more thing you should know: they told me that at least half of the AQIM forces manning the fort are away right now, on a mission. He mistook us for some of their number returning.'

'That's until he saw the whites of my eyes. At least that makes less of 'em to fight, anyway.'

The fort's flaming silhouette was no more than 250 yards away now. Tak was powering onwards and making a beeline for the front gate, but the fortress was set on a slight rise, and the track leading up to it was a slew of soft sand. If Tak pushed the Toyota too hard it would lose traction, and so he had to nurse it up this final incline.

Tak half turned his head towards Range. 'Hand me the M240,' he growled. 'Cover's blown. Time to get fucking serious.'

Range levered up the big GPMG and passed it forward to Tak, with the belt of ammo wrapped around the gun's mechanism several times. Tak took it one-handed, and leant it against the Toyota's central seat within easy grasp. With all the windows smashed out of the vehicle, Tak could put down fire to the front and left, if he could manage to operate the big machine gun single-handed.

'Chuck me my webbing an' all,' Tak added. 'If we're going in overt we may as well dress for war.'

Range threw the big Fijian his webbing kit, and fished out his own. But before strapping it on, he needed to do something about his stomach wound. It was seeping blood, and Range could feel it soaking warmly into the lower half of his robes.

'On the dashboard, in amongst the grenades, there's a combat dressing,' Range yelled at Gadaffi. 'Throw me one over.'

He'd stuffed some there for just such an eventuality – someone getting hit in the vehicle, and needing to patch himself up in a hurry. Range had one hand pressed tight into the knife wound, so as to try to stem the bleeding.

As Gadaffi passed Range a dressing, he handed him in return his M249 squad assault weapon. 'Take this. You know how to use it, right?'

Gadaffi nodded. 'I have watched you at work with it.'

'You'll need some real firepower. It's set to auto, and it packs a 200-round mag. Here's a couple spare.' Range handed him two fresh drums of ammo. 'Keep them handy.'

Gadaffi stuffed the bulky mags onto the seat beside him, next to Tak's M240. He eyed it for a second, then glanced at Tak and Range.

'I would be better, I think, on the M240,' he ventured. 'More firepower, plus I can operate it two-handed. Tak can take your Maximi.'

'Perfect,' Range declared. 'Tak, you good with that?'

The big Fijian grunted an affirmative.

'And chuck me your AK,' Range added, 'plus any spare

mags of ammo. I'll need a secondary.' He slapped the Dushka. 'Can't exactly go mobile with this thing.'

Range grabbed Gadaffi's assault rifle and threw it on its sling over his shoulder. He'd just finished strapping the dressing around his torso – it made a passable bandage that should stop the bleeding for now – when there was an unmistakable burst of static in his radio earpiece.

'We're on the roof above the entrance tower.' O'Shea was yelling to make himself heard above the noise of the battle. 'The Kiwi's down. Get here. Now. Or they'll take us.'

'Put your IR strobe where I can see it,' Range yelled back. 'We're coming through the gate now!'

The men on the four vehicles had agreed a simple plan of attack. Once through the entranceway, Range's wagon was to head directly for the gate in the fort's central wall, and from there to the tomb where the gold was stored. Vehicles two and three were to break left and right, hitting targets on the fort's outer walls, whilst vehicle four would secure the main entranceway.

If all went well, the others should have the fort secured as Range's team took the tomb where the loot was hidden.

Chapter Nineteen

The lead vehicle careered around the final bend in the track and the gate tower hove into view. For several seconds Range scanned the roof area with his Sophie sight, but there was no sign of the IR strobe. And then he had it, flashing away steadily on the battlements atop the structure.

Range dropped the Sophie into his Bergen and pressed the 'send' switch on his radio: 'O'Shea's positioned on the tower gateway roof, on the battlements western side. Mallet every other fucker that you see. Jock, take the gateway, relieve O'Shea and hold it. Watch for Tuareg trying to counter-attack. Defend the gateway from within and without. It's vital you hold it, for that's our only exit point. Vehicles two and three, attack as planned.'

Grabbing the Dushka's handles, Range swung it around towards the open entranceway, the knife wound to his stomach screaming blue murder at him as he did so. Forcing the pain to the back of his mind, he raised himself onto the balls of his feet so he was ready to swing the big weapon from side to side, smashing rounds into the enemy wherever he met them.

There was no point trying to use NVG: the fires raging in the fort would white-out any night-vision kit, blinding the user. Battle was going to be fought using pure aggression and guile, plus the mark-one human eyeball. The only advantages Range and his men would have were shock and surprise, plus their skill at firing weapons accurately from vehicles moving at high speed. So be it.

The lead wagon was one hundred metres out now, and Range could see a confusion of figures clustered in the gateway. They were clearly trying to fight their way up onto the tower roof, where he now knew O'Shea and a badly injured Kiwi were positioned. Range steadied the big weapon, pulled the trigger and opened fire.

He hammered a long and savage burst into the very midst of the enemy fighters. The formal name for the Dushka is the Degtyarov Krupnokalibernyi, or DShK for short. Dushka is its nickname, which translates from the Russian as 'Sweetie'. It struck Range that there was nothing particularly sweet about it as he unleashed that first burst – apart from the effect it was having upon the enemy.

The first few rounds ripped the remains of the shattered wooden gate to shreds. The big, armour-piercing bullets chewed into the stonework all around the gate, blasting chunks of masonry asunder and creating a storm of deadly shrapnel that swept through the archway. It tore the AQIM fighters clustered there limb from limb, blowing them clean away.

Behind him, Range heard and felt the other wagons open up as they raced towards the entrance with a fifty-yard gap between them. Range's vehicle made the gateway first, and after slowing to take the impact, Tak powered the technical over the scattered debris of splintered wooden planking and shattered fragments of stone. They passed into the archway and Range was forced to cease firing. It was Tak who struck the next blow.

With Tak's massive arm holding the steering firm the wagon bucked and forced its way through as he reached forward with the other, grabbed a grenade from the dash, ripped out the pin and threw it into the tower stairwell. It exploded to their rear, punching a whirlwind of shrapnel into the tower, as smoke and debris billowed into the archway. That should have done for any surviving enemy trying to reach O'Shea's position on the roof.

Ahead of them the interior of the fort was a scene of dark chaos and mayhem. Flames licked skywards from the blasted remains, showing where O'Shea and The Kiwi had done their work, and the dark night was shadowed with clouds of billowing, oily smoke. Sporadic explosions ripped through the air as ammo in the arms store was cooking off. Figures darted to and fro across the fort's open interior, but few seemed to be moving with any sense of order or collective purpose.

A surprise attack in the depths of the night by an unseen assailant: it was the perfect means by which to seriously mess with your enemy's head. That, coupled with fast-moving vehicles packing serious firepower, were the tactics used to perfection by Stirling's SAS during their operations in the Libyan desert seventy years earlier. Such were the eternal certainties of war.

Facing a demoralized and confused enemy – and one hopefully bereft of their commanders – Range reckoned the fort was theirs for the taking. Winning this fight was all about keeping the wagons moving at speed now, and about the volume of concentrated, accurate fire they could put down from the vehicle-mounted machine guns.

Tak floored the accelerator, and the wagon sped towards the open interior of the fort.

'Gadaffi, COVER RIGHT!' Range yelled. 'COVER RIGHT.'

He'd given Sultan Gadaffi the western wall of the fort, largely because the eastern wall was where the barracks was situated. Range figured O'Shea would have hit that with a massive charge of explosives, but still there would be survivors. In which case, he expected the fiercest enemy resistance to come from that direction. Gadaffi couldn't fire to the left in any case, or he'd be engaging targets across Tak in the driver's seat, and it made total sense to divide their fire this way.

As the wagon surged ahead, Range detected the sickly-sweet smell of scorched human flesh, which more than likely was coming from the burning barracks block. The stench made him gag. Fighting back the urge to vomit, he swung the massive barrel of the Dushka around to the left, as Sultan Gadaffi readied the M240 out of the right-hand passenger side of the vehicle.

If Range had been defending the fort's gateway, he'd have fallen back into the cover of the tower, waiting to hit the incoming vehicles side-on the moment they emerged. This was going to be a battle of raw firepower now, and it was one Range knew would be won or lost in the first few moments.

The Toyota thundered out of cover, and a split second before he could open fire Range heard Gadaffi unleash with the GPMG. The instant the Dushka's barrel cleared the massive wall of the tower, Range let rip. He saw rounds from the weapon ricocheting and sparking all along the tower wall, as spent cartridges spewed out of the breech and went spinning through the air.

The simple, flip-up iron sights of the Dushka were silhouetted against the harsh flare of its firing. Dozens of muzzle flashes were blasting back at Range from the shadow of the fort wall. As he poured rounds into those targets, seeking to sweep them away in a whirlwind of shrapnel, Range heard the distinctive 'tzzzinnnggg-

tzzzinnnggg-tzzzinnnggg!' of bullets cutting through the air barely inches from his head.

The night had erupted in a maelstrom of tracer. From the nearest enemy positions at the base of the tower fire rippled backwards, until the entire eastern wall seemed to be awash with flame. Range could only think that the Toyota was getting riddled with bullets, but the noise from the Dushka was so deafening that he couldn't tell where they were getting hit.

Within seconds the flat bed of the vehicle was awash with hot, smoking brass shell cases. Range could see stick figures darting in and out of his line of fire, and silhouetted against the harsh glare of the enemy's muzzle flashes. He kept his finger hard on the trigger, as each second ten massive rounds from the weapon tore into target. Yet still the roar and thump of the enemy fire punched over the wagon in a pounding, crushing shock-wave.

A few yards to the front of the speeding vehicle Range could see tracer rounds sparking and ricocheting off the dirt, as the AQIM fighters put down a murderous rate of fire. They were overcompensating for the speed of the Toyota, but within seconds they were bound to readjust their aim. They'd have packed their magazines with one tracer round per three bullets, so what Range could see now was just a fraction of the weight of their fire.

Range aimed at the central point of the nearest

enemy fighters, knowing the Dushka would plaster all around it with death. He saw bullets from the weapon sparking off metal and ripping into stone, kicking up plumes of vaporized masonry as they tore the wall to pieces. Human figures exploded under the impact, bodies being torn apart and thrown backwards into the shadows.

Range ramped the weapon further to the right, blasting fire into target after target, as every inch of the wall to the east of him seemed alight with flame. He poured rounds into muzzle flashes, silhouettes of gunmen, and the odd gun slit spitting fire. A short burst and he was on to the next target, doing what he'd learned to do so well during his years in the Regiment, and since on numerous B6 operations.

He didn't have time to think or to feel fear. He was operating on automatic now, and that was the beauty of the years of training and elite soldiering. The Dushka juddered and shook with each burst of fire, the smooth, gunmetal steel of the weapon lit up by the latticework of tracer tearing past all around him, the barrel practically glowing red with the heat.

The Dushka packed a one-hundred-round mag, and Range was painfully aware of having to kill the enemy whilst at the same time conserving his ammo. *One burst, one kill*. If he pulled the trigger and all he got was an empty click, they would be finished. Doing a belt-change right here and right now would be the end of them, for it was only the rate of firepower being put down by the Dushka that was keeping them alive.

All the same, he could feel the tearing, juddering impact of rounds ripping into the wagon. Right to his front a burst of well-aimed fire stitched a line of holes through the Toyota's metal side, and he couldn't understand how it hadn't taken his legs off. For an instant the vehicle faltered, and Range feared it had suffered a terminal hit. Or maybe Tak was down. In response, Range upped his rate of fire, hurling a solid stream of armour-piercing rounds at the enemy.

An instant later the engine seemed to catch again and the Toyota powered onwards. It was halfway across the open area and speeding towards the gate in the central wall, when Range saw wagons two and three come powering through the entranceway. The instant they did so, one broke left and one right, and the vehicle-mounted Dushka and the PKM opened fire, plus a pair of M240s, which were being operated by Jock and Tiny from the wagons' glassless windows.

Now, battle truly had been joined.

Seconds later Range's Toyota was swallowed up in a mass of thick oily smoke. The acrid, choking cloud was billowing forth from the ammo store, on the far side of the fort's central wall. Range felt the harsh fumes burning into the back of his throat, and he was momentarily blinded. He experienced a vicious spike of claustrophobia. The years spent locked up in the kids' homes had made him hate being enclosed or blinded or trapped in any way.

For several seconds the Toyota went speeding through this dark, eerie, suffocating tunnel, one lit a ghostly red by the fiery streaks of tracer rounds and the explosions from the outside. It took a massive mental effort for Range to get a grip on himself. But somehow he managed to keep his surging panic and nausea in check, as he forced himself to keep a grip and to hold his fire.

There was no point trying to hit the enemy when you couldn't see them. Worse still, if he opened up, his muzzle flash would only serve to give their position away. Right now, much that he hated being trapped and hemmed in like this, the thick smoke had cast a protective cloak around them. The enemy had all but nailed them as they'd emerged into the fort, and this was providing much-needed respite for them and their bullet-riddled vehicle.

Range held his fire for another reason too. He figured the heavy machine gun's belt was pretty much done. He used the momentary break in the action to reach forward and grab a spare. As he did so he almost lost his balance. The floor of the vehicle was a sea of spent bullet cases, and he had to boot them out of the way to maintain a foothold.

Range lifted the breech of the weapon, flipped the fresh belt of rounds across, slammed shut the mechanism, pulled back the cocking handle, and the Dushka was good to go. One of the great things about having served in the SAS was that he had trained with just about every weapon ever used in modern warfare.

There were dozens of Dushka variants sloshing around the world's war zones, and all had their unique peculiarities. Those made in China were knock-off copies that were as likely to kill the weapon's operator as they were the enemy. They were welded together from various plates of sub-quality steel, and were prone to blowing up in your face.

Luckily, Sultan Gadaffi's father had had the money and the means to purchase the very best. This was a Russian-made DShK-M – 'M' for modernized. Machined from one chunk of metal, the weapon Range was operating was bulletproof, and its mechanism was as sweet as a nut. He hunched over the big machine gun poised to open fire, and urging Tak onwards.

Tak had to be steering from instinct alone as he aimed for the fort's central gateway. Range felt him slow the vehicle, and as he did so Tak lifted the Maximi off the seat until the gun's bipod was spread-eagled on the vehicle's bonnet, the muzzle pointing forward in the direction of travel. Keeping one hand on the pistol grip and trigger mechanism, Tak used the other to steer for where he guessed the gateway had to be.

The sounds of battle were ferocious, the noise of war too deafening to hear the individual bullets strike. In every direction the dull, opaque wall of smoke was lit with explosions, as if a lightning storm was raging all around. Range could sense that their vehicle was still taking hits, although they were no longer suffering sustained and murderous fire. But all it would take was for one lucky round to shred a tyre, and they'd be immobilized and as good as finished.

Finally, the wagon thundered out of the cover of the smoke. The instant it did so Tak opened up with the Maximi, spraying the gateway in the fort's central wall with a savage barrage of suppressing fire. Range swung the Dushka around to meet the next threat, the long barrel searching the fortress ahead for targets.

Atop the wall adjacent to the gateway Range spotted a cluster of figures, hefting some kind of a weapon. He swung the Dushka around, but Tak was quicker, a burst of rounds from the Maximi smashing into the enemy fighters. Still, there was the violent flash of a detonation, and an instant later Range could see a flaming rocket-propelled grenade (RPG) coming right at him.

In the warhead came, the exhaust trail appearing like an angry comet roaring through the night. Time seemed to freeze. From the trajectory of the flaring rocket, it looked as if it was aimed right at Range's head. Instinctively he ducked, as the warhead thundered across the front of the Toyota, missing it by a bare few inches. It went right over the bonnet, metal scraping on metal, a great big fuck-off rocket before their very noses.

It passed over the wagon's cab, practically taking

Sultan Gadaffi's head off where he was on his feet up front operating the M240. It exploded against the western wall of the fort, the white heat of the blast lighting up a wide stretch of the grounds in this eerie, smoke-filled halo of light.

Range couldn't believe it. How the hell had it missed the wagon? Targeting a vehicle moving fast at night was extremely difficult, even with an assault rifle. Doing so with an RPG across terrain thick with smoke was next to impossible, but that had been horribly close.

As Tak gunned the vehicle for the open gateway, Range fixed the RPG team with the Dushka and opened up. Rounds hammered into the top of the wall, smashing great holes into it and blasting nameless bits of bodies into the air. Range saw the RPG operator flipped off the wall like a scarecrow, the launcher still gripped in his hands, and he followed the body down with his finger hard on the Dushka's trigger.

The next instant they were powering through the gateway. The moment the wagon emerged, the sky to the right of them dissolved into a sheet of flame, where a massive firestorm was blazing in the fort's weapons store. Away from the blaze, all was pitch black. But as the wagon powered ahead it passed just a few metres from the inferno, and Range could feel the heat roasting those parts of his face not covered by the *cheche*.

A few seconds in the burning heat – the smell of

blistering rubber, scorched metal and fire-blown munitions fierce in his nostrils – and they were speeding away from the blown-up ammo dump. The heat was on Range's back as Tak pushed the Toyota onwards. For an instant it crossed his mind that the fiery eruption now behind them had to represent all of AQIM's spare weaponry and ammunition, which must mean that they were running low on ammo. No doubt it was going to prove a battle-winner that O'Shea and The Kiwi had blown the place sky-high.

As Range swung the Dushka back and forth across the empty expanse of the southern half of the fortress, it struck him how devoid of fighters it was. He guessed this was another bonus of O'Shea and The Kiwi's stealth attack: by retreating to the entrance tower they had drawn the bulk of the surviving AQIM fighters that way. Range figured that was how The Kiwi must have got wounded – in drawing the enemy on to himself and O'Shea.

A yell of excitement brought him back to the present.

'THERE!' Sultan Gadaffi yelled. 'STEER TO THE RIGHT OF THE STABLES! THE TOMB WILL BE DEAD AHEAD!'

Tak flipped the steering wheel right and the Toyota swung that way, the vehicle roaring around the edge of the fort's stable block. One end of the building was completely burned out and the wall had collapsed inwards. Inside, Range could see several Toyota-style vehicles, their gutted shells spitting fire and spewing out great gouts of black, oily smoke.

They crawled past the first wagon, the paint blackened and blistered from the scorching heat. Here and there great rents had been torn in the soft-skinned vehicle, as the high-explosive charges set by O'Shea had torn into it. As Range searched the inside of the stables, he noticed one or two wagons down the far end that looked as if they might have escaped the fire. He made a mental note to lob a couple of grenades into them before departure. No point leaving any means via which the enemy might launch a pursuit.

As they came around the far side of the stable block, Range got a glimpse through the burned-out remains of what had once been the entrance – a kind of large, wooden, garage-style door. Inside, a pile of flaming tyres was pouring out thick clouds of smoke which were billowing into the night sky. Forward visibility was down to near zero here, which made this the perfect ambush point.

As the Toyota nosed ahead through the smoke, Range was hyper-alert to any enemy presence. The stable block must have been one of the first buildings to get targeted by O'Shea. Coming into the Fort of the Great River from the south-eastern corner, where the ancient structure met the pool of the oasis, O'Shea would have emerged somewhere around here and set his first charges.

For a split second, Range wondered where it was that The Kiwi had been hit, and how badly injured he might be, and how they were going to get him out of there. From the northern end of the fort, the noise of battle was still raging, though Range figured the intensity of the fire being traded both ways had lessened. The shock and surprise of the assault, plus the sheer weight of firepower, seemed to be winning the day. The sooner they could get to the gold, haul it out of there, and get themselves back to the waiting Chinook, the sooner they might get The Kiwi to some proper medical facilities.

Of all the men in his team, Range felt closest to his New Zealand operator. If he were ever forced to go on the run in the Libyan desert, he'd choose The Kiwi to fight back-to-back with. Tak might be physically stronger. He could outlift The Kiwi at weights any day of the week. So could Range, for that matter. O'Shea might be more technically skilled where the minutiae of weaponry were concerned, and Jock could definitely drink The Kiwi under the table.

But when the shit went down, it was mental hardness and durability that mattered most. The Kiwi's psychological stamina was second to none, as was his ability to take punishment. He'd keep going no matter what had happened and what wounds he'd taken. He'd share his last mouthful of water with you, but he'd also be able to out-think, outfight and outwit the enemy. Plus he was a natural with weapons, as if he'd been born with a shooter in his hands.

Up until now, Range hadn't even considered that The

Kiwi's injuries might be life-threatening. But right now, as he scanned the southern expanse of the fortress with his gun sights, and Tak powered them onwards toward that hidden gold, the horrible thought struck Range that they just might be.

He punched 'send' on his radio. 'O'Shea, Range: sitrep,' he mouthed into it. 'How's The Kiwi–?'

His words were cut short as an RPG round came flaming out of the smoke and darkness. As Range tried to swing the Dushka around to engage, the round struck the dirt to the right front of the wagon, skipped up a few inches and shot beneath it. He braced himself for the devastating impact of the explosion, but instead the warhead tore out the far side of the vehicle, flared across the fort's grounds, and impacted in a punching ball of flame against the eastern wall.

Range could barely believe it. The RPG round had passed clean beneath their wagon. How the hell had it missed? He brought his weapon to bear and opened fire, pumping bullets into the patch of smoke-filled darkness from where the rocket had been fired. As Range knew only too well, RPG teams often operated as a unit of three. Two guys each with a launch tube shared one loader between them, who also carried the spare rounds.

Sure enough, as Range pumped in the fire, there was the flare of a second RPG launching – a violent burst of orange-yellow, like a mortar flash, only horizontal and aimed right at him. In the flash of the second launcher firing Range spotted the RPG team. They were crouched in a sandbagged bunker right in the entranceway of what he presumed must be the tomb building.

There was zero time to readjust his aim and to kill them. The RPG roared towards the Toyota like an express train, and this time Range just knew it was going to hit.

KABOOOOOM!

The blast came from the rear of the wagon, lifting it up as if a giant's hand had grabbed it. Range felt the vehicle flipping over, and there was a sickening falling sensation, followed by a tremendous, crushing impact.

Chapter Twenty

Range struggled to open his eyes. He felt a massive weight on his legs. He seemed trapped in the pitch darkness with some form of crushing mass lying on top of him. He had his back to the dirt, and he couldn't seem to move. He had this piercing, ringing agony shooting through the centre of his skull, with lights popping and fizzing in the darkness before his eyes, and a screaming whine inside his head.

Yet outside of his agonized body, all was silence and shades of grey, as if the battle had faded away into stillness. He tried to move one arm, so he could press his fingers into his eyes to try to stop the pain. The distinctive smell of explosives hung heavy in the air, plus there was the rich, oily scent of leaking diesel.

Range's first lucid thought was that he'd been blown up. Or rather, their vehicle had been. He figured it had to be lying upside down on top of him, and probably suspended on the roll bar that looped around the top of the cab. Right next to him was the hot steel of the Dushka, still smoking from the recent battle. The breech of the weapon was jammed into the dirt, the rear of the wagon perched above it.

The vehicle shifted slightly and let out a groan of tortured metal. Range hoped to hell it didn't fall further and crush him with the impact. His next thoughts were for his fellow operators, Tak, plus Sultan Gadaffi – for that's how he'd come to view the only surviving Gadaffi son. He searched with his eyes, frantically scanning the wall of drifting smoke that surrounded him. He couldn't see either of them.

His next thought was that he needed a weapon. He reached behind, lifted his head, and his hand found the sling of the AK-47 still draped over his shoulder. He dragged it out from under his torso, cocked it, chambered a round and prepared to fire. Out there somewhere was that RPG team, and right now they were sure to be reloading for the killer blow.

And then Range saw him. A massive figure came sprinting out from where Range guessed the front of the Toyota had to be. It was the unmistakable form of Tak, and he had the Maximi levelled at the hip. He surged forward, powering towards the enemy bunker, and as he did so he opened up, a long tongue of flame stabbing out from the weapon's muzzle as he raked the target with fire.

Tak covered the ground like the rugby player he was, his legs flashing and his feet jinking from side to side as he made of himself a shifting target. But his main focus was on the storm of lead that he was hammering into that enemy bunker some forty yards in front of him. From his position lying prone beneath the truck, Range saw bursts of tracer lancing back at Tak, but the giant Fijian just kept powering forward.

Long bursts from the Maximi ripped out the rounds at approaching one thousand metres per second muzzle velocity, and at the rate of sixteen bullets per second. The barrage of fire smashed into the bunker, and at the distance Tak was pumping rounds into it he'd be hitting it with a cone of concentrated fire. Bullets from the Maximi sparked off metal and ripped into the sand-bagged walls, kicking up plumes of dirt as they tore the place to pieces.

The closer Tak got, the fiercer the concentration of fire became, and Range saw sandbags and bodies exploding under the impact. Range tried to raise his AK to put down covering fire, but the big Fijian was too close to the bunker for him to risk doing so. In any case, Range had a hopelessly limited arc that he could cover, trapped under the wagon's rear as he was.

An instant later Tak went down. For a split second Range feared he'd been hit, and then the big Fijian's arm came up from the cover of a low wall and he let loose a grenade. It looped lazily through the air, dropped like a stone and tumbled into the entranceway to the tomb, right at the rear of the bunker. A second later the grenade exploded. There was the blinding flash of the detonation, and a wave of shrapnel tore through the position.

Twisted figures were thrown into the air, and a thick cloud of choking smoke billowed out of the bunker's open sides. With that, Tak was on his feet again, charging forward the final few yards. He reached the sandbagged wall and sprayed a murderous burst of rounds all along the inside of the fortification. If anyone had been left alive in there, they sure as hell were dead now.

Range saw Tak sink down behind the cover of the sandbagged wall. He heard a squelch of static over his radio.

'Range,' came a breathless voice. The big guy was panting heavily. 'You hear me?'

'Nice work,' Range replied. 'I'm trapped under the wagon, but I've been watching your every move.'

'Can you move forward? I'm at the tomb's entrance.'

'Negative. My legs are trapped. I don't know what by and I can't feel any pain. In fact, I can't feel my legs at all.'

'Can you cover me?'

'Yeah.'

'Right, I'm coming back your way.'

Range saw Tak rise from the bunker, and the big Fijian began to sprint back the way he'd just gone. He'd covered half the distance when a burst of fire tore out from one of the tomb's gun slits, set just above ground level. Tracer arced around Tak's form, the rounds groping for a kill. Tak hit the deck, which cleared the line of fire for Range. He opened up on auto, spraying a long burst into the slit-like aperture.

As Range ceased fire Tak was up and running again, and he sprinted back the final few yards, diving into the cover behind the vehicle. Range could hear Tak's chest heaving and his lungs dragging greedily at the night air.

Keeping one eye and his weapon on the tomb building, Range felt down around his legs. He couldn't feel any breaks in his skin, and there didn't seem to be any blood. But right at the level of his knees something heavy was pinning them to the dirt. It had the feel of cold, angular steel.

For a moment he wondered which part of the wagon's rear had him trapped. He tried to shift around, but his body was too constrained and he couldn't seem to gain enough leverage to do so.

'Tak,' Range called, 'try and free my legs, mate.'

Range felt hands reaching under the upturned wagon and scrabbling about.

'Ammo tin,' Tak snorted. There was the grunt of a heave. 'You're free.'

A box of 100 12.7mm rounds had fallen with the vehicle and smashed into the back of Range's legs. With 16 kilograms of weight behind it, the box had dealt a crushing blow, temporarily cutting off the blood supply from the knees downwards. With the ammo box removed, Range felt the first jabbing twinges of pain, as the circulation returned and the nerves started to come back to life again.

Within minutes he was able to drag himself out from under the wagon and get himself into a sitting position propped against it. He glanced to his right, and Tak was crouched behind the upturned engine block, which was about the only proper cover from fire provided by a vehicle. Range dragged himself across to him.

'Can you walk?' Tak grunted, without taking his eyes or his aim off the enemy position.

'Not yet. Give me five. Life coming back slowly.' Range paused. 'Where's Gadaffi?'

Tak shrugged. 'Not a clue. Been too busy fighting.'

Range glanced about him. In the light of the burning stable block he figured he could see a slick of blood leading off in the direction of the only other scrap of cover. Maybe thirty yards to their left was a circular stone wall about four feet high, with some kind of a pulley system arranged above it. O'Shea had said there was fresh water piped into the fort. Maybe this was some kind of a well forming part of that system.

Sultan Gadaffi must have been wounded when the grenade hit, or perhaps as he was thrown clear from the wagon. He'd crawled away into the one patch of cover he could see. Range glanced into the truck's upturned cab, and there was the M240 GPMG, the weapon that Gadaffi had been using. It looked as if he was out there all right, injured and unarmed.

Range caught Tak's eye. He nodded in the direction of the well. 'I reckon he's over there. Injured. I'm going to get him.'

Tak shook his head. 'I'll go.'

'He didn't save your life.'

'He didn't need to. Anyway, you can't walk.' Tak handed Range the Maximi. 'Take this.'

With one hand Tak reached into the upturned wagon and grabbed hold of the M240. He dragged it out, checked it over, wrapped the belt of link around his torso, and prepared to move.

'Cover me.'

Range leant around the front of the wagon, flipped the Maximi's tripod out, and prepared to open fire. He hadn't the faintest idea how many rounds were left in the drum magazine. For a second he considered crawling back under the Toyota to retrieve a fresh mag, but he knew that he'd never make it. His lower legs were still popping and fizzing with pain as the life came back into them.

Tak crouched like a sprinter, the big machine gun cradled in his right arm. He glanced at Range. 'Ready?'

'Hold it. How about a change of plan? How about we all fall back into the cover of that well. This thing's almost killed me once, it's pissing diesel, and one round and it could blow. We'll fall back and regroup.'

Tak nodded. 'Cover me. Then I'll cover you.'

'Go!' Range squeezed the trigger, sending a burst of rounds ricocheting off the roof of the tomb building. There wasn't a sniff of answering fire. He knew the enemy was in there, for there was only one way in and out of the underground structure. They were clearly holding their fire, most likely in an effort to conserve their ammo. One thing was for certain: they wouldn't be getting a resupply any time soon from the fort's arms store.

Tak reached the well-like structure and dived into cover. 'Go!' he yelled across at Range.

As Range got to his feet, his legs all but gave out on him. He bit back the cry of pain and forced himself to keep shuffling forward. Thankfully, Tak kept a solid stream of rounds hammering past, which had to be keeping the enemy's heads down. Range stumbled to the well, hobbling like an old man, and collapsed into its cover.

'You look like my granddad,' Tak snorted.

'You fucking fight like mine,' Range shot back at him.

'This is more English humour?' came a weak voice. Range recognized it at once as the guttural tones of Sultan Gadaffi.

The Libyan was lying against the well, a bloodied leg stretched out before him and his face racked with pain. From the angle that the lower part of the limb was lying at, Range could tell that it was broken.

'Tak's a bloody foreigner,' Range grunted. 'He doesn't do English humour. And you're injured.'

'My left leg. I tore it as I was thrown from the vehicle.'

'Can you move?' Range asked.

'I can crawl. I crawled here.'

'It'll have to do.' Range leaned over to inspect the wound. 'I'll patch it up to stop the bleeding. But it'll need a splint.' He fished around in his webbing for a field dressing. 'Tak, keep a close eye on that tomb. Make sure no one sneaks off with any of our gold.'

Having patched up Gadaffi's wound as best he could, Range put a radio call through to O'Shea. First off, he asked for a status report on The Kiwi.

'He'll live,' came back the reply. 'Just.'

'Shit, I was hoping for one less greedy bastard to share the loot with.' Range glanced around himself to get a clear fix on his position. Apart from the odd burst of gunfire, the battleground seemed to have fallen silent. 'We're in the southern end of the fort, on the approach to the tomb. Our wagon's lying on its roof, and we're thirty yards to the east of it, in the cover of something that looks like a well–'

'Cylindrical, stone-built structure, about waist-high?' O'Shea cut in. 'Know it well, buddy. That's where we came up from the duct into the fort.'

'Right, you got us. Grab as many blokes as you can, and muster on our position. Bring maximum ammo and firepower. The enemy's hunkered down in the tomb, and it'll be like Waco unless we can root them out of there.'

'What, they're all about to commit suicide?' O'Shea fired back.

'Nelson will get his eye back before those fuckers slot themselves,' Range growled. 'Just get over here.'

'We're on our way,' O'Shea confirmed.

Range glanced at Tak, who had his eyes glued to the tomb. 'Any sign of life?'

Tak shook his head. 'They're waiting for us.'

Range shifted his gaze to Gadaffi. 'Only the one entrance in and out of there, right?'

'Beyond the bunker, a stone archway leads down a set of rock-hewn steps,' he replied. 'They lead into an underground chamber. The tombs lie off the chamber radiating out from it. What you can see of the chamber above ground belies its size below. It is cut deep into the rock, and there are maybe thirty steps leading into it. The entranceway is narrow, like a slice into the rock, and one man alone can defend it. There is no other way in or out.'

'What about those slits they keep shooting from?' Range asked. 'How do they work?'

'They are positioned at ground level and mostly for ventilation and light, but they double as gun ports. There are stone slabs set horizontally into the walls, so the tomb's defenders can stand on those and use the slits to fire through.'

'In the immortal words of The Kiwi, *I'd kill for some sarin,*' Range muttered. 'A couple of canisters lobbed through the vents, and we could knock out the guard force and take it uncontested.' Range paused. 'What about the gold? Where's it stored, exactly?'

'They moved me from this place six months ago. That is when I was taken to the Fort of the Mount. But last I knew, it was stored in the tomb to the very rear of the chamber.'

'The other tombs? What're they used for?'

'Believe it or not, the guards sleep in them. There is a twenty-four-hour watch—'

'Isn't that against their beliefs?' Range cut in. 'I mean, disrespecting the dead and all that?'

'Those who built this fort were only nominally aligned to any religion we recognize today. In the walls and floors of the tomb are carved the images of four river gods – the Fort of the Great River, remember – plus the goddesses of Adornment, Foundation and Renewal, and wild images of sea-monsters, crocodiles, and many of water . . .'

Range fixed Gadaffi with a piercing look. 'Any of fire? Any images of fire?'

'Probably. But in a desert such as this water was the main priority—'

Range raised a hand to silence him. 'At a time like this I reckon it's fire that we need.'

CHAPTER TWENTY-ONE

Ten minutes later, two battle-worn Toyotas pulled to a halt on the far side of the well and cut their engines. They'd parked up spaced fifty metres apart and in positions from where their machine guns could cover the tomb. With a two-thousand-metre effective range, the lone Dushka would be devastatingly accurate at less than three hundred metres, the distance at which it would be putting down fire onto the enemy's subterranean stronghold.

Conversely, the tomb's defenders would be armed mostly with AK-47s, which were rendered all but inaccurate at that kind of range. Leaving Tiny manning the Dushka, O'Shea jogged across to Range.

'You guys look shot to shit,' he remarked, as he dropped into cover. 'How you doing?'

'Never felt better,' Range retorted. 'What's the status of the battle?'

'Pretty much gone our way. Those me and The Kiwi didn't blow up – they've been shot to pieces by the mobile force. Figure a few got away, just like they did at the Fort of the Mount. There was no stopping them.

There was a lot less than six hundred here, that's for sure, even before we hit them with the explosives.'

'We've been lucky all right. Any sign of the Tuareg joining the show?'

'Not yet. But Jock's on the gate, just in case.'

'Injuries?'

'Two with flesh wounds, nothing fatal. The Kiwi's more serious. Took a lump of grenade frag to the thigh. He's lost a lot of blood, but we've got him stabilized. One advantage of him being a medic is that he's able to treat himself. I had my hands full there for a while, keeping the fuckers from taking us at the tower.'

'I'm sure you did. Great work, by the way.' Range paused. 'Now, tell me, what is the melting point of gold?'

'Gold? Not high for a metal. About 1,064 degrees Celsius. Why?'

'I'm asking the questions. At what heat does diesel burn?'

'Around 210 degrees. But it's hard to ignite. Kerosene's a lot easier, if you have any, and it burns around the same temperature. There's plenty around this fort. No electricity, obviously, so they use kerosene in their lanterns.'

'D'you know where their fuel dump is? Stumble across it when you were planting your charges?'

'As it happens, yeah. But why all the questions?'

'It's like this,' said Range. 'We can't fight our way into

that tomb, 'cause there's only a few of us left fit to fight and we'll all get killed. Plus there's only the one way in, and it's a death trap. We could lob in grenades through the slits, but that might bring the roof down, in which case we can kiss goodbye to the gold.'

'Which is what we came for. And what Randy died for.'

'It is.' Range paused. 'So, I figure it's time to get medieval on the fuckers. Remember the castle sieges of old, when they poured down boiling oil on top of the enemy? And they used massive catapults to hurl burning rocks over the walls?'

'Know it well. Trebuchets – that's what they called the catapults . . .'

'Well, whatever they called them, mate, it's time to take a little lesson from history. We're going to burn them out. Here's the plan. We lob in a couple of smoke grenades, just to get 'em turning and burning and drive them away from the gun slits. Next, we pour in a few gallons of kerosene. We chuck in a white phos grenade to ignite it, and then we're cooking on gas.'

Twenty minutes later his men were ready. Range had spent most of that time massaging the life back into his legs so he could lead this, the next stage of the assault.

He, Tak and O'Shea scuttled forward from one patch of cover to another, their Bergens laden with grenades, spare mags of ammo and a gallon drum of kerosene each. As they neared the tomb, muzzles sparked defiantly from the gun slits, and rounds snapped angrily around their ears. But those bursts of fire were met with a savage onslaught from the vehicle-mounted machine guns, which quickly silenced the enemy's guns.

The three men darted forward, each taking cover against a wall of the tomb adjacent to one of the narrow openings. Range unclipped a smoke grenade from his webbing, pulled out the pin, and lobbed it through the slit, letting the lever fly free as he did so. Three seconds later there was a muffled pop from inside the building, and the clearly audible hiss of the grenade releasing its load. That was followed by two further detonations as Tak and O'Shea's grenades went in.

Moments later, the sounds of frenzied choking and heaving broke forth from deep within the tomb, as thick grey smoke started billowing out of the slits. By now, Range had got the plastic drum of kerosene ready. He tilted it up and started to glug the colourless liquid through the narrow slit, which was still gushing out a thick cloud of acrid smoke. Some of the liquid splattered onto the ground, and the smell hit Range's nostrils.

He waited several seconds so the kerosene had a good chance to evaporate, for it was the fumes that would ignite, as opposed to the liquid itself. That done, he pulled the pin from a white phosphorus grenade and leaned across to lob it in. As he did so, he saw a muzzle spit fire as one of the tomb's defenders squeezed off a long burst on automatic. Rounds tore past, barely inches from Range's arm and face. If the enemy gunman had been able to see to aim properly, he'd have nailed him.

Keeping well back, Range released the pin and threw the grenade. It struck the side of the stone slit, bounced off and tumbled into the smoky darkness. Range was on his feet and edging backwards when he heard the sharp crack of an explosion from below. An intense white light burned out of the gun slit, illuminating the cloud of smoke that enshrouded it. A second later there came a hollow, echoing whump from below ground, and fire swept through the tomb like a wave.

Almost immediately, thick flames started licking out of the entranceway and the gun slits, and a pall of greasy black smoke billowed over the building. Range and his men used the thick smoke and the fierce roaring of the fire as cover under which to withdraw. The conditions below ground had to be lethal by now. The flames and the fumes would quickly take effect, burning and asphyxiating the surviving enemy fighters.

Range had retreated well past the tomb's entranceway when he heard a series of frenzied cries from below ground. He turned to see a group of figures come powering up the steps, screaming at the tops of their voices. They leapt across the sandbagged barrier at the top of the steps, and as they charged forward – their faces soot-blackened and their robes scorched by fire – he spotted what they were holding in their hands: grenades.

Range dropped to one knee and opened fire, the AK he'd taken from Sultan Gadaffi juddering and smoking in his hands. From across the fort came the throaty roar of the Dushka opening up, and Range saw the heavy rounds tearing into the enemy figures, but still they kept coming. Range got the leader nailed in his sights, and for a split second he saw a crazed figure rushing towards him brandishing a grenade in either hand, his mouth set in an animal snarl.

As Range squeezed his trigger, the enemy fighter let out a spine-chilling scream of hatred and released the lever on his grenades. He was barely twenty yards away, and there was a blinding flash and the deafening roar of an explosion. As Range dived for cover, further blasts rang out as the first grenades set off those that the other fighters were carrying.

Through the swirling smoke Range saw the bottom half of the man's torso toppling slowly to the ground. His head, arms and body had been completely obliterated in the blast. He searched with his weapon, scanning for any remaining enemy fighters. All he could see was the sandy earth littered with shattered human remains and soaked in blood and gore. Severed arms, legs and heads were scattered across the ground in front of him, where the tomb's defenders had blown themselves to pieces in one last desperate act of defiance.

As Range scanned the terrain all around him, it was

obvious that the fight for the Fort of the Great River had descended into one of ancient, brute barbarity. In spite of the modern weapons of war, the battleground resembled a scene from some castle siege in the Dark Ages. A thick cloud of smoke hung over the northern end of the fortress where the ammo dump still burned fiercely. To that had now been added the clouds of smoke billowing out of the subterranean tomb. And everywhere, there were the blasted remains of the fallen.

It took a long, dragging hour for the smoke and flames at the tomb to die down. It was 0315 by the time the kerosene was sufficiently burned out for the place to be accessible. Following Gadaffi's directions, Range led his team through the narrow, fire-blackened archway and into the darkness below.

With his flashlight attached to his weapon Range probed the darkness. It was unthinkable that anyone had survived down here, but still he raked the shadows with his gun sights, alert to the slightest sign of resistance. There was nothing; only silence. His foot set something metallic spinning across the solid stone steps and echoing around the tomb. It was a used smoke grenade. As he hit the floor he half stumbled over a soft, shapeless form lying on the ground – the remains of an enemy fighter who had succumbed to the fire and fumes.

He pulled up his *cheche* to cover his nose and filter out

the sickening stench of burned bodies. Fighting down the gag reflex – not to mention the sense of claustrophobia he felt in such cramped darkness – he pushed ahead. O'Shea and Tak fanned out to either side of him, and there, directly before them was the arched entranceway to the rearmost tomb – where Sultan Gadaffi had told them was the gold.

The archway rose from the stone floor to no more than chest height, the roof itself consisting of a solid slab of stone laid crossways between the rock walls. Range flashed his light to either side, and vaults of similar shape and construction ran off the main room. There was nothing in particular to single this one out as being remarkable.

A stout wooden door sealed the vault's entrance, though it was scorched and soot-blackened from the fire. It was closed with a single massive padlock, but even so it seemed laughably inadequate to safeguard what supposedly lay within. For a moment Range wondered whether he was going to roll back the door and find only a pile of old bones, or worse still the doss-sack of one of the tomb's guards. And then he remembered the suicidal ferocity with which those guards had sought to defend this place.

As long as the Fort of the Great River had been occupied by al-Qaeda in the Maghreb, the gold had needed no special security measures to safeguard it: no laser-triggered alarms, no metal cages, no massive steel-walled safe. Those stationed here had relied upon the fort's utter isolation, coupled with secrecy over the gold's whereabouts, and the diehard nature of its defenders.

It had taken so many factors to come together to make the hoard as vulnerable as it was now: a team of men like that assembled by Range; a mission like that launched by HMG (or whoever might be the driving force behind it); a pilot like Walters, with a compelling personal reason to buy into their crazed plan; plus the last surviving Gadaffi son with a body of secrets and lies known only to himself, a need to win his own survival, and the knowledge to buy it.

Range stepped a few paces away from the door and levelled his weapon. 'Ready?'

O'Shea and Tak nodded. He could see the light of eager anticipation burning in their eyes. Range pulled the trigger and a bullet slammed into the lock, blasting it away.

He nodded at O'Shea. 'You do it. You and The Kiwi – you took this place pretty much single-handed. You've earned it.'

The ex-SEAL reached out and pulled at the door's iron handle. There was a creaking of the hinges as O'Shea put all his weight against it, but still it refused to budge. He glanced at Tak, and without a word the big Fijian took hold and flexed his muscles. The seal broke under the pressure, and the thick door swung outwards, revealing the darkness inside.

Range flicked his flashlight into the opening. The beam of light came to rest on a blocky outline, about the size and shape of your average desk. The angular edges were softened by some kind of a blanket or throw-over. O'Shea reached in and yanked it aside. It caught for a moment, he struggled to unsnag it, and then he had it free. The instant he did so the three men were practically blinded by the intense flash of the wall of solid gold that lay before them.

For all that Range might have anticipated this moment, he was rooted to the spot by what lay before them. In this place that had been so ravaged by fire and smoke and blood, he had somehow imagined the bullion might be corroded or discoloured or have lost some of its purity and intensity. But not a bit of it. After the darkness of the tomb, the hoard shone with a dazzling golden fire.

Range reached in and pulled out the first bar. He all but dropped it due to the incredible weight of the thing. He cradled it in the one hand as he brushed off the few specks of dust with the other. It lay there, perfect, unsullied and shining like pure sunlight. Due to the density of the metal, it was almost cold to the touch, and the very heft of the thing took his breath away.

He knew well what he was holding. It was a London Good Delivery bar, the standard configuration for gold bars traded both between banks and commercially. It weighed in at exactly 400 troy ounces, or 12.5 kilograms.

In terms of its size, it wasn't a great deal bigger than the magazine of an AK-47. Yet incredibly, the value of that one bar alone was pushing a million dollars.

For a few short moments Range turned it over and over in his hands, admiring the pure beauty and feel of the thing. The topside of the bar was slightly curved at the edges, and it was smooth and clear of markings. The underside, by contrast, displayed the London caster's name and stamp at one end, consisting of a very royal-looking crest. Below it were the letters 'PN', which Range presumed stood for 'production number', and the serial number of the bar: 00786.

Range checked the bar next to it. It had the same manufacturer's stamp, plus the serial number 00799. They'd rolled off the company's London production line, one after the other. At the bottom end of each bar was stamped 99.99, referring to the purity of the gold in the bar.

By rights, there should be a little over one hundred bars to shift, some 1,250 kilos of bullion. With The Kiwi and Sultan Gadaffi out of action, plus Randy gone for good, Range had ten men left to shift the gold, though they'd have to alternate standing guard on the fort walls. They were battle-worn, but they were still capable of pitching in. There were five hours left until daybreak, and a two-hour drive to get back to the Chinook, which left three hours of darkness in which to load up the gold and get the hell out of there.

Range turned to O'Shea. 'Get the two wagons which are the least damaged, and back them up to the entrance of the tomb. The stair's too narrow for more than one person, so we'll form a line and pass the bars hand to hand. Call in all the guys you can pull off the walls.'

'Got it,' O'Shea confirmed, as he turned and made a beeline for the stairs.

Range locked eyes with Tak. 'Come on, big man, let's get moving.'

Chapter Twenty-two

One very intense hour later, Range and his team had loaded up the two wagons with the gold bullion. It sat in the rear of one of the Toyotas, stacked up against the bulkhead of the cab, in amongst the steel feet of the Dushka's tripod, and with a similar amount piled up in a sister vehicle.

The pumped-up adrenalin buzz of the battle, plus the incredible rush of finding the gold, was all that was keeping Range going, and it had helped him to blank the pain. But with the gold loaded and the wagons good to hit the road, Range found the stabbing pain of the knife wound to his stomach bleeding through to his consciousness again, plus the throbbing ache where his legs had been crushed under the upturned wagon.

In loading up the gold he'd put far too much strain on his injuries, plus the bullet wound to his leg, but there had been no avoiding it. Most, if not all, of his men had taken flesh wounds from bullets or lumps of shrapnel, but nothing serious enough to stop them extracting the loot from its underground lair.

With the gold loaded, Range slapped a couple of fresh

field dressings on his injuries. It was the vicious knife slash to his stomach that was causing him most trouble. It set his mind to thinking about the Tuareg with whom he'd fought that brutal hand-to-hand battle in the rear of the speeding Toyota, and the fact that they were very likely going to be waiting for him and his men as they exited the fort.

If Range were the Tuareg commander, he'd have set ambush positions all along the track that wound through the palm tree oasis. Doubtless, they'd look to hit his convoy hard and from positions of good cover, seeking bitter and bloody revenge. As he surveyed his vehicles and his men, Range realized how ill-suited they were to be driving into further battle, and especially against a well-armed enemy like the Tuareg, who knew the desert like the back of their hands.

The first vehicle in the convoy was bereft of a mounted machine-gun. It was an ancient-looking but massive Ford Bronco pick-up, one that they'd salvaged from the Fort of the Great River's stable building. Two vehicles to the rear of the fire-ravaged structure had escaped the worst of the flames. The paintwork was blistered and scorched, but otherwise the Ford was in far better condition than the remainder of the wagons, whose bodywork was peppered with bullet holes.

Range was travelling in the lead wagon, which was also carrying the worst of their wounded. The Kiwi was laid against the tailgate, his injured thigh tied tight with a tourniquet to stop the bleeding. Next to him was Sultan Gadaffi, his broken leg bandaged and bound with a makeshift splint, and stretched out before him.

In spite of the fact that the lead vehicle would be the first into any ambush, Range had put the Bronco at the front of the convoy because there was just a chance it might sneak through without getting hit. He had O'Shea at the wheel, for Tak had returned to his fire team. Range had reclaimed his Maximi, with which he could put down fire as he rode shotgun next to O'Shea, and both The Kiwi and Sultan Gadaffi had their weapons at the ready.

Wagons two and three – driven by Tak and Tiny – could cover the lead vehicle with their heavy machine guns, and put down a serious amount of fire onto any Tuareg attackers. Those were the vehicles carrying the gold, which meant the loot was sandwiched between the front wagon and the one at the rear.

Vehicle four was the last in the convoy, and it was commanded by Jock. Arguably, that wagon would be the most vulnerable, for by the time it came to pass any ambush point, every man and his dog would have been alerted to the convoy's presence. But Jock had volunteered for the position, and Range had been glad to accept. It gave him huge peace of mind to know the big, unshakeable Scot was backstopping the convoy.

Before setting out into the unknown, Range and O'Shea mounted the stairs that led onto the entrance tower. Using his Sophie sight, Range gazed out from the battlements, scanning the terrain below. Just as he'd anticipated, there were few, if any, of the glowing heat sources of camp fires any more. The Tuareg had extinguished them. Oddly, he couldn't seem to pick up any human heat sources either, which he'd hoped might give him a sense of where the desert nomads had set their ambush points.

'Fires more or less gone,' he remarked to O'Shea.

'Yeah, Sultan was explaining how they sleep close by the fires at night, for the warmth,' O'Shea replied. 'Plus they use the fire to brew up tea early in the morning. Guess if they've doused the flames, there's none of them sleeping any more.'

'Enemy awake, alert and ambushes set, I'd say,' Range grunted. 'Weird, though – can't seem to pick up any human heat sources.'

They descended the stairs, and Range gave a quick heads-up on what he'd seen from the tower roof. Whilst he'd failed to pick up on any human heat sources, he felt sure the Tuareg were out there and waiting.

'They sleep wrapped in these thick woollen blankets,' Sultan Gadaffi volunteered. 'That's how they will be lying in their ambush positions. The blanket acts as insulation, and that will mask their body heat from your thermal-imaging systems. Perhaps that is why you cannot see them.'

Range shrugged. 'Maybe. The mujahideen did

something similar in Afghanistan, to hide from the heat-seeking systems of overflying helicopters. Either way, that Tuareg lot haven't gone away, that's for sure.' He turned to O'Shea. 'You got any of those PE4 charges left?'

'A couple. Why?'

'Set 'em under whatever weapons and ammo you can find. As soon as they blow we get the wheels rolling. That way, it may look as if there's still battle being fought here at the fort, as all the ammo cooks off. It'll cause a distraction, and it might just make the Tuareg less ready to hit us.'

'Plus we roll out lights-off,' came The Kiwi's voice from the lead wagon's rear. He was deathly pale from the loss of blood, and the words were spat out through gritted teeth. All the B6 team were carrying ampoules of morphine as a painkiller. But morphine is a slightly less refined form of heroin, and it would fry the taker's mind and send him to planet Zog – which was largely how it killed pain. The Kiwi had refused to take any, so as to remain sharp and able to operate his weapon.

'We drove in lights-on, and they'll expect us to come out the same,' The Kiwi continued. 'There's ambient light enough to drive by NVG.'

'We go out dark,' Range confirmed, 'and hope we can sneak through. But we go out expecting to get hit like fuck.'

Few if any of the men believed that they would manage to slip past the Tuareg desert warriors, but it was always worth a try. In any case, going out lights-off and on NVG would make themselves a far less visible target, for headlamps gave a perfect firing point for any ambush team. It would buy them time, and get them nearer to any hostile force, which meant they might just get the drop on them.

'One last thing,' Range added. 'We do this run without stopping. Unless a wagon gets put out of action, we keep driving no matter how badly wounded anyone is. The priority is to make that helo before sunup, and to get us and the gold out of here. We fail to do that and we're pretty much dead anyway.'

It was 0430 by the time O'Shea had finished setting his explosives beneath a mountain of captured ammo and weaponry. Range watched his figure come sprinting across the northern end of the fort, and then the first charge blew, the white-hot flash of the explosion silhouetting the wiry American as he dived into the lead vehicle. He hit the driver's seat, fired up the Ford's engine and swung its nose towards the fort's battle-scarred entranceway.

As the big Ford Bronco growled through the arch of the entrance tower, Range checked for one last time that he had a round in the chamber of his Maximi. He glanced around the wagon's rear to see The Kiwi doing likewise with his MP5 sub-machine gun. Range had been locked and loaded ever since driving in to assault the fort, but it never hurt to double-check, especially when others had been using his weapon.

They left the cover of the fort with a cacophony of explosions kicking off behind them as the ammo went up. Range tensed himself for the battle he knew was coming. The seconds dragged by in a nervous silence, the only noise being the rush of the wind as O'Shea eased the wagon down the rise. There was nothing worse for any soldier than driving into a known ambush, and facing an enemy by which you were far outnumbered and outgunned. But right now Range's fear was buried by the pure animal aggression of the coming fight, and the burning conviction that no one was taking those gold bars off them.

The lead wagon reached the location at which Sultan Gadaffi had blasted the Tuareg out of the Toyota pick-up. O'Shea was keeping the speed down so as not to get too far ahead of the wagons laden with the gold. Range was able to search with his eyes for any sign of the desert nomad's body, but there was none. They pressed onwards, and Range flipped down his NVG to scan the surrounding terrain. Apart from their vehicles it seemed utterly devoid of life.

After the insane intensity of the battle for the fort the silence was deafening. The lead vehicle pushed onwards for several seconds, the only noise being the swish of sand under the Bronco's fat tyres. Range could feel his heart beating like a machine gun, his pulse thumping in his ears. He was hunched behind the Maximi, continuously sweeping his arcs and seeking targets amongst the thick and shadowed vegetation, his finger white as bone and tense on the trigger.

A voice kept screaming inside his head: *Where the fuck are they?* But everywhere he looked there was nothing – just empty bush, with the skeletal silhouettes of palm trees etched in the darkness. The tension was unbearable. As his senses tuned in to the environment, Range realized there was a new scent in the air now: the reek of burned cordite from his weapon was mixed with the sharp, salty tang of iodine. Before leaving the fort, Range, plus The Kiwi and Sultan Gadaffi, had poured the brown-yellow liquid over their wounds in an effort to sterilize them.

Range swept the desert night with his weapon. It felt like the ominous, ringing silence was almost mocking him. He knew the Tuareg were out there somewhere, and he sensed in his bones the battle that was coming. Yet knowing that he and his men were all in this together, that they were a brotherhood of the best, gave Range something powerful and unbeatable to conquer his fear. He presumed it was the same for every other man on that mission.

He was torn out of his thoughts by a few words from O'Shea. 'Up ahead. Roadblock.'

Range strained his eyes to detect whatever O'Shea had seen. In the eerie green glow of his NVG he could just make out three hot engine blocks a couple of hundred yards ahead. The vehicles had been parked up sideways onto the sandy highway to form a makeshift barricade. Their motors were still warm, throwing off the heat sources being picked up by their NVG.

As they drew nearer Range could make out more details. The Tuareg had left a gap between the vehicles, one that appeared to be just about large enough to squeeze the Ford Bronco through. It didn't make much sense to Range to have thrown up a roadblock leaving a space for the wagons to pass. Or, thinking like a wily desert nomad-warrior, maybe it did. Maybe they had the gap covered by a couple of thumping great Dushkas. Maybe if Range took the bait and went for the gap, they'd unleash the big machine guns and blow them all to hell.

Or maybe they'd booby-trapped the gap with grenades. Or maybe they had an RPG team waiting just to the far side of it, to smash a rocket-propelled warhead into his wagon as they went to speed through. Whatever, there wasn't much point wasting time and energy thinking about it. With thick vegetation bordering the track to either side, there was only one way through for the convoy – especially when carrying over a tonne of gold bullion – and that was dead ahead.

'Put your foot down, mate,' Range told O'Shea. 'No choice but to run the fucker.'

O'Shea put his pedal to the metal, and the old Ford

responded with a throaty roar. The one advantage of the Bronco was that it was built like a tank, and it probably weighed only a fraction short of one. It was the ideal vehicle for smashing through a roadblock, not that Range had set the line of march with that in mind.

O'Shea got the big Ford hammering forward at increasing speed. Within seconds Range could feel the big, mud-eater tyres slewing through the soft sand, as the heavy vehicle thundered towards whatever was coming. The roadblock was looming closer and closer by the second. They were going to run it, or die trying.

Muzzles started sparking amongst the shadows between the vehicles blocking their way, and from out of the palm trees to either side. There was little point in trying to remain covert any more, for the Tuareg knew well what was coming. As one, the guns on the wagons opened up and tore into the thin metal skins of the vehicles forming the roadblock and the bush all around it.

Range had his Maximi barrel-front and spewing out the rounds. He could see his empty cartridges spinning out of the weapon's breech as he kept his finger hard on the trigger. He figured the Bronco must be getting riddled with enemy fire – bullets tearing metal and punching into steel.

The Ford was almost upon the roadblock, driving down the enemy's guns, when the central vehicle exploded in a blinding sheet of flame. Range had been targeting the area of the fuel tank and it had detonated, the massive blast throwing the vehicle half out of their path. Range felt O'Shea going for the gap, and an instant later the Ford's massive bull-bar smashed into what remained of the enemy vehicle, punching the flaming wreckage out of their path.

As they careered through the scattered debris, Range kept pumping rounds into what was left of the road-block. They sped out the far side, leaving the twisted wreck of a burning pick-up on the one side, and the bullet-torn carcasses of two vehicles on the other. Range was poised for a follow-up attack, expecting a blocking group to have been set behind the roadblock to hit any vehicle that might make it through. But as he scanned the wall of thick vegetation to the left and right of him, there was nothing. It was as if the enemy had melted back into the shadows, allowing them to power through.

Range flicked his eyes across to the cracked wing mir-ror on the Ford, and in the light thrown off from the burning roadblock he could see the three wagons fol-lowing behind. It seemed too good to be true, but somehow they'd all made it through. Range figured he might have injured blokes on the wagons to the rear, or maybe even a guy who was bleeding out, but there was no way of knowing. Unless he got the call on the radio to pull over, the imperative was to keep moving.

Range felt a crazy blast of euphoria as O'Shea gunned

the vehicle into the safety of the darkness. The Tuareg should have nailed them at that ambush. Instead, they had somehow smashed a way through. Range glanced across at O'Shea. He was hunched over the Bronco's wheel, totally focused on urging it towards the comparative safety of the open desert. As the Bronco crested the lip of the wadi at the far end of the oasis, Range saw O'Shea lift his one hand from the wheel and his clenched fist pumped the air.

'WE FUCKIN' MADE IT! WE FUCKIN' MADE IT THROUGH!'

Range couldn't help but share in O'Shea's sense of euphoria. He felt high on the pure adrenalin rush of being alive. As the lead wagon powered away from the kill zone, its big engine growling throatily, O'Shea kept thumping the steering wheel in sheer exhilaration. Range knew exactly how he was feeling. Yet at the same time he couldn't help thinking that somehow the Tuareg hadn't given up the fight.

As he swept the empty, moonlit expanse of the open desert with his weapon, he couldn't shake off the feeling that the real battle was still to come.

Chapter Twenty-three

The Kiwi had his pain-racked eyes fixed on the east, where the sun was painting the horizon a faint duck-egg blue. It was an hour or more before sunrise, and the sky was barely lightening. But nevertheless, as the lead wagon tore through the deserted landscape he figured maybe he'd seen something.

They were less than forty minutes away from the Chinook rendezvous point, and well into the flat, featureless desert terrain that stretched to the far horizon, but still The Kiwi was haunted by the fear that they were being hunted by an unseen adversary.

He searched the horizon with his eyes – eyes that had spent a childhood scanning the New Zealand mountain wilderness for wild animals. There it was again: just the faintest hint of a column of dust far to their rear, silhouetted against the grey-blue of the breaking dawn.

With some difficulty he leaned forward until he was in yelling distance of Range: 'Stop the wagon.'

'What? Mate, we're in a real hurry . . .'

'Stop the wagon,' The Kiwi repeated, his teeth grinding with the pain. 'Now.'

'O'Shea, pull up. The Kiwi needs a break.'

On Range's word the lead vehicle ground to a halt, the wagons behind it doing likewise. The four wagons had been driving across the open desert in staggered formation, so that each avoided the dust thrown up by the one in front, but still they had stuck rigidly to the order in which the vehicles had left the fort.

'Help me down,' The Kiwi said to Range.

'Mate, you're injured. You can have a piss from the wagon . . .'

'Lower the fucking tailgate and get me down,' The Kiwi snarled. 'Kill the engines, and get the rest of the blokes to keep dead quiet. Not a fucking word.'

Range did as requested. He knew better than to mess with The Kiwi on the rare occasion when he got like this: a steely-eyed bringer of death on some kind of a mega-kill mission.

With a supporting arm around The Kiwi's shoulder he helped him hobble a good few dozen metres away from the vehicle into the open desert. This far from the wagons, there was an eerie, open emptiness and quiet to the place, an absence of human life like he had never experienced anywhere else on earth.

'Help me down,' The Kiwi told him.

Range lowered the injured man gently to the earth.

'Now, fuck off back to the wagon, or stay completely

still and silent,' The Kiwi grated. 'I don't care which.'

He lowered his head until it was laid flat on the smooth surface of the desert sand. He nestled himself down still further, turning slightly so that his ear made firm contact with the earth. A fierce light of burning concentration swept across his eyes, as The Kiwi focused everything on the one sense that truly mattered now – his hearing.

Several seconds passed in utter silence. It was so quiet, so absolutely devoid of sound, that Range found the silence oppressive. He couldn't wait to get the convoy back on the move again, and make the RV with the Chinook. He went to check his watch, but The Kiwi spat out a curse that stilled him.

'I said don't fucking move!' The Kiwi lay there for several seconds more, before flicking his eyes up at Range. 'Help me stand.'

Range levered him to his feet, and together they began to hobble back to the lead wagon.

'Vehicles in pursuit,' The Kiwi grated through the pain. 'Unsure exactly how many, but I heard the vibrations through the sand. Faster than us, but not trying to catch us. Can only mean one thing.'

'Which is?'

'Following us at a distance, so we lead them to the helo. They'll hit and take the lot of us, Chinook and all.'

'Shit.'

'They'll sit two klicks back if they're packing

Dushkas, and blast the Chinook as it lifts off. They'll sit further back if they're packing SAMs, and strike as soon as the helo's heat spots are visible to the missile's homing system.'

The Kiwi sank back exhaustedly into the rear of the Toyota. 'Call Walters. Get him to get the rotors turning, and the ramp down, so we drive right in. Forget loading the gold across from the wagons. Walters needs to get the drive into his flight computer, and his radar operational, before we lift off. He needs to get a fix on their wagons before they see us, and he needs to hit them with the Chinook's miniguns. They're the only thing with the range, the accuracy and the firepower to take out the kind of force that's coming after us.'

'The roadblock in the oasis,' spat Range. 'It was a fucking come-on.'

'It was,' The Kiwi confirmed, the pain and fatigue writ large upon his features. 'They had us there, but they melted away and let us through. How else to get us to lead them to the helo? Get on the blower to Walters. We've got a dozen wagons in pursuit, maybe more. We've got no choice but to lead them to him . . .'

'I'm on it,' Range confirmed.

He reached into the inside pocket of his Bergen, pulled out the Thuraya, and dialled up the Chinook to issue Walters a warning.

As the convoy pushed ahead, he couldn't help but flick his eyes across to his passenger mirror. Range kept scanning the blank expanse of terrain to their rear, and checking for any sign of vehicles in pursuit. But the desert behind them seemed totally empty. Yet he hardly expected the Tuareg to be driving across the night-dark terrain with their headlights on, and he didn't doubt for one moment that they were there.

They were a kilometre out from the CH47 when Range first picked up the distinctive, juddering thock-thock-thock-thock of the Chinook's rotors beating the still air. The noise would have been audible from an even greater distance away, had it not been for the dramatic rock walls of the volcanic crater that served to shield the aircraft.

The crater provided cover behind which the Chinook could get airborne, but as soon as it popped up above the level of the rock wall it would be visible, which meant it could be targeted by a Dushka or a heat-seeking missile. In a sense the 12.7mm armour-piercing rounds fired by the Dushka were just as worrying as a SAM, for no defensive system had ever been developed to combat bullets. They were aimed by eyesight alone, and the only sure defence against cannon fire was to kill the weapon's operator.

O'Shea led the convoy into the crater the way that they had come, driving on memory alone. The big Ford swung around the southern side of the spine of black volcanic rock that towered out of the desert, and there was the Chinook. The camo-netting had been rolled away, and the drooping rotors of the giant helo had been spun up to what looked like three-quarters speed. With the sun clawing towards the eastern horizon, it had lit up the wide expanse of the sky above the aircraft a cloudless, azure blue.

The faint shadows thrown off by the spinning rotors were flashing hypnotically across the desert sand. O'Shea pulled the Ford to a juddering halt in the lee of the aircraft. He and Range gathered up the weapons and Bergens from the Bronco, and rushed them into the aircraft's hold. That done, they half-carried The Kiwi and Sultan Gadaffi – the barely walking wounded – up the Chinook's open ramp, and with the loadie's help got them laid on a row of fold-down seats.

Range went forward to Walters. 'Here you go.' He passed him the flight drive. 'Glad you could wait for us.'

Walters took one look at the bloodied, dirtied bandage wrapped around Range's midriff. 'I won't ask how it went.' He reached forward and slotted the drive into place. 'Now let's get us bloody airborne!'

'Fucking amen to that,' Range replied, as he turned to leave.

'What about the booby trap you set with the Claymore?' Walters called after him.

'Safe as houses,' Range yelled back. 'I'll grab it anyway. Best not to leave any evidence behind.'

Range returned to the hold to find Tak and Tiny manoeuvring the two vehicles laden with the gold into the Chinook. With the loadie waving them forward, first Tak and then Tiny powered the wagons up the steel ramp and into the belly of the beast. The loadie started anchoring them with thick nylon cargo straps, ones that ratcheted tight to steel eyelets set into the helo's floor.

Range dropped down from the tail ramp and hurried across to the Ford. He pulled the pins on a couple of white phosphorus incendiary grenades, dropping one in the front of the wagon and the other in the rear. Old habits died hard, and it was a golden rule of his days in the Regiment never to leave any telltale evidence behind.

'Grenade!' he yelled, as he legged it across to the other vehicle and did likewise.

There was the thud of the grenades detonating, the explosions throwing out fingers of white-hot phosphorus that engulfed the vehicles, and within seconds they were burning fiercely. Range turned back to the helo and raced beneath its body, his figure bent double to avoid the rotor's downdraught. He unhooked the dummy booby trap, and with the Claymore in hand he charged up the ramp into the Chinook's interior.

'Twelve pax, two vehicles aboard,' the loadie radioed Walters. 'Good to go!'

Range heard the turbines' animal scream rise to a fever pitch as Walters boosted them to full power. He glanced at the aircraft's door-gunners, tensed over their weapons. No doubt the Chinook's miniguns could deliver maximum lethality. The aircraft boasted two M-134 miniguns, each an electrically driven six-barrel Gatling gun that could churn out a staggering rate of fire – some 6,000 rounds per minute.

The M-134 was 'only' a 7.62mm weapon – as opposed to the far larger 12.7mm calibre Dushka – but the miniguns' murderous rate of fire would saturate any target with leaden death. And that was exactly what Range prayed that the gunners would do to the convoy that was bearing down on them.

Then a thought struck him. Range had to presume that the door-gunners were the best in the business, for they flew with the RAF's 47 Special Forces Squadron. But even so, there was no harm in adding some extra firepower to their arsenal. He grabbed his Maximi and made a move towards the aircraft's open ramp.

'Tak, O'Shea, Jock, Tiny – on me!' he yelled, showing them his weapon as he went.

He strapped himself onto the aircraft's steel ramp using one of the loadies' restraining belts, and lay prone on the floor facing the opening. He saw Tak do the same, followed by Jock, Tiny and O'Shea, each man hefting either an M240 or, like Range, a Maximi. They lined up facing to the rear of the aircraft, each with their weapon's bipod splayed out to lend stability and added long-range accuracy to their fire.

Range felt the Chinook rise from the floor of the

desert, the rotors beating up a fierce cloud of dust. As a last-minute thought he grabbed a set of the aircraft's headphones so he could listen in on the chat. Walters backed the aircraft towards the west, and away from the rock. As it pulled into a graceful turn the Chinook was flying barely fifty feet above the floor of the crater and heading towards its eastern wall.

Range had to presume the terrain-following radar had kicked in, as had all the other state-of-the-art navigational aids on the aircraft, but for an instant it seemed as if the giant twin-rotor helo was about to crash into the rock wall. Seemingly at the last moment Walters piled on the power, and the Chinook popped up over the crater rim and hove into view of the desert beyond.

As he pulled out of the cover of the sheer rock wall, Walters noticed a line of vehicle-shaped icons on his flight screen, moving rapidly through the desert towards his position. Only one thing gave a radar signature like that: fast-moving vehicles. The convoy of a dozen Toyota-type gun-wagons was weaving its way through the open desert at breakneck speed. By the sheer pace and confidence of the driving, it was obvious that those at the wheel knew the terrain intimately.

The convoy was closing on the Chinook fast, most likely being drawn to its position by the column of smoke that was billowing forth from the vehicles that Range had torched. Walters was acutely aware of the far greater reach of the weapons their attackers would be fielding. The Dushka had twice the range of the Chinook's miniguns, and if they did have Igla-S SAMs, they would outshoot the miniguns by a factor of six.

His only hope lay in lurking behind the cover of the rock face and waiting for the convoy to come within range – at which point they would pop up and saturate the entire target with overwhelming firepower. That's if his door-gunners were forewarned with accurate target coordinates and if they were good enough, but Walters had no doubt that they were amongst the best in the business.

Keeping the helo no more than fifty feet above the desert floor, Walters began to track south around the crater rim, sticking well below its cover. Presumably the Tuareg commander would be expecting him to head north, for southwards stretched only the vast continent of Africa. The trouble was that in keeping his heavily laden aircraft in a slow-moving, low-level hover like this he was fast eating up the gas.

As he nursed the Chinook around the crater's edge, he got Mike, his co-pilot, to program in the targeting coordinates to the in-flight computer, and to predict exactly where and when the enemy force would come into range. That done, Walters got on the radio to his crew in the rear.

'We've got company. Coming in from the east on a bearing 070 degrees. Target consists of twelve technical-type vehicles, sporting HMGs and very possibly IR-guided SAMs. They will be coming into our line of fire in approximately sixty seconds' time. When you see me pop up over the crater rim, be ready to engage on the bearing I will provide. Give it all you've got, for there's no doubt these forces are hostile and very well armed.'

Two kilometres to the east of the Chinook, the Tuareg leader Moussa ag Ajjer's eagle-eyed gaze had missed nothing of the scene up ahead of him. Travelling in the passenger seat of the lead vehicle, he'd been amongst the first to spot the smoke thrown up by Range's white phosphorus grenades, which had given him a pinpoint fix on their position. He'd altered course and ordered his men to make all haste, the vehicles behind him building up speed.

It was then that he'd seen the distinctive form of the twin-rotor helicopter rise from the rim of the volcano like a spectre, and just as quickly drop back down again. Moussa ag Ajjer presumed the pilot had seen his force, and that it was trying to find an exit point from the crater which was further from his line of approach, taking them north towards safety. Either way, it wouldn't put his aircraft out of the range of the kind of weaponry his men had at their disposal. The crater was no more than a kilometre across, and the Igla could engage a target at six times that distance.

'They have led us to their means of escape,' he declared, triumphantly. 'But there is no escape from our anger or our thirst for vengeance.' He turned to a figure at his rear. 'You are ready with the Igla?'

'I am, *amghar* – chief,' the fierce-eyed individual replied, excitedly.

'Do to this aircraft as you did to the French,' the Tuareg leader commanded. 'If God wills it.'

'If it is God's will,' the figure echoed.

Moussa ag Ajjer spoke to his driver. 'As soon as we see the aircraft exit the crater you will signal the vehicles to a halt, so as to give our missile operators a firm platform from which to fire.'

'I will, *amghar*,' the driver confirmed.

'Tell me, how many Iglas are made ready?'

'Twelve, *amghar*,' the missile operator in the vehicle's rear replied. 'When we received your orders, most of us were on the high plateau, where we had taken our cattle to graze. But still we made ready.'

'It is enough.' Moussa ag Ajjer smiled. 'Whatever kind of machine this twin-bladed black warplane might be, I would like to see it outrun twelve Igla-S.'

'I vow it will take only the one,' the missile operator volunteered. He patted the long cylindrical weapon lying beside him. The warhead was already inserted into the tube, the launcher armed to automatic and ready to fire.

As the Chinook edged closer to the lip of the southern rock wall, Walters checked his timing once more. The sixty seconds was all but done. He piled on the power and the aircraft began to rise. He ran his eyes across his targeting screens, then spoke into his radio.

'Door-gunners, prepare to engage on a bearing of 055 degrees, range 1,000 yards.'

As the twin rotor blades hauled the aircraft out of hiding, Walters could see the downwash whipping a cloud of sand and loose rock off the crater's jagged rim. To his east the enemy convoy began to slow. Knowing how much easier it was to engage a target from a stationary vehicle, Walters presumed they were preparing to open fire.

'Engage! Engage! Engage!' he yelled, as he rotated the aircraft to present the minigunners with a clear field of fire. 'Confirm bearing of target is 050 degrees, range 900 yards. Engage!'

As Walters held the giant aircraft rock-steady, the Chinook's defenders seized their few precious seconds of advantage and the gunners swung their miniguns onto target. The aircraft was swept by a storm of vibrations as the pair of M-134 miniguns opened fire simultaneously. There was a long, thunderous 'brrrrrrrrrrrrrrrrrr', as the roar of the six-barrelled weapons thundered around the hold.

The thick, stubby barrels of the Gatling guns were spitting fire, and for every second the gunners kept their fingers on the trigger mechanism, one hundred rounds tore towards target. A cascade of spent shell cases rained down below the aircraft, turning the predawn sky beneath it dark.

From the helo's open ramp Range saw the gunners'

rounds falling just short, sparking off the desert to the front of the lead wagon, which was braking hard in an effort to come to a halt. The minigunners leaned into their weapons, raising their muzzles a fraction on their pivot mounts, and fired again.

This time, rounds hammered along the length of the lead vehicle, tearing out windows and sending fountains of glass into the air. Shredded seating and jagged chunks of bodywork spewed across the desert, along with the remains of the vehicle's human occupants. A second line of vehicles was hit, but not before the occupants had opened fire with wild bursts.

As the miniguns tore into the convoy, one of the wagons swerved violently to the right and careered out of the line of fire. It rolled over several times, and Range followed it with the sights of his Maximi until it stopped moving. Then he opened fire. The Toyota had come to a rest on one side, and by the time Range had ceased firing there were no more muzzle flashes coming from the wreckage.

He swept the hot, smoking barrel of his Maximi back towards the main body of the convoy. Range could see kneeling figures silhouetted in the glare of their muzzle flashes, as they sprayed off long bursts and tried to smash rounds into the Chinook. As one, the four machine guns on the aircraft's open ramp tore into them, whilst the miniguns chewed up the wagons further to their rear.

Range and his men concentrated their firepower on the human targets, pounding rounds into them. All of a sudden, there was an angry burst of flame from a wagon to the rear, as one of the miniguns practically tore its diesel tank in half and set the whole vehicle ablaze. Within seconds the entire rear section of the convoy was obscured by a thick blanket of choking smoke.

As the dark and oily cloud drifted across the desert, Range swept the nearest vehicles for further targets. The lead Toyota was lying in the dirt with its roof staved in, and the window struts buckled from the impact. Bodies were hanging out of shattered glass, with others lying face-down amidst spreading pools of blood. There didn't seem to be a figure moving, but he continued to rake the targets with suppressing fire. The more rounds they could put down the more likely they were to keep the enemy's heads down and ensure their own getaway.

Walters had seen the miniguns tear apart the target, and he saw the smokescreen that had been thrown across the enemy convoy. He figured now was as good a time as any to make good their escape. He dropped the aircraft's nose, turned towards the north in a graceful, banking dive, and using the cover of the volcano's rim he pushed the Chinook towards its top speed of 259 kph.

He planned to exit the crater at the northernmost point, then drop down to treetop level and set a bearing north-west, so using the cover of the crater to hide them from any surviving enemy.

As the Chinook swept north along the crater rim, a figure staggered away from the wreckage of one of the lead vehicles. The tall, wiry Tuareg had the long, tubular form of a missile launcher clutched in his left hand. For a moment he turned to survey the scene of carnage left by the Chinook's miniguns, and his eyes came to rest on the mangled form of his chief, Moussa ag Ajjer. He felt blind rage sweep over him.

'*Amghar*, I will kill them all for you!' he screamed. 'They will all die!'

As he sunk to one knee and raised the Igla, he almost thought he saw the Tuareg chief smile, as if he had heard those words and understood them. The thought gave him untold strength as he steadied the missile launcher in his hands and waited for what he knew was coming. An instant later the squat black form of the Chinook hove into view, as Walters brought it up over the northern end of the crater, setting a course for safety.

At that moment there was a blinding burst of yellow flame, and the missile operator fired.

CHAPTER TWENTY-FOUR

The moment the warhead left the tube Range spotted the missile launch, and he opened up with his Maximi. He was still lying prone on the Chinook's open ramp and covering its rear, the position offering him a perfect fire platform. A long burst from the Maximi tore into the Igla operator, but by then it was too late: the deadly heat-seeking missile was already well on its way.

'*Fox One*! *Fox One*! Infrared lock-on!' The Chinook's helicopter integrated defensive aids suite (HIDAS) began screaming out a warning, *Fox One* being the NATO brevity code for an infrared-guided surface-to-air missile. 'SAM launch! SAM launch! SAM launch!'

As the aircraft fired off a blinding burst of decoy flares, Walters put it into a stomach-churning dive. With a massive cloud of heat sources blooming all around it, he hoped the flares would draw the missile's IR sensors whilst he got them out of the danger zone. But with the Igla boasting an advanced guidance system, and an independently swivelling infrared-seeker head set within the glass nose of the missile, there was every chance it would remain glued to the main target regardless of what decoys were deployed.

The Igla streaked through the dawn sky at 570 metres a second. To Range perched on the open ramp, it looked as if a deadly comet was flaming towards them. As the Chinook swept down the far side of the crater and hugged the desert terrain, Range saw the missile sweep through the cloud of decoy flares undeterred, and arrow forward.

It was tearing in to strike when Range opened up again with the Maximi, his fellow B6 operators and the minigunners following his lead. They met the missile's inrush with a solid wall of lead, the combined rate of fire being 16,000 rounds a minute, and all of it unleashed in the path of the Igla. There was a seemingly impossible moment when it looked as if the rounds were having no effect, but an instant before the warhead was about to slam into the side of the speeding aircraft it exploded in a ball of seething fire.

The Igla-S packs a 2.5 kilogram high-explosive fragmentation warhead. As it detonated, fragments of jagged shrapnel were blasted in all directions, most tearing through the open desert sky. But a good number ripped into the MH-47, punching through its armour plating and smashing into the vehicles fastened in the aircraft's hold.

The blast wave tore across the Chinook's open ramp with a force like a whirlwind. Range lifted his head from the cold steel, and for an instant he wondered how the hell they were still airborne and still alive. He glanced across at Jock opposite him to make some form of a comment.

It was then he noticed the ugly hole where Jock's forehead used to be, and the blank, lifeless stare in his eyes.

A long flight lay ahead of them to reach their refuelling point in the western Libyan desert, and Walters was forced to nurse the battle-damaged helo northwards at well below optimum speed. It left Range plenty of time to reflect on Jock's death, and to mourn his passing.

A fragment of shrapnel from the missile had passed clean through the big Scot's head, killing him instantly. It could have been anyone, and Jock had just been unlucky, but still there was a dark atmosphere in the aircraft's hold. The loss of Jock just as they had begun to believe they had made it out of there had hit them all hard. With Jock and Randy gone, that was two families to whom Range was somehow going to have to deliver their share of the loot – that's presuming they got the gold away to safety – plus the news that their man wasn't coming home.

Though he'd not admitted as much to his men, Range was very much making this up as he went along now. Whilst he had a plan of sorts forming in his mind, it was dependent on so many variables – one of which now included a Chinook shot to pieces, and how long

Walters was going to be able to keep his damaged aircraft airborne.

Four nerve-racking hours later the Chinook touched down at the remote refuelling base. Camp Stirling – Wadi Idhan to the locals – was just as Walters had described it: some godforsaken desert outpost in the midst of nowhere. But after losing Jock, none of the men had much interest in the scenery.

The refuelling done, the Chinook began to taxi out to the helipad once more for take-off. It would have made perfect sense to ground the damaged aircraft, were it not for Range and Walters's orders. Come what may, Sultan Gadaffi was to be delivered into the hands of whoever had orchestrated this mission, and well outside of Libyan territory. The Colonel had been adamant about that when he'd first briefed them on the mission, and he was even more so now.

Walters had kept his communications with base extremely short, in spite of The Colonel's obvious alarm that the mission had been delayed and gone 'off radar' for twenty-four hours. He'd had his hands more than full trying to fly his shrapnel-riddled aircraft, without a bunch of irate mission commanders breathing down his neck and yelling in his ear.

He'd cut his response to any radio calls to two brief words: 'Wait out.'

This was military speak for 'I hear you but cannot communicate right now.' Repeated often enough over the air, Walters hoped it would get those in command to back off and give him the space to concentrate on trying to get the mission home.

'Home' wasn't going to be the UK base they'd set out from. Walters had insisted that he bring his crippled aircraft into the nearest secure British airbase, which was situated just across the Mediterranean, in Gibraltar. They would be flying into Headquarters British Forces Gibraltar, not far from the army garrison based at Devil's Tower Camp. The Colonel, The Fixer and a good few other top brass were apparently flying out to meet them.

With the drive slotted into his flight computer Walters couldn't exactly turn off his comms systems, and The Colonel and others had made it very clear to him that there were to be no further delays in bringing his aircraft home. But as he prepared the Chinook for take-off from Camp Stirling, and for the three-hour hop north-west to Gibraltar, he was aware that Range had asked him to hang on for as long as he possibly could.

Walters didn't exactly want to know the reason for the delay. As Range had said, what he didn't know he couldn't tell, and he knew too much already, as far as he was concerned. Another body was scheduled to join the aircraft here at Wadi Idhan, and Walters didn't want to know who it was or why.

To the rear of the aircraft Range and Sultan Gadaffi

were perched on the open tail ramp, scanning the airstrip for movement. Where the hell was he?

'Tell Walters we're still awaiting one more pax!' Range yelled at the loadie. 'And Walters had better not get airborne before he gets here, or one day he's going to run into me down a darkened alleyway.'

The loadie spoke into his radio, exchanging a few words with the pilot up front.

'Captain Walters says he can hold on for a further five minutes,' the loadie yelled in response. 'He can push it for five. Any longer, and The Colonel and those above him are going to crucify him.'

Range's eyes flashed murder. 'Wait here. Keep a watch out for two or three blokes, one who'll be joining us.'

Range strode forward to the cockpit and stuck his head through the door.

'Walters, I should have kept your fucking aircraft hijacked!'

'Probably,' Walters snapped back at him. The tension was clear in his features. 'I'll hold for as long as I can, Range, but you've not got The Colonel and a bunch of other high-ups going spare in your ear.'

'Tell them to piss off,' Range rasped. 'Tell them you've been hijacked, shot up, whacked by missiles, the works. Tell them you've got The Joker plus us lot on board, and that you'll be back with them in your own good time. Tell them we've lost two good men on this fucked-up mission of theirs . . .'

'It's not what I tell them that matters,' Walters cut in. 'The drive's back in the flight computer. They can speak to us, but more importantly it shows them exactly where we are. They'll know the refuelling's complete, and I'm on the helipad about to get airborne. They've already been screaming at me to get airborne.'

'Listen, I want ten minutes, minimum. And don't get airborne without warning the loadie.'

Walters shook his head in frustration. 'Ten. But no more.'

Range hurried back to the tail ramp. The seconds dragged by, but still there was no sign of any movement out on the airstrip. Finally the loadie received the call from Walters. Range was all out of time and he was about to get airborne. Above him, Range could hear the turbines spooling up to speed. At the last moment he grabbed Sultan Gadaffi, slung him over his shoulders, thundered down the open ramp and vaulted to the ground.

He ran a few paces away from the aircraft's howling downdraught. 'Let's see 'em get airborne without us!' he yelled. 'Without you, anyways!'

'Thank you,' Gadaffi yelled back, his faced racked with pain. 'Whatever happens, Mr Range, even if we do not make today's rendezvous and you have to hand me in, I will always remember what you did, and tried to do, for me and for what was right.'

Range gave a grim smile. 'And for the gold. Don't forget the gold.'

'Yes, that as well. But I am not so certain you are driven only by greed alone.'

From behind him Range heard a screech of tyres on loose gravel. He spun around and the distinctive form of a British army Land Rover was powering toward them. It came to a halt in a cloud of dust. A figure emerged. He was wearing desert camos, and leading a second figure by the arm – one dressed in a Western-style shirt and trousers, but with an Arab headscarf mostly obscuring his features. It helped keep the wind-blown dust out of his mouth and eyes, but mostly it was being done for the purpose of disguise.

Range strode across to them and gave the first figure a crushing bear hug. 'Better late than never Planky, mate! I owe you . . .'

'You owe me enough beer to get me totally wankered,' growled Planky, his SAS mate based here at Camp Stirling. 'I don't know who that guy is and I don't want to know. The Hogan delivered him, which was a ballsy move in itself, but I've had a total bollocks getting him through security. You better fucking believe it – you owe me.'

'Yeah, enough beer to get you plastered for a month. Won't cost me too much, though. Seem to remember two beers and you're anyone's . . .'

'Piss off, mate.'

Range grabbed the mystery figure, and got him up the aircraft's open ramp and strapped into a seat. He returned for Gadaffi, carried him in and left him conversing in hurried Arabic with the newcomer.

'The Bergens?' Range prompted, once he was back with Planky.

In response Planky heaved down the Land Rover's tail ramp. 'Give us a hand!' he yelled, as he chucked out the first of a dozen backpacks. Together, they got them loaded into the Chinook's hold, before shaking hands briefly.

'We lost two,' Range added, a darkness sweeping across his features. 'One, an ex-SEAL named Randy. Top bloke. You didn't know him. The other you knew well. Big Jock McGregor . . .'

Planky shook his head. 'Fucking unbelievable. Jock – he was indestructible.'

'We'll expect you at the wake.' Range turned to mount the Chinook's open ramp. 'Later!' he roared. 'We'll drink to Big Jock's memory!'

With that the loadie gave the signal and the Chinook pulled into the air. Range made straight for the cockpit, striding past the newcomer who was firmly strapped into his seat beside Gadaffi. As he squeezed by the two vehicles anchored in the helo's hold, he did a quick visual check on the gold.

The two piles of bullion looked totally unremarkable in the vehicles' rear, sheeted over as they were with lengths of tarpaulin. To a casual observer they'd look like any normal pile of lumpy gear stored in the rear of a desert pick-up: jerry cans of extra fuel, a spare wheel, inner tubes, some wooden blocks for jacking up the vehicle in loose sand, tool kits and the like.

Range reached the cockpit and leaned in. 'Thanks. The delay. It's appreciated.'

Walters grunted an acknowledgement. 'Not a lot of choice, with the two of you mooching around like dicks on the apron.'

'Gives you a good excuse, though. You couldn't take off 'cause Range, the lunatic, had pulled The Joker off the aircraft.'

'Great. Thanks. Now, if you'll excuse me, I've got one very shot-up MH-47 to fly home.'

'One more thing. Leave the ramp down, will you, all the way to Gib.'

'Any particular reason? Or shouldn't I bloody ask?'

Range gave a hard smile. 'We need the air.'

Range returned to the hold and gathered his men around him. In effect they were nine now, for The Kiwi had maxed out on the morphine just as soon as the Chinook had got airborne, and Sultan Gadaffi – having finished briefing the aircraft's mystery newcomer – had just been injected with a first phial.

With the noise of the rotors thrashing above their heads and the wind pounding in via the open tail ramp, Range presumed neither the loadie nor the door-gunners would be able to overhear what he was about to say. Either way, he didn't particularly care.

They'd pulled together pretty much as one team, not knowing quite what kind of mission they had been flying, and Range was determined to look after the Chinook's crew. But at the same time, he'd prefer to maximize the aircrew's ability to deny any knowledge of what was coming. After all, the aircrew still served with the military and might wish to continue doing so for some time.

'Right, Walters has got clearance to fly into Gib,' Range began. 'That'll route us over southern Spain. He's taking the helo up to 10,000, in case it piles in on us and we have to make an emergency landing. That way he can auto-rotate from altitude, and as long as we're over land we should stand a decent chance of surviving.'

Auto-rotation was a way to make a controlled crash-landing from altitude with a disabled helicopter. As the helo fell through the air the uprush would drive the rotors ever faster, which would create lift, so slowing the aircraft's rate of descent. In essence, the pilot would use the rotors as a giant parachute under which to break the aircraft's fall.

'Presuming we make it to the Spanish coast,' Range continued, 'I've got a burning question for O'Shea.' He eyed the American. 'You've got a house somewhere in the Spanish highlands? What's it like and where is it exactly?'

'Been inviting you out for years now. It's a *finca*: an old farmhouse set in the hills around Andalucía, on the outskirts of a village called El Barca.'

'Great. Sounds lovely. Very scenic. Point is – it's remote and private, is it?'

'Very.'

'Here's why. If we jump out of the Chinook at 10,000 feet at the nearest point of the flight path to your *finca*, could we HAHO into it, or at least to as near as we can get?'

'At that height, we'd make twenty, maybe thirty klicks under the chutes,' O'Shea replied. 'Plus the wind direction would have to be just right. So it's unlikely. Doesn't really matter, though. Once you're away from the Spanish coast the highlands are very lightly populated. We land on some remote mountainside, I call up Maria, she gets in the four-by-four and RVs with us. Maria's my 27-year-old live-in Spanish lover–'

'Whatever,' Range cut in. 'But can she keep her mouth shut?'

'If I tell her to, she can.'

'So, if it doesn't matter where we put down as long as it's reasonably remote, we can just as easily HALO?'

'Yeah. If we jump out over the mountains, we'll find an empty spot to put down no problem.'

'Great, 'cause HALO's quicker and far less visible, which is all the better for what I've got in mind.'

Range paused and eyed his men. Their smoke-blackened features were streaked in grime and cordite burn marks. In their ripped and blood-and-sweat-stained combats, and with bandages wrapped around heads, legs, arms and other flesh wounds, they resembled a band of diehard mercenaries that would make The Hogan proud.

They looked like a bunch of utter desperadoes, which was what Range figured they were right now – and especially considering what he had in mind as the next stage of the operation.

Chapter Twenty-five

'Right, here's the plan,' Range announced. 'As you may have noticed, a dozen fresh para-packs were loaded aboard at our Camp Stirling refuelling stop, courtesy of Planky. At 10,000 feet you can jump without oxygen, and each pack is a HALO rig. Dump everything out of your Bergens that you don't need, and I mean everything. Replace it with the gold. We've got 1,250 kilos to shift, and there are nine of us, so that's 138 kilos, or roughly eleven bars, per man.

'Two guys will be jumping with blokes tandemed to them – that's you, O'Shea, plus you, Tak. Tak, you'll go with The Kiwi, 'cause he's too badly injured and too stoned to make the jump. The Kiwi must weigh 70 kilos, or thereabouts. A bloke of your size should be able to tandem a 70-kilo bloke, plus ten gold bars – that's around 190 kilos all told. You good with that?'

It was a massive amount of weight to carry, but Tak simply grunted an acknowledgement, like it was going to be any normal kind of a jump.

Tak and O'Shea were among a tiny number of elite American and British operators who'd been trained as military 'tandem masters'. They were able to freefall another human being from high altitude with that person attached to their torso. They'd jump with the bloke strapped to their front, the chute on their back and their Bergens suspended below them. Not counting their own body weight, they'd normally be steering some 130 kilos into the exact spot onto which they intended to land – including survival gear, food, water, ammo and weapons.

'O'Shea, you jump with Gadaffi. He's a 65-kilo bloke, so take eight bars in your Bergen – which puts you up around the 160 kilos mark. You good with that?'

'Good to go.'

'The remainder we share around us. We'll each have around 150 kilos of bullion, but it makes sense to squeeze in a personal weapon if you can. Those who have pistols, pack 'em – just in case any Spanish peasant gets it into his head to go grab his shotgun and try to rob us.

'Now, someone's bound to see us make the jump,' Range continued. 'There's always one. Let's say he's two sandwiches short of a picnic and he figures Spain is being invaded by aliens. Let's say he calls the local cops. Here's what we do. First priority when we hit the ground: we stash the gold. We find a patch of cover and hide it good. Three blokes – O'Shea included – get into a hide alongside the stash, and remain with it for as long as it takes for Maria to make an RV. O'Shea, take the Thuraya so you can guide her in.

'If the cops turn up, let me do the talking. We tell them we're a British Special Forces team that had to bail out of a Chinook that was going down. We tell them we were en route from a mission in Libya, and heading for Gib. We tell them that's all we can say, unless they can get us to the nearest British consulate.

'O'Shea, you know what to do with the loot. You stash it at your *finca*, and no one breathes a bloody word.' Range paused, checked his watch and eyed his men. 'If everyone's good, let's get sparking. It's coming up to 1430 hours – we should be over the Spanish coast in less than thirty minutes, and there's a shedload to do before then.'

There were a series of curt nods, all except for Tak.

'What about Jock?' the big Fijian demanded. 'A dead man can't jump.'

'We leave his body here,' Range replied. 'I don't like it, but he'll get repatriated from the British base in Gibraltar, so he'll be returned to his family. I'd prefer to take him home, but we can't.'

'First Randy and now Jock,' O'Shea muttered. 'It doesn't seem right . . .'

'Yeah, and I'd give my right arm to have them still with us,' Range cut in. 'But they're not. They died for the gold and for Gadaffi's secrets. And if their loss is going to mean anything we've got to jump, and that means we can't take Jock with us.'

Range's words silenced all further objections.

'O'Shea, you call the jump,' he added. 'You call P-Hour on your GPS when you figure we're over the LZ.'

Some fifty minutes later Range stood on the edge of the Chinook's ramp, the cold air tearing at his battered combats. The end of the dirtied bandage wrapped around his torso was flapping free, and being grabbed at by the helo's slipstream. Jumping from a helicopter was never ideal, due to the powerful downdraught of the rotors, but doing a HALO jump they'd freefall through the turbulence and only pull the chutes at a much lower and calmer altitude.

HALOing had the added advantage of getting them onto the ground the fastest way possible, and largely unseen. Range had been torn as to whether he should warn Walters about what they were about to do, but on balance he felt it best to keep quiet. For sure the loadie and the door-gunners had to know what they were up to, and they could fill Walters in later if need be.

For want of a better option, O'Shea was acting as the team's parachute dispatcher. Tak was leading the stick out of the aircraft, and he'd shuffled to the very brink of the ramp with The Kiwi strapped to his front. The wiry New Zealander had a spaced-out look in his snake-green eyes.

O'Shea was counting down the seconds to the moment they had to jump. He had his eyes glued to his GPS as it tracked the Chinook's flight path through the hazy Spanish cloud. Walters was holding the helo rock-steady and on a bearing heading almost due west, and the conditions outside seemed as good as they'd ever be for such a jump.

The nine men – eleven including the stoned-out forms of The Kiwi and Gadaffi – shuffled forward, trying to tighten up the space between the bodies. It was next to impossible to move weighed down by the bullion each man was carrying, but once they'd made the jump they'd unhook themselves from the deadweight of the Bergens.

Range heard O'Shea give a yell from his position at the rear: 'Ten, nine . . . three, two, one: GO! GO! GO! GO! GO!'

On his 'GO' the stick surged forward as one, and the men plummeted into the howling void. Range was too exhausted and too on the edge to baulk at the jump. He dived out, hit the Chinook's slipstream, and the powerful blast of the rotors threw him into a twisting, spinning fall. He tore out of the slipstream, pushed his weight forward onto his Bergen and accelerated into a head-first dive.

Directly below him was the bulky form of Tak plus The Kiwi, forming a darker spot against the terrain. Range brought himself to within fifty feet of Tak, getting his arms and legs into a star shape to slow his fall. He turned his head into the roaring slipstream to check on those behind him. He counted seven dark human-shaped blobs strung out in the air above, and silhouetted against the mid-afternoon Spanish sky.

Having made sure the line was complete, Range did a quick check of his altimeter. Jumping from 10,000 feet they'd be just twenty seconds in the freefall, and he needed to keep a close eye on their release height, which was set at 3,000 feet above ground level. As they plummeted earthwards he noticed a figure overtake him. It was O'Shea, with Sultan Gadaffi strapped to his front.

O'Shea had got the two of them formed into a streamlined delta shape to increase the speed of their dive. He was shooting past the other jumpers, who had arms and legs outstretched to slow and stabilize themselves. O'Shea knew the ground here, and he would lead the stick into an impact point of his choosing.

Range saw O'Shea hit the 3,000-feet mark, and there was the flash of a canopy blossoming above him. He reached down and grabbed for his own release. His fingers found the 'throw-away' – the mini-parachute-shaped piece of material that deploys the main chute – and he pulled hard and let it fly into the air. It caught, blossomed and dragged the main chute after it, and all of a sudden Range felt himself yanked upwards by a massive force.

An instant later he was left floating in the silence and stillness of mid-air, and suspended beneath the silk canopy. They had just a couple of thousand feet to go, and below him O'Shea would be searching for the ideal landing spot. He needed a patch of terrain clear of trees or other obstacles, and as far away from human habitation as possible.

The men formed up in line, and began serpenting after O'Shea as he led them in. At 500 feet of altitude Range released his Bergen, and the 150-odd kilos of gold – twelve London Good Delivery bars, each wrapped in whatever blankets and sheeting Range had been able to find on the helo, to prevent their weight tearing through the Bergen's tough nylon exterior – plunged downwards on the chute's pulley system, until it was suspended below him.

The Bergen struck the ground first with a massive thud, but at least it had taken the weight of the bullion off Range's legs. He hit the deck a few seconds later, landed badly, rolled, recovered and let the chute come down beside him. The LZ that O'Shea had chosen was far from flat, being on a mountainside, but at least it seemed to be remote. The only signs of life that Range could see in any direction were the few sheep grazing on the open, grassy hillside.

Range gathered up his chute and did a proper visual scan of the terrain. A hundred yards to their north he spotted a patch of stunted oak woodland. That's where he figured they would stash the gold.

Once all of the jumpers had made the LZ, Range gathered the men. They orientated themselves to north, after which O'Shea gave them a quick talk to familiarize themselves with the terrain. The nearest human settlement was a tiny Spanish hamlet some ten kilometres to their east. The only people who ever came into these grasslands were a few local shepherds, plus the odd rambler trekking the mountains.

'The *finca* is a good forty klicks north-east of here, which equates to an hour or more on the local roads,' O'Shea explained. 'The nearest route navigable by four-by-four is a farm track, maybe five hundred yards that way. Maria could bring the jeep across the grassland to RV with us there.' O'Shea indicated the woodland. 'That's where I'm guessing we'll stash the loot?'

'It's the only place,' Range confirmed. 'Tak, when you've made The Kiwi comfortable, take Tiny and go recce the woodland. Find a good hiding place, plus somewhere nearby to establish a hide from where you can keep eyes on the loot. We'll stash the chutes, then start ferrying the bullion across to you.'

Tak nodded and they were gone.

'O'Shea, best you make the call to your girl,' Range suggested. 'We're also going to need some favours from the locals, so I hope they're bloody friendly. One, is there a doctor who can take a look at The Kiwi and Gadaffi, and without asking too many questions?'

'The local medic's a guy called Alberto Franco. He's Spanish to his boots, which means he'd treat the devil himself as long as the price was right.'

'Second, we're going to need to get Gadaffi before

someone from the British media. You've got contacts with the press, right?'

'Yeah. There's a journalist guy I know who ghost-writes stories for several guys who are ex-Special Forces.'

'Right. Once we've got the main priorities sorted, you need to get on the line to your guy, so Gadaffi can blow what he knows to the world's media.'

'No problem,' O'Shea confirmed. 'Let's get the gold stashed, the guys patched up, and I'll get onto it.'

With Tak signalling that he'd found a hiding place, the men began to ferry the bullion across to the woodland. Halfway through the exhausting task Range paused to catch his breath and he glanced toward the west. The Chinook would have reached Gibraltar by now, all being well. He wondered what kind of reception Walters and his crew, plus their mystery passenger, might be getting.

He'd just finished lugging his portion of the bullion across to the hiding place, when Range heard a trilling on the Thuraya. He checked the caller ID, half expecting it to be O'Shea's girlfriend, Maria, reporting that she was on her way. Instead, he had a call incoming from The Hogan.

He punched 'answer' and lifted the Thuraya to his ear. 'Range.'

'Welcome back, old boy,' The Hogan purred. 'I take it you *are* back?'

'We are.'

'Fantastic,' The Hogan enthused. 'Now, I've just taken a call from The Colonel. He's in Gibraltar and appears to be rather mystified as to what's taken place with your mission. He says they've got The Joker, or someone who he presumes is The Joker, but otherwise you and your team have disappeared, and the pilot seems to have no idea where you are. He says you were in the Chinook when it took off, but you weren't there when it landed a few minutes ago.'

'It's still mission accomplished,' Range replied. 'They asked us to bring the Gadaffi kid in. We delivered.'

'Which is exactly what I told him.' The Hogan paused. 'The trouble is, there's this twenty-four-hour period wherein your team went totally off radar. There's also the little issue of an RAF Chinook apparently being hijacked, and it being shot to pieces as it extracted from whatever mission you'd hijacked it for. I've told The Colonel these allegations seem a little wild, even for you, and that it's best he hears an explanation from the horse's mouth. But for now, I'd suggest you keep a low profile . . .'

'That's exactly what I intend to do.'

'Quite,' The Hogan chuckled. 'Once you've done what you need to do, let me help bring you in. There will need to be a debrief with The Fixer and his ilk. It's unavoidable, and Blackstone's future business depends upon it. But before that takes place you and I will need to get our heads around everything that's been happening. And perhaps a one-on-one with The Colonel might be useful, to help explain things from your perspective and to bring him on side?'

'Yeah – as long as you think he's still one of the good guys,' Range confirmed.

'Any sense of a timescale, old boy? I just have this feeling I'm going to have the lot of them on my back until I can bring you in and give them some answers.'

'Give me seventy-two hours,' Range told him. 'In three days' time and at this hour we'll RV in the usual place.'

'Perfect. I'll have a glass waiting for you on the bar.' The Hogan paused for an instant, and when he continued speaking Range could detect a hint of tension that had crept into his voice. 'You *are* sure we've got this one right, old boy? We've made the correct call?'

'As certain as I can be. There was no other way to call it. I'll fill you in when we meet. This is insecure means, so enough said. Thanks for everything.'

The call done, there was nothing left to do but to watch and wait. Maria was on her way, and all being well they'd start ferrying their injured and the loot out of there shortly. If necessary, Range was happy for those who could walk to trek the route to O'Shea's *finca*. It had to be possible off-road, which would hide them from the view of any curious onlookers, and it was fine weather for a stroll. All they needed the jeep for was the bullion and the wounded.

O'Shea joined him in the cover of the long grass at the edge of the woodland. From there they had a commanding view of the terrain below, a series of sweeping ridges and humped folds, descending in dramatic steps to the lowland valleys, the greens becoming ever more brown and hazy as the distance lengthened.

'You sure letting Gadaffi blow this thing wide open is the right thing to do?' O'Shea asked, voicing the worry that was foremost in his mind.

'Right like how?' Range grunted. 'Morally right? I don't give a shit about that. Right for Gadaffi? That I do give a shit about, and for him it's the only thing to do. But most importantly, right for us? Right for B6, for the team? For Randy and for Jock, and for their families? Far as I can tell, it's the only way to protect us all.'

'How so?'

'Think about it. We went AWOL. Hijacked a British military asset and its crew. Booby-trapped the lot of them. Blew up a Libyan fortress on an unsanctioned mission and wasted a lot of bad guys in the process. We picked up unsanctioned personnel en route, parachuted into a sovereign European state without the right to do so, and all to smuggle one hundred million dollars of gold in. You could say that those who commissioned this mission would have every right to crucify the lot of us. Or get us locked up for a very, very long time.'

'Yeah, you could say that,' O'Shea agreed.

'But no one's going to be doing any locking up or crucifying of us lot if Gadaffi has his say. Instead, those who commissioned this mission will be running for the fucking hills. Or maybe they'll be locked up behind bars themselves, which if Gadaffi is right in what he told us is exactly where they should be. As to us lot, we won't have any questions to answer, because there'll be no one around any more to do the questioning.'

'If Gadaffi's right,' O'Shea echoed.

Range threw him a look. 'You doubt him? Everything he's said to date has stacked up, one hundred per cent. And bear in mind those who sent us in to get him sent us in on a lie. At the Fort of the Mount there was no gold, remember? They knew that. Without Gadaffi, we wouldn't be lying here next to one hundred bars of gold bullion. So on that basis alone, who do we owe our allegiances to?'

'Sultan Gadaffi, I guess.'

'Sultan Gadaffi,' Range echoed. 'Plus he is no war criminal. There are no war crimes to stand trial for. Every which way you look at it, the mission was bullshit. And this way, we get to the truth and we flush out the bad guys.'

Chapter Twenty-six

'I just need to do a white-balance check,' the TV cameraman announced, 'and we're done.'

About bloody time too, Range thought to himself, whatever a 'white-balance check' was. They weren't in any great hurry, but it had taken an age for the crew to set up all their gear, and he'd be much happier once they got the interview in the can. He had presumed they'd just point the camera at Gadaffi, start asking questions and press record. Wrong. The camera guy had spent a good hour setting up portable spotlights, to 'light' the interview, not that Range could see anything wrong with the bright Spanish sunshine that was streaming in through the windows.

He'd asked Range to sit in the chair where Gadaffi would be doing the interview, so he could get the lights just right and check his camera angles. Sultan Gadaffi, meanwhile, was off with the one bit of skirt on the crew, getting his face seen to. Range couldn't quite believe that they'd flown out a make-up girl with the rest of the crew, but he was pleased that they had. After Maria, she was now the next-best-looking girl in the whole of El

Barca village as far as he could tell. She had a great set of pins, and tottered about on her high heels very agreeably.

Mostly, it had been her presence that had drawn Range to the interview, which was taking place in O'Shea's converted barn at the far end of the courtyard from the main house. The rest of the B6 team – being innately suspicious, if not downright hostile to the media – had remained in the main building, drinking brews and nattering away about what they were planning to do with their share of the gold.

O'Shea had offered his journalist friend an exclusive on Sultan Gadaffi's story. After he'd been couriered one or two of the documents that Gadaffi had downloaded from his online databank, the reporter had had no problems convincing his editor to send out a team to do the interview. That team had included a print journalist, who'd be doing the main interview, plus a couple of hotshots from their online and broadcast desks, who came complete with video cameras to film the whole thing, plus computer editing and uploading kit.

Range didn't see why the press should be less trustworthy than anyone else in the kind of world he inhabited, and he was curious to see how they went about securing their interview. Not content with getting four spotlights shining into his eyes, the cameraman proceeded to cover two of them with some kind of translucent material, which looked like the greaseproof paper you'd find packed around a brand-new delivery of weaponry. The third and fourth light he'd covered with a blue and an orange plastic filter, so that each threw a beam of colour across the stone wall that formed the backdrop to the interview.

'Lends some atmosphere to things,' the cameraman explained. 'A touch of gravitas, a hint of mystery . . .' He leaned forward and thrust a plain sheet of paper in front of Range's face. 'Hold that there for a second, will you?'

Range did as he was asked. He heard the guy fiddling with a few buttons on the camera, and they were done – white-balance balanced, or so it seemed. It was all mumbo-jumbo as far as Range was concerned. But having watched the set-up for the interview, one thing was clear. There was as much to filming one of these as there was to setting a good military ambush, and each entailed a specific package of skill sets – including loading something, pointing it at someone and proceeding to shoot.

'All set,' the cameraman called through to the adjoining room.

The journalist who was doing the interview appeared. In contrast to the cameraman, who had to be in his late forties and was a down-to-earth kind of a bloke, Range had taken an instant dislike to the cocky young reporter. He marched about as if he owned the place, and Range figured he was full of more shit than a Christmas goose.

Still, he seemed professional enough, and Range could just about put up with the bloke for the few hours they were scheduled to be here, as long as he got the job done.

The make-up girl appeared, leading Sultan Gadaffi by the arm towards the hot seat. Range was amazed at the way she'd transformed him. Via the application of several shovel-loads of make-up, his haggard, battle-worn features had been rendered something pretty close to normal.

'You good, mate?' Range asked him, as he approached.

'I think Alice has made me look almost presentable,' Sultan Gadaffi replied. 'As to the interview – if not now, then when?'

'Yeah. Best to get it over with.' Range levered himself out of the chair, his body aching like hell from his injuries. 'I've been keeping it warm for you.'

Sultan Gadaffi needed Range and the cameraman to help lower him into the seat, for the broken leg was troubling him. They'd eased off on the painkillers that Dr Franco, La Barca's one medical practitioner, had prescribed for him, so he could keep a clear head for the interview whilst at the same time being able to cope with the pain.

The village doctor had to be pushing seventy, and the sparse population of La Barca rarely had call to use him these days. Over several decades the place had become increasingly depopulated, as villagers moved to the cities seeking work. Dr Franco had been more than happy to take a little freelance – and very highly paid work – from the likes of O'Shea. It was only the blow-ins – like the American – who gave him hope that the village had any kind of a future. The foreigners still seemed to appreciate the values of peace, rural tranquillity and privacy, and they brought vitally needed money and energy into the place. He for one had no desire to question how they earned their cash, especially if they were willing to share a little of it around.

The cameraman clipped a tiny microphone onto Sultan Gadaffi's collar, running the lead over his shoulder and back along the floor to the camera. 'Mind telling me what you had for breakfast, Mr Gadaffi?' he asked, as he slipped on a pair of headphones, presumably to monitor the volume. 'Just as a sound check.'

'The delightful Maria cooked a Spanish omelette, if you know what that is?' Sultan Gadaffi replied. 'I had not tried it before, but it was delicious. Eggs mixed together with some vegetables, tomatoes and a little meat, I think . . .'

'That's fine,' the cameraman smiled. 'You're making me feel ravenous.'

'Right, if we're ready?' the reporter prompted.

'Rolling,' the cameraman replied. 'And . . . speed.'

Range was standing behind the cameraman now, well out of shot, and watching as the interview unfolded. As in the military, it seemed, this TV business had a language all of its own. He glanced across at the make-up girl, and they exchanged a quick smile.

'Great job on the face, Alice,' he whispered.

'As I've said, I'll need everyone to keep absolutely silent during the interview,' the reporter snapped. 'And Mr Gadaffi, if you will answer looking directly at me, and ignoring the camera . . .'

The reporter cleared his voice, then slipped into interviewer mode. 'If you would identify yourself for me, and explain what role you played in your late father's regime?'

'My name is Sultan Moussa Muammar Gadaffi,' he answered. 'I am my late father Colonel Gadaffi's only surviving son. During the time that I served under his regime I was known as "The Laundry Man", and this was because . . .'

Range listened for a while as Sultan Gadaffi began to outline for the interviewer the same story that he had first revealed to him in the battle-torn Fort of the Mount. He'd heard most of it before, and fairly quickly the novelty of the TV interview process began to wear off. He heard a faint click of the door behind him as O'Shea entered the room.

Range joined him. 'Keep an eye will you, mate? I need a break and a brew.'

He slipped quietly from the room, and made his way across the cobbled yard towards the main house. As he did so, he glanced around himself admiringly. O'Shea had some kind of a set-up here, that was for sure. The American was a good few years older than Range and considerably more wealthy – or at least, he had been prior to this mission going down. Unlike Range, he'd managed to stick his full term in the US military, and earn a handsome pay-off and pension at the end of it all.

Range hadn't lasted his twenty-two years in the British military, and at the end of the day even the SAS hadn't been able to contain him. Those years growing up in the children's home had been both a curse and a blessing. They were a blessing in that the total deprivation of his childhood had given him a burning desire to succeed and to be the best, no matter what. Without that kind of a hunger to triumph against the odds and make something of his life, he doubted if he ever would have made it into the military elite.

But they were a curse in the sense that he always hungered for new horizons and the next challenge. Plus the years spent getting abused by authority had left him with scant regard for his superiors, no matter what their rank or unit. Eventually, even the SAS had baulked at his maverick, unconventional ways – not to mention his disregard for rank and privilege – at which time Steve Range had moved on.

It was only in Blackstone Six that he had found a place where he really felt he had come of age. The Hogan was no pushover. There was cold steel beneath his old-school charm and impeccable manners. In terms of background, upbringing and appearance, he and Range couldn't be more opposite. But deep down, they were remarkably alike: they were united in their willingness to think the unthinkable and to break every rule in the book, if that's what it took to get the job done. And that was why Range figured however many millions the gold might net him, he'd not be leaving B6's payroll any time soon.

In any case, it was one thing having a pile of bullion stashed beneath a tarpaulin in one of O'Shea's empty sheds. It was quite another turning all of that into clean, usable ready cash, but there had to be a way. Gold was pretty much untraceable, so who would ask any questions? They'd need to hold fire, use their contacts and manage it all just so, and Range felt certain it wasn't going to happen overnight. But at least when the time came, in The Hogan they had a bloke with the confidence and stature to front up the business of turning the gold into readies. He had a big interest in doing so as well: a proportion of the loot was rightfully his.

'So, which of you sorry lot's buying the first yacht?' Range demanded, as he took a seat around the long table that dominated O'Shea's kitchen.

'Tiny's getting himself a canal barge,' Tak rumbled, with perfect deadpan delivery. 'He's calling it the Blackstone Belle.'

'Fuck off,' Tiny laughed. 'Nah. It's going to be a villa somewhere in the sun for me. Tax-free. Maybe a boat. Why not? That's the life . . .'

'I was thinking about that dive business back home in Fiji,' Tak remarked. 'The one me and my brother always had our eye on.'

'So, Blackstone's losing the lot of you?' Range prompted. 'You know what, I don't think so. You'll be back. The boredom. The lack of action. The rules. The laws. You'll never stick it.'

The men eyed Range silently. Deep down, they all knew the truth in what he was saying. The type of operators who made it into Blackstone stayed with the outfit because it was the best. What could ever top a B6 mission like the one they'd just undertaken? What could ever come close? With B6, every normal rule or law of war was subordinate to getting the job done – no holds barred. Sure, the money was good, but it wasn't what drew them in like moths to a candle flame.

'So you're staying put?' said Tak.

'Nope,' Range replied. 'Having watched that TV crew at work I'm going to retrain as a cameraman and focus on my white balance . . . Only joking. Yeah – I'll give it a few more years, that's for sure. So should the rest of you. Buy that yacht. And the villa. But stay on B6's payroll. After all, the gold's not going anywhere any time soon. And anyway, The Hogan would be lost without the lot of us.'

The conversation was interrupted by Maria, who placed a pot of steaming coffee in the centre of the table, plus some fresh-baked olive bread.

'Coffee,' she announced, flashing her dark eyes

around the table. 'Hot and strong, as we like it here in España. And I have made the bread – in case any of you men are feeling the hunger.'

'I'm feeling the hunger all right, Maria,' Range grinned, 'but it wasn't exactly bread I had in mind . . .'

'Now, now, Mr Range,' she scolded, playfully, 'Patrick would not like to hear you talking so . . .'

'Well Patrick, as they say in America, can blow it up his arse.'

Maria laughed. 'For forty-seven years old, Patrick has a very cute ass, I think. So maybe I will be doing the blowing . . .'

'Whoaa . . . Hold on!' Range exclaimed. 'I'm going to blow a fucking gasket with much more talk like that. Now, Maria, on a more serious note, I need your help on something. See this?' He pulled the Thuraya satphone out of his pocket. 'I need this and one other like it disposed of somewhere that no one will ever find them, not in a million years. Got any ideas?'

Maria eyed the phone. 'Well, not in the trash, for sure. There are too many of the Somali and Moroccan illegals living on the municipal dump. They would be sure to find it. But if I drive to the coast there is the certain place where the sea is very, very deep . . .'

'Sounds perfect, Maria. I'll break them into their parts, and if you could do the honours and hurl them into the ocean depths that'd be great.'

Chapter Twenty-seven

Forty-eight hours had passed since Range and his men had stashed their golden haul at O'Shea's *finca*. By now the reporting was done and dusted, and the story was poised to break online and in print versions of the broadsheet, plus on the TV news in less than twenty-four hours' time. The journalist who'd led the interviews predicted that an explosive story with such massive international ramifications would attract blanket press coverage worldwide. Now was the calm before the storm.

Meanwhile, Range had had to make his rendezvous with The Hogan. He'd left his team at the farmhouse, and under strict instructions to maintain total communications silence until the story had hit the media. At that time, they could start to emerge from hiding. Range had flown from Malaga to London direct, and made his way to The Beaujolais wine bar, a venerable watering hole tucked away on a side street in the heart of the West End.

The Hogan was such a regular there that his name was at the top of the wine bar's blackboard, with a permanent 'IN' chalked beside it. It was a standing joke that he could always be found there, propping up the bar. When Range met him – bang on time three days to the hour after their short Thuraya phone call – The Hogan was already a third of the way through a bottle of fine French Bordeaux.

Range had joined him for a glass, and proceeded to fill him in on the mission. Even for an old hand like The Hogan, the finer details of this Blackstone operation had blown him away. And when Range had revealed to him the media storm that was about to break, The Hogan had begun to seriously question Range's judgement. But eventually he'd been convinced that this was the best way – in fact the only way – to safeguard their own interests, and maybe even their lives.

As to who had really commissioned their mission, it remained a mystery, and at the end of Range's tale neither of them was any the wiser. But one thing was clear: the media storm would flush them out of hiding. Would Blackstone's reputation be tarnished in the process? It was a possibility, but unlikely, The Hogan reckoned. No one would find it in their interests to expose the role that Range and his team had played, for that would only serve to open up a fresh can of worms.

More than likely, Blackstone Six would continue to do business as usual. And even if they didn't, with one hundred million in gold bullion to bank, they could more than ride out a few lean years. They'd been promised the gold at the start of the mission, so who could blame Range and his team for using all possible means to go get it? And in the process, they'd dealt a deathblow to al-Qaeda in the Maghreb, a group that was preparing to build a dirty nuke and to use it.

Whatever way The Hogan looked at it, who could ever accuse Blackstone Six of doing anything other than the right thing? The conversation with Range more than cheered his spirits, and the two men left for their meeting feeling more than a little reassured. The next twenty-four hours was going to be a rollercoaster, but so be it. They'd just have to sit back and try to enjoy the ride.

The black cab threaded through the busy London streets, taking the two men towards a nondescript building set on an unremarkable street somewhere between Victoria and Whitehall. Range had had countless such meetings on Blackstone business, more often than not at buildings resembling private residences, and they never seemed to meet at the same location more than a few times. He presumed it was all part of the need for deniability, but it made it hard to gauge who exactly you were dealing with, which brought him to the issue of The Colonel.

'You still trust him?' Range asked. 'The Colonel?'

'Yes, old boy, I do,' The Hogan confirmed. 'How long is it now that we've been doing business with him? Ten years? Twelve, maybe? And we've never had cause to doubt him. His role is to take what our political taskmasters demand and to try to deliver that militarily, using people like us where appropriate. That's a very difficult pair of shoes to fill.'

'Maybe The Colonel's still on the side of the angels,' Range conceded. 'But somewhere there's a divide between those who sent us in believing the mission was bona fide, and those who knew full well it wasn't. I'd like to know where that divide lies, and who's on the wrong side of it. Remember, had that first fort held the gold Jock would still be with us, and maybe Randy too.'

The Hogan threw Range one of his shrewdest glances. There was steel behind those fiercely twinkling eyes. 'One thing's for sure – you won't find out by asking the people we're going to meet. This afternoon is all about you giving them some answers, so we get them off our backs. You'll get your answers once the media storm breaks, and you'll see then who amongst them are the bad eggs.'

'We'll watch to see who disappears?'

'Yes, exactly – those who run for the hills.'

The cab pulled up and they dismounted. The Hogan pushed the bell and was buzzed into an entryway. From there the two men were led into a large and spacious lounge, which had wooden shutters half drawn across the windows. Gathered around a table were a group of four people, most of whom were standing. Range recognized The Fixer immediately, but the rest of them were unfamiliar to him.

'Range! At last.' Nigel Champion strode across to greet him. Range noticed an unusual urgency in The Fixer's step, plus a taut look that flashed across his features. 'So good of you to put in an appearance . . . eventually.'

'Who're the suits?' Range asked, glancing towards the mystery figures, and ignoring the hand that was extended towards him.

As far as Range was concerned, this was the man who was responsible for Jock's death, and maybe that of Randy as well. He didn't do niceties with those who put his fellow operators and closest friends in needless peril.

'They are people who need to be here, and who are eager to hear some answers,' The Fixer replied stiffly. 'It's not your need-to-know.'

'Who's the lady?' Range enquired, nodding in the direction of the lone female, whose elegant suit somehow marked her out as a foreigner.

The Fixer gave a thin smile. 'Even less of your need-to-know, I'm afraid, so if you'll just take a seat . . .'

'So much English secrecy,' the mystery lady interjected. 'No one here is, I think, Mr James Bond. And Mr Range's mission is, I think, over. I see no reason why not to share a little Gallic intimacy.' She stepped closer. The rich aura of her expensive French perfume did little to make her seem any less dangerous, in spite of her being decidedly easy on the eye. 'Madame Enée, Operations Director from the Direction Général de Securité – the DGSE. You know of us?'

Range shrugged. 'DGSE? Like GCSEs, only harder? Never managed to get any of either, myself.'

The Frenchwoman stared at him blankly. She'd clearly not understood a word.

'Only joking,' Range added. 'DGSE: you have a habit of sending planeloads of Igla-S missiles to any bunch of desert nomads who do the asking. Seems nuts to me, but then again I'm just the hired help.'

Madame Enée stiffened noticeably at the mention of the abortive missile drop. The memory of it, plus the aircraft and the operators she'd lost, still rankled.

'Yes, well, I expect not every mission *you* embark upon goes faultlessly, does it, Mr Range?' Her tone was noticeably icier. 'Like the one from which you have just returned.' She glanced in the direction of The Fixer. 'From what I understand, it didn't quite go to plan. No, no, no – not to plan at all.'

The door opened and a figure bustled into the room. 'Tony, Range – good to see you at last,' said The Colonel. 'I'd begun to worry the Libyan deserts had swallowed up your entire team.'

'The Libyan desert should be so lucky,' Madame Enée murmured. '*Eh bien*. So, shall we . . .' She gestured at the table. 'To the business at hand.'

Chairs were pulled up to the table and those present took their seats.

'So, Range, it's time for some answers,' The Fixer began. 'Tell me how a twenty-four-hour mission became a six-day extravaganza, one that got a Chinook shot to pieces and forced it to make an emergency landing in Gibraltar. It's fortunate we have a base there, or where would the aircrew have put their damaged helo down? You returned with the HVT . . .'

'Sultan Gadaffi, you mean?' Range interrupted.

'Yes: High Value Target. HVT. Sultan Gadaffi. Him it seems you did deliver. But in the meantime you were off radar for several days, in which time you appear to have lost all of your men . . . Or at least none turned up via the helicopter, yourself included. So, where in God's name are they? Dead? Bodies scattered across the Libyan sands? Captured?' The Fixer turned his cold gaze on Tony Hogan, who was seated beside Range. 'I mean, Tony, old chap, it's hardly what we commission Blackstone for, is it: quiet, under-the-radar black ops. Untraceable business . . .'

Tony let out his signature chuckle, rumbling and unashamedly warm-hearted. 'It does seem a little dramatic a return that Range has made this time. But let's hear him out. I'm sure there are good reasons . . .'

'Fine. Where were you, Range?' The Fixer demanded. 'And what on earth happened? What were you doing during those missing days? And bear in mind there are others right now asking very similar questions of the Chinook crew, who are the only others on this mission apart from you who seem to have returned.'

'To cross-check our answers, you mean,' said Range. 'To check if anyone's lying?'

'That kind of thing, yes,' The Fixer snapped. 'This isn't a bloody game, Range. This is deadly serious. People's lives and a whole lot more are at stake – far more than you could ever imagine – and your going off the radar for several days has been hugely bloody unhelpful, to put it mildly.'

For a fleeting second Range wondered whether Walters and the rest of the Chinook crew had unpacked their flight bags yet. He felt sure they must have done, in which case they'd each have discovered the one London Good Delivery bar secreted in their baggage. It seemed the least he and his men could do, after the way the Chinook crew had rallied around. And as an added bonus it would tend to militate against any of the air-crew blowing the gaff on what they knew about the unsanctioned elements of Range's mission.

'Range, we need answers,' The Fixer prompted, irritably. 'We need to get to the bottom of this, and sharpish. If we can't, I'm afraid Blackstone's hitherto excellent working relationship with HMG is likely to go into terminal decline. Oh, and I almost forgot – you did return one of your team. Jock, I think you call him, was also on the Chinook.' The fixer threw a furtive glance at Madame Enée. 'He was dead, apparently killed by a fragment of an Igla-S missile.'

Range saw a shiver of revulsion pass across the Frenchwoman's face, before the mask of elegant inscrutability came down again.

'I take it you'll repatriate Jock's body and return him to his family?' Range demanded.

'There's not a lot left of the man that's recognizable, but yes, we'll return what remains.'

Range fixed Nigel Champion with a stone-cold, deadening look. 'It's wrong to speak ill of the dead.'

'Of course we'll get Jock home and he'll be reunited with his family,' The Colonel interjected, from where he was seated opposite. 'We're all supposed to be on the same side, and the man's a decorated war hero, and from long before anything that may have happened on your mission. But I think you owe us this much in return – to provide some answers.'

'Well, correct me if I'm wrong,' Range began, 'but you sent us on a mission with the stated aim to bring back Sultan Gadaffi. You got him, which means it's mission accomplished. As it happens, we ran into a shedload more resistance than we expected. Some of the lads plus your MH-47 got a bit shot up in the process of extracting Gadaffi. But exactly how we went about getting him – that's our affair. That's the deal with B6, isn't it? You send us in to do your dirty work, and you don't want to know how it's done. It's called deniability.'

'That's as may be, Range,' The Colonel countered, 'but no two missions are ever the same, and sometimes we do need answers.' He glanced in the direction of the suits, who so far had remained a grey and watchful presence. 'Sometimes, there's a risk that HMG will be drawn into something nasty and embarrassing and ugly, and in an effort to avoid all that we do need some details. Now, please.'

'HMG or the French government?' Range glanced from The Colonel to Madame Enée. 'Oh, I forgot, we're best of friends and allies now, aren't we? Or maybe this isn't so much about governments? Maybe its more a group of individuals we're trying to protect here?'

At that The Fixer's head snapped around, his eyes bulging furiously. 'And what the bloody hell is that supposed to mean?'

'Answers, Steve,' The Colonel cut in. 'From mission departure until now – just a quick heads-up on what you've been up to. We deserve to know, and this time – trust me – we need to.'

For an instant Range eyed The Hogan. The man at the helm of Blackstone Six shrugged imperceptibly, then rolled his eyes – as if to say: go on, give it to them with both barrels.

'Truth is, there was no gold at that fort, was there, Nigel?' Range began. 'You knew that all along, and you sent us in on a lie, as your satellite photos prove. Lot of very angry blokes on my team as a result. Had I brought them back to Gib, they'd have liked nothing more than to string you up and make you hurt real bad, especially since we'd lost Randy and Jock in the ensuing carnage. I felt that was best avoided, and hence we never made it to Gib. But the bottom line is you got your HVT. You have the Gadaffi boy, and you never know who—'

There was a sharp knocking on the door. A head appeared and spoke a few hurried words to The Fixer. 'Sorry, sir, to interrupt, but you need to pull up your Skype-Mil link right now. I'm told it can't wait, sir, and that's taking into account present business and company.'

From the tightness in his shoulders as he stalked across the room, Range could see the enormous amount of tension that Nigel Champion was under. They seemed to suspect Range and his team of a good degree of subterfuge, though he doubted if they had any idea of the shitstorm that was about to break.

The Fixer punched a keyboard on his laptop, and the military's own version of the live internet-hosted Skype videophone link came up on screen. Skype-Mil made use of the same kind of software that the civilian Skype service employed, only with a few more layers of security built in.

The Fixer spoke into his computer. 'Champion here.'

'Nigel, it's Major Hammond,' a voice responded from the screen. 'We've just got an answer of sorts, but it's far from being the one we were expecting. The answers the guy was providing were well off the mark, but not because he was trying to hide anything . . . Well, it's probably better if you hear it from the horse's mouth, as it were.'

The speaker shifted the screen slightly and a new figure came into view.

'Sultan Gadaffi,' Range announced, determined to get the first hit in. 'Glad to see you haven't managed to lose him.'

'No, no, Mr Range, but you see I am not Sultan Gadaffi at all,' the figure objected.

'Yeah, nice one, and I'm the frigging Pope,' Range snorted, feigning disbelief.

'No, no, as I have just been telling the Major, I am truly not Sultan Gadaffi,' the figure repeated. 'You see, every dictator has his body double. Saddam Hussein had several – men who could stand in for the Great Leader, as a precaution against kidnap or assassination. Well, Colonel Gadaffi had several for himself and one each for all his family. I may look like Sultan Gadaffi, but I am his double. I am Sultan Gadaffi's double – for The Laundry Man needed a stand-in perhaps more than anyone else in the late Colonel Gadaffi's household.'

There was a stunned silence in the room. All present were staring at the figure on the screen as if they couldn't – wouldn't – believe what he had just been saying.

Chapter Twenty-eight

Range was trying to act as if he was as much in shock as anyone else in the room. The deal they'd cut with Abdel Al-Khofra, the man who was speaking via the video link, was that he would hold out for twenty-four hours before revealing his true identity. He'd managed three times that amount, which was saying something after what his interrogators must have put him through.

Range was the one who broke the silence. 'You're trying to tell us we brought back the wrong guy? You got any proof you aren't who we thought you were?'

'I have given the Major my blood sample, so he can run a check on my DNA. But of course, I know nothing – none of the answers to the questions they have been asking me. I may have been Sultan Gadaffi's double, but I was privy to few, if any, of The Laundry Man's secrets.'

'So why the fuck didn't you tell us this at the time?' Range grated, doing his best disbelieving act.

'Simple: I wanted to get to Britain. What kind of future d'you think there was for me in Libya, a close friend of the Gadaffi family and The Laundry Man's double? None. You gave me the opportunity to get to

Britain, and now I intend to claim the asylum. I have told the Major I am claiming the asylum. Maybe one day I will be the British citizen, and then I will bring my family here also, and I will be beyond the reach of those in Libya who would come after us and do us harm.'

'But the man in the Fort of the Mount was the real Sultan Gadaffi,' Nigel Champion exploded. 'We had copper-bottomed intelligence from multiple sources.'

The figure on the screen shrugged. 'But I am not him. My full name is Abdel Al-Karim Al-Khofra, and I wish to claim the asylum in Great Britain, now that you have brought me here.'

'Well right now you're in bloody Gibraltar, which is far from being home and bloody dry!' The Fixer snapped. 'So you can stop harping on about claiming bloody asylum.'

'But Gibraltar is a British Overseas Territory, is it not?' the figure continued, doggedly. 'And that is still part of Great Britain, I think, so legally I am entitled to claim–'

'Major Hammond, shut the damn prisoner up!' The Fixer snarled. 'And do you have the results from the damn DNA test?'

The Major shook his head. 'We expect them in about an hour's time. But it does seem to make complete sense. I mean whoever the guy is, he seems to know absolutely nothing in answer to our key questions. And legally speaking, sir, he does have the right to claim–'

'Major, call me again only when you've got those DNA

tests.' The Fixer killed the video link. He swung around to face Range. 'Let me get this straight: am I honestly supposed to believe that you parachuted into the Libyan desert, fought your way into that fort and brought us back the wrong man? Is that really the story here? Or am I bloody missing something?'

Range shrugged. 'He looks like Sultan Gadaffi, talks like Sultan Gadaffi and walks like the bloke. As my troop commander in the SAS used to say: if it walks like a duck and talks like a duck, it probably is a duck.'

'Well in this case it seems that it isn't a bloody duck, doesn't it?' The Fixer cursed. 'Fucking hell, Range . . .' He threw a desperate glance at the lady from the DGSE. 'Sorry, Madame, for the language, but–'

'So, Mr Range, after all of this, are we to presume that the real Sultan Gadaffi is still at liberty?' Madame Enée interjected coolly. 'And if we are, it is hardly what we in France would consider mission accomplished, is it, Mr Range?'

'We were shown some mugshots and given the name of a target,' Range replied. 'We went in, and against all odds we got hold of the guy shown on those photos and named as our target. Like I said, I'm just the hired help. The rest of all of this shitty business is way above my pay grade.'

The Operations Director of the DGSE gave a Gallic kind of a snort. 'Mr Range, you are excellent at playing the simpleton. But somehow, I am not so sure . . . In any case, if we are to believe Mr Al-Khofra – and I see no reason why we would not – the question is, where is the real Sultan Gadaffi? And does he know about the nature of Mr Range's snatch mission, for if he does–'

'If he does, I shudder to think what he might do,' The Fixer cut in. 'We need to find him, and fast, for this means just about anything's bloody possible.'

Minutes later the meeting broke up amidst heated mutual accusations and acrimony. The Fixer had tried to task Range with finding the real Sultan Gadaffi, without whom no one from B6 was getting paid for the job, but Range had basically told him to stuff his mission where the sun doesn't shine. The Fixer had tried to threaten Range with prosecution and worse if he didn't take the mission, at which point it had become clear that Steve Range didn't scare so easily.

Things had turned very ugly between the two of them by the time The Colonel had managed to steer Range and The Hogan out of the building. They accepted The Colonel's offer of sharing a black cab. They knew it to be his way of asking for a private kind of a chat. The Colonel directed the taxi to nearby Hyde Park, where the three men alighted. After all, The Colonel suggested, it was a fine late February day and the crisp afternoon sun invited a stroll, one that it was best to ensure wasn't disturbed by any mobile phone calls.

'Tell me, where did you make the switch?' The Colonel asked Range, just as soon as they'd each dumped their cell phones in the nearest waste bin. Even when turned off a mobile could still be used by those in the know to monitor a conversation, with the right kind of technology brought to bear.

'What switch?' Range countered.

'I guess at your Wadi Idhan refuelling stop,' The Colonel remarked, answering his own question. 'Al-Khofra could have made it there, just, I guess, in the time available, though he'd have needed someone to get him access to the base.'

The Hogan gave a cough. 'Yes. Exactly. Erm . . . that was me. We intended to let you know – it's just that there never seemed to be the right moment.'

'In which case, that just leaves the why,' The Colonel continued. 'And that is a question only Range can answer, I presume?'

Range swung around to face the older military man. 'If I tell you, I need some guarantees. One, you'll hear me out. Two, you'll investigate and act upon what I say. And three, you won't try to stop the shitstorm that is coming.'

'Agreed,' The Colonel replied. 'So, let's hear it.'

They'd paused at a bench, and Range lowered himself into it exhaustedly. Suddenly he was feeling overwhelmingly tired, as the tension and pace of the last few days crept up on him.

He glanced up at The Colonel. 'It's like this. You sent us in to assault a fort and to seize Sultan Gadaffi. That we did. Lost a good man in the battle, but we got our target. Trouble was, there was no gold in that fort, and that got the Gadaffi boy and me talking.

'I showed him the satphotos you'd given us of the location of the gold.' Range paused. 'Gadaffi recognized them. Trouble was, they showed another fortress several hundred miles away. Gadaffi knew the hiding place all right, for he'd once been held there himself – that was before the Tuareg had sold him up the chain to AQIM.

'So, we decided to go get the gold,' Range continued. 'There was one added bonus. The French had built Sultan Gadaffi's father a secret nuclear facility, which used uranium from their mines across the border in Niger. And when our previous government found out about it, a series of deals were done to hide the fact from the international authorities. Apparently, Gadaffi bought off our people with lucrative arms and oil deals, or at least he paid off certain individuals.'

Range cast a searching glance at The Colonel, but the look in the man's eyes betrayed only a calm and honest integrity. It was an expression that put the man beyond suspicion, just as The Hogan had suggested he would be.

'Once Colonel Gadaffi's regime fell, the country was in chaos, his secrets leaked out, and AQIM decided to get its hands on some of his fissile material. All they needed was enough to build a dirty bomb or two. The second fortress we hit was their main base, and the one from which they were planning their raid on his nuclear facility. The deal we did with Sultan Gadaffi was to let him go free. We did the switch at Wadi Idhan, just as you deduced. Oh, and we hijacked the Chinook, just to make sure they'd act as our trans-Saharan taxi service.'

The Colonel fixed Range with this steady, unwavering gaze. 'That was some mission. Congratulations. And the shitstorm that is coming?'

'Sultan Gadaffi's somewhere in Europe. He's not in the UK, put it that way. He's given extensive interviews to the media, with documents to back it up. The story breaks tomorrow.'

'You HALOed out somewhere over Spain, I take it?' The Colonel asked. 'It was the only way you could have exited the Chinook in any safety, between your Libyan refuelling stop and Gib.'

'We did.'

'And he's told everything?' The Colonel prompted. 'To the media? Best to be fully prepared, especially when a spot of trouble like this is about to break.'

'I sat in on the interview. I'm no journalist, but it seemed as if he'd pretty much covered it.'

'He duly nailed our friends, the French?' The Colonel prompted. 'Left nothing to the imagination, I hope.'

'Nailed them like a pig in the guts,' Range confirmed.

The beginnings of a smile crept across The Colonel's features. 'Some kind of operation you run here, Tony,' he remarked to The Hogan. 'And with some kind of operators. But with a storm like the one that's presently brewing, I'd better get back to my desk and start doing some contingency planning. Probably have to brief the PM at some stage over the next few hours. I suspect one or two of his closest enemies may be implicated.'

The Colonel levered himself off the bench. It seemed to Range there was a new vitality to his step, which was heartening.

'The deal stands?' Range asked.

'Absolutely,' The Colonel confirmed. 'The deal stands. Never one to break my word.' The smile broadened. 'And sometimes, you know, you need a storm such as this to shake the bad apples from the barrel. When the rot's as bad as it can get at the top, you need the shitstorm of all shitstorms to do so. But take my advice, Range: get well out of the country, at least until the dust has settled. Leave those of us with the clout to finish fighting this one, not to mention the top-cover to protect us.'

'I'm out of here,' Range confirmed. 'Flight's booked in a few hours' time.' He paused, and eyed The Colonel. 'You planned it all in the hope it'd turn out this way?'

'No, no – not planned.' He shook his head, amusedly. 'How could one ever plan to control a mission undertaken by Blackstone Six, and headed up by Steve Range? No. It was more a case of sheer desperation. When all else fails, to paraphrase William Shakespeare, you cry havoc and let slip your dogs of war.'

For a moment Range found himself remembering his bitter fight to the death with the Tuareg warrior, and the shot fired by the Gadaffi son that had saved him. 'Sultan Gadaffi is his father's son, but he's still a good enough guy,' he remarked. 'We couldn't have done any of this without him. If there's a way to protect him, and maybe to bring him in, then I'm for ever in your debt.'

'As far as I am concerned, every man on your mission deserves a high valour medal,' The Colonel told him, 'and that includes the son of the late Libyan dictator. We'll make sure he's looked after. You tell him that from me, wherever he may be.'

There was a twinkle in The Colonel's eye as he said those last words. Range felt certain the wily old bird knew exactly where they had Sultan Gadaffi stashed, and possibly also the gold.

'This used to be an honourable country,' The Colonel added. 'If enough of us keep striving, we might make it so again. Go catch that flight, and lie low until you get the call from Tony. And in the next forty-eight hours, get ready for some very senior heads – and all the right ones – to roll.'

The Colonel turned to leave, but paused momentarily. 'One more thing, Range: don't spend it all at once, eh? We can't guarantee we can roll up all the bad apples, and there are bound to be people watching. Save most of it for a rainy day sometime a good while in the future. That would be safest, mark my words. And in the meantime, there may be a little follow-up job I just might need doing . . .'

Two hours later Range settled into his seat as the Air France passenger aircraft lifted off from London's City Airport, routed direct to Malaga. For a moment he reflected on the irony that he was flying by the French national airline, but he comforted himself with the thought that there would be no Tuareg warriors poised to unleash an Igla-S missile into the belly of this aircraft.

An instant later he had fallen into an exhausted sleep, as the Airbus A360 powered into the darkening skies.

'Hard eyes stare out of massive beards, their faces marked by the scars of battle. With these guys their webbing looks like it belongs to them, rather than it's been hung on a pair of reluctant shoulders. There's not a word been said to us, but the ante has clearly been upped. There's a dark and sinister feeling in the air. It doesn't take a genius to figure it's about to kick off.'

Former SAS soldier Phil Campion tells it like is in this brutally honest account of his insanely dangerous life as a private military operator. From playing chicken with a suicide bomber in backstreet Kabul, to taking on pirates with his bare hands, this is true-life action-packed drama at its best.

'One of the best first-hand accounts
of life in combat ever written'

ANDY McNAB

'A great book from a true hero'

ROSS KEMP

Available now priced £7.99

ISBN 978 0 85738 378 5